About the Au

Ellie Darkins spent her formative years devouring romance novels, and after completing her English degree she decided to make a living from her love of books. As a writer and editor her work now entails dreaming up romantic proposals, hot dates with alpha males and trips to the past with dashing heroes. When she's not working, she can usually be found at her local library or out for a run. You can visit her blog at elliedarkins.com

Lucy Gordon cut her writing teeth on magazine journalism, interviewing many of the world's most interesting men, including Warren Beatty and Roger Moore. Several years ago, while staying in Venice, she met a Venetian who proposed in two days. They have been married ever since. Naturally this has affected her writing, where romantic Italian men tend to feature strongly. Two of her books have won a Romance Writers of America *RITA®* Award.

Cathy Williams is a great believer in the power of perseverance as she had never written anything before her writing career. From the starting point of zero, she has now fulfilled her ambition to pursue this most enjoyable of careers. She would encourage any would-be writer to have faith and go for it! She derives inspiration from the tropical island of Trinidad and from the peaceful countryside of middle England. Cathy lives in Warwickshire her family.

Irresistible Italians

Irresistible Italians:
A Holiday Proposal

ELLIE DARKINS

LUCY GORDON

CATHY WILLIAMS

MILLS & BOON

First Published in Great Britain 2023
by Mills & Boon, an imprint of HarperCollins*Publishers* Ltd,
1 London Bridge Street, London, SE1 9GF

www.harpercollins.co.uk

HarperCollins*Publishers*
Macken House, 39/40 Mayor Street Upper,
Dublin 1, D01 C9W8, Ireland

ISBN: 978-0-263-31934-7

MIX
Paper | Supporting
responsible forestry
FSC™ C007454

This book is produced from independently certified FSC™ paper to ensure responsible forest management.

For more information visit: www.harpercollins.co.uk/green

Printed and Bound in the UK using 100% Renewable Electricity at CPI Group (UK) Ltd, Croydon, CR0 4YY

CONVENIENTLY ENGAGED TO THE BOSS

ELLIE DARKINS

For Mike

CHAPTER ONE

'COULD YOU HELP me with this zip, or are you just going to watch?'

Instinctively Joss shut the door behind him, wondering if anyone else had seen, and glanced through the window of the office to make sure his father wasn't nearby.

'Sorry, Eva. I was looking for my dad. What are you doing in his office? And why does it involve being undressed?'

Eva shrugged—he watched her shoulder blades move under pale, exposed skin where the dress's zip was gaping at the back.

'Edward's already gone to the boardroom. Shouldn't you be there too? Never mind. Could you help? I should have been there five minutes ago, but I spilt a cup of coffee over myself and now I've got the zip stuck.'

'Okay, okay—sure,' Joss said, with a glance back at the closed door. 'My dad wanted to see me in here before the meeting, but I couldn't get away from my last call.'

He reached Eva and gently batted her hands away

from the zip, pulling the slider to the top as quickly and impersonally as he could manage.

Eva turned her head to look over her shoulder, and as his eyes met hers he felt the tug of attraction that was ever-present around his father's executive assistant.

'Um… Joss, I meant *un*zip.'

Oh, no, that was *not* what he'd signed up for. No way was he that stupid. He'd been keeping his eyes, hands and mind off this woman for years. He knew the limits of his self-control, and just this proximity to her was pushing it—never mind anything else.

'I'm not sure that's…'

'Joss, would you just do it? Shut your eyes, if you want, but get me out of this thing! It's not like I'm naked under here, in case you're worried about your delicate sensibilities.'

He took a deep breath and unzipped, but the teeth snagged halfway down her back.

'It's stuck.'

'Still? Brilliant. I was hoping it was just the angle I was pulling it. Can you unstick it?'

He wasn't sure he wanted to—not when unsticking it meant exposing more creamy skin and finding out exactly what she'd meant when she said that she wasn't naked under there.

Joss fiddled with the zip, passing the teeth slowly through the slider and unpicking the threads that had got caught. Finally it gave way and slid smoothly down Eva's back, revealing a silk slip in a soft pink colour, edged with delicate cream lace. Worse than naked, perhaps, to be so close to seeing the body that he'd dreamed of, only to find it tantalisingly out of reach.

'At last! Thank goodness for that,' Eva said, stepping quickly out of the dress and reaching for another, which Joss had just noticed draped over his father's chair. As the fabric was sliding over her head he turned for the door, but Eva stopped him. 'Wait—can you zip up this time? I don't want to be any later than I already am.'

Joss let out a sigh, but crossed the office again and reached for the slider of the zip, his fingertips very close to the rose silk at the base of her spine. He lingered for a moment as he swept her hair away with his other hand, revealing the wispy baby hairs at the nape of her neck and the invitingly soft skin behind her ear.

But before he could cover her safely, the door behind him opened.

'Eva, are you in—?'

Damn his father and his terrible timing.

'I'm sorry, Edward. I'll be right there,' Eva said, reaching for the zip herself and pulling it further down in the process of twisting round.

'No, no—I can see I'm interrupting,' Edward said. 'I trust you're both on your way.'

Joss couldn't bring himself to look, but he could almost *hear* the huge grin on his father's face, verging on a full-on laugh.

'We're waiting for you.'

His father left the room before Joss could explain that nothing had been going on between him and Eva. He shot a look at her, and saw she looked as taken aback as he did as she struggled with her dress. He pulled the zip up for her—no lingering this time—and strode for the door.

'What are we going—?' Eva started.

'I'll handle it,' Joss said.

He walked into the boardroom, still fighting images of Eva's lingerie-clad body and the look of intrigue and delight on his father's face when he'd so clearly misinterpreted what had been going on in his office.

He was more used to seeing disappointment from his father, especially when it involved him and women. Since Joss's first marriage had failed, his father had tried to hide his disappointment that he'd not been able to settle down with anyone else. He knew that when he'd first told his parents he was getting a divorce, they'd blamed the break-up on him.

And then, when he'd walked into the office as a single man, emerging from the dark clouds of clinical depression and divorce, he had realised the strength of his attraction to his father's executive assistant.

He'd told himself that he would not be going near her—under any circumstances. His father doted on her, and would not take kindly to her feelings being hurt. And after what Joss had done to his marriage—the destruction he'd been powerless to prevent—he knew that he couldn't expect to make any woman happy.

At least his father respected him professionally. He'd been working for the family's chain of luxury department stores since he was in primary school, and had earned his position as Vice President of UK Stores. But professional respect and personal pride were two very different things, and Joss knew that an abundance of one would never compensate for the lack of the other.

All eyes turned to him as he entered the full boardroom, with Eva right behind him. They found a couple of spare chairs in the corner. Sunlight flooded in through the old lead-paned windows, brightening the panelled room, which could feel oppressive on a gloomier day.

Joss tried to catch his father's eye, but he was either deliberately avoiding his gaze or so entranced by the view out of the window that he couldn't bring himself to look away. The well-heeled streets of Kensington were bustling below, and Joss could tell just from the hum of the traffic that the pavement outside the store was filled with shoppers and tourists, stopping to take in the magnificent window displays for which the store was renowned.

Eventually, though, the old man cleared his throat and looked around the room, glancing at each of the board members in turn.

'I'd like to thank you all for being here,' Edward began, with a smile that Joss couldn't interpret. 'Especially at such short notice and on a Friday afternoon, when I'm sure you'd all rather be at a long working lunch. I'm afraid that, as some of you may have guessed, an emergency board meeting is rarely called to share good news, and today is no different. So, it is with regret that I have to announce that due to ill health I will be resigning from the company in all capacities with immediate effect.'

Joss felt fear and dread swell in an all too familiar

fashion in the base of his stomach as the deeper meaning of his father's words sank in. His father *must* be ill—seriously ill—to even consider leaving the business.

But Edward carried on speaking, leaving him no time to dwell.

'You all know that over the years we have taken steps to ensure a smooth transition when the time came for me to hand over the reins, and so—if you are all still in agreement—I will be leaving you in the capable hands of my son, Joss, who will become Managing Director and Chairman of the Board in my place. Eva, of course, will be assisting Joss in his new role, as I suspect she knows more about my job than I do. I know you will continue to support them, just as you have supported me. Now, I imagine there will be questions, so I'll answer them as best I can. Who's first?'

The room sank into silence as Edward finished speaking. Joss looked closely at his father. Ill-health? His father hadn't taken a day off sick in his life, and yet now he was resigning completely? Yes, they'd talked about succession plans. Any sensible businessman had contingencies for all eventualities, and Edward would not have wanted to leave the company in chaos if anything had happened to him. But had there actually been more to it than that? Had his father known that he would soon be stepping down?

The dread in Joss's stomach twisted into stark fear as the implications of the announcement sank in and he realised what this must mean. His father wouldn't resign because of a dodgy hip or 'a touch of angina', as he'd once described a health scare. He'd always sworn he'd be carried out of a Dawson's department store in his coffin. For him to resign must mean he had had some terrible news.

Panic and grief gripped his throat as he noticed for the first time the slight grey tinge to his father's skin, and the lines around his eyes that suggested a habitual wince of fatigue. Why hadn't he noticed before? Why hadn't he been looking? His father wasn't exactly a spring chicken, and he was still working sixteen-hour days long past the age when most people would expect to retire.

He should have made his father take things easier—should have taken more off his plate.

He met his father's eye and saw sympathy and understanding in his father's gaze. He wanted to rush to embrace him, but something froze him to his chair, chilling his blood.

And then warmth crept from the tips of his fingers as a hand slid into his and he heard Eva's voice.

'Edward, are you in pain? What can we do to help?'

Joss's eyes swam and he clenched his jaw, determined not to allow a single tear to fall, to keep control over his emotions. Besides, swiping a falling tear before anyone saw would mean taking his hand from Eva's, and at that moment he couldn't see how he was meant to do that.

'Perhaps we should speak in my office?' Edward said to Joss, his voice gentle. 'And you lot—' he addressed the remaining members of the board 'you have a good gossip while I'm gone and think of what you need to ask me. Head back to the pub and finish your lunch, if you want to. But get your questions to me sharpish, because I'm planning on being on a sun lounger by the end of next week.'

Edward rose and Joss noticed, as he hadn't before, that his father leaned heavily on the table for support.

Joss snapped out of his trance and back into business mode as they walked down the corridor and back to Edward's office, firing questions all the way.

'Dad? What's happening? Are you okay? Was this what you wanted to talk to me about?'

Edward collapsed into the chair behind his desk and rested back against the padded seat. 'Yes. I'm sorry, son. Of course I wanted to tell you first, but you didn't arrive for our meeting—'

'Dad, if I'd known—'

'I know.' He softened the words with a smile. 'I know. But it was difficult for Eva to get everyone here at such short notice. I couldn't delay it any longer.'

'Couldn't delay? What's wrong with you, Dad?'

'Sit down, son.' His father indicated the chair opposite. 'And you, Eva. You both need to hear this. It's cancer, I'm afraid, and there's nothing they can do about it. I ignored it for a bit too long, it seems. So I thought it was about time I took that holiday I've been promising myself for the last thirty years and let you get on with running the business while I'm still around to answer your questions—there's no deadline for you two, of course.'

Joss stared at his father, unable to take in his words. His hand found Eva's again and he gripped it hard, taking strength from the solid presence of her, the warmth that always radiated from her.

'How long, Dad?'

'Oh, you know doctors. Never give you a straight answer. A few months, it seems. Long enough to have a little fun before I go. I love this business—you know that I do—but news like this makes you rethink, and I don't want these four walls to be the last thing I see before I go.'

'I'm so sorry, Edward.'

Joss could hear the tears in Eva's voice, and he squeezed her hand. He knew how fond she was of his father, and that her grief must mirror his own. 'Are you sure you're comfortable? Is there anything we can do?'

'Quite comfortable for now, my dear. Thank you for your concern. Now it's my turn to ask the questions.' He glanced at their clasped hands. 'Is there anything you two would like to tell me?'

Eva sat in shock, silenced by Edward's words. She couldn't believe that the old man was dying. Sure, he'd looked a little creaky around the joints lately, but he'd never complained of so much as a runny nose. It just didn't make sense that he could be terminally ill.

Joss had taken hold of her hand and she could feel the contact burning her skin. She hadn't thought about it when she'd slid her fingers between his back in the boardroom. Hadn't thought about all the times she'd imagined the slide of his skin against hers over the years. All she'd been able to feel was the grief and fear radiating from him, and she had acted on instinct, trying to ease it in any way she could.

And now Edward was calling them on it. Under normal circumstances she'd have cleared up the understanding with Edward the minute it had happened. But this was Joss's father, and they had both just been hit with shocking news. It was Joss's place, not hers, to explain.

'I'm sorry you saw that, Dad—' he started.

'Oh, don't be sorry—I'm delighted. I *do* remember what it was like to be young, believe it or not. I'm just pleased that you two have finally found each other. I can't deny that I've been waiting for this for some time. I take it that if you're bringing your personal life with you to work then it's serious?'

Eva felt her mouth fall open and waited for Joss to correct his father, to sum up what had happened with the dress and the coffee and the zip. But expressions chased across Joss's face faster than she could read them.

She was just about to jump in and explain for herself what had happened when Joss finally spoke.

'Yes, it's serious,' Joss said. 'In fact, we're engaged.'

She was about to call him on being completely ridiculous when she clocked the look on Edward's face. A smile had brought a glow to his face, and he was beaming at them both. Just a moment she was so shocked she couldn't speak. And then real life kicked in, and she remembered the news that Edward had just delivered, that Joss had just received. She found that she couldn't contradict him.

Still, she gently withdrew her hand. She had to maintain some semblance of control if she was going to keep her head.

She'd been trying to pretend to herself for years that she didn't have an enormous crush on this man. That he didn't enter her mind when she was out on a date with any other guy. And now he had to go and pretend to be in love with her. And the only result of calling him on it would be to hurt the man she'd come to care for almost as a parent. She couldn't do it to him. She'd have to talk to Joss in private. He could break it to his father gently.

Funny how being angry with him made him that little bit less fanciable—she'd been looking for something to knock the shine off him for years.

It wasn't as if she *wanted* to be attracted to him— she told herself that often enough. She couldn't think of anyone less suitable for falling in love with than the son of her boss, who spent half his time on the road visiting the UK stores, and the other half in his office, buried in spreadsheets and dodging calls from disappointed would-be dates.

Secretaries talked—hardly breaking news.

As soon as she'd recognised where her feelings were going—the irritating pitter-patter of her heart, the annoying dampness of her palms, not to mention the completely inappropriate but delicious dreams that had her waking flushed and impressed by the breadth of her own imagination—she'd acted.

She'd put space between them at the office, avoided him in the break room and at the pub. She'd thrown herself into dating in a way that was the opposite of

Joss's clinical style: enthusiastically, prolifically, discriminately. She'd found handsome, eligible bachelors who weren't intimidated by her salary or her seven fluent languages—or the handful of conversational ones. She'd dated in Russian, Greek and German, and once—haltingly, but memorably—in Mandarin. She'd gone dancing, cocktail-making, picnicking. Tried blue blood and blue collar.

And not a single one of the men she'd kissed so demurely on the cheek at the end of the night had helped her even start forgetting about Joss. He was beginning to appear annoyingly unforgettable, and now he was pulling her into a deceit that she knew, unhesitatingly, was a BAD IDEA. All caps.

'Well, like I said, I can't say that I'm surprised. I've suspected for a while that you two have a soft spot for each other,' Edward said at last, still smiling.

Eva groaned inwardly. Oh, no, how much of her stupid crush had he seen? How much was he going to figure out? How much was *Joss* going to figure out for himself?

'And it makes me a very happy man to see you settled and in love before I go.'

The three of them sank into silence as the meaning of his words hit home and the reality of his illness intruded once again on the completely insane situation Joss had just created.

'But now I've got work to do—so get out of here, the pair of you.'

Eva kissed Edward on the cheek and mumbled something indiscernible, then let Joss follow her from the room, past the open-plan desks and into Joss's office.

'What the *hell* was that?' she demanded as soon as they were alone, staring at Joss as he sank into his chair and rested his face in his hands.

'Not now, Eva.'

'Not *now*? You just told your father we're engaged— I think I'm entitled to an explanation.'

'He's just told me he's dying. I can't talk about this now.'

She dropped into a chair opposite him, feeling sick to her stomach. Joss was right—he'd just had terrible news. Much as she had every right to give him hell, perhaps now wasn't the time.

'You didn't know anything about it?' she asked gently.

'He didn't say *anything*. Just that he needed to speak to me before the meeting. But I was tied up on a call and I... I missed the meeting. He wanted to tell me.'

'You couldn't have known he was going to tell you that.' She crossed to stand beside him and rested a hand on his shoulder. 'It wouldn't have changed anything. The news would have been the same.'

'It would have felt different if he'd been able to talk to me before having to tell everyone else.'

'You're right. I'm sorry.'

He leaned his head against her arm and she let her hand brush against his hair.

'And I'm sorry for what I told him about us.'

Eva moved her hand away, aware of a sudden change

of the chemistry in the room. She hitched herself onto the corner of the desk, letting her stilettoed feet dangle.

'What was that about? The truth would have been a much simpler explanation. It's going to be a hundred times harder to explain things now. Engaged or not, who knows what he thinks we were up to in his office?'

'I was thinking on my feet. I didn't want him to think that you were involved in something sordid, and my brain went to "engaged" rather than "wardrobe malfunction". You saw his face when I told him that we were getting married. I knew that it would make him happy.'

'Marrying me?'

'Being happy…settled. It's all he wants for me. And since my divorce… You don't want to hear all that. Just trust me on this one. I know my father. I knew it would make him happy.'

'So what's it going to do to him when you tell him there's no engagement?'

And suddenly, from the defiant clench of his jaw and the killer look in his eyes, Eva knew that he wasn't planning on telling his father the truth at all.

'Don't be ridiculous,' she said, keeping her voice low and commanding. 'We have to tell him the truth. I'll tell him about the coffee and the dress. I'll sort this out.'

Joss shrugged, never breaking eye contact, never backing down from the challenge she'd made so clear in her voice.

'We'll explain about the dress. But I see no reason to drop the pretence of our engagement.'

She stood slowly from the desk and took a step towards him, letting him know that she found neither his position in the company nor the six inches in height he had over her intimidating in the slightest. Least of all when he was seated and she could tower over him.

'No reason, Joss? You just panicked and told a bare-faced lie that has implications for us both. I have no intention of lying to your father, so unless you want him to hear from me that you just fabricated a fiancée, I think you would do better to just tell him now.'

'Or we could make him believe that it's true.'

She took half a step back to stare at Joss. 'Have you completely lost your mind? Why would we want to do that?'

'Maybe I have lost my mind. It wouldn't be the first time. I don't know… What I *do* know is that my father has just told me that he's dying, and I—we—can do something to make him happy in the time he has left.'

'By lying to him? Do you think he'd really want that?'

'You saw his face. You tell me if you think the lie hurt him.'

She shrugged, unable to contradict him. 'I know he seemed happy, Joss. But it can't be right. I mean, how long would we have to keep this up?'

She sat down again, losing a little of her anger as she realised what she was asking.

'I'm sorry. I didn't mean…'

'I know. I know you didn't mean anything by it. But, yeah, we would have to keep it up until he dies. Which, apparently, won't be all that long. Don't worry—I don't expect you to actually say *I do*.'

She sat and thought on it for a moment. Remembered the look on Edward's face when Joss had told his lie. She couldn't deny that he'd looked happy. As happy as she'd seen him for a long time.

She loved Edward. He had been the one constant in her life for so long now, and she wasn't sure how she was going to manage without him. A sob threatened, and her hand lifted slowly to her throat as she forced it down. She slumped into the back of the chair, suddenly deflated. Surely if it made Edward happy she could do this. She *should* do this.

'I need some time to think about it,' she said eventually, not wanting Joss to know the direction her thoughts had been heading.

Goodness knew she'd been trying to keep the details of her mind secret from him for long enough. If they were to go through with this completely ridiculous idea, how was she meant to keep that up? To hide the fact that her mouth wanted to part every time she saw him? That she had to stop her tongue moistening her lips and her body swaying towards him?

'Take some time, then. No work's going to get done this afternoon anyway, by the looks of it.'

Eva shook her head. 'Your father will need me.'

'I'm going to my father's office now, and we're going to have a long talk. I'll make sure there's not a problem. If you want, I can say you went home with a headache.'

'While he's still at work with a terminal illness? Thanks but no thanks. Lock yourself in with your father if you want, but I'll be at my desk if either of you need me.'

Joss leaned back in his chair, raising his hands to admit defeat. 'We need to talk, though. And we can't do that in the office. Dinner tonight?'

Dinner tonight.

How many times had she imagined Joss issuing an invitation like that? Though she'd always known that she wouldn't accept. It wasn't even the time that he spent travelling around the country that made her think he was a million miles from boyfriend material. No, it was the fact that even when he was here he wasn't quite...*here*. There was an isolation about him. A distance. Even when he was close enough to touch.

She'd done long-distance before, with people in her life that she'd loved, and she'd hated every second of it. The last thing she needed was a man—a fiancé—who was distant even when he was in the room.

But she couldn't ignore him while he was going around telling people that they had got engaged. She had to convince him to tell his father the truth. And then figure out how they were meant to work together.

'Yes,' she agreed eventually. 'I guess we do need to talk about this. My place? I don't feel like going out after news like this. I don't suppose you do either.'

'No. That sounds good. Eight?'

She nodded, and scribbled down her address.

Walking back to her desk, she grabbed the coffee-stained dress and put it in the garment bag that she'd flung over her chair as she'd raced for the boardroom.

The blinds in Edward's office were drawn—a sure sign that he didn't want to be disturbed—so she sat at her computer, knowing that her work—the one constant she had in her life—was going to change irrevocably, and there was nothing she could do about it.

CHAPTER TWO

EVA CHECKED ON the food and resisted glancing at her reflection in the window. She didn't want Joss to think that she'd made an effort, so she'd not touched her hair or her make-up since she'd got home, and had just thrown on jeans and a comfy jumper. She always wore her skinnies and a cashmere sweater for a Friday night in—that was perfectly plausible.

She didn't even want to think about how the conversation over dinner was going to go, but she had to. Had to be prepared—set out in her own mind, at least, what was and wasn't going to be on the cards.

Joss was crazy, thinking that they could get away with a fake engagement. They'd be under scrutiny every minute they were together at the office. She knew how little fuel the gossip furnace needed to keep it alight. But every time she convinced herself of how terrible an idea it was, she remembered the happiness on Edward's face and the eagerness to please his father on Joss's.

She had to admit to being intrigued.

Joss was a powerful man. A director—now the MD—of a vast luxury group of department stores, with a presence on every continent, property in every major European shopping capital. He was notorious for the coldness of his personal life—the wife and the marriage that he'd neglected, and the transactional nature of the dates he took to industry functions. The women he dated were always clients and colleagues, there to further a business deal or a conversation, and they always went home alone.

She'd always seen something else in him. Something more. Something in the way that he joked with his father in a way he didn't with anyone else. Being so close to Edward, she'd seen their father-son relationship up close. Seen that Joss might not be the cold-hearted divorcee that everyone had him pegged as.

And now he'd invented an engagement just to please his dying father, and her curiosity was piqued again.

The two men didn't have much time left together— and they both seemed happier with this alternative reality than with real life. Who was she to judge? Who was she to tell them they were wrong? If she hadn't been personally involved she'd be telling them to do whatever they had to do in order to enjoy the time they had left together. But to say that she was 'involved' was putting things mildly—and this was *way* personal. She'd be as responsible as Joss if the truth came out and Edward's heart was broken in his last few weeks or months.

And maybe all of this was academic. Because it assumed that they stood a chance of getting away with this charade. Making everyone believe that they were in love. Well, it wouldn't be too hard to convince on her side, she supposed, given the attraction that she'd been hiding for years.

Through the break-up of his marriage—that time of dark black circles under his eyes and an almost permanent blank expression on his face—she was the only one who had seen him lean back against his father's office door after he'd left a meeting, composing his features and erasing all emotion before he went and faced the rest of the office. And in the time since, he'd been working non-stop—not competing with his colleagues but seemingly competing with himself.

It was hard to pinpoint when she had realised she had a heck of a crush growing. Perhaps after the dip in her stomach when she'd won a hard-earned smile, or when they'd argued in the boardroom and he'd held up his hands in concession to her point, never mind that he was a director and she an assistant.

Or when he'd walked in on her today, half-dressed in his father's office, and her whole skin had hummed in awareness of him. She'd had to hide the blush that had crept over her cheeks when his fingertips had clasped the zip and pulled it down—something she'd fantasised about more times than she wanted to admit, even to herself.

But nothing that she had done so far had worked in trying to get herself to forget him.

Perhaps it was time to do something different. She had proved that ignoring this thing wasn't going to make it go away. Maybe getting closer to him was the key. It was easy to maintain a crush, a fantasy, from afar. When you didn't have to deal with wet towels on your bed or dirty dishes left on the table. Maybe what she needed was some old-fashioned exposure therapy.

Because what did she really know about Joss, beyond what she saw when he was occasionally in the office? If there was one sure way to test a romance it was for a couple to move in together.

Was she completely losing her mind thinking that this was even a feasible idea—never mind a good one?

The doorbell rang, shocking her out of her internal debate. Good, she was getting sick of the sound of her own thoughts. At least with Joss here she would have a sparring partner.

She jogged down the stairs to the street-level door, trying to ignore the familiar flip of her heart at the sight of him. Not that he was looking his best—he had clearly come straight from the office. His shirt was creased, his collar unfastened and his tie loosened.

And then she remembered again how his day had been a thousand times worse than hers and had to resist the urge to pull him close and comfort him.

'Hey—you found it okay?'

'Yeah.' He waved his phone vaguely at her. 'Just a little help from this. I've not been here since I was a kid.'

'Of course—your dad used to stay here back then. I'd forgotten you must have been here too.'

She stepped back so that he could get through the door. From her little cobbled mews she could barely hear the traffic from the main road nearby, muffled by the square of white stucco pillared houses around the private, locked garden. She showed Joss upstairs to her apartment—a legacy of the time when the building would have had stables downstairs and living quarters for servants of the wealthy above, all tucked away behind the grand mansions on the square.

Eva loved the understated elegance of her home, with clipped bay trees at the door, original cobbles paving the passage and soft heritage colours on the doors and windows.

'It's beautiful,' Joss said as he reached the top of the stairs and crossed to the living room, where great tall windows flooded light in one side of the room. 'Have you been living here long?'

'Since I started at Dawson's.'

Joss looked intrigued. 'I thought my dad had got rid of this place.'

'He had—sort of,' Eva said, reaching for a bottle of wine and raising a glass in question at Joss.

He nodded and reached to take it from her when it was full.

'He realised it was mostly sitting empty while it was a company flat, so he decided to rent it out. When I started working for the company I was stuck for somewhere to stay. Your dad didn't have a tenant at the time, and needed someone to house-sit, so he offered me this place.'

Joss raised his eyebrows. 'Lucky you.'

'Yeah, I don't like to move a lot, and he offered me a long-term lease. I like it here.'

'So I'm going to have a hard time convincing you to move in with me?'

Eva snorted, and winced at the sting of wine in her nose.

'That part's non-negotiable,' she confirmed. 'This is my home and I'm not leaving it.'

'So you're coming round to the rest of it? Good.'

She should have given him an outright no—told him there and then that there was absolutely no way she was going along with his ridiculous scheme. But somehow, with him here in her home, in her space, she wasn't sure she wanted to. All of a sudden she wasn't sure about anything.

That was what happened when the only stable part of your life upped and threatened to leave. It had sunk in on her short walk home from the office that she could be about to lose her job—the first point of stability she'd ever had in her life. The safe place that she'd built for herself in the twelve years that she'd been with the company.

She would have thought she'd have been used to it by now. She'd had her whole childhood to practise, after all. Every time her mother or her father had shipped out, or they'd all packed up and moved to another army base, she'd told herself it was the last time she'd care. The last time she'd cry.

She'd not managed to stick to her word until the final time. The time her mother hadn't come home at all.

Her father had packed her off to boarding school then, not long after she'd begged him to leave the army, to stop moving her around and give her some stability. She'd taken herself straight off to university after school, and from there straight into business, landing in Edward's team and working her way up to be his executive assistant.

Her parents had never managed to give her the stability she'd craved, so she'd found her own—with Dawson's. It was a family business, its history stretching into the last century and the one before that. The company had been around long before Edward, and she had no doubt that it would continue without him.

But how was it ever going to feel the same after he was gone? And what else was going to change?

The succession plans that had been approved by the board had appointed her as Joss's new EA—she was tied to the job role, not to the holder—but once his father was gone Joss had no reason to stick with that decision. She could be out through the door as soon as Edward was dead.

An engagement to the heir apparent—even a fake one—was another tie to the company. To the family. Another bond to the life that she'd built for herself. An obstacle between her and everything falling away. Was that completely crazy? Maybe. But that didn't mean she didn't feel it.

'Here.' She passed Joss a bowl of potatoes and a salad. 'Can you stick these on the table? The chicken will be just another minute.'

He took the bowls from her and glanced at the pan on the hob.

'That looks amazing. You shouldn't have gone to so much trouble, though. We could have ordered something.'

She shrugged. 'It was no trouble. I'd have been cooking for myself anyway.'

'You cook like this every night?'

She narrowed her eyes as she tried to work out his angle. 'Are you asking if that's part of the deal?'

'I'm making conversation. At least, I'm trying to.'

'I'm sorry.' She shook her head as she grabbed a couple of plates and started serving up. 'Everything just feels so…weird. I can't get my head around it.'

'It doesn't need to be weird.'

'Joss, this afternoon you asked me to pretend to be your fiancée. Now you're asking me to move in with you. How can it be anything *but* weird?'

'Because it's not real, Eva.'

She brandished a set of tongs at him. 'That makes it worse! How can faking something like that not feel weird to you? Lying to your father won't feel weird?'

He held his hands up and shrugged, though his expression belied his casual attitude. 'Do you tell your parents everything that's going on with you?'

'There's just my dad. We're not close. But I've never invented a fiancé.'

Before now, she added in her head. Because this conversation seemed to be gathering momentum, and she wasn't sure she was going to put a stop to it. She hadn't come out and told Edward that it wasn't true yet, so at the very least she was complicit in the lie getting this far.

It was only when Joss had mentioned it that she'd even thought about the fact that she might have to tell her dad. How was it that she'd put more emotional energy into worrying that she was lying to Edward than into the fact that she would also have to lie to her own father? She'd not even considered that going through with this would affect him too.

Maybe it didn't have to. Maybe she could keep the whole thing from him—it wasn't as if they spoke often. Or at all, really.

'You're quiet,' Joss commented as they sat down to eat at the dining table tucked into the corner of the living room.

'Thinking,' she replied, helping herself to salad and potatoes.

'Enlighten me,' Joss instructed, equally economical with his words.

Eva sighed, but he was here to talk and they weren't going to get anywhere if neither of them opened up. And, if what she'd seen of Joss over the years was anything to go by, she would be waiting a long time for an emotional outpouring from his end.

'I'm not sure that this is a good idea.' A good start, she thought. Get her cards on the table. 'We're lying to your father. It's likely we'll be found out. It's a distraction when we should be concentrating on what he needs.'

Joss raised an eyebrow.

'What?' Eva asked.

'We're doing it *for* my father. You saw how happy it's making him.'

Joss had said that they needed to talk, but it was only now she realised that he thought he was here to sort out details—not to convince her. He was assuming that she would just go along with it. He'd taken her decision not to tell Edward the truth from the start as approval, and he was here to iron out the fine print.

'You really think I'm going to go along with this?'

Joss looked up and held her gaze for a beat longer than was comfortable.

'I think you already are.'

A shiver ran through her at the tone of his voice. So commanding. So sure of himself. So arrogant. She'd had no idea before this moment that that did something for her, but the heat between her legs and the tightness in her belly told her it definitely did.

'If you were going to back out,' he continued, 'you would have done it back at the office. Or just told my father the truth on the spot. Why are we bothering to dance around this when we both know you've made up your mind?'

She fixed him with a stare and muttered an Arabic curse under her breath, trying not to show him how right she knew he was. Because she *could* have called a halt to this hours ago. The fact that she hadn't told them both all they needed to know.

'I'm doing it to make your father happy,' she clarified, still holding that gaze, making sure Joss could see that she wasn't backing down or giving in to him. She was making her own decisions for her own very good reasons.

'I know.' He nodded, taking a sip of his wine, breaking their eye contact and cutting into his chicken.

'I mean it,' he said, after he'd polished off half the plate. 'I could get used to this.'

'Good,' she said, standing up and picking up her

plate, suddenly losing her appetite. 'You can get used to doing the washing up as well.'

Joss finished his food and followed her through to the little kitchen. 'You think you're going to scare me away with threats of stacking the dishwasher?'

She gestured around the bijou kitchen. 'You see a dishwasher in here?'

He glanced around. 'Fine. So we'll get someone in. I'll pay,' he added when she started to shake her head.

'It's not about the money.'

'What? It's about me being willing to get my hands wet? Fine. But I'm not a martyr, Eva. If you're hoping to scare me then I might as well tell you now that it's not going to work.'

'You don't want to move in here. There's no space.'

He leaned back against the kitchen counter, a hand either side of his hips. His man-spreading made his intentions clear. It would have been more subtle if he'd marked the doorframe with his scent.

'I decide for myself what I do and don't want, Eva. This is where you live, so it's where I'll live too. You've stated your ground rules; now I'm stating mine.'

She folded her arms and leant back against the kitchen counter. 'There's not even any space in the wardrobe.'

'You can't expect us to live apart.'

'We're going to see each other all the time at work. Isn't moving in together a bit much?'

He took a step towards her, and Eva had to admit that his height *was* a little intimidating in the tiny kitchen.

'And how many people are going to believe our story if we're not living together?'

'We could tell people we're waiting until after the wedding.'

He shook his head and, much as she hated it, Eva knew he was right.

'They'd ask us which century we're living in. Perhaps if this was a real relationship we'd say to hell with what they think. But we need to make them believe us. I don't want to give them any reason not to. I'll start moving some stuff in on Monday.'

He moved to leave, and somehow, although it was what her rational brain wanted, it seemed her body wasn't expecting it. Disappointment washed through her. It wasn't as if she wasn't used to living alone. She loved having her own space. But they'd been through a lot today, and she wasn't particularly keen on being left alone with her thoughts.

'Do you want a coffee before you go?' she asked, flicking on the kettle behind her.

'Sure,' Joss said, watching her carefully. 'Something wrong?'

'No,' she replied, rubbing her forehead and realising she wasn't being very convincing. 'Just a lot to take in. Weird day.'

'Tell me about it,' Joss said, leaning back on the counter.

Eva looked up and realised that it wasn't a figure of speech.

'No, no—it's fine,' she said.

'I can listen. Even help.'

'I can't, Joss. He's your dad. You don't want to… It should be me asking if you're okay.'

'I don't get an exclusive on it, Eva. I know you care for him too.'

'I just can't believe I didn't know…you know.'

She made two coffees and carried them back through to the living room. Plonking them on the coffee table, she just had time to wish she had space for a bigger sofa before Joss appeared behind her.

'Do you sit and spy on your neighbours?' Joss asked, pointing out the way the sofa was angled towards the big picture window out onto the mews.

'More like bask in the sun. I get enough gossip at work.'

He looked surprised.

'What? Don't tell me you hadn't noticed.'

He shook his head. 'What do people gossip about?'

'Oh, you know—the usual. Who's sleeping with who. Who's angling for a promotion. Who's getting fired.'

'So why don't I hear any of this?'

Eva rolled her eyes. With all his expensive business education, did he seriously not understand how an office worked? She was clearly going to have to spell this out to him.

'Of course you don't hear the gossip,' she said. 'One, you're practically the boss. No one gossips in front of the boss. Two, you're hardly ever in the office. And three, you're not exactly Mr Friendly over the coffee machine when you *are* there.'

'People don't think I'm friendly?'

'*I* don't think you're friendly. I can't speak for anyone else.'

He folded his arms and fixed her with a stern look. She was tempted to laugh.

'What's so unfriendly about me?'

Should she go for it? Unload all his faults? All the reasons she'd been telling herself for years why he was a million miles from boyfriend material.

Why not? Perhaps it would be the final straw in this idiotic deception.

'Fine—if you want to hear it. You're not exactly an open book, are you, Joss? You don't talk to people unless it's directly about the business.'

'I don't do small talk. There's a difference.'

'Right: the difference between being friendly and not friendly. It's not a criticism. Just an observation.'

'You think I should be friendlier?'

She sighed and shook her head. Seriously, this man's emotional intelligence didn't even register on the scale. 'I didn't say that. I don't think you need to change. But just don't be surprised if people don't open up around you.'

'Well, *you* don't seem to be having a problem with that.'

She shrugged and gave a resigned laugh. 'Proposing to a girl will have that effect. If you didn't want to know, you shouldn't have asked.'

'Might as well know what people think of me. So—office gossip. Is there going to be a lot of it. About us?'

'Are you kidding?' She laughed properly, genuinely

amused for the first time all day. 'I'm going to be grilled like a fish about this on Monday morning.'

'You could just not go in,' Joss offered. 'Take a few days off. Benefits of dating the boss.'

The smile dropped from her face as the insult hit. As if she could just not show up for work, with no notice, and it wouldn't make a difference to anyone.

'I think we need to get a couple of things straight, Joss. One—I work very hard with your father. My job is important, and I can't just swan off because you say so. Unless you fancy handling his correspondence in Arabic, Italian and French on Monday morning, I'll be at my desk as usual. Two—we are not now, nor will we ever be "dating". If I'd wanted to date you, I'd have asked you out for dinner. I'm going along with your little charade because I care about your father. Don't confuse the two.'

'Would you?' He leaned into the arm of the sofa with a smile that was verging dangerously on smug.

'Would I what?'

'Have asked me out for dinner?'

She sighed. Bloody man. 'The key part of that sentence, Joss, was *if*. I've never asked you because I don't want to date you.'

'You know, you sound like you've given that quite a lot of thought. Should I be flattered?'

'Honestly. Only a man with your ego could find a way to take that as a compliment. Listen to me carefully, Joss. I don't want to date you. I don't want to be engaged to you. I'm going along with it for now. But when the time comes we'll both extract ourselves from this situation with as much dignity as we can muster and forget it ever happened.'

CHAPTER THREE

EVA SPENT THE weekend in a daze. The further she got from having seen Joss the more ridiculous the whole thing seemed. So when she pitched up at her desk at eight o'clock on Monday morning she was almost surprised to see him there waiting for her.

'You're in early,' she commented, unwinding her scarf from around her neck and draping it over the coat-stand. 'Trying to impress somebody?'

'I told you—my father wants to start handing things over today. I thought we'd need an early start.'

'Well, we've both beaten the boss in.' She glanced through the blinds to Edward's darkened office beyond. 'Did you see him at the weekend? How is he?'

'*He* is marvellous, Eva, dear,' Edward said, bowling up behind her. 'Thank you for asking. And I was out of the city this weekend, so I've not seen anyone since I left the office on Friday. How about you two? I hope you did something nice with your weekend and didn't spend it worrying about me.'

'Dinner on Friday night,' Joss supplied truthfully.

'And Borough Market on Saturday,' Eva added.

No need to mention that she'd gone alone. She disliked the taste of the half-lie in her mouth, but the smile on Edward's face softened the blow.

'And arriving together on Monday morning. Were you this indiscreet before or am I really getting old?'

'Actually,' Joss said, 'we thought that now everyone will be finding out our news there's no reason we can't arrive together. In fact, I'll be moving my things over to Eva's place tonight.'

'Well, that's marvellous. Wish it had all worked like that when your mother and I were that age. Now, I'm glad I've found you two alone—I've been thinking, and there's something I want to say to you. I don't know what your plans are, but I don't want you to rush them for me. I know my news has been upsetting, but I don't want you hurrying anything up for my sake. Please?'

It was perfect, in a way, Eva realised. They wouldn't have to find an excuse not to marry before he died.

'But enough about that. I need the two of you in Milan as soon as you can get there. The store manager's feeling jumpy, and we have a couple of major suppliers over there as well who would probably appreciate a visit. I need you to smooth things over. Let people see that you're more than ready for the big job.'

Joss's eyebrows drew together, and she knew he wasn't happy at the implication that his employees didn't trust him.

'Dad, I met Matteo at the conference earlier in the year and it was all fine. The managers all know me. Surely you want me here? I'm not sure now's the time for me to be travelling.'

'Now's the perfect time, son. We need to steady things. You're going to have to visit all the flagship stores. The big suppliers too. They're worried—it's been a long time since this company faced big changes. This is part of your job now.'

'But what if something happens here?'

Eva winced. She knew exactly what Joss meant.

'What if I pop my clogs, you're asking? It's not going to happen overnight, son. We have some time. And I'd like to see the old girl looking straight before I go. I promise if anything changes you'll be the first to know. If it helps you make your mind up, I'm not planning on hanging around London waiting to die. Some places I want to see before I go. But you two need to be on a plane before lunchtime, and I've got an inbox the size of Milan Cathedral to work through with Eva before you go.'

Joss walked away, leaving Eva and his father huddled around his computer monitor. Eva was making notes on a pad and occasionally reaching across to touch the screen. It was clear to him how fond she was of his father, and how distressed at the news of his illness.

And now he'd told them that he didn't want a hasty wedding. Yes, it got them out of having to take this charade too far, but Joss saw something else in it.

How much did his father know about his last marriage? About how he had felt rushed, unable to stop the oncoming commitment even after he'd realised it was a bad idea. More than he had let on at the time, it seemed.

He'd been rash and stupid announcing their non-existent engagement to Edward, and he supposed that he should be grateful that Eva had agreed to go along with it.

She'd told him that it was because she cared for the old man, and Joss didn't doubt that. But that didn't mean he believed she'd given him the whole story. There were things that she was hiding. Layers of secrets, he suspected, from the frequently veiled expressions that crossed her face. Well, he was going to find out what they were—they had hours of travelling ahead of them, and she couldn't dodge his questions the whole way to Italy.

Or maybe he'd sleep instead of quizzing her, because that definitely hadn't been happening enough since his father had dropped his bombshell. He'd have liked to say it was grief over his father's illness that was causing his insomnia, but he knew that it was something else.

It was sleek chestnut hair and hazel eyes. The memory of a rose-pink slip under a serious navy dress. It was the thought of his holdall of clothes stashed in his office, destined for her flat just as soon as they got back from their trip. The thought of living in such close quarters with a woman he'd determinedly avoided since he'd noticed his attraction to her.

Back in his office, he dug out his toothbrush and a change of clothes from the holdall. If they weren't on a plane until lunchtime, he knew that they'd need to stay over. With his dad sending him off in such a hurry, he guessed it wasn't going to be a short meeting at the other end.

A noise caught his attention and he looked up to see

Eva, stalled at the entrance of his office. He felt that familiar pull, the heat in his body he knew was inevitable when he was near her. Again he silently cursed whatever impulse it was that had made him lie to his father.

He felt a twist of pain in his belly. He knew how dangerous secrets could be—keeping his feelings bottled up had turned toxic before, and lying to his father felt unnatural now.

Intellectually, he understood the reasons he'd done it. Because he'd let his father down so many times over the years. He'd married his university girlfriend, a friend of the family, because she was 'the right sort of girl' from 'the right sort of family', and everyone had expected it to happen. He'd done what he'd thought was the right thing—stood up in front of their friends and their family and made the commitment that was expected from him, no matter how wrong it had felt inside.

As his depression had grown and his marriage had darkened, he'd ignored the problems. Blinkered himself against his wife's pain and buried himself in his work rather than go back on his word and end a marriage that was never going to make either of them happy. Until she'd upped and left, and he'd seen the disappointment in his parents' eyes that he had failed. Failed his wife. Failed both their families.

It had only been after the breakdown of his marriage that he'd realised he needed help. He'd gone weeks with barely a couple of hours' sleep a night. Seen his weight drop and his appetite disappear. It had only been when he'd looked up his symptoms on the internet that he'd realised they were classic signs of depression.

As soon as he'd read that, everything had fallen into place—that was the dark tunnel that he'd found himself in as his personal life had hurtled towards marriage while he'd buried his head in the sand, concentrating on the business.

So he'd gone to his doctor, worked hard at therapy. Eaten and exercised well. Taken the meds he'd been prescribed. And he'd recovered from his illness with a clarity and a focus that he'd not felt in years.

He shouldn't have been in that relationship to start with. He should have called it off as soon as he'd had doubts—before his illness had blinkered his vision and left him feeling that he didn't have a way out.

His parents had hinted over the years since his divorce that he should start seeing someone else, get back out there. But he knew he didn't want to be a bad husband, a bad partner, again. He couldn't risk doing that to someone else.

But he also knew that his father wanted to see him settled and happy—that was what had made it so easy for those words to slip out of his lips in the heat of the moment. And it was what made him burn with guilt now, knowing that he was misleading him. He suspected his father felt partially responsible for Joss feeling he had to go along with family expectations. If this lie made Joss feel uncomfortable, it would be worth it if it meant that his father could let his guilt rest before he died.

The recent spate of sleepless nights was a worry, though. It was years since he'd felt this drag of fatigue, and it reminded him of a time in his life he had absolutely no wish to revisit. This time it carried with it an extra shade of dread. He didn't want to be ill again. Didn't want his world to shrink and pale as he fought with his own brain chemistry to feel even the smallest amount of hope.

And right there was another good reason not to listen to the pull of his body when Eva was near. No. They had to keep real life, real feelings, and their charade separate. Regardless of how attracted they were to each other.

He considered his own thoughts. Was he right? Was she attracted to him as he was to her?

'Hey, come in,' he said, remembering that she was still standing, watching him from the doorway.

She shut the door behind her and Joss shifted in his chair at the sudden charge in the room that their isolation created.

'How's Dad getting on?' Talking about his father seemed like the safest option.

'He's great. Same as always. If he hadn't told us, I still wouldn't know there was anything wrong. Says he's looking forward to some more time out of the city. You?'

'I'm good. Could do without this trip, if I'm being honest.'

'Yeah.' She glanced at her watch. 'That's what I wanted to talk to you about. Your dad's asked me to book us a room. Said he thought the meetings might go on a bit. I need to go home and pack a bag, so I'll just meet you at the airport.'

'It's easier if I come with,' Joss said, leaning back

in his chair. 'You're only around the corner. We'll get a cab from there. It means I can drop my stuff off too.'

'You brought it to the office?' Eva looked horrified.

'What? Are you still worried about the gossip?'

'It's easy for you to joke about it. You've not been grilled about our grand romance every time you've so much as looked at the coffee machine.'

'I'm sorry you're getting the brunt of it. Do you want me to say something?'

She sighed and shook her head. 'What? A formal announcement about our fake relationship? A little weird, Joss.'

'Fine. Well, we'll be out of here in an hour. Think the news has reached the Milan store already?'

'Oh, I can guarantee it'll travel faster than we do.'

As the plane lifted from the runway Joss itched to reach into his bag for his laptop, hoping to relax in the familiarity of a working journey. He'd travelled between stores more times than he could count, and he knew he could get plenty of work done before their meeting. Plus staring at the screen of his computer was safer than glancing across at the woman sitting beside him.

He remembered the first time he'd seen her. Well, the first time that he'd really noticed her. For so long during his marriage and his illness, he'd not been able to see any beauty in the world, never mind in a woman. And then one morning, newly divorced and with a fresh hold on his psychological wellbeing, he'd walked into his father's office and heard Eva speaking in quick-fire Italian—to the Milan store, perhaps. Or one of the luxury fashion suppliers. She'd burst into laughter, and as she'd thrown her head back in amusement she'd caught his eye.

Something had caught inside him, too. A spark of intense attraction he couldn't remember feeling since… Forget that. He'd *never* felt anything like that before— the intense pull not only to a beautiful woman, but to one he knew could joke and laugh in half a dozen languages when he was struggling to do it in one.

There had been a time in his past when an attraction like that would have felt like a red rag to a bull. But he knew better now. He knew where a relationship with him would leave a woman, and he had no desire to inflict that on Eva.

The 'Fasten Seatbelt' light was switched off, and Joss kept his eyes down as they both pulled out their laptops. Eva started muttering under her breath as she read through a document, the sound almost lost in the rustle of her hair as she tucked it behind her ear.

Please, not Italian, he pleaded silently. He wasn't sure what it was, but the sound of that language on her lips was his weak spot. He breathed a sigh of relief when he caught an Arabic phrase—something to do with the Dubai store, perhaps. It wasn't Italian but, *God*, she made it sound sexy.

He remembered the last time he'd heard her speak Arabic—at the conference of all their international store managers—the way the sounds had rolled around her tongue, and the confidence and speed with which she'd spoken. It was too much, eventually, and he glanced up from his spreadsheet, promising himself just a quick look at her expression.

But when he looked at her, her eyes were already focussed on him, and once he realised that he couldn't look away.

'What?' she asked him, breaking off from reading, and he knew he'd been staring too long.

He raised his eyebrows and shook his head. 'Nothing. Just wondered if you knew you were talking to yourself.'

He returned his gaze to the columns of numbers that had been dancing in front of his eyes since he'd loaded up the file.

He kept his eyes decisively on his screen until he heard his name pass Eva's lips and couldn't help glancing up to see her expression—he wished he hadn't when he saw the exasperation there. She rubbed her forehead and he glanced at her screen, but couldn't make out any of the Arabic she was reading. From her frustration, it was pretty clear that there was a problem, and he suspected he knew what it was.

'Trouble in Dubai?' he asked.

'They're worried,' Eva replied. 'Your father was due to have a phone conference with the manager of the store tomorrow. Edward's cancelled and asked me not to reschedule yet and the manager is worried about business continuity. I'm going to have to call your dad. See if he'll rearrange.'

'I'll take the meeting,' Joss said. 'What?' he added when Eva grimaced slightly.

'I'm not sure that'll work. In fact, I already tried that. They say they want to speak to Edward.'

'Well, if Dad's taking time off it's not like he doesn't have a good reason.'

'I know that. We'll talk to him about it when we're back in the office. But this is two stores just this morning who are going into crisis mode. I think we have to assume that others will react in the same way.'

Joss stared her down, not appreciating her doubting his ability to do his new job. 'I'm perfectly capable of running this business. I've been preparing for it for long enough.'

'I know that, Joss.' Eva relaxed back into the seat as she spoke. 'Your father does too—and every Dawson's employee, really. But knowing it and feeling it aren't necessarily the same thing. As a rule, people don't like change, and—like it or not—you at the head of the company *is* change.'

He shrugged off her concerns. 'So I'll go to Dubai too. To every single store worldwide if I have to.'

'It might help,' Eva said. 'In Dubai at least.'

Joss nodded, trying to mentally rearrange the next couple of weeks to accommodate another overseas trip. Dubai was too far to hop on a plane for just the day.

'You should come,' he said, thinking how valuable having his father's right-hand woman by his side would be in showing the store that nothing was going to change with him in charge. Yes, that was the only reason he was inviting her along. 'As a show of continuity. They might not know me well, but they know you. It will be reassuring.'

'I don't know, Joss.'

Eva didn't look convinced by his reasoning.

She leant forward, her elbows resting on the table in front of her. 'I never went with your dad. I can make the time to be out of the office for this one meeting, but I can't be constantly on the road or in the air.'

He watched her closely for a minute. The way she shifted in her seat and wouldn't meet his eyes. She might be worried about the business, but that wasn't really why she was refusing to go.

'That's not why you don't want to go. What is it—afraid of flying?'

She snorted a laugh. 'Did I miss you dragging me on here kicking and screaming? As if! And I'm an army brat, remember.'

'You *were* an army brat,' he corrected her. 'You look all grown up to me.'

He could have cringed at his cheesy line, but when her gaze finally locked on to his he didn't care—it was the truth. He didn't want to talk about her childhood. He wanted to talk about them on an all-night flight to Dubai and then getting hot and sweaty together in the desert.

He shook his head, hoping to scatter those dangerous thoughts. Eva was strictly off-limits, and he'd do well to remember that. Even if she agreed to this trip, as she'd agreed to the engagement, it would be strictly business. There would be no hot and sweaty—in the desert or anywhere else.

'So it's not the flight,' he said. He was intrigued. Who would turn down an impromptu trip to Dubai, with a visit to the city's most luxurious shopping mall guaranteed? 'What is it, then? Fear of catching some tropical disease?'

'It's nothing remotely exciting, Joss.' Eva flicked her fingers at an invisible piece of fluff. 'I prefer not to travel much. I love living in London and I like to stay there.'

Joss laughed with incredulity. 'But you speak six languages. Don't you ever want to use them?'

'Seven, actually. And, hello? How long have we been working together? I use them every day.'

'But is that really the same? Just saying the words, I mean. Or reading emails? Don't you want to go and experience the different cultures? Hear the dialects and the slang on the streets?'

Eva shrugged. 'I've done different cultures, thanks. I've done trying to learn what slang the cool kids are using. I'm happy where I am.'

'So why learn the languages at all?' He knew that talking about something so personal was probably a bad idea. But he couldn't help being intrigued by her. Couldn't help wanting to know more. 'There are plenty of jobs you could do without them.'

'It was a case of necessity at first, I guess,' Eva said. 'When we moved to Germany I wanted to do more than speak to the other kids on the base and at the army school. If I was going to be dragged to another country, I was determined to learn how to express myself there. The same when we went to Cyprus. And, to be honest, it came naturally. I loved learning to speak other languages. Maybe my brain likes the patterns of different grammar. Or hearing sounds that we don't even have in English. Words that can't be translated, because speaking another language makes you think in another language.'

'Okay, so German and Greek I get. But what about Arabic? Did you live in the Middle East?'

There was something more to this, he realised. Something about her parents. Something they'd never talked about before.

She shook her head. 'No, we were based here while Mum and Dad did their tours in Iraq. I'm not sure why I decided to learn. I quite liked the challenge of another new alphabet. A completely different written form of language.'

'And maybe it made you feel closer to your parents?' Joss asked gently. 'To speak the language they would be hearing around them every day?'

Eva remained silent, her eyebrows pulling together in a frown. Had she never considered that? he wondered.

'So, anyway, these meetings this afternoon,' Eva said, shaking off any suggestion of a personal conversation. 'What do you need from me? I've already requested an update from the supply management team on any issues they've had in the last few months, and pulled together the minutes from relevant meetings. As for the manager of the store, Matteo Lazzari, I've put all the correspondence between him and Edward in a folder and given you access. Is there anything else you need me to prepare?'

Joss looked at her closely, noting the swift change of subject but not pushing back. If she didn't want to talk about her personal life, then that was up to her. If this had been a real relationship then maybe he'd have encouraged her to open up, but this was just for show. She wanted to draw a line and that was fine by him.

He drew his eyes back to the spreadsheet in front of him, determined that the rest of the flight would be spent working, rather than trying and failing to guess what was going on in Eva's head.

When the announcement came to pack away all electronic devices and return their tables to an upright position, Joss congratulated himself on his self-control. Just as he'd promised himself, he'd got his work done with barely a thought for Eva.

He glanced sideways, to see if she was still working too, and realised the reason he had been so free from interruptions was because at some point, with her fingers still resting gently on her laptop keys, she had fallen asleep. Perhaps he wasn't the only one to have struggled with insomnia last night.

The cabin crew were making their way down the centre aisle, checking that their instructions for landing had been complied with, so he gently shifted Eva's hands from the computer onto her lap, then closed the laptop and folded up the table. She stirred a little in her sleep, shifting to get comfortable, and then eventually rested her head on his shoulder, letting out a deep sigh and settling back into sleep.

Joss watched her for a moment, unsure whether he should move her. But he thought it was unlikely he could do that again without waking her. So he left her where she was: with the gentle weight of her head against his arm and the smell of her hair temptingly close. The armrest between them was up, and as she fell deeper and deeper into sleep her body pressed closer, relaxing into him as he grew more and more tense.

He couldn't allow himself to enjoy this.

He mustn't allow himself to think about how he had seen that body covered only by the fine silk of a slip. How he'd wanted to run his hands inside her dress to clasp her waist, to pull her back against him as he slid her zip all the way down.

He couldn't allow himself to think about all the places his mind had taken him after he'd left her flat that night. Alone at home, he'd imagined pushing her dress off her shoulders, it gliding down to the floor and landing at his feet...

Another announcement from the cabin crew broke into his thoughts and was loud enough to wake Eva, who sat up with a start.

'Did I—?' Eva began, smoothing down her hair with a shaking hand before she stopped herself. 'Sorry—must have fallen asleep,' she said, briskly this time, looking around her in confusion. 'Did you put my laptop away?'

'They put the lights on for landing,' Joss offered by way of explanation.

'You should have woken me.'

He shrugged. 'Looked like you needed the sleep. I know the feeling. We'll be landing any minute,' he added, keen to move the conversation away from the question of them sleeping even in the same vicinity as one another.

An hour later their car passed the extravagant frontage of the Milan store on its way to their hotel, and he looked up at it in wonder. It didn't matter how many times he saw it, it never lost its magic. He thought of his great-grandfather, who had built up this business in a different century, a different world. And not for the first time he thought how lucky he was to be part of this family, to have such an inheritance, such a legacy to care for. His determination to continue that success, to prove himself, rallied.

And, much as he might protest to Eva that he had spent his life preparing for the top job, and much as that might be true, the job was his far sooner than any of them had imagined. He had thought he had a few more years to work on his relationships with the managers of the overseas stores. To build the connections that would be so important when his father was no longer around.

He was certain he had the experience and the expertise to continue the family success—now he had to prove himself to the rest of the business.

CHAPTER FOUR

EVA STEPPED UP to the desk at the hotel and pulled out the paperwork with the details of their reservation. The receptionist took their reservation number and tapped the screen of the computer for a seemingly endless time, until eventually she looked up with a smile and called over a bellboy.

'Thanks so much,' Eva said, excited to be speaking Italian face to face, despite everything she had said to Joss on the plane. 'Could you send some lunch up to the room?' she asked as the bellboy took their bags.

Their meeting was in an hour, but with the prospect of Italian cuisine when they arrived she hadn't been able to face the thought of airline food.

'Something quick and simple, please.'

She hovered behind the bellboy as he jiggled the key card and opened the door into their room. As she followed him in, she realised that there must have been some sort of mistake, in spite of how long the receptionist had taken to check them in.

Her eye was first caught by the extravagant bouquet of flowers on the beautifully polished table in the centre of the suite's foyer. A bottle of champagne and a note sat beside it, with her and Joss's names picked out in a stylish copperplate hand. Through the open doors leading from the foyer she could see at least one bedroom, a marble-lined bathroom, and a terrace overlooking the city. It was luxury far beyond anything she'd ever experienced. Was this what she had to look forward to as part of the Dawson family?

Not that she was part of the family yet. *Or ever would be*, she reminded herself. This engagement was all for show, no matter how real this suite was making it feel.

She picked up the envelope and turned it over, feeling the heavy weight of the paper in her hand. She read the note inside, fighting against the tear that was threatening at the corner of her eye.

Dearest Joss and Eva,
Consider the suite a little engagement present
from me. Enjoy Milan and don't hurry back.
Love,
Dad

Those last two words made her feel something she had been looking for for as long as she could remember. Included. Accepted. Part of a family. Something her own family had never managed.

Some parts of her childhood had been so privileged she knew she shouldn't complain. She'd always had a roof over her head and food on the table. While her mother and father had taken turns to be away on tour, among families and homes torn apart by conflict, whoever had been left behind had tried their best to fill the space that was left.

But that didn't change the facts. Both her parents had been happy to leave her for months at a time. Hugging her goodbye and promising to be home soon, all the while aware that they had no way of knowing if they could keep their promises. And then—inevitably, it had seemed—her mother had kissed her goodbye, told her she would be home soon, and instead they'd had a visit from a sombre-looking man in uniform. Eva had been left with the knowledge that her mother had never loved her enough to want to spare her the pain that her death would bring, even though she'd tried to convince herself that she didn't care enough to hurt.

She'd thought that would be it for her father. That he would be repulsed by the thought of leaving her again. Of taking the chance of making her an orphan.

She'd been wrong.

Joss came up behind her and took the note gently from her hand.

'The old romantic,' he said, with the beginnings of a laugh. He stepped around her to examine the champagne, but when he caught sight of her face he replaced the bottle in the ice bucket and reached to touch her cheek. 'What is it?' he asked, alarm evident in his expression.

'It's nothing,' Eva said, painting on a fake smile. 'You're right—it is romantic. Shame it'll be wasted on us.'

A knock at the door signalled lunch arriving.

'You show them in, I'll be back in just a minute.'

In the bathroom, she patted cold water on her cheek-bones and took a few deep breaths, trying not to think about romance, or the suite, or Joss. It was probably a good job that they were going to be in meetings all the time they were out here. It didn't matter what Edward said—she would be hurrying home. The less time they spent closeted in a luxury hotel suite the better. Or safer, at least. There were a lot of reasons why she might enjoy being locked away with Joss, but it was absolutely not a good idea to think about them. Definitely safer not to.

She left the bathroom and grabbed a couple of pieces of ciabatta from the tray the waiter had left on the table. Eating while she worked, she sifted through the files that she had brought with her, stocking her bag and ensuring that her tablet had enough charge to last the rest of the day. She had access to all the information that Joss might need for their meetings. This was his first test as Managing Director of the company, and it was a matter of professional pride for her that nothing went wrong for him.

She glanced at her watch as she pulled on a jacket. 'Are you ready?' she called to Joss, who had disappeared into one of the bedrooms.

'Be right out,' he called back.

She checked her phone as she waited by the door and was relieved to see a text from their driver, letting them know that he was waiting for them outside.

Joss emerged wearing a fresh shirt and she deliberately averted her eyes, not wanting to give herself any excuse to appreciate the way that man wore simple white cotton. It was a thought that she'd blocked out a lot over the years—when she'd caught sight of Joss in a meeting or walking through the office and tried to work out exactly what it was that made this man so attractive to her.

It wasn't as if he was even *nice*. Sure, he was courteous. He was professional. She couldn't think of a time when he had been outright rude. But definitely not nice. He wouldn't go out of his way to make someone feel comfortable. Wouldn't remember her birthday and drop something small and wrapped on her desk in the morning without a word.

He was nothing like his father, whom she adored. So how was it that for years she hadn't been able to get him out of her head? Why was he the man she measured every date against and found them lacking?

She reached behind her and grabbed the door handle, opening the door into the corridor and stepping out of the suite when Joss was a few feet away. A buffer zone: that was what was needed. Safe space between them that couldn't be breached.

But would people think that was odd? she wondered. She had no doubt that news of their engagement would have reached the Italian store before they did. Her standoffishness might cause more gossip—make people start to question whether the relationship was real. Make them ask what she hoped to get out of it.

She shook her head. It was far more likely that people would see that they were two professionals at work, acting professionally. No one would expect them to be all over each other. Respectful distance worked *for* their story, rather than against it.

'So, when was the last time you met with Matteo in person?' she asked Joss, determined to keep their conversation on a work footing after their earlier diversion into her personal life.

'In the spring,' Joss said. 'But it was at the conference for all the international store managers. You know what that thing is like—between meetings and presentations there's hardly time for a business conversation, never mind anything more personal.'

'Well, we should have lots of time today. You two have all afternoon pencilled in, and there's nothing in your diary for tonight either, so you can always take it to dinner if you feel you need to. Just remember you're trying to make a personal connection. He knows that you're capable. You've been with the company for ever. Just show him that you're someone he's going to enjoy working with.'

Joss caught up with her in the hallway. 'What? You want me to flirt with him? Seduce him?'

Here she was, trying to be professional, and he had to mention flirting and seduction pretty much the minute he opened his mouth. Was he determined to make this impossible for her?

'You know, I think he's been happily married for the last twenty years or so. I'm not sure flirting will get you anywhere.'

Joss tutted. 'You know what I mean. You think I should charm him. That's what he wants?'.

'I don't think he wants to be charmed, Joss. I think he wants to get to know you. You could be friendly. That would be a start.'

Friendly. There was that word again. Was that what she wanted from him? For him to be friendly to her? Hardly. That would make things impossible. At least when he was terse and short and—well, *un*friendly— she could remind herself of all the reasons why she shouldn't indulge this crush of hers. If he were to actually start conversing, or—God forbid—laughing like a normal human being, then she was going to be in big trouble.

'I thought we'd already established that I can't do friendly.'

'No, we established that you *don't* do friendly. Only you know whether that's out of choice or not. Do you try to be unfriendly?'

'I just try and get the job done, Eva. It doesn't normally require chatting over a cup of tea.'

'Well, your new job does, Joss. People need to see you, to get to know you. Your dad's illness has been a big shock to everyone. They're going to miss him enormously. It's a big gap to fill.'

Joss stopped in the hallway and fixed her with a stare.

'I'm well aware of that, thank you, Eva.'

She let out a breath and reached out a hand to his arm. 'I'm sorry, Joss. I know you are. And I'm not trying to criticise. Just trying to fill you in on what your father's relationship with his store managers is like. I'm not saying that you need to do business in the same way—I'm just giving you the information that you need to manage this transition. We're all trying to manage this situation as best we can. Myself included.'

He turned back to the lift and pressed the button to take them to the lobby. 'Well, thank you for the information. I'll take it under advisement.'

So that was how today was going to be. Icy cool. Well, that was fine by her, but she wasn't sure what Matteo would make of it.

They walked into the grand entrance of the Milan store to see Matteo waiting to greet them. 'Eva, *bella*. It is always such a pleasure.' He greeted her with a kiss on each cheek and warm enquiries about her health. 'And Mr Dawson, of course.'

He held out a hand to Joss and received a brusque handshake in return.

'Please, call me Joss.'

Unfortunately Joss's tone didn't match the friendliness of his sentiment, but Eva resisted the urge to roll her eyes in front of Matteo.

'And I hear from a little voice back in the office that congratulations are in order! You are to be married?' He kissed Eva again on both cheeks and shook Joss's hand again. 'An office romance. How lovely.'

He picked up Eva's left hand and let out a murmur of dismay.

'Oh, but no ring?'

'Oh, no,' Eva said, trying to think on her feet. 'Everything happened rather quickly, and with Edward's news...'

She let the sentence sit in the air and hoped that her allusion to terminal illness would do away with the need for further explanations.

'Oh, but you have some time now,' Matteo exclaimed with pleasure. 'And you are in the most beautiful store in the world! If you will forgive the slight to your English stores, Mr Dawson. I absolutely insist you come and choose something before our meeting.'

Eva looked at Joss, expecting him to shut down any discussion of shopping and insist they all get to work. But he wore an inscrutable expression that was heading towards a smile, and somehow she knew that meant trouble.

'If you're sure you don't mind waiting a little longer for our meeting, Signor Lazzari. Eva and I would love to do that.'

As they walked through the lobby towards the fine jewellery department, Eva grabbed Joss's hand and hung back a little, allowing the distance between them and Matteo to stretch beyond his hearing a whisper.

'What are you doing?' she asked out of the side of her mouth, glancing round to make sure that no one else could be listening in.

'Being friendly,' Joss replied with that same almost-smile.

'If you're doing this to make a point to me, it's fine. I get it—you're Mr Friendly. Time to drop it.'

Joss shook his head. 'Matteo wants to spoil us in his store. Show it off at its best. I thought it was politic to go along with him. Anyway, we will need a ring. If we wait too long people will start to talk.'

'You know,' she said, a touch of sharpness in her voice, 'some people think of that before they pop the question.'

'Yes, well, I'm not "some people", am I? I have the feeling that you never would have agreed to this if I was.'

She stopped, a hand on his arm turning him towards her. 'And what's that meant to mean?'

'Oh, nothing, darling,' Joss replied as he realised they had reached the gleaming glass counters of the jewellery department and Matteo was looking at them expectantly. 'So—where do you want to start?' he asked.

Matteo pulled out a few rings from the nearest cabinet—diamond solitaires all of them, ranging from the shockingly big to the tastelessly huge.

'Something classic, perhaps?' Matteo said, handing her a platinum diamond ring that must be a good three carats.

Eva held it between her fingertips and then looked up to Joss. He must have sensed her discomfort, because he took the ring from her and placed it back in the tray.

'Something a little more unusual for Eva, I think,' he said, reaching for an equally huge stone, this time flanked with pretty yellow pear-shaped diamonds. 'What about this,' he asked, meeting her eyes as he slipped the ring onto her finger.

She stood staring at it for a moment, reality and make-believe clashing. She knew this wasn't real. She knew it was all for show. But with this rock on her finger the lines were less clear than ever before.

She couldn't deny that she'd fantasised about this moment. All she wanted in her life was constancy... stability. Perhaps, one day she'd meet a man who she wouldn't want to let go. He'd slide a ring onto the third finger of her left hand and she would know without doubt that it was staying there for life.

It wasn't meant to feel like...*this*. It was never meant to be temporary. All she could see when she looked at this ring was the day when she would have to take it off. When Edward was gone, and she and Joss gave up their pretence, she'd have to return it to its snug velvet box and hand it back to him.

Her eyes filled with tears, but she fought them back, knowing that she couldn't lose it in front of Joss, never mind in front of Matteo.

'Ah, look at you. This is a special moment,' Matteo said with a smile. 'And I see I am not quite needed here. If I say I will see you again in an hour, will that be enough time for you?'

He handed Joss the keys to the jewellery cabinets and clapped him on the shoulder. 'I leave you two young lovers alone. Choose something special, yes?'

They both watched in silence as Matteo crossed the jewellery hall, waiting until they were alone and could speak safely.

'You don't like it?' Joss asked eventually, picking up her hand again and examining the ring.

'It's spectacular,' Eva replied with honesty.

'Then why the tears?' he said, gently this time, brushing a finger across her cheekbones.

'I'm not crying.'

'You're not letting them fall. I can see that. But you're upset. Why?'

'It's nothing, Joss. It's just that this is all a bit unnecessary. It feels strange. Wrong.'

'Why?'

There was no impatience in his voice, nor in his expression, as she took her time choosing the right words.

'Because it's all a lie. And a ring like this—it deserves something better. It's meant to be a symbol of love and commitment. We both know that we're not promising either of those things.'

He looked down at the ring for a moment, and then gently pulled it over her knuckle. 'Nothing that looks like an engagement ring, then. That narrows our options. What about this?' he asked.

'That's an eternity ring, Joss. Same problem.'

'You know, I don't think the ring is going to mind.'

She shook her head, not sure if she could make him understand without revealing too much of herself. '*I* mind. I might want one of these things for real one day. When I buy my engagement ring—or an eternity ring for that matter—I don't want to be keeping the receipt for when I have to return it.'

'So that's the problem.' Joss nodded, looking as if he had cracked a particularly difficult problem in the budget spreadsheet. 'You don't want something you like because you won't want to give it back? You can keep the ring, Eva. With everything you're doing for my father, for the business, it's the least I can do.'

Eva let out a breath in frustration. 'It's not about the money, Joss. It's the symbol. It's what the ring's meant to mean. I can't accept an engagement ring when there is no engagement.'

He looked thoughtful, and remained silent for a few long minutes, before reaching for her hand and pulling her gently to another case. 'What about if the ring symbolises something else, then? What if it's a gesture—a friendly gesture—of thanks. Thanks for caring for my father enough to go through with this. Thanks for looking after him and the business for so long. It's a gift—from a friend. The meaning doesn't change, whatever happens between us. And I absolutely won't accept it back from you when this ends.'

She looked at the case of jewellery he had brought her to, and thought about what he had said.

A gift like that she could accept, she thought. A ring was part of making this engagement look realistic, but these didn't look like engagement rings. They looked more like garlands of flowers, or boughs of blossoms. Tiny diamonds, sparkling and weaving their way across bands of yellow gold.

Joss unlocked the case and brought out one of the rings, with pink and blue sapphires scattered amongst bigger diamonds. He slipped it on to her third finger and they both stared at it in silence for a moment, taking in the effect.

'What do you think?' Joss asked.

'Better,' Eva said. 'It feels…friendly.'

Joss breathed a laugh. 'You old romantic. You're right. It's better. But it's not perfect. It's too heavy for those slender fingers. Too busy.'

He slipped it off again, and swapped it for a more delicate one—just diamonds this time, set in a meandering line like a trailing spray of flowers. This time when Joss slipped it on her finger she had no doubts.

'It's the one,' she said, gazing down at her finger.

'Perfect,' Joss agreed.

And before she realised what he was doing he had lifted her hand to his mouth and the warm heat of his lips was pressing against her knuckles.

She stood and stared at him, not quite sure where to begin with her line of questioning on this one.

'Joss… I don't think…'

His lips left her hand and he looked up, meeting her eyes with his intense gaze. She forgot what she had been going to say. Something about how this wasn't a good idea, probably. Except with her hand still encased in his, with the ring warming on her finger, it suddenly felt like the best idea they'd had for a while.

Joss's other hand landed lightly on her waist and for a moment neither of them breathed. Then, as one, they took in a sharp breath, and nudged closer towards one another.

Joss's hand snaked around her back, taking hers with it, twisting her until her back was against the jewellery cabinet. And it would have been so, so easy to relax into him, to loosen her body and let his arms take her weight. Take her anywhere he wanted to go.

Another half-step closer and his body met hers, pressing lightly against her from knee to chest, setting off fireworks everywhere in between.

This was all for show, she reminded herself. Joss was playing a part. For him, all this was just a way of making his father happy. Nothing about this was real for Joss—not in the way that the feelings she could feel growing for him were real.

At that moment she heard Matteo's voice from somewhere behind Joss and pushed gently against his chest, putting some much needed distance between them.

'Ah, I see you two have chosen something. Come—let me see.'

Eva held her left hand out to Matteo, hoping that she would be able to control the slight shake she could feel deep inside.

'It is beautiful,' Matteo said. 'A wonderful choice. But then I would expect nothing else. So, perhaps now we are ready to get to work?'

'Of course,' Joss said, his voice brusque, nothing like the soft tones she had heard when they were discussing her engagement ring.

She hoped that Matteo would put it down to an excess of emotion over their engagement rather than unfriendliness, otherwise the whole 'choosing the ring' exercise would have been wasted.

'And I have just spoken to Signora Lazzari—Giulietta—and she insists that you join us for dinner tonight,' Matteo said.

'Oh, I'm not sure if we—' Eva started.

'We'd love to,' Joss said, interrupting Eva's plan for a polite refusal.

But Joss was probably right. He was here to show the manager that he was the sort of man they could work with. It made sense for them to have dinner together. Eva herself had suggested that they might spend some time together this evening. But eating together as a foursome—that was inviting a world of trouble.

When they were working, it would be simple to explain away the lack of intimacy between them. They *should* keep a professional distance when they were in the office or one of the stores. But at dinner, perhaps at Matteo's home, that would be personal. They would be expected to look like a couple—and they'd have to make it convincing.

But now that Joss had agreed she didn't have much choice. She could hardly *un*accept a generous invitation from the man they were here to charm.

'But I insist that you allow us to take you out,' Joss said, allaying one of her concerns.

At least if they were safely out in public then they would be expected not to indulge in too many displays of affection.

CHAPTER FIVE

EVA PULLED ON the black dress that she always packed in case of emergencies. There was no situation she'd discovered yet that a simple black shift couldn't handle. She caught sight of the diamonds on her left hand and decided to leave off the statement necklace she'd also packed—it would be a shame to overshadow the pretty, understated ring that she and Joss had chosen together.

They'd agreed on dinner in the hotel restaurant downstairs. Its reputation was unparalleled in the city, and Matteo and his wife had happily accepted Joss's suggestion.

She checked her reflection quickly in the mirror and rubbed away a smudge of eyeliner. She'd kept her make-up simple, professional: a subtle reminder to herself that she hadn't knocked off for the day. She still had a part to play.

She heard the shower being shut off in the other bathroom and wondered whether Joss had thought to pack something to wear out to dinner. If it had been Edward taking the meeting she would have provided him with an itinerary of their trip—including likely social possibilities as well as all the meetings that were confirmed in the calendar. She hadn't found that familiarity with Joss yet. That closeness. A way of anticipating his needs even before he did.

She shivered slightly at the thought of developing such a thing with Joss. Even without their fake engagement, the changes at work would have been enough to turn their relationship completely on its head. To break down those careful barriers she'd built to keep herself distant from him at work. To keep her mind from wandering in his direction.

With everything else that had happened, she hadn't stopped to consider the alternative reality that might have existed if Edward had never walked in on them in the office and got the wrong idea. It wasn't as if her life would have carried on unchanged. She and Joss would still be in Milan, for a start. In separate rooms, though, instead of this suite. And Joss would still be moving in to Edward's office, sitting every day in her direct eyeline, on the other end of an intercom, occupying a huge part of her work life.

Joss's presence in her life would have grown anyway. So maybe by agreeing to this engagement she'd actually gained more control than she would otherwise have had. More freedom to discuss the nature of their relationship. To make clear to him that, however it might seem, a romantic attachment was absolutely *not* on the cards between them and never would be.

She shook her head. Most people didn't feel the need to have that sort of conversation with their boss. With most people it was just assumed that there would be nothing extracurricular going on. Just the fact that she was thinking it proved that these changes were always going to have caused trouble.

'Are you ready?' Joss called from the other side of the bedroom door.

What a question. She was ready to jump in a car, get on the first plane home, and pretend that none of this was happening. But was she ready to go out and fake a relationship with the man she'd been burying her feelings for since his divorce? She wasn't sure she wanted to admit the answer to that one.

Instead she opened the door, shut out her feelings and faked a smile.

'Ready,' she said, doing a last-minute check on the contents of her bag as they headed to the front door of the suite.

'You look nice,' Joss said as they headed out into the corridor.

He'd barely looked at her, she noticed. But she couldn't fault his manners.

'You too,' she replied, trying just as hard not actually to look at him.

Spending so much time together was meant to be curing her of her crush—but so far all the evidence was that it was having the opposite effect. It really was in no way fair. Perhaps it was the vast suite that Edward had arranged for them. With their separate bedrooms the size of palaces they might as well be living in separate apartments, as they had been back in London.

But this was only temporary, she reminded herself. Tomorrow they would be flying back to London, where there was a holdall of his clothes waiting for them in her spare room. And an empty drawer and a few inches of wardrobe space she'd managed to clear out for him.

They rode the lift down to the lobby in silence, and Eva deliberately avoided meeting Joss's eye in the mirrors that surrounded them. Then she remembered what they were doing here, the lie they were meant to be living, and risked a glance at him. She found him already watching her, and gave him a small smile.

'Ready for this?' he asked.

'No. You?'

'No.'

At that she felt the smile spread from her lips and across her cheeks, and saw it was reflected in Joss's eyes. She even risked a small laugh.

'Well, as long as we're in agreement, I suppose.'

She grabbed his hand as the lift doors slid open, and they were greeted by the sight of Matteo and his wife waiting for them in the lobby. Good job they'd got their faces sorted out before the lift stopped, Eva thought.

She greeted Matteo and Giulietta with kisses to both cheeks, but Joss kept her hand locked in his. She held on, in case he needed the support. Anyway, with her body anchored to his like this it made it easier to remember what she was doing—the part she was supposed to be playing. She wasn't just his assistant, greasing the wheels of conversation, providing snippets of information when they were needed. She was half of a couple.

Even as they were chatting over an aperitif she could still feel the warmth of Joss's hand against her skin, and she wondered if that would ever go. This hyper-awareness of his body whenever it was in contact with hers. In twenty years, would she still be getting fireworks if their fingers brushed when she handed him a letter to sign, or a contract to approve?

Twenty years.

Working with Edward, she'd never had any trouble envisaging her future. She'd felt secure. She'd known— or thought she had known—that she would always have a place with Dawson's. But now… Now she couldn't be sure.

One of the reasons she'd agreed to this charade in the first place was because she'd thought it would bind her more closely to the company, and then Joss wouldn't be able to show her the door as soon as his dad was gone. But was that naïve? Did this fake relationship make it more likely, rather than less, that Joss would want to see the back of her once this was over? Surely it would be more realistic that they *wouldn't* want to work together any more if they 'broke up'.

And if people found out that the whole thing was a sham, of course Joss would want her out of the way.

The thoughts crashing through her brain made her realise how naïve they had been, thinking that they could just start this thing with no idea when or how it was going to end. And how had she thought that Joss would want to keep her around after it was over?

A shiver ran through her, and she felt rather than saw Joss turn towards her.

'Cold?' he asked, dropping her hand and placing an arm around her shoulder.

'Just from this,' Eva said, faking a laugh and gesturing to the Prosecco in her hand, condensation beading on the glass.

As they took their seats at the table Eva was still incredibly aware of her body language, and that of Joss, sitting beside her. Were they playing it too cool? This was a dinner with colleagues, and they were out in public, so no one would expect them to be all over each other. But since she'd shaken off Joss's arm, with protestations that she wasn't cold, she was more aware than ever of his presence beside her, of having him so close but not touching.

Should she do something? she wondered, as she stared at the menu in front of her, unable to take in a single word. She glanced at his hand, resting on the table, and wondered if she should reach for it. She could just slide her fingers between his, the way she remembered doing instinctively the day Edward had announced his illness. It would look like the most natural thing in the world to Matteo and his wife. Or maybe she could rest a hand on his thigh, feel under her fingertips those firm muscles which just a couple of hours ago had pressed her against a jewellery cabinet.

She resisted the urge to sigh and tried to concentrate on her menu instead, picking it up from the table and attempting to focus.

'Oh, what a pretty ring,' Giulietta said from across the table. 'Matteo told me you chose it together today.'

Eva smiled at Giulietta and glanced down at her hand. She remembered what Joss had said about it symbolising friendship, her place in the family, and looked up at him with a smile.

'Ah, but you two are so in love,' Giulietta said with a laugh, and Eva felt her cheeks colour. 'It is good that you can be happy after such sad news. I was so sorry to hear that Edward is not well.'

This time she didn't think about it. She reached for Joss's hand and squeezed it tightly in her own, knowing how raw his pain must be, if it was anything like her own.

'Thank you,' Joss said, carefully steady.

Eva glanced up at him and could see from the set line of his jaw how much of a struggle he was finding that composure.

'I know my father values your efforts here highly.'

'And I know that he is so sorry that he's not able to be here himself,' Eva added, hoping that she'd be able to make up for Joss's lack of warmth.

Edward and Matteo had been friends for years, and she knew that the Lazzaris would be feeling the sadness of his loss too. Joss had his own grief to deal with—but she had to make sure that this meeting achieved everything they needed it to. Matteo *had* to see that he would be happy working with Joss.

'I know that he would love to be at this dinner with us.'

'Ah, we understand,' Giulietta said with a kind smile. 'We are just happy to have *your* company this evening. And to be able to send our warmest wishes with you when you return.'

'Of course we will take them,' Eva said, and glanced up at Joss.

They were here to try and show Matteo a more

human, personal side of Joss, but so far he was too distracted. He seemed more buttoned up than ever, and she still had no idea how to get him to open up.

'If you'll excuse me?' Giulietta said, pushing her chair back. 'I'll be back in a few moments.'

Three at the table felt a whole lot more uncomfortable than four, Eva realised after a few seconds' awkward silence.

She attempted to start up a conversation a couple of times, but nothing was thawing between them. Matteo's phone rang, and he excused himself from the table with apologies, saying that it was his deputy at the store.

'What?' Joss asked, as she turned towards him with a concerned look.

She took a bracing breath, knowing that this conversation had to be quick, discreet and effective. 'We're here to show Matteo a warmer side to you, yes? Well, we're not doing a good job so far.'

He sat up a little straighter in his chair. 'We were talking about my terminally ill father. Would you like me to be cracking jokes?'

She shook her head—a small, efficient movement. 'Of course not. And I understand how difficult it will be. But we've come all this way. If we're not going to make it count, then why did we bother? Do you want to go back to the office having failed to achieve our objective?'

She knew that the business-speak would win him over—she'd worked with him for long enough to understand that the company director in him wouldn't be able to resist the threat of a missed objective or deadline.

Giulietta returned to the table and Eva greeted her with a smile, and an offer to top up her glass. Signora Lazzari took hold of her hand and looked again at her ring.

'Forgive me,' she said. 'I can't help looking. They're pretty stones—and such an unusual design. You really have an eye.'

It was the perfect opening she needed—cue Joss's human side.

'Actually, it was Joss's choice. He understood exactly what I would want.' She turned to him with what she hoped would look to their guests like an adoring smile.

'After a couple of false starts,' Joss added with a laugh.

Eva could hear that it was slightly forced, but from the look on Giulietta's face she hadn't noticed.

'Let's just say that Eva had to point out the virtues of "less is more".'

Joss leaned over and pressed a kiss to her temple, and for that second when his lips were on her skin everything else stopped. The noise of the restaurant… the conversation around the table. Her breathing and her heartbeat. Everything was *him*. His lips, his touch, his heat.

And then it was gone, and the world crashed in again—noisy and brash.

'Well, you must be an attentive pupil,' Giulietta said. 'It's truly beautiful. And have you set a date?' she asked as Matteo returned to the table, tucking his phone into the inside pocket of his jacket.

'It is to be soon?' Matteo asked as he took his seat. 'Your father must be so excited to see you married.'

'We don't want to wait longer than we have to,' Joss said, taking Eva's hand. 'But we're not ready to set a date yet. My father has asked us not to decide anything until we've had time to come to terms with his news and all the changes it will bring. He wants us to concentrate on business at the moment. We feel that's the least we can do for him, to ensure the continuation of his legacy.'

'Ah, well, a long engagement is very romantic,' Giulietta said with a sigh. 'Sometimes I wish we could go back and do it all again.' She looked wistfully at her husband. 'Be newlyweds again.'

'I can drink to that,' Joss said with a smile that looked a little more relaxed. He lifted his glass. 'To engagements.'

'And being a newlywed,' Giulietta added.

Matteo lifted his glass as they all toasted.

'And to Edward Dawson,' Matteo said before they all went to replace their drinks on the table. 'He can never be replaced, but I am looking forward very much to getting to know his son better.'

Eva breathed a sigh of relief, and for the first time since they had arrived in Milan thought that maybe this might turn out not to be the disaster she had feared.

The rest of the dinner passed quickly, with conversation flowing in tandem with the wine. They eventually kissed Matteo and Giulietta goodbye in the lobby, late in the evening, and walked towards the lift, still hand in hand, just in case the Lazzaris should look back and see them.

Except Eva didn't drop Joss's hand once they were in the lift. She felt warm and comfortable, relaxed in Joss's company in a way she hadn't been since the day Edward had shared the news of his illness and Joss had come up with his absurd plan.

Until the lift doors slid shut and they were completely alone.

Not so relaxed any more.

In fact every muscle in her body tensed as she glanced around her, seeing them reflected in the mirrors on every side of them. Still their hands were linked together. She looked up at Joss, to find that he was already staring down at her, his expression inscrutable.

She opened her mouth to speak, but the ding of the lift stopping and the doors opening halted her.

Hand in hand, they turned towards their suite, and Joss dipped his free hand in his pocket for the key card, smoothly opening the door so that they barely had to break stride.

Eva realised she was holding her breath. She wasn't sure when she'd started to do it, but as the door closed behind them, and they were truly private for the first time all evening, she let it out—long and slow. All she could think about was Joss's lips. Warm on her hand that afternoon as he sealed their friendship ring with a kiss. And then tender on her temple over dinner.

She stopped at the door, not trusting herself to go any further into the suite. After all, her hand was still locked in Joss's, and neither of them was showing any sign of letting go.

She leant back against the door and Joss stood in

front of her, filling her vision with the wide shoulders of his exquisitely cut suit.

'Everything okay?' he asked, his voice low and sensual.

Eva nodded, when what she really wanted to do was shout. To tell him that no, she wasn't okay. That things were far, far from okay. This was confusing and terrifying and oh, so much more complicated than she had ever wanted her life to be.

But she couldn't let go of his hand. Couldn't be the one to break that connection between them.

She'd felt it growing as they'd played their parts over dinner. A touch of the hand here. A brush of fingers over an arm there. A quick kiss to the temple and too many shared smiles.

The intimacy had grown and grown between them, in some strange simulacrum of the relationship they had invented. But she had expected them to walk away from it. Expected to leave it at the table as they had their dirty glasses and used tableware. She hadn't expected it to stalk them into the lift and back up to their suite.

Intimacy was safe in public, where neither of them could act on it. But with her back against this door and Joss in front of her—looking serious, smelling delicious—it was a more dangerous prospect. And Joss knew it too. That much was clear from his expression. And she wouldn't be the first person in her family to walk headfirst and knowingly into danger. Maybe she had more in common with her parents than she'd realised.

A shiver went through her as the moment to push

him away, to break their contact, came and went, and she knew that she had made a decision. She closed her eyes and pushed herself onto her tiptoes, then gently, as gently as he'd kissed her, she pressed her lips to his.

For a moment she thought she'd miscalculated, misjudged, and that this *hadn't* been where the evening had been heading since the moment she'd walked out of her bedroom and set eyes on Joss. But then his lips came alive beneath hers, tasting, touching, caressing. She let out a long sigh—her body's relief after so many years of imagining this moment.

But her body wasn't the one in charge here—her brain was, and it wasn't exactly cheering her on. She could feel his restraint, too. It was there in his jaw, when she touched it gently with her fingers. It was there when he lifted his hand and it came to rest on the door beside her head instead of on her cheek or in her hair. It was there in the way he held his body ever so slightly away from hers, instead of pressing her hard into the wood.

And it was there in the way she had her hand on his chest, making sure he couldn't get too close.

She broke the kiss and rested her head back against the door, a chagrined look on her face.

'Bad idea,' she said at last as their breathing returned to normal. 'Too complicated.'

'I wish it wasn't,' Joss replied, and she could tell that he meant it.

Except they'd known each other for years before it had got so complicated, and they had known then, too, that this wasn't a good idea. At least it was a kind lie.

'Goodnight,' Eva said at last, after a few long moments during which one or the other of them might have decided that the complications didn't matter that much after all. But this wasn't a fairy tale, and the realities of their lives weren't going to melt away because of one kiss.

She pushed herself away from the door, determinedly avoiding eye contact, and brushed her hand gently against his arm as she slipped past him and into her bedroom.

CHAPTER SIX

'BAD IDEA,' EVA had said. Joss couldn't argue with that. It would undoubtedly have been a very bad idea. But a bad idea had never looked so good in his life.

They could have just gone for it. One kiss—how much damage could that have caused? But instead they'd both held back, and the whole moment had turned into a glimpse of what it might have been. Stirring his imagination without satisfying anything.

The next morning that kiss was on his mind all through his meetings with the Milan-based suppliers, even as he was reassuring them that there was no reason to think that there would be any drop in demand for their luxury goods throughout the Dawson's network of stores. And there would be absolutely no problems with the transition from Edward's leadership to his.

And on the plane, with Eva so close and so untouchable, the impression of her lips on his remained distractingly present.

It wasn't until they walked into their office at three o'clock in the afternoon and saw his father packing the contents of his desk into cardboard boxes that he was able to push that kiss from the forefront of his mind.

'What are you doing?' Joss barked at his father as he reached his office, though the answer was startlingly obvious.

'Sorry, son,' Edward said. 'I thought I'd be finished before you were back from the airport. You're the boss now—it's only right that you have the office that goes with it.'

Joss folded his arms, looking around the messy office, unable to believe his father was really going to be gone. 'Dad, I don't need your office. I don't *want* your office.'

'Well, I don't have much use for it now, and it would be silly for it to sit here empty.' Edward held up his hands and shrugged. 'And, really, I'd quite like to see you sitting here. If it makes you feel any better, it means Eva won't have to move desks. You'll want her close, believe me. She knows this job as well as I do. Better.'

He'd want her close. Well, there was the problem, wasn't it? It seemed that neither of them knew exactly how close they wanted to be.

She'd kissed him yesterday, all the while keeping him at a safe distance, never really giving in to what she wanted, even when they were alone. And he'd held back too. Warring with himself, telling himself that he had to stop this. He'd not been able to drag his lips from hers. All he'd been able to do was keep some emotional distance and try as hard as he could not to be dragged by those sensations into doing something they would both regret.

He whipped his head around as he heard the familiar click of her heels behind him.

'Edward—no. You can't be packing up already.'

'Ah, my dear, you as well. It is good to see you and my son so in tune with one another but, really, you must both see that I'm not needed here any more. Joss is more than capable of running this company and, to be perfectly honest, I've got places I would rather be. You know how much this business means to me—both of you do. But a prognosis like mine helps you to see what's really important. I've given this business fifty good years. Now, if I only have a few months left, I'm going to spend them doing some of the things I've been putting off for too long.'

He taped up the box with what seemed to Joss to be an unnecessarily dramatic flourish.

'Now…' He glanced at his watch. 'I've got an appointment, so I guess the rest of this will have to wait until tomorrow.' He laid a hand on Joss's shoulder as he passed him. 'I know this is hard, son. I'm here if you need to talk.'

He left the office and Joss couldn't breathe. It was as if he'd taken all the oxygen with him. He sat stiffly against the edge of the desk, among the abandoned staplers and office supplies that Edward had left lying there.

'Do you?' Eva asked.

Joss stared at her, unable to work out what she meant.

'Do you need to talk? Because I'm here too.'

He absolutely, definitely did not want to talk. What he wanted was to go and lock himself in his own office and get on with his job as if none of this was happening. There was a budget spreadsheet in his inbox that he could happily lose himself in for hours.

But he'd been down that route before, and it hadn't led anywhere good. Anywhere healthy. He had no intention of going there again. Talking to Eva… He wasn't sure that was a good idea. But when he thought about it he wasn't sure there was any other good option. She was the only one who knew the secret they were keeping after all. But what about *his* secrets? What about all the things in his past that he'd carefully hidden from everyone around him.

'Maybe I *should* talk, Eva. But I'm not sure that talking to you is the best idea. After last night…'

'What about last night?'

Really? Was she just going to pretend that it had never happened? Maybe they both should. After all, forgetting about that kiss was just about the most sensible—albeit impossible—option at this point.

'That kiss. It was…nice.'

He had a feeling it might have been incredible—if they hadn't both been holding back. He didn't know what her reasons were, but he was going to have to share his if that was what it took to keep them both from the mistake of making this fake relationship real. She had to see what a bad idea it would be, getting involved in a relationship now, with his father's illness and the knowledge that they would lose him soon.

'But I think we were right to stop it when we did. Taking it any further… It just wouldn't be a good idea.'

'Oh!' Eva's left hand flew to her chest. 'You mean

this isn't for *real*?' She subtly waved her engagement ring at him, but the rolling eyes gave her away. 'I *do* know that, Joss. Really, you need to get over yourself.'

'I know I wasn't the only one holding back, Eva. And I don't need you to tell me your reasons. But I want you to hear mine. It's not like I didn't want—'

He stopped himself before he said something stupid.

He started again. 'I want you to understand why. You know that I've been married before?'

Eva nodded.

'Well, it didn't end well. For either of us. The thing is, before I got married I was ill. But I didn't realise.'

She looked curious at that, but didn't interrupt.

'It was clinical depression. I hid it from everyone. From my family. From my then girlfriend, now ex-wife. I didn't get the help I needed, and then the wedding gathered pace around me, and I found myself in the position of being a really terrible husband.'

Her eyes softened with sympathy. 'But you were ill, Joss. It wasn't your fault. Maybe you need to be kinder to yourself.'

He stood stiffly, determined that she would under-stand him. 'I know that depression is an illness, but that didn't make our marriage any easier for my wife. Or our divorce, for that matter. I realised after it was all over how wrong it had been to feel the way I had for a long time and I finally got help. Got better. But none of that changes what I put her through. Or the fact that I know that it could come back. I'll never be completely free from it. And I'm determined not to do to anyone else what I did to my ex.'

Eva took a step closer to him and he took half a step back. 'You don't know that you will get ill again,' she said.

'And I don't know that I won't. What I *do* know right now is that my dad is dying, and that seems as good a recipe for depression as any other I can think of.'

'And don't I get a say in this?'

He looked at her closely. Had he missed something? This had started as a way of getting things off his chest, just to make things clear to her. A way to avoid the bottling up of his thoughts that he knew could lead somewhere toxic. She had been holding back too last night, and he'd assumed that meant that she was as wary of this chemistry between them as he was. But was he wrong? Did she want more?

Her answer unsettled him—he'd never really thought that she'd want a say in it.

'Don't look at me like that,' she said. He hadn't realised he was looking at her like *anything*. 'I'm not saying that we were wrong to stop things.'

He walked away from the desk and she shifted herself up to perch on the edge of it. He couldn't tear his eyes away from her ankles, slender and vulnerable-looking atop her smart spike heels.

'Look,' she continued. 'I think we can both say that there is an attraction between us. After what happened last night it would be stupid to attempt to deny it. But I'm as scared of this thing as you are. No offence— and this has nothing to do with what you've just told me—but a relationship with you would scare the hell out of me. I want commitment and stability, and even

before I knew what you just told me it was abundantly
clear that those things are not of interest to you. I fancy
you—okay. But that doesn't mean that wanting you is
a good idea. We got carried away last night. It was the
first time that we really had to act this thing out, and it
was trickier than I expected to slip in and out of character. We'll get better at it. We have to.'

She fancied him? It shouldn't really be news to
him—not after that kiss last night. But somehow, despite everything else she was saying, that was all he
could hear. And not because it was a nice boost to his
ego. But because it made him question so many things
from the last few years. All those times he'd avoided
her, knowing that she was too much temptation, had
she felt the same?

'But just because I don't think this would be a good
idea, Joss…' she slipped off the desk and came towards
him, laying a gentle hand on his arm, '… I don't think
having an illness in your past is a good enough reason
to shut yourself off from the idea of having a relationship in the future. There's probably some woman out
there who thinks you'll make the perfect boyfriend—
and she should probably be allowed a say in what happens. Why don't you give it a chance?'

He thought for a long moment. Some mystery woman
who might come and convince him that he had been
wrong about the decisions he had made in his life? He
just couldn't see that happening. If he couldn't find it in
himself to bend his rules for Eva, he just couldn't imagine any other woman who would make him want to.

'Well, we don't need to worry about that, do we?'

he said briskly, wanting out of this conversation before he started questioning his own better judgement. 'For now, I'm an engaged man. And one relationship—even a fake one—is enough.'

'Fine.' Eva said, crossing her arms. But then her expression and her body language softened. 'But I meant what I said. If you want to talk, Joss, or if you think your depression might be coming back…you can come to me. I mean, a fake fiancée can still be a pretty good listener.'

Joss smiled. If things had been different—if he hadn't had this illness lingering in his past—he was pretty sure she'd made a damn good *real* fiancée.

'I appreciate that. So, what about you? No luck finding a stable, committed guy to do this for real?'

'Plenty of candidates,' Eva said, with a shrug that wasn't as nonchalant as he thought she was hoping for. 'None that quite match up to my criteria.'

'Lucky for me, I guess.'

'Damned lucky for you.'

CHAPTER SEVEN

Eva sat at her desk, watching the clock on her screen ticking ever closer to seven o'clock. It was already dark outside and the office had emptied a couple of hours ago—everyone except her and Joss were long gone.

She wondered whether Joss was working late for the same reason she was—putting off the moment when they would have to go back to her little apartment and start living together for real. Her stomach gave a growl, and she wished she had picked up something more substantial for lunch.

Well, one of them was going to have to be the first to make a move, and she was too hungry to wait and see if Joss would cave. She shut down her computer and straightened up her files for the morning.

Joss appeared in the doorway to his office, leaning against the frame.

'Heading home?' he asked.

'Yeah, I'm all done for the day. And starving,' she added truthfully. 'I'll see you back there.'

She opened the door to her flat and headed straight for the kitchen. She hadn't shared her living space since she had left university and started working at Dawson's, and she realised that she had no idea how adult flatmates really worked. Or any form of cohabiting other than student living, really. She'd not seen her parents living together often enough to have formed an idea of it at an early age. How *did* a relationship work with both parties present at least most of the time?

She hated feeling so uncertain in her own home. For as long as she had been working at Dawson's she'd felt settled, secure. She'd known how things worked in the office; she'd had her own place to come home to. No one had started changing things up just when she'd got settled. And now her security at the office had gone, and even her home wasn't the safe haven it was meant to be with Joss moving in.

She chucked the leftover sauce she'd found in the freezer into the microwave and tested the pasta. Still way too *al dente*. A glance out of the window showed no one coming up the mews, and she felt relieved. Perhaps she'd be able to eat and zone out in front of a box set for an hour before Joss came home. At which point she could invent some excuse and escape to her bedroom for the rest of the evening.

Really, Eva, she chastised herself. *Hiding? Not exactly your style.*

But then the glow of a mobile phone outside the window caught her eye and she knew that her plans for a solo dinner had just been thwarted.

When she heard the knock at the door she remembered that Joss didn't have a key—something they'd have to fix. As she walked down the stairs it really hit her. He was going to be here. Every day. Even if not in person, his stuff would be here. He was going to be a permanent presence in her life for the next few months at least.

She tried to think of the last time she'd had a relationship, even a friendship like that, and came up blank. The last man she'd lived with was her father. And that hadn't exactly been plain sailing.

She opened the door and stood aside to let Joss pass her on the stairs, but instead he stopped in the doorway and gave her a considering look.

'What's wrong?'

'Nothing,' she replied automatically, trying to shake off the mood that thinking about her parents always caused. 'Just thinking that we need to get you a key cut. Come up—I've put some pasta on.'

'I thought you told me not to get used to being cooked for?'

'You shouldn't. You're cooking next time.'

'Fine. It's a date. I told you—you're not going to scare me off with threats of domesticity.'

A date. She hadn't meant it to sound like that, but intentionally or not she'd just arranged one. Did Joss see it like that too? Or was it just a figure of speech?

She shook her head as she went back up to the kitchen and gave the sauce a stir. Of course he didn't see it like that. He couldn't have been clearer with her that he didn't want to date her. Good, because she'd already told him—more than once, and in no uncertain terms—that she didn't want to date him either.

And where did that leave her? she wondered, thinking back over the last few years of her love-life—or lack of one. If she didn't want to date the only man she had been remotely interested in in years, then was she resigning herself to a lifetime of being alone?

Maybe there wasn't anything wrong with that. Lots of people never married. Stayed single. Perhaps that was the life she was cut out for. When this engagement was over Joss would move out, she would move a couple of cats in, and settle for the next few decades.

But if she really thought that why had she bothered dating at all? Why download the apps and accept the blind dates and chat to the hopeful-looking men in bars if she wasn't looking for something more?

Window shopping—that was what she had been doing. After their visit to the Italian store's jewellery department yesterday, she recognised it for what it was. Looking at all the pretty things on offer, knowing they weren't right for her, and that she would never be interested in actually buying them. So why wasn't she interested in dating Joss either? If the only reason she hadn't wanted those other guys was because they weren't *him*, surely she should want him if he were offered on a plate.

But it wasn't just about him, she realised. Maybe it had never been about him. If she refused to accept anyone who wasn't Joss, but didn't want the real thing either, then that left her where? On the shelf? Off the market? It left her alone, as she had been for all of her life. Where she was comfortable.

Was that what this was?

'Hey, is it terrible to open a bottle of wine on a Tuesday night?' Joss asked, grabbing one from the rack beneath the kitchen counter.

'After we spent most of Monday night on the Prosecco? I don't think anyone will judge us too harshly.'

She was glad of the distraction as she opened the bottle and found glasses.

'So, what have you got planned for the rest of the week?' she asked, trying to keep their conversation on a safe work footing as they went through to the living room and settled with bowls of pasta on their knees and their wine on the coffee table.

'Ah, I actually need to talk to you about that.'

'Sounds ominous.'

She'd expected him to brush the comment off, but he nodded. *Not good.*

'It's Dad. He's invited us to spend the weekend with him. He wanted an engagement party, inviting the great and the good. I managed to talk him out of it, but he still wants us to spend some quality time together.'

'Just the three of us?'

It was a lovely idea, in theory. She couldn't think of a better way for Joss and his father to spend the time they had left. And she loved Edward—of course she wanted to spend time with him. But this charade of a relationship with Joss made everything more complicated. By spending time together, were they going to expose their secret and do more harm than good?

After what had happened in Milan she knew that spending more time in close quarters with Joss and an audience wasn't a sensible idea. Acting out their relationship with the Lazzaris had led to acting out her desires, and they had both agreed that that had been a bad idea. The last thing they needed was a whole weekend of blurring the boundaries.

But they had to put Edward first. And if it was a weekend of quality time that he wanted, then that was what he deserved.

'Yeah, just the three of us,' Joss replied. 'Unless you want half the county and your business contacts list invited too?'

She shuddered. She wasn't sure what was worse—the scrutiny of the single person who knew them both better than just about anyone, or of everyone either of them had ever met.

'The whole weekend?' she checked, thinking that maybe, if they went for just a few hours over lunch, they might be able to keep up the pretence without doing too much harm to her self-control. Being together a whole weekend, there was no way that they'd be able to get away with separate bedrooms—not when Edward thought they were living together.

'That's what he said. And, given the circumstances, I want to go. It's not like we have time to waste.'

'And he wants me there too? Are you sure?'

Joss nodded. 'Of course he does. He thinks you're my fiancée. He just assumed that you would be coming. And you have to admit it would look strange if you didn't.'

Of course it would.

'Okay. And it's just one night, isn't it? Two at most?'

Joss nodded. 'We'll drive down after work on Friday. Be back on Sunday.'

She drew her brows together in confusion. Edward's house was no more than a fifteen-minute walk from her mews, on one of the smart garden squares that filled this part of London.

'Drive there? Wait—where are we going?'

'The house in Berkshire. I thought you realised that's what I meant?'

She sat back in the sofa cushions, temporarily lost for words at the thought of being isolated down a country lane with Joss. Somehow the seclusion of a country house seemed more intimate than being in London all together. If they were in the city she could make excuses to give Joss and Edward time alone together—pop out and fetch them all coffee, suggest a trip to the gallery she knew was opening on Saturday. In the countryside she didn't even know if there would be a pub nearby to escape to if it all went wrong.

She shook her head, but knew that she couldn't refuse. 'Of course I'll come—it'd be my pleasure.'

Oh, she shouldn't have used that word. Because now all she could think of was all the different types of pleasure that Joss could show her in an isolated country house. Hot breath on cold cheeks after a walk to a secluded spot in the woods… Cold hands on warm skin in front of a roaring fire…

'And the rest of the week?' she asked, knowing that she needed to distract Joss from what she was sure was a tell-tale blush on her cheeks.

'Dubai,' he said, giving her a curious look. 'You were right. I need to show my face. Let them know everything's going smoothly. Make sure everyone's happy with how things are going to work from now on.'

She nodded. 'Sounds like a good idea.'

'I need you to let me know if there are any problems here,' he went on. 'Make sure the place is running okay with Dad not coming in to the office any more.'

'I'm your eyes and ears on the ground. I get it. Do you want me to book your tickets?'

'It's done,' Joss said.

Eva felt piqued that he had bypassed her.

'What?' he asked, when he saw the look on her face.

'I know all this fiancée stuff is pretend, but you *do* know that the job isn't? I'm your assistant. I should know about your travel plans.'

'You're angry that I got someone else to book my plane ticket?'

'I'm angry that you're not letting me do my job. The other thing doesn't trump that, you know. I know it's hard, with everything else that's going on, but we have to find a way to work together as well. Otherwise how will that look? Like you've taken over and I'm instantly getting an easy ride.'

'Well, at least one of us is…' Joss said.

Eva didn't want to begin to unpick all the potential meanings of that sentence. Way too dangerous.

'Fine,' he said. 'While I'm away you can take over everything that's needed. When I'm back you can brief me on anything you think I need to know about from my father's desk that he hasn't already covered. Does that meet with your approval?'

'Fine. Good.'

She knew she still sounded short with him as she took another sip of wine, but she prided herself on her professional skills. If Joss was going to work around her at every opportunity she couldn't see herself *wanting* to stay in her job for much longer—a thought that terrified her. If she didn't want to be at Dawson's any more she didn't know who she was, never mind what she wanted from life.

No, she was being silly. Her job at Dawson's went way beyond her relationship with Joss, and mattered way more. She wouldn't even consider leaving just because she and Joss hadn't worked out the finer details of their professional relationship yet.

'So, when do you leave for Dubai?' she asked, wondering when she would get back the safety and security of living alone.

'I thought I'd go Tuesday, then be back in time to drive us down on Friday. Does that work with my diary?'

'You'll have to tell me. Until we get to work tomorrow I'm officially off the clock,' she said, taking a glug of her wine to prove her point.

CHAPTER EIGHT

Eva glanced at the time, hating herself for doing it even as her eyes were drawn once again to the hands on the old wooden grandfather clock in the far corner of Joss's new office.

Three forty-seven. Exactly four minutes after she had last looked.

And at least twenty minutes after she had expected to see Joss back in the office.

He had been on a half-nine flight, which the live arrivals board told her had arrived at Heathrow at thirteen thirty-three. If he'd jumped into the car that she had booked for him he should definitely be here by now.

It was professional concern, she told herself. He had a meeting at four o'clock. She'd told him he would be cutting it fine if they were to leave to pick up his father this evening and get to the house, but he'd insisted that he would be there in time.

Her eagerness to see him was nothing to do with the way she had lain in bed awake, remembering the hard press of his body and the gentle touch of his lips in that hotel suite in Milan. Thinking about the night they had spent together in her flat, knowing that he was just down the hall. Knowing she could bump into him on the way to the bathroom and get a glimpse of those firm, toned abs and muscular thighs.

She shook off the thought. No, it was absolutely nothing to do with that at all.

A noise behind her made her jump, and she turned to see Joss striding through the office, familiar holdall in hand, glancing at his watch.

'I know, I know—you told me it would be close.'

'And you told me you'd make it. I never doubted you,' she lied.

He came up to her desk and kissed her on the cheek, and it was only as the blush rose that she remembered he was only doing what would be expected from a man who'd just spent a few nights away from his fiancée. He was performing for their audience, who—a brief glance out of the corner of her eye told her—were appreciative of his efforts.

'I told him you'd meet him in his office,' she said after a pregnant pause, suddenly struck with stage fright, unsure of her lines.

'Great. I'll drop this bag and head over there now. We'll still be out of here by six. Promise.'

She smiled and waited for him to walk away, but his gaze hadn't broken from hers and the ghost of a smile passed over his lips.

'Did you miss me?' he asked.

She resisted the urge to draw in a shocked breath, keeping her breathing deliberately slow and even. Was he playing with her? Was this part of their act or was he really asking her—the *real* her, not the fake fiancée?

'Not even a tiny bit,' she said, with a proper smile of her own.

Any eager ears in the office could put that down to normal relationship banter, she decided. And it was worth it to see the expression on Joss's face. She liked taking him by surprise.

He reached out a hand to her cheek, just ghosting the tips of his fingers along the line of her jaw. 'Well, I guess that means I need to make more of an impression,' he said, his voice low. Too low to be for the benefit of their audience. 'Give you something to miss next time I'm gone.'

He brought his right hand up in a mirror of his left, bracketing her with his fingers. She should pull away. Turn her face to her computer monitor in an effort at professionalism. But then she might never know. She would be left wondering whether this was for play or for real. And suddenly, dangerous or not, she had to know.

For the fleeting half-second he held her gaze, she wondered if she would be able to tell. And then she remembered that kiss in Milan. The way that they'd read everything the other person was feeling through the touch of their skin. And she knew that his body wouldn't lie to her, whatever he might say out loud.

With the first fleeting, barely there caress of his lips, she knew that it was real. It held all the promise of their kiss in Milan. Set off all the same fireworks. She lifted her hand to his face, felt the same tension in his jaw— the strength of his desire battling with the strength of his self-control. She could feel herself teetering on the edge, just as she had in Italy, knowing that letting a crack in her resolve show for even a second would mean they were both lost.

Which was why—even as it pained her—she pulled away. Again. Put just a millimetre of space between them, waited for him to move further back. He didn't. Instead he leaned his forehead against hers, and she could sense rather than see his smile.

'Now I'm late,' he said, after what felt like an age but couldn't have been more than a second.

Eva bit her lip with a smile, unwilling to let the moment go just yet. 'Told you so,' she said, stifling a laugh.

Joss sneaked one last peck onto her cheek before he strolled out of the office with an irritating degree of calm and confidence.

When the door shut behind him Eva knew she couldn't avoid looking around her any longer. She glanced over the partition of her cubicle and saw that— as she might have guessed—all eyes had been on her and Joss. She waited for the inevitable jokey comments, but instead the women—and half the men—were looking at her wide-eyed.

Eventually her assistant blew out a slow breath in awe, and muttered something that sounded incredibly like, 'Lucky woman.'

If only she knew.

On the dot of six o'clock, Joss closed his laptop and reached for the jacket he'd chucked over the back of his chair. He'd promised Eva that he'd be done in good time for them to leave for his father's country house for the weekend, and he had no intention of breaking that promise. Especially after what had happened earlier.

What *had* happened?

He wasn't sure what had come over him. But as soon as he had walked into the office and seen her it had been as if something that had been missing for three days was suddenly back and in overload. As if he hadn't even known he needed something, and then was drunk on it.

It had been meant as a polite, friendly hello. The sort of public kiss that anyone would offer their fiancée when they'd been away for a few days. To do anything else would have looked suspicious. But as soon as their eyes had locked it had been so much more.

That night in Milan had come flooding back—everywhere that kiss might have led if they had decided to let it. And then it had been too late to back out, and he'd had no choice but to give in to what his body had been begging him to do. Let his fingers trace the soft skin on her jaw, let his lips brush against hers, setting off a chain reaction that was going to lead them somewhere dangerous.

Thank goodness they were in the office, with an in-built safety net of public scrutiny and didn't have to rely on their self-control. Or *his* self-control at least. Who knew? Perhaps hers was still rock-solid, and she'd only returned his kiss for show.

No, he knew her better than that, he realised. He had felt the passion in her, and the iron self-control that was holding her just as fast as it was him. She wanted him, but she wasn't going to let it get the better of her.

And now they were going to be spending a whole weekend together, holed up in an isolated country house. Most people would consider having their dying father there as having something of a chaperone effect—but, as he'd once said to her, they weren't 'most people'.

He had to stop overthinking this. It would only make them awkward. The only thing to do this weekend—if they wanted to keep the lie alive and his father happy— was to jump right in. Forget it was a lie. Live as if they were really an engaged couple, head over heels in love. And lust.

But where could that lead when sustained over a weekend? In Italy it had led to an aborted kiss, when they had both still had just enough self-awareness to keep it from going further. And—importantly—they'd had separate bedrooms to retreat to. When they found themselves alone behind a closed door with a four-poster in the corner how were they going to resist?

Well, they'd just have to find a way. Because the alternative was giving in to this attraction. Getting involved in something real. And he knew that if he let that happen Eva would get hurt—and he wasn't having that.

He opened the door to see that she was still sitting at her desk, concentrating on the screen of her computer, the pen in her hand tapping absent-mindedly at her lip. He couldn't look away, reminded of the feel of those lips less than a couple of hours ago. But she was obviously more aware of him than he realised, because she held up the pen in the universal sign for, *Give me a minute*.

She tapped a few more keys, and then looked up with

a beaming smile. 'Sorry—just had to get that done. Are we ready?'

He nodded, temporarily lost for words. He didn't know how she had that effect on him. But then, why would he? For years he'd been avoiding this. Avoiding finding out the effect that she might have on him. Well, there was going to be no getting away from it this weekend.

He wondered if she was as nervous as he was about them being in such close proximity. His father's house was far bigger than her flat, but there were fewer places to hide. Not when they couldn't drop their act as soon as they were inside the front door and start treating each other like indifferent colleagues again.

Eva wrapped a long scarf around her neck as she stood up, half an eye still on her computer before she finally shrugged her shoulders and shut it down.

'Problems?' Joss asked.

'No...nothing. I'd just hoped to be able to sort something out before we left. It's not a big deal.'

He held out her coat and she slipped her arms in while he resisted the urge to run his hands instead of the sleeves up her arms. To let them rest on her shoulders before brushing her hair aside and pressing a kiss at the nape of her neck.

Eva turned on the spot and was suddenly far, far closer than was comfortable. She barely had to look up to meet his gaze, and he resisted the sensible part of his brain that was urging him to take a step backwards.

'Ready, then?' she asked, glancing past him towards the door.

'As I'll ever be.'

Thankfully the drive out to the house was short and familiar—because, Joss thought, he really couldn't attest to his competency on the road with a car so filled with atmosphere.

His father had seemed chipper when they had picked him up, as Edward had slung his small bag into the boot of the car, but he had been asleep on the backseat within minutes.

'Everything okay?' Eva asked, after they had been driving in silence for another ten.

'Yeah, fine.'

He knew that he was killing any chance of conversation dead with his monosyllables, but for the moment he didn't care. The confined space of his car, with two people keeping secrets from each other, was more pressure than he could take.

It wasn't until he drew on to the driveway of his father's country house, between the old stone gateposts, that he finally felt himself start to relax. It wasn't so much that the pressure of having a fake fiancée was lessened. But out of the city, with space around them, it felt easier to breathe.

He parked close to the front door, and was relieved to see it open before they had stepped out of the car, and Thomas, their groundskeeper, pushing a wheelchair through.

Joss stepped out of the car and stared at the chair for a moment. He hadn't even realised that his father *owned* a wheelchair, never mind needed one. But Edward had slept the whole way here from London, and Joss suspected that he hadn't been entirely honest about how well he was feeling.

He waved at Thomas as he walked up to the steps at the front of the house. 'Thanks for this,' Joss said, gesturing at the chair. 'But he fell asleep while we were driving. We should probably just leave him a few minutes.'

'Probably for the best,' Thomas agreed with a nod. 'And this must be Eva.'

Joss looked behind him to see Eva stepping from the car, glancing briefly through the back window to check on his father. He felt a tug of tenderness at this obvious display of affection for the old man. He had no idea what the next few months had in store for them. How dark things were going to get while his father's body fought and then succumbed to this disease. But, however complicated things might be, he was glad that Eva was going to be by his side.

It was selfish, he knew, to look for her support. Especially when he knew that he wouldn't be able to return it. He was going to need all his strength to look after his father, to look after himself. And that was why he couldn't let this thing with Eva become real. Because she would get hurt.

He had to keep reminding himself of that. It didn't matter how good she looked, how incredible she smelled, how natural it felt to have her skin against his, her hand in his. Her life meshing with his. It didn't matter that it felt right, because it wasn't.

Except… That was not what Eva had said when he'd explained things to her. It wasn't what she believed. He had told her, plainly, the reasons he shouldn't be in a relationship, but they hadn't seemed to be good enough for her. He supposed he was lucky that she had her own reasons for wanting to stay single. Because she hadn't recoiled when he had told her of his depression. Hadn't blamed him when he'd told her about how his last marriage had ended. She had simply told him what he knew intellectually to be true: that he had been ill, and that what had happened had been out of his control.

Well, that might have been true then. But it wasn't now. He wasn't going to let this relationship get out of control. Because when that happened innocent bystanders like Eva got caught in the crossfire.

Eva walked towards him and threw a questioning glance towards Thomas. He loved the way she didn't even break her stride as she held out her hand to shake his. There was something in her posture, her confidence, her self-awareness, in the straightness of her back and shoulders, that he found completely captivating.

'Eva, this is Thomas. He looks after the house and the grounds. And perhaps he looks after my father, too, recently?' Joss said, glancing again at the wheelchair. 'Does he use this a lot, Thomas?'

'Ah…only now and then,' Thomas replied. 'More the last time he was here. He hasn't told you?'

'My father's been keeping secrets.'

'Well, he's not the only one, is he? It's lovely to meet you, Eva,' Thomas said. 'I hear that there are wedding bells in the offing. Congratulations to both of you.'

'Thanks,' Joss said, with a quick side-glance at Eva.

She was still smiling at Thomas, not showing any sign of discomfort at their lie. Once again he was blown away by her self-possession.

The sound of the car door opening behind them caused him to turn sharply on the spot, to see his father stepping out of the car.

'Sorry about that, folks. You know what it's like in the back of a car. Like being rocked to sleep in a cradle.'

Joss took the wheelchair from Thomas's hands and pushed it over to the car, but his father waved it away. 'No need for that, son. But if you don't mind I think I'll go and finish this nap inside. You show Eva around. Enjoy the last of the sunshine—it's been a beautiful day.'

Well, his father was right about that. The sun was low in the sky, casting long shadows over the garden through the leaves, which were just starting to turn shades of red and gold.

'Don't worry about the bags,' Thomas said. 'I'll get those. Your father's right. Go for a walk down to the village. The path's beautiful this time of year, and there's just enough light left.'

Joss turned to Eva with a questioning look, and she smiled. 'Good job I threw some boots in my bag. Sounds like a lovely idea.'

She pulled on her boots as she perched on the bumper of his car, and Joss watched his father walk slowly up the steps to the front door. It had only been a couple of days since he had last seen him, but his father seemed years older. And more sick.

When he reached Thomas he leaned on him for a few

moments before taking the last step up into the house. They would have to talk later. Have one of the difficult conversations they had all known must be coming about what his father wanted for the end of his life and how they could all keep him comfortable.

But for now the sun was just touching the tops of the trees, and he knew that the pub in the village would have good beer on tap. They could keep the real world at bay for an hour longer while his father rested.

He grabbed boots and a coat from the car and looked over at Eva, who was winding a scarf around her neck. Was she going to regret this in the weeks to come? Entangling herself with a man, a family, that was about to reach crisis point?

'Let's go,' he said, heading towards the path at the side of the house that would take them through the gardens and then down towards the village.

He walked quickly around the corner of the house, glancing up at the familiar red brick of the old building. This had never been his permanent home, but it had always been a happy place to escape at weekends and in school holidays. He knew every inch of the brickwork, every hollow and tree in the grounds. And soon it would be his, he realised. Along with the house in London and the dozens of Dawson's stores around the world. A whole portfolio of responsibilities was about to fall onto his shoulders.

'Is it far to the village?' Eva asked, catching up and walking alongside him.

'Not far—about fifteen minutes if we go down the

lane. If we want to stay for a pint we'd better walk the road way back. It'll be dark by then.'

'Sounds good to me,' Eva said, and they fell into silence as they walked.

Joss buried his hands deep into his pockets.

'Your father looked tired,' Eva said eventually. 'I'm glad he went for a lie-down. I was worried.'

Joss stopped for a second. 'Me too,' he said eventually. 'I should have expected it,' he added, walking on.

'Doesn't mean it wasn't a shock. Or that it won't be hard to watch.'

'I'm aware of that.'

As soon as the words were out of his mouth he regretted them. Or his tone, at least. He shouldn't be taking this out on Eva—it wasn't her fault. For a second he had a flashback to his marriage. Fights over nothing, and always with his dark mood at the start of them.

'I'm sorry, Eva. I didn't mean to snap.'

'It's okay. It's understandable,' she said, brushing a hand against his arm.

He shrugged it off. This was exactly what he was trying to avoid. Anyone being in the firing line if his depression came back. He was going to do everything in his power to stop that happening, but if he couldn't do that—if he couldn't beat it again—he was at least going to make sure that he wasn't taking anyone else down with him.

'It shouldn't be. You shouldn't let me get away with it.'

'You're under a lot of stress. I can't imagine—'

'Eva, don't make excuses for me. I don't need them. This shouldn't affect you.'

'If I didn't want it to affect me, Joss, I wouldn't have gone along with this whole charade in the first place.'

Joss turned to her, shaking his head and stopping his stride. 'That's different. Of course Dad being ill is going to affect you. But that doesn't mean that my moods should as well.'

Eva brushed her hand against his sleeve again, and this time he lost the battle to shrug it off.

'We're living together. I'm pretty sure that in a couple the other person's crappy moods are part of the deal. Trust me—give it a couple of weeks and I'll give you a run for your money.'

'We're not just talking about an occasional bad mood with me, though. This is something different.'

'Are you talking about your depression?' Eva asked. 'If you're telling me you think it's returning, Joss, then we can talk about that. We can think about getting you the help you need to get you through a bad patch. But snapping at people is something that we all do. It doesn't have to be a symptom of something bigger.'

'It's no excuse.'

'You're right.' She nodded. 'It's not. So apologise, think about what I've said, and we'll move on.'

'I'm sorry,' he said after a few long minutes of walking in silence. 'I don't want you to be brought down by this.'

'You know, maybe you could trust me to *tell* you when enough is enough. My happiness isn't your responsibility, Joss. I can look after myself. I always do.'

She was right—her happiness wasn't his responsibility. But he'd like it to be, he realised. He'd like his first task in the morning to be to put a smile on her face. He could think of a dozen ways right now that he'd like to try. And then he could spend his whole day keeping it there.

But another person's happiness was too big a responsibility on top of his own. Especially for someone like him, who had so spectacularly failed at the task in the past.

He also suspected there was more in what she said than first met the eye. She had always looked after her own happiness... Well, of course. Everyone had responsibility for their own happiness. But the way she'd said it—there was independence and then there was isolation. He suspected he knew which side of the coin she was on.

'So you always look after yourself?' Joss asked, brushing past some overgrown gorse, the thorns catching on his coat.

'No one else volunteered for the job,' Eva replied, with a flippant smile that didn't reach her eyes.

It was obvious that she didn't believe what she was saying. Which meant she was hiding something. After exposing so much of his own past, his own vulnerabilities, he suddenly realised how little he knew about her. And he hated how unequal that felt. Hated that she might be able to hold that over him. If he was exposed, then she should be too.

That was what was behind him needing to know more, he told himself. It wasn't that he had any other reason to want to know why she hadn't met someone and settled down already.

'Somehow I find that hard to believe,' he said. 'I have a suspicion that plenty of guys were interested and none quite measured up.'

'What makes you think that?'

'Oh, you know. You hear things.'

She gave him a sideways look that told him exactly how unbelievable she thought that was.

'Um… I think we've already established that you *don't* hear things. Try again.'

He shrugged. 'Fine—I'm guessing. Are you going to tell me I'm wrong?'

He watched her carefully, watched her eyes narrow and her forehead wrinkle as she thought hard. So he had hit on something, then.

'Why are you so keen to pair me off, Joss? You're not going to be one of those unbearable people who can't see a single woman in her thirties without assuming there's something wrong with her?'

He'd give her full points for deflection, but zero for accuracy. Well, if he'd hit a fault line it seemed to make sense to keep pushing.

'I don't know. *Is* there something wrong with you?'

Eva threw her hands up and picked up her pace, calling over her shoulder. 'So you *are* going to be one of those people? Great.'

He jogged a few paces to catch her up. 'I just wonder why you think you have to do everything by yourself.'

She slowed down again. 'I never said that I did,' she replied.

'No, but I've watched you. In the office. With me. You like to be in control.'

'So? Who doesn't?'

He gave her a meaningful look. 'But a relationship doesn't work like that, does it? Sometimes you have to give the other person a chance.'

She shook off his comment with a carefully neutral expression. 'Good job we're not *in* a relationship then, isn't it? We're just pretending—which means I don't need to change anything about who I am for you.'

'Right, because *that's* a healthy way to approach things.'

'So now I'm unhealthy? Is that what's wrong with me, or is there something else?'

He tried to reach for her wrist, slow her down, but she dodged away from him.

'I'm starting to think you're impossible—does that count?' he asked.

'Oh, sure—why not add impossible to the list as well? At least you don't have to wonder why I'm single any more. It should be self-evident by now.'

Oh, it was becoming that way. The way she deflected his questions. The way her arms had folded over her body, putting physical as well as emotional barriers between them. The way she was making every effort to appear as unavailable and unattractive to him as possible...

She wanted to be single—fair enough. Relationships weren't for everyone. He knew that. But he recognised something in the way she oh-so-casually brushed off the idea of being involved with someone. He recognised it because it was so familiar. It was the same brush-off he'd given his father for years when he asked if he'd considered dating again, giving married life a second chance. The same expression he'd doled out to concerned friends who asked if he wasn't lonely with his string of meaningless dates.

Something had happened to make Eva feel this way about relationships, and he wanted to know what it was.

'So have you always felt like this?' he asked, as the sun slipped behind the thick hedgerows, leaving them in a twilight that cast murky shadows across her face.

'Yeah, I suppose… Just never thought I'd be the settling-down type.'

'But you do date?' he clarified.

'Of course I date. I'm not a hermit.'

But why bother dating if you didn't want a relationship? He knew that one tended to lead to the other, which was why he had stayed clear of both.

'Why do you date?' he asked.

'I don't know—for fun? To meet new people? Do new stuff?'

'Why meet new people who you're not planning on seeing again?'

He could see from the tight expression on her face that he was annoying her. Well, good—if it meant that they got to the bottom of this issue and she stopped evading his probing.

'I see some of them again,' she said, a note of defiance—or was it simply irritation?—in her voice.

'What—two, three times, I'm guessing.'

'What is this, Joss? Are you stalking me now, or just planning to?' she asked as they reached the end of the lane.

He could see the lights from the pub across the road. They crossed to it in silence, and it wasn't until they were installed at the bar, each with a pint of real ale, that he picked up his line of questioning.

'I'm not stalking you,' he said, just in case she hadn't been kidding. 'I'm just guessing. But I'm pretty sure I'm right, or you wouldn't have reacted that way.'

She took a sip of her beer, and he could see the machinations behind her eyes as she tried to work out what his angle was. Why he was so interested.

'I just don't get why you want to know, Joss. Why it's any of your business, in fact.'

He managed a wry smile. 'You're right. It's not. I mean, if we were *friends* then it would be normal for us to talk about this sort of stuff—the guys you're dating, what you want for your future. But we're not friends.'

'We're not?'

'Of course we're not. How can we be when you're so intent on keeping me at arm's length?'

'Um… I thought we were keeping *each other* at arm's length? I thought we had decided that was the best thing to do? We both know that getting involved romantically is a complication this situation really doesn't need.'

'I'm not talking about romance, Eva. I'm talking about friendship. We've barely spoken since Milan. And I don't know about you but it feels weird to me. We're living together. We're working together. We're spending the bloody weekend together with my dad. If we can't even be friendly to each other it's going to be unbearable. And we don't know how long we're going to be keeping this up. Months in the same house but living as strangers—it just wouldn't feel right.'

'Now you're accusing me of not being friendly? You *do* remember we had this exact conversation the other day, except it wasn't me who was being standoffish.'

'You were talking about being friendly.' He laid a hand over hers, where it was fidgeting with a beer mat. He wanted her to focus on their conversation. He needed her to open up to him, and he didn't want to think too hard about why. 'I'm talking about being friends, Eva. Do you even know that there's a difference?'

'I have friends.' She shrugged his hand away with an annoyed flick of her fingers.

'Do you? Really? People you tell your darkest secrets to? Who know you as well as you do yourself?'

She looked up from the beer mat and met his eye—there was fire in her expression now, and he knew he was close to cracking her. Close to the truth.

'That's a pretty narrow definition of friendship.'

'I don't know... I think most people agree it involves opening yourself up. Being vulnerable.'

'Oh, and you're the expert on that, I suppose? Because you're so open to letting new people into your life. That's why you had to convince your assistant to pretend to be your fiancée rather than find yourself a real one.'

He choked on his beer and then looked at her for a few seconds without speaking. She was right. They had a lot in common—which meant he could tell her the truths he was pretty sure she needed to hear. It wasn't as if *she* was holding back. And she wasn't going to get out of talking about herself by turning the conversation to him. They'd already talked about his vulnerabilities—at length. He had no desire to go over that again.

'That's different. Other people got hurt. I'm protecting them, not myself.'

'You're *so* noble. The fact that you don't have to take a risk on anyone else—that's just a side benefit, I suppose?'

He reached for her hand again, hoping that the contact would bring her closer. Let her see that he was on her side.

'Don't turn this around. We were talking about *you*.'

'We were talking about vulnerability…about letting people get close. I think turning this around is pretty valid.'

'Fine, and we can talk about me later, if that's what you want. But right now we're talking about you. Why is it you don't want to let me in?'

CHAPTER NINE

'THIS ISN'T ABOUT YOU, Joss. It never has been.'

Her hand flew to her mouth as she took in a deep suck of air. She hadn't meant to say that.

Ever since he'd started digging, digging, digging—trying to get her to talk about why she didn't want to get involved—she'd told herself she shouldn't let him in. Letting people in never led anywhere good, and with Joss Dawson it would be downright dangerous.

It had been easier to dodge and deflect his questions when they'd been walking, with shadows to hide her face and the ability to walk off when he hit too close to the bone. But here in the cosy, intimate atmosphere of the pub, with the fire roaring behind them and Joss perching so close to her on a bar stool that she could see the golden flicker reflected in his eyes, she knew there was nowhere to escape.

The only way to shut this conversation down was to give him what he wanted—show him that a relationship wasn't an option for her, the same way it wasn't for him. Perhaps then he'd let the topic lie.

'Look, I know what it's like to have someone you

love leave you and hurt you, okay?' she said after a long pause. 'Is that what you want to hear? Because it's pretty much a description of my entire childhood. Both my parents in the army, taking it in turns to ship out while the other one was stuck at home with me. Me making friends and then being told we were leaving again. Until one day my mother didn't come home from her tour, and my dad—rather than be stuck with a grieving teenager—packed me off to boarding school so he could lose himself in his work. So for the love of God, Joss, don't talk to me about opening up. Some of us have perfectly good reasons for being happily closed books, thanks.'

She watched him as she waited for a response. Fine lines appeared at the corners of his eyes and a muscle in his jaw flickered. He was waiting, weighing, judging. Was he going to push further, or had she revealed just enough to make him back off?

'I'm sorry,' he said. 'I didn't know.'

Bingo. Well, her plan had worked, at least. But with the new information in the air between them, and old wounds exposed for the first time in years, she felt uncharacteristically vulnerable. Small and unprotected.

'It's fine. I just want to drop it now. We should change the subject.'

'Right.'

They sat in silence for a few minutes, while she tried to think of somewhere safe to take the conversation. Work? They had enough of that at…well, at work. His dad? That wasn't exactly going to lighten the mood. And there was no point waiting for Joss to pick up a small-talk baton. They'd already established he was all but incapable of that.

She glanced around them for inspiration and her eyes fell on a framed picture of the manor house, where they had left his father resting. Until she saw the picture, faded behind the bar, she hadn't really thought about the house as being part of the village, of Joss belonging to a community.

'So, has your family always owned the house?' she asked.

Joss's face relaxed immediately with relief at her opening small-talk gambit. Much as he had been pushing, it seemed he was as happy to see the personal topics dropped as she was. Perhaps because it meant that she wasn't turning the conversation back onto him, as she'd threatened.

'No, Dad bought it when I was small,' he said. 'After he and Mum divorced. He wanted somewhere in the country to bring us—get us out of the London fumes occasionally.'

Eva nodded slowly, raising her eyebrows. 'Well, when he wants to escape, he does it in style. How old were you when your parents split up?'

'Young enough not to remember it. It was all amicable. They're still good friends. No deep scars to probe there.'

'I'm glad to hear it.' She smiled, relieved the atmosphere really was lightening between them. 'So you used to come here at weekends?'

'And school holidays. You should see it in the summer—it's beautiful.'

'You're lucky.'

'I am.'

She could tell from the way he said it that he knew how incredibly privileged his life had been. But there was a tinge of sadness there, too. Because next time the house saw summer perhaps it would belong to Joss. And that could only mean one thing. She wondered whether Joss was making that same connection.

She finished her beer and glanced at her watch. 'Do you think your dad will have woken up?'

'Probably. We should head back anyway. I'm not sure whether Dad has asked Maria, Thomas's wife, to arrange dinner. But if he has you won't want to miss it.'

'Another woman who likes to cook for you—should I be jealous?'

Eva could feel a blush rise on her cheeks and turned her face to the fire so she could at least blame her colour on the heat from the flames. Thankfully Joss didn't capitalise on the potential of that sentence to get her confessing more secrets she didn't want to share.

'I'll drink up and you can find out for yourself.'

As they crunched up the gravel driveway towards the front door of the house Eva realised that there was one factor of spending the weekend with Edward they hadn't talked about yet—sleeping arrangements. Thomas had told them not to worry about their bags, which presumably meant that by the time they reached the house they would have been delivered to one of the dozens of bedrooms a house like this must contain—and, despite the copious number, they would have been delivered to the same one.

She could only hope that it contained an enormous bed, large enough for them to share without meeting in the middle at some point in the night. Or that there'd be an elegant chaise longue in the corner of the room that Joss could retire to in a show of gentlemanly manners.

If all else failed there were the flannel pyjamas— long legs and sleeves of course—that she'd packed just in case she found herself needing to protect her modesty.

They walked up the front steps and were met by Thomas at the door.

'How's my father?' Joss asked as soon as the door opened, and Eva couldn't help a small smile at his devotion to his father even in the sad circumstances.

'Still resting,' Thomas answered, with a concerned look. 'I've put you and Eva in your usual room, Joss, and Maria says dinner will be ready at eight. If you look in on your father, could you ask him if he'd like a tray instead and let me know? I think the journey must have taken it out of him.'

'Of course,' Joss said, his voice heavy with worry, and he gestured for Eva to go ahead of him up the stairs.

'Do you think he's okay?' Eva dropped her voice as they climbed, fearful of disturbing Edward, though with the treads carpeted in a lush, thick velvet, she supposed their voices wouldn't carry far.

'I'm shocked,' Joss replied. 'I didn't think that just driving to the country would tire him out so much. Either things are moving quicker than he expected, or he's not been telling the truth about what's going on.'

Eva had suspected as much herself. 'Are you going to ask him?'

'I already have. And I've offered to go to the hospital with him. He brushed me off with barely a word. He said he didn't want me dragged down by it.'

'Sounds like he wants to protect you.'

'Parents, huh?' A grimace crossed his face. 'Sorry, I didn't mean...'

'It's fine. You don't have to apologise for having a great dad. I just feel lucky that I got to know him too. You know, he's something of a father figure to me.'

'It will make him happy to know you think that.'

She shrugged, a little embarrassed. 'Well, let's not go telling him. We wouldn't want him to think we're getting all mushy.'

They reached the top of the staircase and Joss gestured her down the corridor in front of him. His steps slowed as they passed door after door, and eventually Eva had to laugh.

'My goodness—how many rooms *are* there in this house?'

'Last count? Fourteen bedrooms. And half as many bathrooms. Not sure about downstairs. I've never counted...'

'So, fourteen bedrooms and we end up—'

'Here,' Joss said, as they finally stopped and he opened the door.

Well, she'd been right about the chaise longue, at least. It was positioned under the elaborately draped Georgian paned windows, upholstered in a deep navy, with a pattern that caught the light from the chandelier overhead. A fire was set in the grate opposite the bed—a four-poster, naturally. It had a canopy up by the ceiling, and heavy curtains tied back in each corner. Crisp white pillows were piled up at the head of the bed, and instead of the sheets, blankets and eiderdown she'd been expecting there was a fluffy duvet, also covered in simple white cotton.

She turned to Joss and had to suppress a giggle.

'I know. It's a lot. But imagine a normal-sized bed in a room like this. You'd never find it.'

'No,' she said, shaking her head, her eyes wide. 'It's perfect. It's just…'

'Ridiculous? At least I drew the line at frilly sheets.'

'Yeah.' She let out a laugh. 'Yeah, a bit ridiculous.'

She crossed to the bed and had to do a little hop in order to hitch herself up onto the mattress. Joss came and sat beside her as she kicked her heels against the frame, and she turned to look at him, smiling.

'Here I was thinking it was going to be awkward, us sharing a bedroom, and I'm bursting out laughing as soon as we get in here.'

'Not what I'm usually aiming for when I show a woman to my bedroom,' Joss said. 'But I'll take it under the circumstances. You thought it would be awkward?'

'Well, of course. You didn't?'

'I hadn't really thought about it.'

'You're lucky to have me, d'you know that? To do your thinking for you. You really do need someone who knows how to do your job.'

'I never said I wasn't lucky.'

'Good. Let's keep it that way.'

She glanced around the room. Her comments on the decor and the house and the furniture had broken the ice when they'd entered the room but now, as they sat on the bed together she could feel tension mounting between them as they both looked around.

She presumed he was thinking the same thing she was—where were they going to sleep?

'I'll take the chaise longue,' Joss said eventually. 'I'll sneak some stuff from the linen closet.'

'And risk Thomas and Maria finding out that we're not what we say we are?'

'I'll blame it on you. Tell them you feel the cold,' he said, with a laugh that eased the tension again.

Eva pushed him gently on the arm. 'Throw me under a bus, why don't you? You know, the bed's the size of a continent,' she said. 'I trust you not to try anything if you want to share.'

'Wow. You have such a high opinion of me you feel you have to spell that out?'

'It was a generous offer and it comes with an expiry date. Just a warning.'

'Fine. Well I accept your offer.'

'Good.'

'Good.'

And all of a sudden awkwardness was back with a vengeance. She glanced across at Joss, then looked away as soon as she realised he had done the same. Being around this man was worse than being a teenager. At least then you could be pretty sure your crush was as messed up and confused as you were. But neither she nor Joss were hormonal kids. The decisions they made now would have real consequences over the coming days, weeks and months. There was no kissing now and then pretending it had never happened.

Except it was too late for that, Eva realised. Kissing without consequences was what they had tried in Milan, and if the tension between them right now was anything to go by there was no doubt that pretending it had never happened wasn't an option.

'I should check on my father,' Joss said at last, breaking the atmosphere between them.

It was a temporary reprieve; she knew that tension would be waiting for them when they climbed the stairs at the end of the night and found themselves locked in here until morning.

Joss disappeared for a few minutes, and then stuck his head round the door. 'Dad's going to join us downstairs, but I'm going to give him a hand getting ready. Do you need anything?'

She shrugged, and glanced pointedly around the room. 'Well, I didn't pack my tiara. Will I be needing one of those?'

'Oh, don't worry about it. Chuck on any old jewels. Kidding!' he added, when her expression must have shown her surprise. 'I'll see you downstairs.'

Eva descended the stairs, wondering how on earth she was meant to find the dining room without a map or a compass. When Joss had been trying to find her mews house he'd had the benefit of satellites and technology, but she suspected there wasn't an app for navigating your fake fiancé's country home.

She stuck her head around a couple of doors, revealing grand reception rooms with clusters of uncomfort-able-looking furniture. In the end she followed her nose down grand corridors to the back of the house, until the sound of Radio 4 came into hearing and the smell of roasting chicken grew stronger.

She checked another couple of doors until eventu-ally she stumbled into a room with an enormous range cooker and an elegant woman—seemingly in her fif-ties, and certainly in charge—stirring something de-licious-smelling.

The door hinges squeaked and the woman turned around, her face lighting up with a smile. 'You must be Eva,' she said. 'I'm Maria. I try and keep this house in order and keep those men fed.'

Eva returned her smile, feeling instantly welcome. 'And you do a beautiful job of both, by the looks of things. Roast chicken?' she asked, knowing that food was always a safe conversation-starter.

'With lemon and garlic sauce,' Maria replied. 'Now, don't tell me that the three of them have abandoned you to find your own way here?' she said with a tut.

'Oh, Joss is—'

'Never mind what they think is more important. You're our guest. If I'd known they'd left you to wan-der the halls I'd have come and looked after you myself. Now, take a seat and tell me what you'd like to drink. Tea? Or something more appropriate to the hour? A little aperitif?'

'Well, I suppose a gin and tonic would go down well,' Eva said, after thinking about it for barely half a second. 'But only if you join me. The dangers of drinking alone and all that.'

'Oh, well, I think I probably should—seeing as I appear to be in charge of you. Right, then, let me find us a lime. I know there were some in the delivery yesterday.'

Maria disappeared for a couple of minutes and returned with two glasses filled almost to the brim with ice, lime and clear sparkling liquid.

'I'm sorry—I should have asked if you want this in the drawing room,' Maria said, her brow suddenly creasing. 'Edward asked me to set the table in the dining room for dinner, but he normally has a drink in here with us first. You can go through, though, if you prefer.'

'No, not at all,' Eva said, raising her glass in a salute to Maria and taking a long sip. 'A drink in here sounds perfect to me. It's ridiculously warm, for one thing.'

'Decision made, then,' Maria said, opening the door of the Aga and peering inside. She pulled out a perfectly golden chicken and placed it on the warming plate on top of the range before sliding a meat thermometer into the flesh.

'Can't be too careful,' she said, glancing over at Eva. 'With Edward's health being what it is. I've tried to get the rest of the house warm for him, but a heater in his bedroom and the Aga in here seem to be the only things that work.'

Eva didn't have a chance to reply before the door of the kitchen opened and Joss, Edward and Thomas all appeared.

'Ah, about time. You gentlemen abandoned poor Eva,' Maria scolded them. 'We both had to take some medicinal gin for the shock,' she added, with a wink to Eva.

'Excellent idea,' Edward said. 'Think I'll have one of those myself. Anyone else?'

He made to walk away from where he was leaning on Joss's arm, but stumbled with his first step. Joss helped him over to a chair instead.

'You sit down, Dad,' Joss said, sharing a concerned glance with Eva over the top of Edward's head. 'I'll get the drinks.'

By the time they were all seated formally in the dining room Edward was looking tired again, ready for another lie-down. Eva and Joss shared another concerned glance, but this time Edward caught the look between them.

'Enough, you two. If you've got something to say, then just say it. I'm having a tiring day. Not sure why, but I suppose it's to be expected under the circumstances.'

'We're just worried, Dad. You seem more tired than you were last week.'

'I *am* more tired,' Edward said. 'But my doctor's not worried. I called him, you know. I'm not just pretending this isn't happening. He said it's completely normal. I just need to rest more. Which means we should get this conversation done with so we can all eat and get to bed.'

'What conversation?' Joss asked.

Eva felt a shiver of foreboding. She could guess what conversation.

Edward reached for a folder of papers that Eva realised he must have stashed on a chair earlier.

'We need to talk about my will,' he said.

'Dad—' Joss tried to interrupt.

But Edward wasn't having any of it.

'No, son. We need to have this conversation at some point and I'd like to do it now, while I'm still well and no one can accuse me of having gone doolally or anything like that. Not that it matters much *what* you say, actually, because it's all finished already. I just thought you might like to know what's in there.'

Joss pushed his chair away from the table and Eva could see him glancing at the door, wondering if he could bail out on this conversation. He'd better not dare leave it to her—she'd make him pay if he did.

'Dad, it doesn't matter to me what's in there.'

'Well, it matters to me. So you can sit there and listen, if you're quite finished talking.'

Eva shifted uncomfortably in her chair. It was hard enough being caught in a family argument. When it was about a will, and it wasn't even your family, she was all for bolting for the door herself.

'Maybe I should leave you two…?'

'Not at all, dear,' Edward said when Eva tried to excuse herself. 'You're part of this family now, and I'd like you to stay. I know Joss will tell you everything anyway, so this way we save him the trouble. Right, I'm not going to go over every detail, because you know all the business stuff already. But the personal stuff we've not talked about before. It's not complicated, though. I'm leaving your mother a large amount of cash, so neither of us have to worry about her being comfortable for the rest of her life. But most of the rest of it goes to you, of course, Joss. Including the London house and this draughty old place. But the mews house is yours, Eva. It's been your home for many years, and I would hate to think of you having to leave it. I hope that you'll accept?'

'Edward,' Eva protested straight away. It was too much. Too generous. 'I couldn't possibly—'

But Edward shook his head defiantly. 'I don't want to hear anything like that. A simple thank-you would be fine.'

She couldn't accept. Of course she couldn't under these circumstances.

If Edward knew the truth about their fake relationship he wouldn't be doing this. It wasn't fair to let him make decisions like this based on a lie.

'Edward, you don't understand. About me and Joss—'

'No, no.' Edward said decisively. 'I'm quite sure that your relationship is none of my business. Really, Eva dear. This is a gift for you. Quite apart from what you and Joss mean to one another.'

She shared a long look with Joss, and tried to communicate what she was thinking without speaking.

Was he angry with her? She would tell Edward the whole ugly truth if she had to. This had gone too far. It wasn't fair on the sick old man. She'd gone along with his misunderstanding when he'd assumed that she and Joss were a couple because it had seemed a small thing to do to make him so happy. But this—this was different. This was legal—a binding contract and the transfer of property—making their little white lie suddenly seem a whole lot more serious.

'The mews house *should* be yours,' Joss said at last.

She wanted to kick him under the table for continuing to lie to his father. They should just tell him the truth. Come clean. She turned and glared at him.

'I mean it,' he carried on. 'I'd give it to you anyway, if it came to me. I'm serious,' he continued, when she widened her eyes at him, trying to get him to stop talking. 'Don't fight this, Eva.'

His voice was softer now, gentler, and she found she couldn't argue with him when he was being reasonable.

And when she thought of her mews house as being really her own... It meant that she would have a little piece of the city that was always there—a safety net whenever she needed it. She fought back tears as she rose from her chair.

'Thank you, Edward,' she said, walking around the table to give him a kiss on the cheek. 'It means the world to me. It really does.'

'Well, let's hear no more about it,' Edward said, his cheeks flushed a little pink.

Maria appeared at the door with such promptness it seemed inevitable that she had been waiting outside, listening for an appropriate break in the conversation.

'This looks delicious, Maria. Thank you,' Eva said as the platters of food were set down in the centre of the table.

With the difficult topic of the will set aside, they all relaxed into friendly conversation, though she could see that Edward's eyes were fighting to stay open halfway through their main course. She glanced at Joss, and saw that he had noticed it too. As their eyes met she felt a flash of connection between them, and knew that in that moment she could read him completely. She wondered if she was as open to him as he was to her. What he could see if she was.

A warmth started in her chest and sank to her belly as she realised how close they had grown over the past week. How she had really started to know him, with their communication becoming subtler, more personal, more intuitive.

She didn't want to think too much about what that meant. About the risk that she was taking in letting him in. Because that *was* what she was doing. Whether she had intended him to or not, he was getting under her skin, into her thoughts, into her life. And now, when she looked at him, she saw something familiar—something that had been part of her life for so long she would recognise it anywhere. She saw the void that he would leave when he left. She saw her life without him. The spaces she would have to try to fill when he wasn't part of her world any more. The voids that would haunt her at night and occupy her thoughts during the day.

She'd seen those voids around both her parents when she was growing up, and had wondered how her life would look if they were gone—really gone—and she was left behind. And then her mother had been killed on duty and she'd found out. She'd lived longer with the space that her mother had left behind than she had with her mother there. It was like a shadow in the corner of the room, reminding her of what she'd lost. What she'd never had much of a claim on in the first place.

And she could see that void around Joss now. See the hole that would be left in her life when this was over.

She'd never meant to let it get this far. It was meant to be a lie. Their engagement *was* a lie. But these feelings that she was having for him—they were very, very real.

She didn't know what to do with them. Her instincts were telling her to run. To get away from him now, while she still had a chance of plugging that space, of rebuilding her life without him in it. But her heart wanted her to stay. She knew that from the way it ached when she thought about leaving. About what they were going to do when they had to get back to real life. When she thought about a life without him in it—or, worse, a life where they were polite to one another in the office and then tried to forget each other existed the moment they left.

Joss frowned slightly, and she realised she had shown too much in her expression. Even if he couldn't understand the minutiae of the struggle she was feeling at that moment, he knew something was wrong. And she had a suspicion that he was going to expect her to explain herself later.

A clatter disturbed her thoughts, finally forcing her gaze away from Joss's, and she realised that Edward had dropped his knife. He'd barely touched his meal, but now he lay down his fork too, and took a sip of wine.

'I think I'm going to retire and leave you young people to enjoy the rest of the meal,' Edward said. 'I'm sure that Maria will have a delicious dessert in store, so please don't let it go to waste.'

She called goodnight to Edward as Joss took his elbow and helped him out of the room and presumably up the stairs to bed. Left alone, Eva wondered whether she should make her escape. But what would Joss think if he came downstairs and found her not at the table? And even if she decided she wanted to, she had nowhere to go.

She could escape to the bedroom, but Joss would be there as well soon enough. She might remember how to get back to the pub in the village, but what would Edward, Thomas and Maria think of her taking off in the dark? They'd know that there was something wrong between her and Joss, and that was the last thing she wanted for Edward just now.

Joss appeared at the door a few minutes later, and made her glad that she had stayed. His eyes looked heavy, as if he was fighting off emotion, and she knew he needed company. That if he were alone his thoughts and fears would torture him.

'Is he okay?'

'Tired,' Joss replied. 'He says he's not in any pain, but I'm not sure I believe him. I'll check on him later, and if he's not sleeping soundly I'll call the doctor. I'm sorry, Eva. I should never have brought you here. You shouldn't have to go through this. It's not fair on you.'

'I'm glad I'm here,' she said automatically.

But as the words passed her lips she realised that she meant them. Even if it *did* mean facing the sadness of watching Edward fade by the day. Despite her earlier thoughts of escape, she knew that this was important. That if she left these men to fend for themselves at this crucial time she would be hurting both of them, and she didn't want that.

It was dawning on her just how far she had let both of them in already. She had told herself after her mother had died and her dad had sent her away that she wouldn't do that again. She would never let anyone leave a hole in her life that she didn't know how to fill. But somehow the two Dawson men had found a way in.

Her affection for Edward was nothing new, but since he had given her the news of his illness, since her closeness with Joss, it had changed. He was no longer the kindly old boss she'd always thought him. He'd become more than that. He'd become like family.

And Joss? She didn't know *what* to think about Joss and how she felt about him. She had never meant to feel *anything* about him. She'd had a crush, yes. But that was all it had been. An appreciation for a handsome face and an enigmatic attitude. So how, in a matter of a couple of weeks, had he come to be so much more than that to her? How was he suddenly so much a part of her life, a part of *her*, that all she could see was the dark outline of the shape he would leave in her life when he inevitably left her?

What she wanted to know was what she was meant to do about it. She knew it was too late to turn back without getting hurt. Hurting was inevitable now. But she needed a plan to get through it when the time came to end their engagement.

'How can you be glad?' Joss asked eventually, rubbing both his hands on his face and then reaching for his drink. 'I'd rather be anywhere than here.'

'I don't think that's true. I think you're glad to be spending time with your father. And I'm here for the same reason you are, I suppose. Because it's important to be with your dad right now. And because it's hard to do that alone.'

'You're right,' he said, looking up and meeting her eyes with a look that might burn her if she wasn't more careful. 'But it's not just that. It's not that I want *someone* here. I want *you* here.'

'Because your father thinks—'

'For reasons that have absolutely nothing to do with my father. Believe me, Eva. What I'm talking about has nothing to do with him.'

He wasn't kidding. She could read volumes in his expression, and filial duty was nowhere to be seen.

She dropped her eyes, breaking their connection. If she hadn't, there was only one place that the conversation would go, and she suspected neither of them was ready to go there. Yet. *Ever.*

The door opened and Maria appeared with a trolley to clear their plates. They sat in silence as she worked, only occasionally glancing across to one another. When they eventually had *tarte Tatin* and *crème anglaise* sitting in front of them, on elegant white and platinum plates, Eva let out a long breath, determined to start a conversation with something completely non-controversial.

But as she grappled around for a subject she found she was coming up with nothing. Everything felt so loaded with Joss. Their work, their home, their families... They all led to conversations more deep and meaningful than either of them wanted right now. And she hoped to goodness they were beyond the point where they would have to talk about the weather for lack of anything else to say to each other.

She pushed a piece of tart onto her spoon, and let out a sigh of anxious relief when Joss eventually spoke.

'I hear it's going to be a nice day tomorrow.'

So that was where they were. She didn't know whether that made her want to weep or laugh, but at least the ice was broken.

'We should take your dad out,' she said.

'He'd like that, I think. He's always liked to walk in the gardens.'

They fell into silence again, and Eva concentrated on finishing her dessert, counting down the pieces until this awkward dinner would be over. And then, with a mouthful left on her plate, she asked herself what on earth she was doing. The longer she could make this last, the better. At least with six feet of solid mahogany table between her and Joss she was safe from making any huge, irrevocable mistakes. Once dinner was over her safety net would be gone.

She lingered over the last mouthful, and responded enthusiastically and gratefully when Maria asked if they would like coffee. But as she drained the dregs of the drink she knew she couldn't delay any longer.

'Do you want to go straight up?' Joss asked.

And, although she had been expecting it Eva still felt wrong-footed. If she said yes, would that make it seem as if she was desperate to get to their room, into bed with him? If she said no, what would he read into that?

But she could feel her eyelids growing heavy, despite the coffee. It had been an emotionally draining evening, and although it wasn't late she wanted a bed—whatever the dangers of sharing it.

'I think I will,' she replied, stifling a yawn that just thinking about sleep had produced.

'Can you find your own way up?' Joss said. 'I think I'll use Dad's study and just finish up a few things.'

Eva let out a breath, trying not to show how her body had instantly relaxed, relieved at his words.

'I'll be fine. I guess I'll see you in the morning, then,' she said, standing up from her chair.

They both stalled by the table for a moment, and for a second she was unsure what they were waiting for. A formally polite kiss on the cheek? A handshake?

In the end, she darted past Joss, the lure of an empty bed too much to resist.

CHAPTER TEN

JOSS LISTENED TO her climb the stairs, her footsteps elegantly measured despite the way she had darted past him out of the dining room.

He sighed at the thought of having to crack open his laptop and put in another couple of hours' work. Since this thing had started with Eva his schedule had been punishing, with him trying to keep himself busy and out of her way as much as possible. Keeping himself from temptation. And now, knowing he would be returning to a shared bed, not just a shared house, the temptation was stronger than ever.

He wondered whether she had felt it too. That connection when their eyes had met across the dinner table... He shook his head. Of course she had felt it. Something like that couldn't be one-sided. It was the very fact that they were both feeling the same way that gave the moment its energy. Its power. He had to be more careful.

He turned on the computer and pulled up the latest reports from his store managers, scrolling through them without really reading. Despite his earlier concerns over how he was going to shoulder his father's business with so little notice, he needn't have worried. The transition plans they had put in place had worked just as they were supposed to. And, although there was still some anxiety in parts of the business, mostly things were going well.

He forced himself back to the start of the reports and made himself read them properly this time.

When he was done, he glanced at the clock and saw that an hour and a half had passed. Eva had looked pretty tired when she had left the dining room, so surely it would be safe by now for him to go up to bed? Everything would be simpler if she was asleep, he told himself. He could just climb into bed and pretend he was alone. Goodness knew, the mattress was big enough for the both of them.

He climbed the stairs slowly, and remembered the sound of Eva's feet on the treads. Had she been feeling as uneasy as him? Wanting to put off the inevitable?

How on earth was he meant to get any sleep in the same bed with her? Maybe he should stick to his chivalrous guns and sleep on the chaise longue as he'd suggested. If anyone caught him, it could be easy enough to explain away. An argument. Snoring. A dispute over the duvet. A sudden conversion to a conservative religious order. Or just a reminder that their sleeping arrangements weren't anyone's business but their own.

Who was he kidding? Sleep was in short supply these days, and if it was going to be difficult in bed with a woman he was attracted to, it wasn't going to be any easier a few feet away, freezing cold, wishing he were closer to her.

He turned the handle of the door to his room slowly, trying to remember where the hinges squeaked and where the loose floorboards were. If he could get into bed without waking her, maybe he could do an okay job of pretending that she wasn't there at all.

Fat chance of that.

He crept through the door, opening it as little as possible, and saw that Eva had left a bedside lamp on for him. He smiled involuntarily at the small gesture of consideration; it was probably more than he deserved.

Her dark hair was spread on the pillow, shiny with just a hint of red, like a conker, in the warm light from the lampshade. He silently gave thanks that the duvet was plump enough to hide any suggestion of what her body might look like beneath the covering.

And then cursed when his brain reminded him that he'd already seen enough to give him plenty of sleepless nights. That day in his father's office. Pale skin and delicate lace. Pink silk just skimming over the curve of her back.

He shook his head and turned his back to her as he slid open a drawer, careful to ensure that the wood didn't stick and make any unnecessary noise. He pulled out a T-shirt and started unbuttoning his shirt, trying not to think about the fact that he was undressing with Eva barely a couple of metres away from him.

If she were to wake up, open her eyes, what would—?

No. He stopped himself. There was no way he could let himself finish that thought. It wasn't fair on Eva, who had offered to share the bed on the understanding that he would be a gentleman.

It wasn't fair on himself either. He needed sleep, and it would never come if he was thinking about Eva watching him undress…maybe moving to kneel at the edge of the mattress as she watched, and then reaching out to help…

He struck a hand against his forehead. He really had to get this under control, he thought, taking a couple of deep breaths. Usually control was not something he struggled with. Since his diagnosis with depression he had taken back control over his life, bringing order to all those areas he had let his illness take over. Structured goals and routine had woken him from the fog that had clouded him for too long. Focussing on achievable objectives, sticking to his plan—even when he didn't feel like it—that was what had got him better. It would be foolish to slip now, to give the power back to his untrustworthy emotions rather than the techniques that he knew worked for him.

He flicked the lamp off, gently pulled back the duvet and slipped between the sheets, gasping at their icy touch on his feet and legs. For a moment he was jealous of the thick cotton pyjamas he had helped his father into earlier, though he hadn't owned anything like that in his life. Even the T-shirt was an out-of-character nod to decency for Eva's sake.

He glanced at the fire in the grate; it was burning low and doing as little as the central heating was to warm the room.

He shifted on the mattress, stretching his legs and wondering how far he could spread out without disturbing Eva. He needed to know where she was so that he could be sure he wouldn't touch her by accident. He reached out a leg experimentally, and breathed a sigh of relief when it encountered only more shiveringly cold sheet.

He turned on to his side, stretching out his arm as he did so, and his hand encountered warm softness. He froze, but the sharp intake of breath from beside him told him all he needed to know. Well, he'd worked out how much space he had—not enough. Eva must have rolled over at the exact moment he had turned, and landed on his hand. The weight of her was soft and heavy, and as he gently flexed his fingers he had to stifle a laugh. Turned out she had better protection against the cold and their attraction than he did.

'Flannel pyjamas?' he whispered.

He felt a shudder of laughter against his hand in return.

'Are you kidding?' she muttered, her voice heavy and slow with sleep. 'Of *course*, flannel pyjamas. It's freezing in here.'

Her voice was not much more than a breath, and the intimacy of whispering in bed with her made him ache.

She shifted and he acted on instinct, wanting to keep her near. As she turned over to face him he drew her closer, so when she eventually looked up they were practically nose to nose. He ran his free hand down her arm, feeling the cotton soft and warm beneath his fingers. The sensation made him achingly hard.

Who knew? he thought. *Flannel.*

Eva sucked in a breath and he realised she was feeling exactly what he was. That she was as keyed up as him, and had the same reservations.

'Still cold?' he asked, testing the waters.

'I've got goosebumps.'

It didn't necessarily answer his question, but it made him throb with the need to pull her even closer. His hand was still trapped beneath the curve of her waist, and finally it was too much to bear. He slipped it under her, until his arm encased her completely and his fingers could brush against the indentation of her waist.

'Better?' he asked.

She took so long to reply he was scared she'd changed her mind. That he was losing her.

'Hot.'

When she eventually spoke he closed his eyes with a groan. She had to know what she was doing, saying that. It was an invitation—or an acceptance. He wasn't sure who was leading this little dance. And he didn't care, because now his other arm was curving around her waist, drawing her against him until she could be in no doubt about how hot *he* was feeling right this second.

He nudged his nose against hers, asking a question he was already pretty sure of the answer to.

He wasn't wrong. Her hand came up to cup his face and she pressed her lips softly to his. Barely a whisper of a kiss at first. He held still, his arms squeezing her to him. It killed him, but he waited. Waited to see if she'd change her mind, as she had in Milan. If she was still holding back. Doing the sensible thing.

But the noise that came from deep in her throat told

him this was nothing like Milan. Her lips found his again—harder this time, demanding a response.

So he responded the only way he could, by possessing her mouth with his, exploring the textures and contours of her lips. Brushing soft kisses, tasting, touching with his tongue.

His hands bunched the soft fabric of her pyjama top at the base of her spine, pulling it tight across her breasts and revealing a couple of inches of bare skin above her waistband. She gasped softly as he did so, and then louder when his hands slipped beneath the cotton, desperate to know the feel of her skin.

'Okay?' he asked breathlessly, drawing away from her for a moment. It felt like ripping away a part of his own body.

'Freezing!' she said, with a gasp and a laugh.

She reached behind her back for one of his hands and drew it between them, rubbing his fingers and his palm between her own, blowing hot breath onto cold skin. He shivered and it had nothing to do with the temperature of the room. She kissed his palm and her lips branded him.

He barely had time to recover himself before she slipped his hand beneath the covers, cupping it around her breast.

'Better?' he asked, barely controlling the shake in his voice.

'Warm,' she replied, pressing another kiss to his lips, snaking her arms around him. 'Good. *Really* good.'

And then her hands were on his back, exploring, pulling at his T-shirt, and he didn't care whether they

were fire or ice—he just knew that he wanted them.
Everywhere.

He sat up so he could pull his shirt over his head
and Eva rolled beneath him. When he looked down
he could just make out her features in the warm glow
from the fire. Her eyes were closed, her face relaxed,
her body open and languid beneath him. He pinned her
with his elbows either side, dipping his head to tease at
her neck and her collarbone with his mouth and tongue
as he unbuttoned her pyjamas, one tiny awkward button at a time.

With each inch of skin that was revealed he dipped
his head lower, determined to learn every inch of her.
And as the last button came open he kissed her navel,
revelling in her gasp of appreciation.

He hooked his fingers into the waistband of her pyjama trousers, barely able to let himself believe that this
was really happening. But her fingers were in his hair,
encouraging, demanding. And as he skimmed the fabric
down her thighs he kissed her lips again, hard. Knowing that every second of this night would be burned into
his memory for ever.

CHAPTER ELEVEN

EVA WOKE WITH a delicious fatigue in her muscles, her head so heavy she could barely lift it to turn her other cheek to the pillow. She fought against the fluffy cotton duvet, which had formed a cocoon around her face, and stretched out a toe. The sheets on the other side of the bed were cold.

'Joss?' she called into the still room, lifting her head and propping herself onto her elbows. She strained her ears, listening for water running in the bathroom or footsteps on the landing. Nothing.

She reached for her pyjamas, where they had fallen by the side of the bed, and shrugged her arms into the soft flannel, which had long since turned cold, abandoned on the floor. Pulling on socks, she crossed the enormous bedroom into the en suite bathroom, where there were signs of a hasty exit from Joss. His toothbrush had been flung on the side of the cabinet, his T-shirt was still in a heap on the floor.

But there was no note. No explanation of his absence. No apology.

Nothing to explain the huge empty hole he had left in their bedroom or the ache in her chest as reality sunk in.

He had left her, just as she had always feared he would.

What on earth had she been thinking, going to bed with him?

She hadn't been thinking at all. Or at least not with her head. She'd woken up to find Joss behind her in the bed and herself practically rolling into his arms. He'd laughed about her flannel pyjamas, and then she'd gasped and sighed as they'd had precisely the opposite effect to the one she had intended.

In Milan she had held back, certain that giving in to her lust for Joss would lead to disaster. But things had been different last night. She had already accepted that he had a place in her life. That, however he left it, he was going to leave a space behind that was going to be hard to fill. But the way he made her feel when they were together—it would be worth it. She had never thought she would find a man worth that risk.

And now he had walked away from her without even a word.

Had he at least regretted it when he'd shut the door with her sleeping soundly on the other side?

She felt tears prick at her eyes and turned away from the mirror, not wanting to see them fall. A thick dressing robe hung on the back of the door and she pulled it on, aware how even her heavy-duty pyjamas weren't managing to keep out the chill.

She left the bathroom and glanced at the fireplace. She had no idea how to get any heat back into those dying embers, so she pulled the fabric of the robe tighter around her, holding her breath to avoid Joss's lingering scent trapped in the collar. Dropping on to the chaise longue, she glanced out of the window.

No sign of Joss's car—just neat parallel lines in the gravel leading away from where he had parked it yesterday. A shadow. A reminder that he had been there.

Eva shook her head, trying to shake off the gloom that had settled over her since she had woken in an empty bed. Was she overreacting? She hadn't even checked her phone. Her thoughts had flown straight to her parents—the way they had left her, as they always had. Her fears that anyone else she loved would do the same. She was going to feel pretty bloody stupid if there were half a dozen messages from Joss, explaining what was going on.

She crossed to the bedside table and picked up her phone, checking the screen. Nothing.

Well, she had never sat around waiting for a guy to call before, and she didn't much fancy starting now. She dialled Joss's number and felt her heart-rate jump when it started ringing. Once, twice—and then the voice-mail kicked in.

She frowned. It hadn't rung long enough for it to have redirected automatically. But the fact it had rung at all meant it was turned on. Which meant that he had to have rejected her call. He had seen her name flash up on the screen, known that she had woken without him, and then rejected her call rather than explain himself.

Nausea rose in her belly as she realised that he had really meant to abandon her. To leave her with no explanation at all. She fought the sickness down, forcing herself up from the chaise longue and formulating a plan for what to do next. She found her suitcase in the bottom of the wardrobe and started throwing things into it. If Joss didn't want her here—and he couldn't have made that much clearer—then fine. She would go.

She had tried and tried with her parents, had carried on loving them when they'd left her time and time again. And she had ended up with her heart broken. She had learnt her lesson—there was no point sticking around to let Joss do it to her again. She would get away and make a head start on building those walls she would need in place next time she had to face him in the office.

Eva jerked upright at the sound of footsteps on the landing, but it took only a split second for her to realise they were too light to belong to Joss. The gentle knock at the door confirmed her suspicions.

'Come in,' she called out, and knew before the head poked around the door that it must be Maria on the other side.

'I thought you might like some coffee,' Maria said, shoving the door open with a tray and setting it down on the table beside the chaise longue. 'And Joss asked me to fill you in on what happened last night.'

Mortification spread through Eva's veins. What on earth had Joss said to her? Had he told her what had happened? That they had slept together for the first time?

Then the reality of her situation started to sink in. No, Maria wasn't here to talk about what had happened between them in bed; she was here to make Joss's excuses for him.

Eva had fallen asleep last night, satisfied and safe in his arms. And at some point, when she had been reliving their passion in her dreams, he had sneaked away and arranged for Maria to do his dirty work.

'He didn't want to wake you or worry you,' Maria said.

From the hesitation in her voice, Eva guessed she wasn't any happier about the position Joss had put her in than Eva was.

Maria didn't know the half of it, she thought. Leaving unannounced was ungentlemanly at the best of times. In the middle of the night, following the first time they'd made love, when Joss knew exactly how big a risk she was taking on him... She didn't want to say it was unforgivable, but that was certainly how it felt right now.

'Edward was taken ill,' Maria said. 'We called the out-of-hours doctor and he called an ambulance. He's going to be in hospital for a few days.'

Eva nodded slowly, taking this news in. Perhaps she should have guessed that something like this had happened. She tried to get her head around the news and work out where this left her and Joss. So he had had a good reason for leaving. But none, she could see, for doing it without saying goodbye. Without a quick kiss and an explanation.

Had it not occurred to him that she would want to support him? That she would want to be there for him and Edward—especially when things were tough?

And it didn't explain why he'd rejected her call. Why

he'd not found the time in the last however many hours to drop her a quick message, letting her know what had happened. It seemed he had found time to keep Maria informed, after all.

Her heart ached for Edward, and for Joss watching his father fade. But it ached for herself as well. For the trust she had finally managed to put in Joss, only to see it trampled. To find herself abandoned, with her worst fears coming true.

She went to the tray to pour some coffee, wanting something to focus on.

'I'll leave you to your breakfast,' Maria said, her voice kind, and Eva guessed she had picked up on her distress even if she didn't know the cause.

As Eva sat and drank her coffee she wondered whether she was overreacting. Joss was at the hospital. Perhaps it had just been an inconvenient moment for her to call.

She watched the screen of her phone, wondering if he would call back, and then remembered that she was far too old to be playing those sorts of games.

CHAPTER TWELVE

JOSS REACHED INTO his pocket for his phone, and guessed before he looked at the screen that it was Eva calling. He was tempted to fire it off to voicemail again, as he had the last time, but knew that there were only so many times he could do something so cowardly.

As he had sat by his father's bedside last night he had gone over and over his decision to leave without waking her. He had taken his phone out of his pocket and replaced it again, wondering what he could say that would lessen the blow of her waking up alone in the morning, knowing he had left without a word.

It couldn't be undone now. He could apologise, explain that it had been an emergency, he hadn't wanted to worry her.

But he didn't want to lie.

The truth was he hadn't been thinking at all. He had been acting completely on instinct—looking after his father, looking after himself. And that was what worried him the most. Because in a time of crisis his selfish instincts had led to Eva getting hurt.

He'd not taken the time last night to think about how

his actions might affect her. It was what he had been afraid of all along—his selfishness. His instinct to look after his own needs was evidently incompatible with a relationship. They had only tried it for one night, and already Eva was paying the price. He had to put a stop to this before he did any more damage.

'Eva?' he said, hitting the green button on the screen.

'Hey,' she said, her voice neutral, flat. 'How's your dad?'

'Better, thanks.'

So Maria must have let her know what had happened. At least she had opened with a topic that he knew how to talk about. He could give her the facts, repeat what the doctors had said.

'They've made his breathing more comfortable. He'll be discharged in a couple of days. Maybe even tomorrow.'

'That's good news.'

He waited as the silence between them grew awkward.

'Can I come by and visit?' she asked.

The question was inevitable, but his answer had to be more than that. It had to protect her, to show her that they had got too close last night and needed to find some safe space between them again.

'That's not a good idea,' Joss said. 'He's still very tired. He's been asleep most of the time.'

'Okay,' Eva said, and they fell into silence again.

He thought back to being in bed with her, how they had moved and sighed and breathed as one body, and wondered how it was that intimacy like that could be lost. Easily, he realised, when one of you had walked away with no care for the damage they were causing. This wasn't something that had happened *to* them. It was something *he* had done.

'I'm sorry I had to leave in a hurry.' There—the apology was out. 'If you want to go back to London…' Joss continued, not sure whether or not he wanted her to take the hint, to be gone when he was eventually able to leave the hospital.

'I'll book a taxi to the station,' Eva said, and this time she couldn't hide the slight shake in her voice, that little tell of emotion.

He was doing it again. Being responsible for another person's emotions was too much. The people he loved were always going to be disappointed. Always going to get hurt. Even when he was trying to protect Eva, everything he did just meant she got hurt. It was better to end it now, like this, he told himself. The sooner he did it the better. He'd proved last night—to himself as much as to her—that he wasn't relationship material. If he didn't do this now, he was only going to end up hurting her more in the long run.

On Monday morning Joss pulled his car up to the front of his father's London house and rested his elbows on the steering wheel. Was it two days ago that he had done the same journey in reverse with Eva, or three? With the bright fluorescent lights and the constant noise of a busy hospital, it was hard to tell how much time had passed. Perhaps it was only two nights that he had spent sleeping uncomfortably in a straight-backed chair, aching to be home, to be back with Eva.

Except he'd known she wouldn't be waiting for him at the country house—not when he had all but told her to leave. And he couldn't go back to the mews. It wouldn't be fair to pick up as normal when he knew that they both needed to back off—for Eva's sake.

He'd not called her again. It was spineless, he knew, avoiding her hurt and recriminations like this, but what more was there to say? He didn't need her to tell him how badly he had acted. But now his father had been discharged, and they were back in London, he knew he couldn't put it off for ever.

He would have to see her at work. Tell her that they had to stop this. See if he could persuade her to keep up the pretence to his father, but forget that incredible night had ever happened. He wasn't sure how she was meant to do that—not when his own efforts had been so dismal. But they had to try.

He settled his father in bed and headed down to the kitchen to make them both a drink. When he returned, he eased open the door to his father's bedroom slowly, not wanting to wake him if he'd fallen asleep. But Edward was sitting up in bed.

'I thought you were going straight to the office?' Edward said, his eyebrows high with surprise.

'There's no hurry. I want to make sure you have everything you need first.'

Nothing to do with wanting to delay the inevitable confrontation, he told himself.

'From the way you crept in here, you thought I was sleeping—not likely to need much, in that case.'

So his father could see through him. Could see he wasn't telling him everything even if he didn't know the details of the evasion.

'It doesn't matter,' Joss said, refusing to engage with his father's probing. 'The office can manage without me for one morning.'

'And what does Eva think about this?' Edward asked.

Joss tried not to let his emotions show on his face, tried to keep his voice light. His dad was like a dog with a bone when he got an idea in his head. He wasn't going to be able to shrug his way out of this, he suspected.

'She didn't drive back with us.' Edward continued his line of questioning. 'I take it she left while I was in hospital?'

'One of us needed to be in the office,' Joss said. 'But she sends her love. I'm sure she'll visit soon.'

'Of course.' Joss could tell from the tone of his father's voice that he knew he had hit a fruitful line of questioning. 'Everything okay there?' he asked with fatherly concern. 'With you and Eva, I mean.'

'Of course it is,' Joss said, not wanting to worry his dad with the problems in his fake relationship.

He wished he could sound more convincing, but the truth was that things between him and Eva had never been worse. And their lie was meant to be making their father happy, not making him worry about them.

'I know all this must be putting a strain on things,' Edward said, reaching across to the chair beside his bed and patting the seat.

Joss sat down stiffly, recognising an order when he saw one.

'It's bound to. It's normal to have problems. Do you want to talk about them?'

'We're not having problems, Dad.'

He felt a wrench in his gut at lying to his father. Except he didn't even know at the moment what was a lie and what was true. He and Eva had started as something pretend, but this pain he was feeling—this was real. More real than anything he had felt through his actual marriage.

'And if you were you wouldn't talk to your old man about them anyway, isn't that right? I've been here before, Joss. Watching you struggle, keeping things to yourself. I don't want to do that again. I wished there was more I could do to help last time. I don't want to die wishing the same thing all over again.'

Joss dropped his head into his hands. 'I never knew you felt that way. I know I let you down with the divorce…'

Edward reached out and took his hand. 'Whatever gave you that idea? It broke my heart to see you struggling and not be able to do anything to help. But you have *never* let me down, son. You recovered, and now you have the opportunity to be happy. Please don't waste it.'

He couldn't lie to his father any more—even for his own good. He couldn't go on letting him think he was something that he wasn't. There had been too much unsaid between them over the years. Too many truths hidden.

'This is different, Dad. I'm sorry. Me and Eva—'

'You haven't told me everything about your relationship. I know that. I'm not simple, Joss. I don't need the details, because it's clear that you two care about each other very much. I think that was clear to me before it was to you. You love her, don't you?'

Joss didn't know what to say. He had tried so hard to convince himself he didn't—that it would be better for Eva if he didn't. But he couldn't lie to his father—not after what he had just told him.

'Yes. I do.'

'Then I want you to go to her and tell her that. And no matter what is happening with me, or what is happening with the business, I want you to remember to tell her that often. Okay? Nothing is more important.'

Joss wished it were that simple. That loving her would be enough.

CHAPTER THIRTEEN

EVA'S BACK AND cheeks ached with keeping her spine constantly straight and her expression neutral as she ghost-walked her way through Monday morning in the office, determined not to let memories of Joss break her perfect composure.

She'd been there since before the sun was up, and the streets were still quiet. If anyone had asked she would have chalked her early start up to commitment and professionalism, rather than the fact that she'd woken at five and been unable to bear the silence of her empty house any longer.

It was just the change back from the big, staffed country house to her little mews that had her spooked, she told herself. Nothing to do with the fact that the house didn't feel quite so much like a home now without Joss in it. Without knowing whether he had any intention of coming back to it.

She was completely in limbo. She hadn't spoken to him for three days, but as far as their colleagues were concerned they were still engaged. *Were* they still engaged? Or as much as they had ever been, anyway? She just didn't know. And it wasn't as if she could ask.

Under normal circumstances she would have no problem asking the man in her life what he thought was going on between them, but these were about as far from 'normal circumstances' as you could get.

As the last person left the office for lunch she let out a long breath and pulled in a lungful of air. It felt like the first she had taken in days. Her shoulders dropped from where they had been up by her ears, and as she tapped away at her keyboard she felt the rest of her body follow their lead and start to relax.

Which was why she jumped when she heard the all too familiar tread of his footsteps behind her, spookily loud in the silent office. She froze where she sat, fingers still on the keyboard. Taking a deep breath, she sent it to her shoulders again, forcing them into a state of relaxation that she didn't genuinely feel but she hoped would look convincing.

She turned slowly in her chair, delaying the moment when she would have to face Joss, lift her gaze to meet his. When she eventually did, anger and sympathy warred within her.

He looked like hell.

It was clear from the black bags under his eyes and the deep lines on his forehead that he hadn't slept properly since she'd seen him last, but worse than that was the expression of pain so clear in his features.

He'd obviously been going through hell. And he'd chosen to go through it alone rather than let her into his life and trust her to support him. To be there for him.

'We need to talk,' he said, his voice cold.

Her blood ran colder as she thought he must have terrible news about Edward. But she followed him through to his office and closed the door behind them.

'How's your dad?' she asked, bracing herself for the worst.

'Better,' Joss said. 'Home now.'

The air left her in a rush of relief, and she collapsed back into one of the chairs by his desk. 'Oh, thank God for that. From your face, I thought you were coming to tell me that he'd…gone.'

Joss sat beside her his expression still grim. 'No, he's home now. That's not what I need to talk to you about. It's us.'

All of a sudden she felt that chill again. The hairs on the back of her neck prickled, and she had a sudden premonition of where this conversation was going. Or where Joss thought it was going, at least.

'What happened on Friday night—it was a mistake, Eva. I should never have let it go that far.'

'Let it?' she asked, not able to keep the note of derision out of her voice. 'I don't think you were *letting* anything happen, Joss. I think you were making it happen. We both were.'

He leaned back against his desk and looked straight at her. She felt a shiver go through her at the emptiness in his expression.

'Then that was the mistake. However it happened, Eva, it was wrong.'

Surely he couldn't feel as blank as he looked about that night. She hadn't imagined the intimacy they had shared, or the ecstasy they had found together. And she wasn't going to let him repaint it all as flat and empty just because he had got scared.

'It felt right to me,' she countered. She knew she hadn't been alone in thinking that. Not at the time at least. 'It felt pretty good for you too, if I remember. I know you, Joss. You can't fake that with me.'

'How it felt isn't the point,' Joss said, refusing to engage with her. No eye contact. No acknowledgement that what she was saying was spot on the truth, whether he wanted to admit to it or not.

Eva stood and took a step towards him, planted her hands on her hips and forced herself into his line of sight. No hiding.

'It felt right, Joss, because it *was* right. There's something between us, and I know that you know it. Whatever it was that spooked you, that has you scared and running from this connection, we can talk about that. But I will not stand here and listen to you talk about it like it meant nothing. Like I mean nothing to you.'

'I want it to be nothing, Eva. It shouldn't have happened. I wish it never had.'

The words were so unpolished, so simple, it was impossible to hide from their blow. Eva felt the blunt impact square in her chest, and had to fight not to look defeated.

'And that's why you left me—even though you knew how much that would hurt me? This is because of your divorce, isn't it?' she said, deciding that nothing short of tackling this head-on was going to get through to him. 'Your depression.'

'This is because of *you*. Because I don't want you to get hurt.'

Oh, so noble while he was breaking her heart.

'Then don't hurt me again.'

It was as simple as that. He could give up on them now, walk away as if this connection didn't mean anything to him. Or he could try again, face his past and his fears, and vow to make his future different. He could accept that this depression might return, but that if it did this time he'd find support in a relationship, rather than seeing it as a burden.

'I'm trying, here, Eva. I'm not standing here saying this because it feels good. Or because I've somehow forgotten everything that happened on Friday night. It's burnt into my memories and my retinas and my skin and I'll never be rid of it. I'm doing this for *you*. Because I want to protect you.'

'And I'm meant to stand here and take it? While you push me away when we both know that we can make each other happy? I'm sorry, Joss, but no deal. You're going to have to try harder than that.'

She didn't know where it was coming from, this fire inside her. When she had woken to that empty bed, that empty room, that empty heart, she had been sure that this was over. That nothing Joss could say to her would make up for what he had done.

But as the days had passed she'd realised she was angrier about what he was doing to their future than what he had actually done the other day. If she'd had another chance with her mother she knew she would have jumped at it. She wouldn't walk away just because she had been hurt once. She would keep trying, keep fighting to keep the ones she loved in her life.

'I didn't want to hurt my ex-wife, Eva, and look what happened,' Joss said. 'I don't want the same thing happening to you.'

'I *know* what happened.' She took a step away from him now, raising her voice and throwing her arms up—anything to try and get through to him. 'You got ill, and your behaviour while you were unwell was a symptom of the disease. When you recognised that you saw a doctor and you got better. It's sad—of course it is—that by the time you realised what was happening it was too late for your marriage. But last time I checked permanent celibacy wasn't prescribed for depression.'

'There isn't a cure.'

Joss's voice was still infuriatingly flat and she stilled for a moment, studying him, looking for any sign of the man she had spent that incredible night with.

'Perhaps not. But there's treatment. There's hard work. There's support, if you'll accept it. Most importantly, Joss, there are second chances, and they're generally not to be sniffed at. I want to be with you. I want to try loving you. Believe me, I'm going into this with my eyes wide open.'

Joss met those eyes now, staring her down. Maybe using the L word had finally got through to him.

'The last few days—'

'Have been pretty terrible. It's taken a while for me to feel ready to have this conversation. To forgive you. Believe me, if you'd asked these questions on Saturday you would have got a very different reaction.'

'The one I deserved?'

'Probably. But this is the one you're getting now. I'm not letting you off the hook, Joss. I'm not going to be complicit in you walking away. If you want to break this relationship you're going to have to try harder.'

'I'll end up hurting you again. You know it's true.'

'Would you stop talking in prophecies, Joss?'

Ugh! If she didn't feel so frustrated she'd be close to giving up on him and his fatalism right about now. There were only so many rejections her ego could take, and whatever that number was they were getting dangerously close to it. She was going to walk out of this office with dignity, whatever Joss decided. So this was it. All her cards on the table. Then Joss could take it or leave it.

'Yes, you might do things that hurt me,' she started. 'You'd be a saint if you got through any sort of relationship without occasionally doing that. I'm pretty sure I'll hurt you too. Soon, actually, if you don't start listening to me rather than talking at me. A relationship comes from moving past that. Recognising that you've done something wrong, apologising for it and trying harder next time. If you're willing to do that, Joss, then I'm still game. Because, quite frankly, I can't imagine how I could walk away from this—from you—now.'

She stood watching him as he remained leaning against his desk, still scowling, still silent. Then he looked up and met her gaze.

It was clear to see how conflicted he was. There was something about the expression around his eyes that reminded her of how passionate he'd been that night, when he'd had her beneath him in his arms, ready and wanting him. But there was a tension in his jaw that she knew meant he was still fighting it. That her words hadn't had the effect she'd wanted. He was still afraid—of himself, not of her.

'This is a lot to take in,' she said, her voice hard but not angry. 'I cleared your diary for the day. I didn't expect you to be in the office at all. Why don't you go back to the house? Rest. You look like you've not slept for days. We can talk again later.'

He ran a hand through his hair and glanced at his watch, as if it held magical answers. 'You're right. I need to sleep.'

He stood upright and took a couple of paces towards her. He was about to step past her when he stopped, laid a hand on her cheek, and she drew in a breath, wondering if everything had changed in that last fraction of a second. But when she looked up she saw from his expression that he was still holding back.

He stroked her cheek with his thumb, and Eva had to resist the urge to turn her face into the warmth of his hand. She had made her position perfectly clear; it was up to him to come closer if that was what he wanted.

'I'm sorry for hurting you,' he said.

His voice trailed off and she knew he wasn't ready yet. He didn't understand his own feelings enough to share them with her.

She pressed her lips gently to his, cutting him off before he could undo what he had just said.

'That's a start.'

CHAPTER FOURTEEN

JOSS WATCHED EVA leave his office with the touch of her lips still burning on his mouth.

She made it sound so simple. As if everything they had felt the night they'd slept together was enough to base a relationship on. As if that were enough to cancel out what he had done afterwards.

It wasn't just that he'd left. It was that he'd cut her out completely. He hadn't been able to bring himself to talk to her on the phone, knowing that just the sound of her voice would make his resolve crumble. He'd kept it up for three days, falling back into old habits and isolating himself.

When he'd walked into the office and seen her sitting there, clearly aware of his presence, his breath had frozen in his chest. Waiting for her to turn around and look at him, he had felt every emotion he had been trying to bury over the last few days flood back, hitting him with a tidal wave of longing.

And then she'd been so angry, so fierce, and so sure of what she had been saying it had been impossible to argue with her. He'd walked into the office convinced that the best thing he could do for her was get as far away as possible—emotionally, at least, even if they couldn't manage it physically. It had never occurred to him what *she* might want. That she might be prepared to give him another chance.

He thought back to the dark days of his marriage. All the times his wife had tried to offer support and he'd thrown it back at her. Retreated more and more into himself, telling himself it was for the best, that he was protecting her. And where had that led them? She'd been hurt, and he'd had to carry the guilt of that. Was he just repeating himself now?

He turned the corner to Eva's mews and looked up at the big picture window of her apartment. He'd been looking forward to getting back here, he realised. It wasn't his own home he had been wishing for when he'd been trying to sleep in that crippling hospital chair. It had been Eva's. And he wasn't so stupid to think it was the bricks and mortar he'd been missing.

Nor was it her delicious body in his bed, because a sturdy wall separated them in this house. No, it was just *her*. Being close to her. Sharing his life with her. That was what had made this feel like his home.

He traipsed up the stairs and into the bedroom, shedding his jacket and shirt as he went. By the time he reached his bed he was down to his underwear and he collapsed onto the duvet, letting his muscles relax, finally, into the bed.

As his eyes drifted closed moments from his conversation with Eva back at the office drifted through his mind until one caught at him—*I want to try loving you.*

Not the first time he'd heard that word today. He'd told his father that he loved her, but he hadn't told Eva.

And in the moment when she'd all but told him she loved him too, he'd been so intent on telling Eva what he thought she needed to know that he hadn't listened to her. Her words hadn't reached him somehow. But he was listening now. *Did* she love him? Was that what she had been trying to say?

He couldn't stop the broad smile that crossed his lips as that thought sank home. It should have been scary. It should have set off warning beacons and alarms and flashing lights. Instead it filled him with warmth, a feeling of fullness that he couldn't remember ever having before. It filled him with hope.

And as he drifted into sleep he suspected that his world had changed.

He awoke to the sun low in the window, and creases from the pillow on his face. He'd fallen quickly and easily into sleep—something that had been a trial ever since his father had given him the news of his illness. His body felt refreshed and his mind was energised, full of Eva—still going over everything she had said to him at the office. Every retort to his omens of doom. Every argument against his careful reasons why they shouldn't be together.

She actually wanted to do this. She knew the risks. She knew who he had been before. She knew that the situation with his father could only ever get worse. And she still wanted to try.

The smile that had formed on his face before he had fallen asleep was fixed in place now, because he knew what he needed to do. He couldn't let her go. Not when he felt like this. She had put everything on the line for him, told him exactly how she felt, and he owed her the same in return.

He pulled on some clothes and went through to the kitchen, pulling open the fridge and glancing in cupboards. He was certain Eva would be able to create something from what he could see, but it was definitely not his forte.

He pulled out his phone and placed a call to one of his favourite restaurants, and arranged for them to deliver something worthy of Eva's palate. With glasses and cutlery and a nice bottle of red in hand he went through to the other room and laid the table, and then dug around in drawers to find candles for every surface. If he was doing this, he was going to do it properly.

She deserved that.

She deserved everything from him.

She had shown faith in him when he had deserved it least. When he hadn't even had faith in himself. And for once he believed her more than he believed the voices of self-doubt in his head. The voices that told him he was better off alone. That no woman deserved to have to put up with him again.

He was curious too. She had seemed so strong when she was talking to him back in the office. But he knew she feared being abandoned. That it was something that had haunted her life. And then, when he had gone and done it—had left her as she had feared—she'd seemed to come out of it stronger, rather than more shaken.

A knock at the door told him the food had arrived,

and he jogged down the stairs, returning a few moments later laden with foil containers. He placed them in the oven, as instructed, and then glanced at the clock. Quarter to seven. She could be home any minute.

He had barely sat down when he heard her key in the door downstairs. He jumped up and glanced around the room to make sure he had got it right. Candles flickered, reflected and refracted in the glass of the windows. The music was low and atmospheric. And the smells coming from the kitchen rivalled anything that Maria or Eva had rustled up for him.

There was nothing more he could do to prepare. It was time for them to talk.

'Something smells good,' he heard Eva call as she reached the top of the stairs and her footsteps turned towards the kitchen. She appeared in the doorway, and he stood completely still as her eyes widened when she took in the table and the candles.

'You've been busy,' she said, and he could tell from the careful modulation of her voice that she was taking care to keep her tone even. She wasn't going to give anything away, then. Wasn't going to make this easy for him.

'I might not cook, but I can order as well as anyone,' he said, trying out a smile, wanting to break the tension between them.

This afternoon he had been so sure this was right that he had forgotten how the tension in the atmosphere ratcheted up when he and Eva were in a room together. It was never going to be the case that they could sit and have a detached, impersonal conversation about where their relationship was headed. He shook his head: what would be the point of detached and impersonal? That was the last thing he wanted. It had taken Eva to show him how stunted that had left his life. How much he was missing out on.

He wanted this to be personal, and he didn't care if it got messy. He didn't care if he got hurt. He just wanted it to be real.

'Have a seat. I'll get us a drink,' he said, heading for the kitchen and buying himself a couple of minutes to decide what he wanted to say first.

He thought back to what his dad had said to him about how he should tell her what he felt. How he had been able to see through the complications of their relationship to the fact that they cared about each other. And he was right. Whatever else was fake about their relationship, the feelings he had for her—the strength he felt from knowing he had her support—that was real.

He hoped it was for her too.

He brought two gin and tonics through and set them on the table, taking a seat opposite Eva, noticing how the shine of the waves in her hair caught and played in the candlelight.

'Did you sleep?' Eva asked. 'You look better.'

'Yeah, I did, thanks. I feel it. Everything okay in the office?'

She looked slightly disappointed at the question, and he could understand why. He was disappointed in himself for asking it. He didn't want small talk. He wanted more than that. He wanted to talk about them: what they were to each other and where they were going.

'Everything's fine. Any news from your dad?'

'He's fine too. Look, Eva, this afternoon you asked me to think. And I have. Since I left the office I've done nothing *but* think. About you.'

She gave a small nod and lifted her brows, encouraging him to go on.

'And you're right. I've been scared. Scared of history repeating itself. Scared of hurting you. When I left you alone the other night I knew what I was doing. I don't think I get a free pass on that just because Dad is sick.'

'I didn't say anything about a free pass,' Eva said, her voice steadier than his. 'Yes, you hurt me. I expect you to learn from that. And to try extremely hard not to do it again.'

'Did it make you think of your parents?' Joss asked.

It wasn't where he'd planned on this conversation going, but he was curious. Something about her had changed in the days that he'd been at the hospital with his dad, and he wanted to understand her better.

Eva nodded. 'Of course it did. But knowing what you were going through with your dad also made me think harder about them than I have before. When I was a teenager the "poor abandoned me" routine was easier to maintain. But I'm an adult now, and I don't expect the world to revolve around me. There are other things going on, and lots of interests that compete with mine. I want to be with someone who makes me a priority. But I'd rather be alone than with someone who doesn't put the needs of their sick parent above mine. My parents did what they thought was right: they lived trying to balance all of the lives they felt were their responsibility. And for them the lives of people caught up in conflict were just as important as mine. They protected me from the effects of that as much as they could, and I never gave them credit for it. I think they genuinely did the best they could, and it wouldn't be fair of me to expect more than that of them.'

Joss leaned back in his chair and took a sip of his drink. So *that* was what had changed. 'That's quite a realisation to come to after so many years.'

'Yeah, well, I had a bit of a push.' She gave him a meaningful look. 'And a weekend with nothing to do but think.'

He leaned forward and reached across the table for Eva's hand. When she turned her palm to meet his and threaded their fingers together he couldn't hold back the smile that spread across his features.

'Eva, you said earlier that you want to try loving me. Well, I want that too. I want you to try desperately hard—because I'm already so in love with you. I want to be with you, here, every day for the rest of our lives. I want to feel *this* ring...' he turned their hands over and kissed the diamonds they had chosen together '...every time I hold your hand, and remember how I felt the day we chose it. How I feel right this second.'

He paused, and looked up from her hand to meet her gaze.

'I want to hear you say I love you in every language you know. I want you to teach me to say it back, so that I'm never lost for a way to tell you exactly how I feel. I want you to be my wife, Eva.'

Her hand gripped his a little harder, and he knew he

had taken her by surprise. Well, no wonder. He'd surprised himself. He already knew he wanted to be with her, but he hadn't planned to ask that question just yet. Now that it was out there, he realised how desperate he was for her to feel the same. He looked into her eyes, tried to read her answer from the shape of her mouth, the expression in her eyes.

'Yes,' she said eventually, a smile breaking her features at last. 'Yes,' she said again as she rose from the table and took a step towards him. *'Oui.'*

At the sight of her pursed lips and the sound of those breathy vowels, he ached to pull her into his lap, but she wasn't done yet.

'Sí, sì, naí, ja,' she added as she reached him, and placed a hand on each of his cheeks.

She leaned in close, so close he could have met her lips with the tiniest movement. But this moment was all hers, and he wanted to hear her tell him yes in every language she could.

'Ano, tak, ie, na'am. I love you, Joss. Of course I'll marry you.'

At last her lips met his, and heat swept through him as he pulled her into his lap, threaded his fingers through her hair and kissed her with all the passion he'd been holding back for weeks. Part of him—no surprise which part—wanted to pick her up, carry her to the bedroom and never let her go. But there was more to this than just wanting her.

'I love you,' he told her again as he wrapped his arms tight around her waist, holding her hard against him.

'I've never wanted anything more than I want to make you happy and to deserve you.'

She smiled down at him, and he felt the connection that ran between them pull at him deep inside.

'We're going to work so hard to deserve each other,' she said with a smile. 'Every day. For the rest of our lives.'

He tipped her face down to his, and poured his whole heart into their kiss.

* * * * *

A PROPOSAL FROM THE ITALIAN COUNT

LUCY GORDON

I dedicate this book to my Italian husband, Roberto, who taught me so much about Italy, and whose love inspired me to set so many books there.

PROLOGUE

'I DID WRONG. I didn't mean to, but I couldn't help it. All in a moment I found that I could be wicked.'

The old man lying on his deathbed spoke weakly, for his strength was fading fast. Vittorio, the young man sitting beside him, grasped his hand and spoke urgently. 'Don't say such things, Papà. You're not wicked. You never could be.'

'Try saying that to George Benton. He was the man I robbed of a million, whose life I ruined, although he never knew it.'

Vittorio rubbed a frantic hand over his eyes and said fiercely, 'But that's impossible. How could he not have known?'

His father's eyes closed and he turned his head, as though too full of despair to say any more. Vittorio rose and went to the window, looking out onto the grounds. They were lavish, extensive, perfectly suited to the Counts of Martelli, their owners for five hundred years.

Franco, the present Count, lay still as his life slipped away. Vittorio knew that his father's mind had often been confused recently. And surely this was merely another example. Yet there was a desperation in the dying man's manner that warned him of something different; something fearful.

'Don't worry about it. Papà,' Vittorio urged, sitting by the bed again. 'It's all in the past.'

'It will never be in the past until it's put right,' the Count murmured. 'We were friends. We'd met here, in Italy, when he came on holiday. We became friends, and when I went to England a few weeks later I visited him. He was younger than me, and that made him fun to be with. We enjoyed a good time, going out for the evening, having a drink, charming women. And we placed a bet. It was just innocent fun—until his gamble paid off! He didn't know. He was too woozy with drink by then. So I cashed in his winnings, then supported him home and put him to bed.'

'What did you do then?' Vittorio asked quietly.

'I'd had the bank draft made out in my name. I did intend to cash it, and pass the money over to George once he was sober, but I fled before he could wake up.'

'And he never suspected?'

'How could he? I never told him about winning. The next day I cashed the draft and returned home to Italy. I never meant to do wrong. I'd just succeeded to the title, but my pleasure was tempered by the discovery of the debt hanging on the estate. Now suddenly I could clear the debt. The world was bright again. It was wonderful to have people showing me respect, calling me Count Martelli.' He managed a wry smile. 'Vittorio—my son—you'll soon know that feeling.'

'Don't, Papà,' Vittorio said with soft violence. 'I don't want you to die.'

The elderly Count squeezed his hand. 'You're a good son. But my time has come.'

'No,' Vittorio said fervently. 'You must stay with me a little longer.'

The thought of losing the father he loved was intolerable. His mother had died giving birth years ago. His father had raised him since then, and together they had been a team, each meaning more to the other than anyone else ever could. Now the man who was the centre of his life was to be snatched from him, and the pain was agonising.

'Fight it, Papà,' he pleaded. 'Another day, another month, another year. I'm not ready to do without you.'

'You won't have to. I'll always be there with you—in your mind, your heart, wherever you choose.'

'I choose to keep you with me in *every* way,' Vittorio whispered.

'My son—my son—there's just one thing I would ask of you.'

'Whatever it is, I'll do it.'

'All these years I've got away with what I did, and now that the end is near—' he shuddered '—I must seize my last chance to make amends—with your help. Promise me— swear.'

'I'll do anything I can. My word.'

'Find Benton. Ask his forgiveness. If he needs money—'

'I'll give him whatever he needs. He'll forgive you and you can rest in peace.'

'Peace? I can no longer remember how that feels.'

'But you will have it, Papà. Wherever you are. I promise.'

'Thank you—thank you.' Franco whispered the words over and over.

Vittorio rose quickly to pull the curtains across the window.

'Don't do that,' his father begged. 'You'll shut out the light.'

'I was afraid the sun was too dazzling for you.'

'It won't be for long.' He gave a sigh. 'Sunlight never lasts. You think it will. You think the light has come into your life for ever. But suddenly it's gone and there's only darkness.'

Vittorio sat down again, taking his father's hands in his. 'Darkness can be fought,' he said. 'I'm going to fight this for you.'

'One day you'll have your own darkness to fight. You

can never tell when it will come, or what will cause it. You must always be ready for what you've never expected. Take care of yourself, my son. Take care—when I'm no longer with you...'

His voice faded.

'But you will always be with me. You must be. Can you hear me? Can you hear me Papà? *Papà!*'

But there was no response. Franco's eyes had finally closed and he lay still.

Vittorio dropped his head against his. 'I promise,' he whispered. 'I gave my word and I'll keep it. Wherever you are—hear me, believe me, and rest in peace.'

CHAPTER ONE

THE WORLD WAS full of light and glamour. Excitedly Jackie danced this way and that, rejoicing in the vision of her beautiful self that appeared in the mirror. Music played in the distance, inviting her into a universe in which she was the heroine.

But abruptly the dream ended. As she opened her eyes the real world fell back into place. The mirror's reflection showed not the luscious beauty of her fantasy but Jackie Benton, a slender young woman with a face that was intelligent, but not beautiful.

She sighed, easing herself out of bed.

Surrounding her was the austere bedroom where she spent every night. By now she had hoped to leave it behind, move to a new home and a more exciting life. But fate had arranged things differently, confining her to Benton's Market—the little shop where she lived and worked.

She'd spent most of her life in the tiny apartment over the shop that her father, George Benton, had started twenty years earlier. He had fought to make it a success, always struggling with money worries, and raising his daughter alone when his wife had left him.

In his last years Jackie had been forced to run the shop alone—something that had given her an unexpected satisfaction.

She was clever and hardworking, able to retain information about all the stock, and produce it at a moment's notice. Something which had at first impressed her father.

'You really remembered all that?' he would exclaim. 'Well done! You're in the right business.'

'I get it from you,' she had reminded him. 'I remember when I was a child there were lots of times you made people gulp at what you could remember without having to look it up.'

It had been a happy moment, uniting father and daughter. He had been proud—not only of her memory but her ability to choose the best stock. Knowing this, she had felt her confidence grow, and she had begun to see herself as a serious businesswoman.

Just occasionally her father had given her a little warning advice. Once, when a temporary employee had flounced out in a temper, he'd said, 'Did you have to be so hard on him?'

'I wasn't hard on him,' she'd protested. 'I just pointed out that he'd got something wrong. And he had.'

'You might have been a bit more tactful.'

'Oh, come on, Daddy,' she had said, in a teasing voice. 'What you mean is that a woman mustn't tell a man that he's wrong in case he's offended. But we're not living in the nineteenth century.'

He'd patted her hand. '*You* may not be, darling, but a lot of men are. You're a bit too fond of giving orders.'

'Too fond for a woman, you mean? You think I should just go along with him? Even when I know he's an idiot?'

They had laughed fondly together, but she'd come to understand that he had been making a fair point. She had learned to speak with more care, but it was still exasperating to have to do so when she knew she was an expert.

She had gradually come to enjoy the feeling of being in command—not merely of their employees but of the whole running of the place. She had chosen stock and it sold well. She'd had the instincts of a talented businesswoman, and they had given her hope for the future.

But her hard work had come too late. Matters had started

getting worse, owing to the mountain of her father's debts that had piled so high that even her commercial success could not completely deal with it. Finally her father had been forced to sell the shop.

By then his life had been drawing to a close. Rik, the new owner, had reluctantly allowed them to stay in the little apartment upstairs, and Jackie had continued to work in the shop—but only part-time, so that she could always hurry upstairs to check that her father was all right. She nursed him gladly, giving him everything in her power in return for the loving care he had always shown her.

'It's so hard for you…to be caring for me and working downstairs as well,' he had said once. 'Such a burden.'

'Stop it, Dad. You could never be a burden to me. *Never.*'

'Bless you, darling. I wanted to leave the shop to you. I'd have been proud to give you a legacy. I hoped once— But there. It just didn't work out.'

She would have loved to own the shop. So much of its success was due to *her* work, and it still held the atmosphere created by her beloved father. But she had known she must abandon that dream.

Her father had died a few days later. And then Rik had offered her a lifeline.

'You're welcome to stay if you become full-time. You can go on living here.'

She'd thought carefully before agreeing. She disliked Rik— an ill-tempered man in his forties—But she had accepted the job because it would give her a little time to work out her plan to escape into a new life—one in which she would have her own business, organising everything, using the talents she'd so gladly discovered.

Her dislike of Rik was well-founded. He had a high opinion of his own knowledge and skills, but Jackie felt that he actually knew very little. He made silly mistakes for which he blamed *her*.

She had tried to save money, hoping that soon she would be able to afford to leave and explore new possibilities. But it had been a hopeless task. Following George's death had come the discovery of more debts that he hadn't managed to pay, even with the money he'd made from selling the shop. Her savings had soon been swallowed up by them. And she had no hope of saving much more, given the meanly low pay Rik allowed her.

'I give you a fair wage,' he would say. 'You live here for nothing. If you worked somewhere else you'd have to pay for accommodation.'

It was true. Frantically she had hunted for another job, but hadn't been able to find one that paid enough to solve the problem. Now she felt trapped, and with no obvious way out she just had to hope for a miracle!

She showered and dressed carefully. She presented a picture of efficiency—ideal for the work that consumed her life—but her looks didn't please her. She considered herself far too plain.

She opened her laptop and logged on to her bank to check the state of her account. The result made her groan with despair. She had very little money, despite her attempts to live frugally.

Dispirited, she opened an astrology website, and read her prediction.

The fates are planning a startling new beginning for you. The sun in Jupiter will bring things you never anticipated, and decisions that will change your life.

In her dreams, she thought wryly. Last week it had said she was going to be a millionaire. And look how *that* had turned out.

She read the prediction again, trying to see it as the approach of the miracle she longed for, and then hurried downstairs and opened up the shop. She served a couple of customers, then spent some time looking around.

The shop had a variety of stock, including home wares and groceries. She often wished she could persuade Rik to show a little more imagination about the stock. But he had no sympathy for her ideas.

'This is a practical place, full of practical items,' he'd once told her sternly. 'You're too fanciful, Jackie. That's your trouble. You want life to be fun, and it isn't designed that way.'

'Not always fun,' she'd protested. 'Just a little bit of excitement now and then. I remember Daddy felt the same.'

'You father spent too much time looking for fun. It was his ruin.'

'*Something* ruined him…' She'd sighed. 'But I don't think it was that.'

'Get on with your work and stop wasting time.'

On the flight from Rome to London, Vittorio sat sunk in thought, wondering where the search for George Benton would finally lead him. Common sense told him he need not search at all. If he simply refused, who would ever know?

But his conscience would know. His promise had brought his father peace in his final moments. If he broke his word the knowledge would be with him for ever. And somewhere in his heart he sensed that his father's reproaches would always haunt him.

Everything had changed with Franco's death. He'd spoken of the pleasures of being Count Martelli, and Vittorio had soon discovered that it was true. The first time someone addressed him as 'Signor Conte' he had hardly been able to believe he'd heard correctly. His employees now treated him with deference, almost awe.

But his father had also spoken of other things—of the

hidden problems behind the glamour, that the rest of the world knew nothing about. And here, too, he had been right.

Vittorio had gone through Franco's things, seeking clues about his father's past life and George Benton. He'd found a photograph of the two men together, which must have been taken during their meeting in England many years before.

How old would Benton be now? Middle-aged? At the height of his powers? Ready to take revenge on the family that had cheated him out of a fortune? He wasn't looking forward to their meeting, but there was no choice.

Franco's papers had also included a newspaper cutting, mentioning a shop called Benton's Market. There was a picture of a small, shabby-looking shop, and one of George Benton, looking older than in the other picture.

That was Vittorio's clue. He had a lead.

At the airport he hired a taxi and spent the journey studying a map of London. The area he sought was just north of the River Thames in the east of the city. As they approached the area Vittorio asked the driver, 'Is there a hotel near here?'

'There's one just around the corner. Mind you, it costs a lot.'

'Fine. Take me there.'

The hotel was pleasantly luxurious. He booked a room for the night, then went out to explore.

Almost at once he saw a corner shop with its sign proclaiming 'Benton's Market'. He took a deep breath, clenching his fists, vowing not to lose his nerve now.

Nearby was a small café, with tables outside. He found a seat, ordered some coffee and took out the photograph of Benton. From this angle he could see through the shop windows clearly enough to know if the man was there.

But time passed and there was no sign of him—only a young woman arranging stock in the main window. Much of it was already in place, but she was intent on reorganising it, giving it all her concentration.

He admired the woman's dedication and artistic flair. He would value such an employee himself, to work in the department store he owned and managed in Rome.

Suddenly he tensed as a man appeared from the rear of the shop. Could this be Benton? But he looked nothing like the picture. His face was thin and severe. His manner to the woman suggested ill temper. When he spoke Vittorio could just make out the words through the open door.

'*Must* you waste time faffing about over this? There's a pile of stuff at the back needs unpacking.'

'But I thought we agreed—' she began to say.

'Don't argue. Just do as I tell you. Get going.'

Looking exasperated, she retreated to the back of the shop.

Vittorio approached the shop, entering with the air of an eager customer.

'I'd like to buy some apples,' he said.

'We've got some here,' the man said. 'No—wait. They *were* over there. What has that stupid woman done with them?'

'I'd also like to talk to Mr Benton, please.'

The man glanced up, scowling. 'What do you want with him?' His tone became suspicious. 'You're not another debt collector, are you?'

'No, it's a personal matter.'

'Well, you can't see him. He's dead.'

'Dead?' Vittorio froze, feeling as though he'd heard a thunderclap. 'When?'

'A year ago. But his daughter still works here.'

'Was that her I saw? Can I talk to her?'

'You can, but not just yet. She's got work to do. You'll have to wait until she's finished for the day.'

Feeling depressed, Vittorio departed. Returning to the

café he settled again to watch the shop, trying to get his thoughts in order. Everything he'd planned was in a shambles. He must talk to Benton's daughter and just hope that she was a sensible woman who would accept financial compensation and let the matter end.

Throughout the afternoon he saw many customers go into the shop. The young woman dealt with them efficiently, always smiling and friendly. Every one of them bought something from her.

Benton's daughter was a natural saleswoman, it seemed.

He stayed there for four hours. He read the paper and then busied himself sending and receiving emails from his smartphone. The frustration of waiting was hard to endure but he forced himself. So much depended on this.

Inside the shop Jackie was working hard. Often she glanced out of the window, puzzled to see that the strange man was still there, sitting outside the café. She concluded that he must be a tourist, albeit a very well dressed one!

At last it was closing time. As she was preparing to leave, Rik arrived.

'Don't go yet,' he said, scowling. 'We need to have a talk about making new orders.'

'But I can't stay,' she protested. She gave him a wry smile, saying, 'And, let's face it, you don't pay me enough to make me want to do overtime.'

'Don't be impertinent. I pay you a fair wage. If you did better I might pay you more.'

'It's not *my* fault profits are low,' she said indignantly. 'I don't think you're buying enough of the right stock.'

'And *I* don't think you're making a big enough effort,' he said coldly.

In his anger he spoke with a raised voice.

Vittorio, a few feet away, heard him through the open

door. He rose and headed for the shop, from where Rik's grouchy voice could still be heard.

'I'm not asking. I'm telling you to stay where you are so we can discuss these orders.'

'*No!*' Jackie said furiously.

Once before she'd agreed to this demand and it had stretched to two hours, without so much as a penny being added to her wages.

'Now, look, Jackie—'

'We can talk tomorrow,' she said desperately.

Unable to bear any more, she fled blindly—and collided with a man entering through the front door. She began to fall, nearly taking him down with her.

'I'm sorry—' she gasped.

'No, *I'm* sorry,' Vittorio said, holding her firmly.

'Come back here,' Rik snapped, reaching out to take her arm in a fierce grip.

'Let me go!' she cried.

'I'll let you go when you do what you're paid to do.'

The last word ended on a yelp that burst from him at the feel of Vittorio's hand gripping his wrist.

'Let her go,' ordered Vittorio.

'Who the hell do you think you are?' Rik wailed.

'I said let her go, and you'd better do so if you know what's good for you.' Vittorio's voice was harsh and unrelenting.

Jackie felt Rik's painful grip on her arm loosen, until she was able to free herself.

A glance back at Rik showed he was scowling. She hurried away, following Vittorio, who put his arm protectively around her.

'Sorry about that,' he said. 'I didn't mean to get you in trouble with your boss.'

'Don't blame yourself.' She sighed. 'He's always like that.'

'I'm afraid I tripped you.'

'No, I tripped *you*. I wasn't looking where I was going.'

'But you stumbled. Are you sure you aren't hurt? I thought you might have twisted your ankle.'

'Just a little.'

'You should sit down. Let's go into the café.'

Once inside, he took her to a table in the corner, summoned the waiter and ordered coffee. When it was served he took a deep breath.

'*Signorina—*'

'My name's Jacqueline Benton. People call me Jackie.'

'Thank you—Jackie.'

'You called me *signorina*. Are you Italian?' She sounded hopeful.

'Yes, my name is Vittorio.'

She seemed pleased at the discovery. Smiling, she offered her hand. '*Buon giorno*, Vittorio.'

'*Buon giorno*, Jackie.'

'I really thank you for what you did—rescuing me from Rik.'

'He must be a nightmare to work for. But I guess you're out of a job now.'

'Probably not. You're right—he *is* a nightmare. But things like that have happened before. He always apologises afterwards.'

'He *what*? I find that hard to believe.'

'So do I, in a way. But if I left it would be hard for him to find someone who'd put up with his horrible behaviour while knowing the place as well as I do.'

'So he knows how to act for his own benefit?' Vittorio said wryly.

'Oh, yes. Mind you, I suppose you could say that of everyone. We all do what suits us, and we don't really think about anyone else's feelings.'

He knew an uneasy moment. Was it possible that she suspected the truth about his arrival?

But she was smiling pleasantly, and he told himself not to panic.

'I find it hard to believe that of you,' he said gently.

'Oh, I can be selfish when it suits me.' She gave him a cheeky smile. 'You wouldn't *believe* the lengths I go to just to get my own way.'

He smiled back, charmed by her impish humour.

'I'll believe whatever you care to tell me,' he said. 'But you don't need to go to any great lengths. Just say what you want and I'll take care of it.'

That could be quite a temptation, she thought, remembering what she had read on the astrology site.

The fates are planning a startling new beginning for you. The sun in Jupiter will bring things you never anticipated...

Certainly she hadn't anticipated a charming, handsome man declaring himself at her service.

Watching her face, Vittorio managed to read her expression fairly well. He guessed she was trying decide how much fun they might have teasing each other.

And it might be *really* good fun, he thought. As well as humour there was a warmth in her eyes that tempted him to move closer.

'Rik said a man was asking after my father,' she said. 'Was that you?'

'Yes. I was sorry to hear that he was dead.'

'Why are you looking for him?'

Vittorio hesitated, sensing the approach of danger. Suddenly he was reluctant to disturb the delightful atmosphere between them.

'My own father knew him several years ago,' he said carefully.

'How did they meet? Did your father try to sell him some Italian goods for the shop?'

'No, he wasn't a salesman. He was Count Martelli.'

He waited for her to react with delight to hearing his status, as he was used to, but she only said ironically, 'A count? You're the son of a *count*? Are you kidding?'

'No, I'm not. And, since my father has died, I *am* the Count.'

She burst into a delicious chuckle. 'You must think I'm so gullible.'

'Why don't you believe me?'

'Because my father never once mentioned knowing a *count*—or even admitted meeting one. I just can't imagine that my father was ever friends with an aristocrat, not when we were so poor.'

'Was he really poor? He managed to start his own business.'

'He borrowed a lot of money to buy the shop. And it was a big mistake. He never really made the profit he needed, and we always lived on the edge of poverty.'

'That must have been a very sad life for you,' Vittorio said uneasily.

'Not for me as much as for him. It destroyed his marriage to my mother. She left him for another man. For years Daddy and I had only each other. I adored him. He was a lovely man…sweet-natured, generous. I went to work in the shop, to help him. It wasn't the life I'd planned—I'd dreamed of going to university. But I couldn't abandon him. And in the end he was forced to sell. Rik beat him down on the price, but he offered me a job and let us go on living there. I did all I could for Daddy, but it wasn't enough. A couple of years ago he had a heart attack.'

Vittorio dropped his head, staring at the floor. In his

worst nightmares he'd never imagined anything as bad as this. If George Benton had received the money that should have been his everything would have been different for him. He might even be alive now.

What would she say when he told her?

He clenched his fists, trying to find the courage to do the right thing.

But his courage failed him, and to his relief the waiter appeared.

'We're about to close, sir.'

'Then I guess we have to go,' he said hurriedly, trying not to sound too relieved.

It was dark outside. He walked Jackie to the shop door and waited, wondering if she would invite him in. But she only said, 'I'm glad we met. It was nice to have coffee.'

'Yes, it was. Jackie…' He hesitated, uncertain how to go on.

'Yes?'

'Nothing. Perhaps we can—see each other again. I'd like to talk.'

'So would I. Tomorrow?'

'I'll look in.'

She went inside, locking the door behind her. For some moments Vittorio stood in silence, trying to come to a troubling decision.

He should have told her everything, but he knew the truth would hurt her greatly. He felt that in his heart, and flinched from striking that blow.

He'd planned every step of the way how he would confront George Benton, explain, apologise, and draw a line under it. Instead he found himself confronted with a woman whose sweetness and vulnerability touched his heart. And the truth was he didn't know how to respond.

After standing there hopelessly for several minutes he turned and hurried away into the darkness.

CHAPTER TWO

NEXT MORNING VITTORIO awoke early. The clock said half past five and suddenly there seemed no point in staying in bed. Showering and dressing quickly, he headed straight out.

It felt good to enjoy the fresh air and the fast-growing light. But then he saw something that alarmed him. A young woman walking away in the distance. It was hard to be certain of details, but she looked strangely like…

Jackie.

Wanting to be sure, he hurried after her, but she turned a corner out of sight.

Cursing, he ran desperately through the streets. He didn't know London at all. It was hopeless, he thought frantically when he found himself by the River Thames. She must be walking along the embankment—but in which direction?

Then luck was with him. After a hundred yards he could see her, sitting on a bench, staring out over the water. He moved closer, struck by the way she seemed sunk in another world. It reminded him of himself the night before.

He stayed silent, unsure whether it was right for him to disturb her, but after a moment she glanced up.

'Vittorio? What are you doing up this early?' she asked.

'I couldn't sleep so I thought I'd stretch my legs. How are you this morning, Jackie? Are you worried about facing Rik today?'

'I'm fine—honestly.'

'Forgive me, but I don't think you are.' He lifted her chin with his fingers, looking at her face. 'You've been crying.'

'Just a little.'

He put his arms round her, overtaken by a desire to care for her. Protectiveness was a feeling he'd seldom, if ever, known before, and now it was almost alarming. He had to tell her something that would break her heart, and suddenly he wasn't sure that he could do it.

'Hold on to me,' he whispered. 'It'll be all right.'

'Sometimes I think things will *never* be all right,' she said. 'I'm sorry to dump all this on you, but I can't talk about Daddy without—'

'Without remembering all the bad things that happened to him?'

'I don't know why, Vittorio, but I feel I could tell you anything.'

She looked up again and the sight of her vulnerable face swept him with a desire to kiss her. He yielded—but only to lay his lips on her forehead.

'Do you want to tell me any more?' he murmured.

'You can't want to hear such a terrible story,' she said.

She was more right than she could imagine, he thought wretchedly. But he owed it to her to listen.

'You can tell me *anything*, Jackie.'

She brushed the tears aside from her face. 'I don't really know what to say... It isn't my tragedy.'

'In a way it is. You lost too. You wanted to go to university. What did you want to study?'

'I wanted to study languages. They just seem to come easily to me.'

He regarded her wryly.

'Buon per te, signorina. La maggior parte delle persone non possono far fronte con le lingue.'

He spoke in Italian. His words meant, 'Good for you *signorina*. Most people can't cope with languages.'

'Italian is the language I manage best,' she said. 'I took a few classes at night school, because we were planning to take a holiday there together. My father longed to travel to Italy. He'd been there once as a young man.'

'Did he tell you a lot about his visit?'

'Yes, he said it was such fun.'

'Did he never mention meeting my father?' he asked.

'He mentioned an Italian friend, but said nothing at all about him being a *count*! They met in Italy and then again in England a few weeks later. From what Daddy said I gather they got on really well and enjoyed each other's company.'

Vittorio nodded. 'Yes I remember Papà saying something like that—I gather they had quite a few adventures together whilst he was there.'

'Daddy said things like that too. He had such a lovely time with his Italian friend. Only then—' She checked herself.

'Then?' Vittorio said tensely. He had an uneasy feeling that he knew what was coming.

'Then suddenly it was all over. One day they were close buddies—the next day his friend disappeared. He left a note but it didn't say much. Just *Goodbye my friend. Franco*'. No address, nothing. Daddy couldn't contact him and he never heard from him again. It left him very unhappy after what they'd been to each other.'

'He told you that? Didn't he tell you any more about who the man was?'

'No, just that his name was Franco. If he'd known more he'd have told me, I'm sure. Maybe your father never let him know that he was a count?'

'Maybe…' he murmured.

Their eyes met, and what Jackie saw took her breath away. There was an intensity in his gaze as though nothing but herself existed in the world. It was something she'd never seen in any man's eyes before, and she became suddenly conscious of the soft thump of her own heartbeat.

'Jackie—' Vittorio checked himself, unsure how to continue. This was taking more courage than he had anticipated.

'What's the matter?' she asked. 'Are you all right?'

'I'm fine—but there's something I must—'

She felt a sudden sense of brilliant illumination—as though the clouds had parted on a rainy day. She'd hardly dared to hope that the vibrant attraction that possessed her possessed him too, but now she let herself wonder if perhaps it did.

A memory returned to her. That astrology prediction had said, *The fates are planning a startling new beginning for you. The sun in Jupiter will bring things you never anticipated, and decisions that will change your life.*

It was happening. This was the great moment that fate had planned for her. Now surely he would tell her how their meeting had affected his heart, and that was something her own heart longed to know.

She clasped his hand between hers.

'Whatever you have to say, I know I'll like it,' she breathed. 'We've understood each other from the first moment, and—'

'Yes…' he murmured. 'Yes—*yes*—'

He knew the next few minutes would be tense, but something in her seemed to reach out to him, drawing him into a circle of warmth such as he'd never known before. It was what he needed most in all the world, and he knew a moment of fear lest his revelation ruin things between them.

He raised her hands and brushed his lips against them. 'I hope so much that you're right,' he said. 'But you can't imagine—'

'I think I can. Daddy always said you had to be ready for the unexpected.' She met his eyes, her own full of happiness and hope. 'And I'm ready for anything. Say it, Vittorio, and you might like my answer.'

He drew a sharp breath. Now the moment had come when he must find the courage to tell her everything.

But the sight of her eyes shining up at him caused his courage to fail. Suddenly he could see how that light would fade when she knew the terrible truth behind her father's suffering. The thought of her pain made him shudder, and he knew he could not force himself to speak.

'I have to go,' he said uneasily.

'What? But—'

'I'm expecting an important phone call. I have to get back to the hotel.'

He rose to his feet and she followed him reluctantly. Suddenly a moment filled with magic had dissolved into nothing, leaving her desolate.

As they walked back beside the river it began to drizzle.

'Better get back quickly, before it really starts to rain,' he said.

They hurried the rest of the way, until they reached the shop.

'I'll see you again soon,' he said. 'We'll talk then. Take care of yourself.'

Then he fled, devoured by thoughts whose bitterness was aimed accusingly at himself. He was no better than a coward!

His own words came back to him.

You can never tell what fate has in store for you.

It was more true than he could have dreamed. His plan for this meeting had never included the desire to hold her, comfort her, protect her—do anything rather than hurt her. It had overtaken him without warning, reducing him to helplessness. And there was no turning back.

Inside the shop, Jackie hurried up the stairs and looked

out of the window in time to see Vittorio vanish around the corner.

She sighed sadly. It was obvious what had happened. He'd been about to kiss her but had changed his mind at the last moment.

Did he want her or not? He had seemed to be trying to tell her something without words. Had she misunderstood him? But he *had* seemed on the verge of telling her something.

What could it possibly be?

She busied herself opening up the shop. Saturdays were always busy. But somehow she couldn't get stop thinking about him. He was there in her mind, his eyes glowing with a look that made her heart beat faster.

Next day was Sunday, which meant the shop was closed. Fearful of missing her, Vittorio hurried there early. He'd lost his nerve the day before, but he couldn't risk losing it again.

A window opened above him and a voice said coolly, 'Good morning, Vittorio.'

Jackie was looking down at him.

'Morning!' he cried, smiling brightly. 'Can you come down?'

'I'm not sure—'

'Please, Jackie, it's important. We really have to talk.'

'We could have talked yesterday.'

'Please.'

'All right. I'll just be a moment.'

She hurried down, full of hope that her tense wait would be over. He seemed to have come close and then retreated, and now she couldn't bear any more. It *must* be the dream she'd longed for. They had known each other such a little time, but what did time matter when their hearts reached out to each other?

Perhaps his feelings were stronger than he'd known before, which was why he feared expressing them. But she would open her arms and her heart to him and they would both know happiness.

As soon as she appeared downstairs he put his arm about her shoulders.

'Let's have some breakfast in the café. It's nice and comfortable in there.'

'And we can talk,' she said eagerly.

When they were settled she waited for him to speak, but again he felt silent, as though attacked by doubt at the last moment. Her heart sank. Her hopes had risen so high. She couldn't bear to lose them again.

'Vittorio, please tell me,' she said. 'Whatever is on your mind I can tell it's important.'

'Yes, it is…' he said hesitantly.

'Then please be brave and say it. Are you afraid of what I'll say?'

'I might be,' he said. 'I don't think you can imagine—'

She touched his face. 'Tell me, Vittorio. Let's get it out between us and then tell each other how we feel.'

'Yes,' he murmured. 'You're right. Do you remember—?'

'Remember?'

'How we talked about our fathers yesterday.'

'Yes, I remember, but—'

'I should have told you then. It's a terrible story, Jackie, but I have to tell you. Your father once placed a bet that won a million pounds.'

'But that can't be true! He'd have told me—we'd never have been in the situation we found ourselves in if that had been the case.'

'He didn't know. My father and yours were out together one night. Your father got tipsy, and he was dozing when the results were announced. When he awoke my *papà* had taken the winnings and kept them.'

Jackie had a terrible feeling of having crash-landed. The words reeled in her head. Only one thing was clear.

This wasn't what she'd expected to hear.

'What on earth are you saying?' she demanded. 'You *can't* mean that he didn't tell Daddy he'd won? That would be dishonest, and surely—'

'It was the only dishonest thing he ever did, and it tormented him. He told me about it just before he died.'

'Is this—this what you've been trying to say?' she stammered.

'Yes, it took me this long to pluck up the courage to tell you that my family has damaged yours. I'm sure you'll find it hard to forgive. Right at this minute you probably hate me.'

That was closer to the truth than he could possibly know. As her dreams collapsed, leaving her in the middle of a desert, she felt a terrifying rage begin to take her over.

'There's something else I have to tell you,' Vittorio said. 'I'm not sure how it will make you feel.'

'Try me,' she whispered, with a faint flicker of renewed hope.

'Papà made me promise to find your father and sort things out.'

'Sort things out? What do you mean by that?'

'I planned to give him the money Papà took from him. A million pounds. I hoped it would make everything all right.'

She stared at him, barely able to believe what she was hearing.

'You hoped *what*?' she said furiously. 'You really hoped things could be made *"all right"* after so many years? After Daddy suffered so much from poverty and it made his wife abandon him? After the way he died in despair? You can't give him your money *now*.'

'But I can give it to you.'

'You think that will make his suffering *all right*?'

'I didn't mean it that way,' Vittorio said tensely.

'Oh, yes, you did. You think money can solve everything—but when a man's dead it can't solve anything at all. You don't understand that, do you? Hand over a cheque and everything's settled! Maybe that's true in business, but not in real life. But you don't know anything about real life.'

'Jackie, please—let me explain. I only want to—'

'You only want to make yourself feel good.'

'I don't think money solves everything, but I'd like to pay the debt my family owes.'

'This is a con. Do you *really* expect me to believe that you can hand over a million pounds, just like that?'

'You think I don't have that much? You're wrong. My father didn't waste the million he gained.'

'You mean the million he *stole*,' she raged.

'Very well—he stole it. But he wanted to pay it back. He invested it successfully, so that it made several more millions. I can give you back every penny—plus a few thousand for interest.'

'Oh, you think it's so easy, don't you? I wouldn't take money from you if I was starving. This conversation is at an end.' She stood up. 'And don't you dare follow me.'

He'd reached out a hand to stop her, but something fierce in her manner made him draw back.

'Please—' he began.

'No. Don't you understand? *No!*'

She fled, fearful lest her true feelings become too plain. Instead of the loving emotion she'd hoped for he'd offered her *money*. If she'd stayed a moment longer she was afraid she might have done something violent.

Her departure left Vittorio in a state of total confusion and misery. Nothing had worked out as he'd intended. He'd failed to fulfil his father's dying wish. Guilt tore at him.

He paid his bill and went out into the street, walking back in the direction of the shop. There was no sign of her.

There was nothing to do but return to the hotel and do some serious thinking about what he was going to do next.

But he found that serious thinking was very little help in a situation he didn't understand.

The rest of Jackie's day and night was tormented. The incredible events of the morning whirled through her brain, and at the end of the day—even though she was exhausted and wrung out when she finally got to bed—she couldn't sleep. Instead she sat up in bed and opened the laptop she always kept with her.

She did a search on 'Count Martelli'. She was half ready to learn that he didn't exist, that the whole thing had been a con, and for a moment it seemed that her suspicions were correct. The picture that appeared on the screen was of a man in his sixties.

He's lying, she thought furiously. *That's the real Count.* But then she saw the text.

Count Franco Martelli, taken just before his death four weeks ago. His heir is his son, Vittorio Martelli, latest in a line stretching back five hundred years.

She clicked the link marked 'Count Vittorio Martelli' and and at once saw a photograph of the man she recognised. There was no doubt.

Her temper surged once more at the memory of Vittorio trying to pay her off to assuage his family's guilt. But had she been too hasty? Had she let her temper get the better of her once again?

Vivid in her mind was the memory of her father's suffering. He'd tried to put on a brave face for her sake, but he hadn't always been able to manage it. Often she had found him in tears. He'd smiled and reassured her, but over time she had come to understand the problems. Her heart had broken for him. She had become his comforter, intent on giving him some kind of happiness.

But the last year of her father's life had been the saddest she had ever known. She still wept when she remembered his suffering.

Vittorio thought money was the answer to everything!

And yet she knew there was another reason for her rage. When she remembered how her hopes of winning Vittorio's feelings had risen, and then been smashed to the ground, she felt capable of murder.

He had just been playing a game until he had what suited him. He hadn't spared a thought as to what it was doing to *her*.

So accept the money, said a voice in her head. *He offered you a million—more than a million with interest.*

Because he thought it would put right what his father had done. If he wasn't such a heartless monster he'd know that nothing could *ever* make it right.

What would her father have done? If he were still alive it would be so different. Then of course they would have accepted the money. It would have been his due. But now he was gone would it be right for her to accept it on his behalf?

She closed the laptop and went back to bed. At last she managed to nod off, sinking into a deep and dreamless sleep.

Vittorio's night had also been troubled. He'd fallen asleep easily, but found his dreams haunted by Jackie's contempt until they were practically nightmares that woke him in a cold sweat.

He rose out of bed. He had no desire to go back to sleep lest the alarming female return to torment him. Day was breaking and he felt the need of a fresh air. Dressing hastily, he went downstairs and out into the street.

His thoughts were full of the promise he'd made to

his beloved father. Come what might he *had* to make this right—for everyone's sake.

Almost at once the shop came in sight. It was time for it to be open, so he went closer and looked through the glass door, but he could see no sign of anyone. Moving quietly, he opened the door and slipped inside. At once he heard the sound of voices coming from deep within. One was Jackie's, and the other he recognised as the weasely boss who had appeared during his first visit. His voice was raised in annoyance.

'Jackie, you're *mad*. You should have got all you could out of the Count and then invested in this place. I could do with some money to cover the debts. You could have helped me out and you just turned it down? How could you be so *stupid*?'

She replied in a voice filled with rage that reminded Vittorio of the way she'd spoken to him with equal fury during last night.

'You think I should have taken his money and used it for *your* convenience?' she raged at Rik. 'I'm not *that* stupid.'

Vittorio stepped a little closer, careful to keep out of sight but wanting to hear everything.

'You just can't recognise reality when it's under your nose,' came Rik's reply. 'You had the chance of a fortune. You could have taken it. But perhaps your fantasies are fixed on something else.'

'What does that mean?'

'It's *him*, isn't it? You refused his money because you're hoping for a better offer! You think you can lure him into marriage, but you're wasting your time. A man like that wouldn't marry *you* in a million years.'

'And I wouldn't marry *him* in a million years. He's cold—and arrogant enough to think that money can solve anything.'

Vittorio made a wry face. A wise man would have slipped

away at this moment, but he didn't feel wise. He felt as though Jackie had seized him and was holding him at her mercy in whirls of confusion.

'It can solve a great deal,' he heard Rik say. 'It could pay a lot of my debts—many of which are *your* fault.'

'How can you say that?'

'If you did a better job this shop would be doing well, instead of sinking into debt.'

'The shop was in a bad way when my father sold it to you. That's how you got it so cheap. I heard you—beating him down on the price when he was too weak to fight you.'

'Don't try to blame me for your father's failings. Luckily it's not too late. You've still got time to find this Italian Count and tell him you'll take the money.'

'You think I'd—? You're mad.'

'I'm *telling* you to do it.'

'And I'm telling *you* to go to hell.'

'I warn you, Jackie, you're walking a very fine line. Perhaps I'd better see him myself—'

'Perhaps you should,' Vittorio said, stepping out so that they could see him.

Rik noticed him first, and the shock on his face alerted Jackie, so that she looked behind her, also appalled at the discovery.

Rik assumed a severe manner. 'We have business to discuss,' he said.

'The only business we have is for you to listen to what I have to say,' Vittorio said bluntly. 'For you—not a penny.'

'But you have a debt to pay,' Rik squealed.

'Not to *you*.'

'Jackie, tell him,' Rik whined. 'Tell him he's got to pay you what he owes you.'

Jackie looked intently at Vittorio, but did not speak.

'Do it now,' Rik snapped. 'Let me hear you say it.'

'I have nothing to say,' she replied coldly. 'The Count's

debt is impossible to repay.' She met Vittorio's gaze and said emphatically, *'Ever!'*

Rik looked from one to the other, scowling.

'So *that's* it,' he raged. 'You two are in this together. As soon as I'm out of earshot you'll take the money and cut me out.'

'You can't be cut out because you were never *in*,' Jackie said fiercely. 'You bought this business fair and square, and any debts are now your responsibility. Besides, I will never take a penny of his money.'

'You're insane!' Rik seethed. 'What kind of fool turns down that sort of money? Well, if money's of no importance to you then you won't be needing this job. *Or* the accommodation I've provided for you. You're fired. I'll give you one hour to clear out your stuff from upstairs.'

Rik stormed out, pausing at the front door.

'One hour!' he yelled. 'I mean it.'

Then he was gone, slamming the door behind him.

Vittorio turned swiftly to Jackie. 'Good riddance.' he said. 'Forget him. He isn't worth bothering with.'

Jackie was shaken, but determined to maintain her dignity. 'How long were you there, listening?'

'I came to see you and arrived just as you were telling him what had happened.'

'I never meant to tell him, but he made me so angry that I said it to knock the smile off his face. I could have strangled him.' She gave a bitter laugh. 'I'd have enjoyed that.'

'Don't worry. He's bound to give you another excuse. He's a pig, Jackie, and you're better off without him.'

'But this isn't just my *job*. I've lived here all my life and now I've lost my home, too.'

'Then we must find you another one. Get packing and we'll be out of here—fast.'

'I've nowhere to go.'

'Trust me to arrange that.'

She knew an instinct to rebel against him. This catastrophe had happened only because he'd come to England and caused trouble. Now she'd lost her job and her home, and he was to blame.

But was he really? If she hadn't been silly enough to tell Rik about the money this wouldn't have happened. When was she going to learn to control her temper?

Never, she thought fiercely.

'Let's get you out of here,' Vittorio said. He took her arm and ran up the stairs with her and began opening drawers and cupboards, working hard to help her.

'Is that your only suitcase?' he asked, regarding the one she had produced.

'Yes, but I've got some plastic bags.'

Luckily the bags proved enough to take her few possessions.

'Anything else?' he asked at last.

'No, that's all.'

'You have nothing else?' he asked, looking astonished.

'This is all I need,' she said defiantly.

He gave her an odd look, as though wondering what madness had made her refuse his money when she seemed to own so little, but all he said was, 'Then let's go.'

She looked around nervously as they went downstairs, but there was no sign of Rik.

'Where are we going?' she asked as they went out into the street.

'I'm staying in the Davien Hotel, a couple of streets away. We'll get you a room there for tonight, then make our plans.'

She knew the hotel. It had a reputation as being costly.

'I don't think it's quite the right place for me,' she said uneasily.

'If you're worried about the money, don't be. I'm paying. I landed you in this mess and it's my responsibility to get you out.'

Suddenly she recalled Rik's warning to her. He'd suggested that Vittorio was hoping to lure Jackie into bed with the empty promise of a great fortune.

Suddenly she was uneasy. Was that why Vittorio was taking her to his hotel at his own expense? Did he mean her to share his bed?

Only recently that thought would have excited her. Vittorio attracted her powerfully. The thought of lying with him in bed would have been a pleasure. But now everything was different. Was he trustworthy? Could she be sure?

A short walk brought them to the hotel. Vittorio went to Reception and chatted with the woman there as she typed something onto the keyboard. Nodding to her, he headed back to Jackie.

'I've managed to secure you a room on the second floor.'

He escorted her upstairs, leading her to a door for which he had the key. She held her breath.

But when the door opened she knew she'd done him an injustice. There was only one single bed.

'Th-thank you,' she stammered.

'If you need me I'm three doors along the corridor.'

He departed at once, leaving her standing alone, trying to take in everything that had happened. Only yesterday she had quarrelled with this man, and today he had come to her rescue and she had accepted his help gladly.

It doesn't make any sense, she mused.

But nothing had made sense since she'd met him. Perhaps nothing ever would again.

He returned just as she finished putting her things away.

'They do a good lunch here,' he said. 'I'll have some sent up.'

'Couldn't we eat downstairs in the restaurant?'

'Do I make you feel nervous, Jackie? Are you afraid to be alone with me?'

'Of course not,' she said uneasily. 'I have no feelings about you one way or the other, actually,' she lied bravely.

'So you didn't mean it when you said you wouldn't marry me in a million years? Or the bit about me being cold and arrogant and a person who thinks money can solve anything?'

For a moment it was as though her worst nightmares were coming true. But then she saw he was grinning, and that his eyes were full of friendly humour.

'Forget it,' he said. 'People say things in the heat of the moment. And it's not far different from what you said to me yesterday. But it's time we drew a line under that. We have to work matters out between us and be friends—if that's possible.'

It was still embarrassing to know that he'd heard her, but his unexpected humour made it bearable.

'So—can I have some food sent up?' he asked.

'Are you asking my permission?'

Again he gave her a cheeky grin. 'Isn't that what you prefer a man to do?'

'Stop trying to make me sound like a bully.'

'Not a bully. Just a woman who knows her own mind—as Rik would tell us after the way you stood up to him. He's a nasty bully, but you really dealt with him.'

'Yes—and that was so successful that now I've got to start looking for another job and a home.'

'But where? You'll never get another job around here. He'll make sure of that.'

She groaned, recognising that Vittorio was right. Rik would spread the word that she was unreliable, destroying her prospects.

'I still feel that I owe you any help I can persuade you to accept,' Vittorio said.

'You have a job to offer me?'

'Not here, but in Italy. I could find many opportunities for you there. Why not come back with me?'

CHAPTER THREE

JACKIE STARED AT him in disbelief. 'Italy? Did I hear right?'

'Dead right. I want you to work for me in my family's department store in Rome. Your talents will be valuable.'

'But I've only ever worked in a little shop. I'd be useless in a department store.'

'Not in our glass and china section. It's a new department, and it isn't doing brilliantly because nobody really understands it. But you could bring it to life and make it profitable.'

'According to Rik, I was lousy at making profits.'

'Were you? Or did *he* make a lot of stupid decisions?'

'Yes, he buys all the wrong stuff.'

'So I can rely on you to buy all the *right* stuff?'

'Mightn't the language be a problem? I never got to finish my Italian course at night school. I had to stop when Daddy became ill.'

'A lot of people there speak English. Some of our customers are tourists, and your English would be a blessing to them. Your Italian seems already pretty good, and you can work to improve it.'

'It's very kind of you—' she began uneasily.

'No, it isn't. I'm not being kind. I'm a businessman and I'm doing what any sensible businessman does—turning the situation to my own advantage. I could make a lot of money out of you, and I'm not passing up the chance to do that.'

'But how—?'

'You won't just have that one department. I want you to cast your expert eye over the whole store and tell me how it looks to you—because that will tell me how it looks to our customers. Tourists are profitable, and you can help me attract plenty of them. And it could open some new doors for you, Jackie. I'll pay you a decent wage—far more than Rik paid you—and you'll have a position of authority.'

Authority. The word seemed to sing in her ears. This would truly be a new, more satisfying life—exactly what she had longed for. Again she had the mysterious feeling that Vittorio could read her mind.

'Authority?' she echoed. 'Do you really mean that?'

'You'd be in charge of your department. You'd have a team that would take your orders. Or don't you feel up to giving orders?'

'Oh, yes, I do. That was always my problem with Rik. And with my father too sometimes. He complained that I argued with him too much.' She gave a brief laugh.

'Don't worry. When you're working for me you can give all the orders you want. I'll make it clear to the team that *you're* the boss. You need never fear another bully like Rik.'

It sounded too good to be true, she thought, trying to suppress a flicker of confusion. Knowing the terrible truth about how her father had been treated had made hostility flare between them, but there were other feelings too— some warmer, some interested, all confusing.

But what else could she do? Where else was there for her to go? What other life was possible for her? It was as if all other doors had slammed shut and fate was driving her irresistibly into this man's power.

Surely she could take advantage of the situation, just as *he* planned to do?

Here was a chance to learn new skills and gain new experiences that might open up a world of fresh opportunities for her.

'All right,' she said in a daze. 'I'll go to Italy with you.'

'Good thinking. I knew I could rely on you.'

She ventured to say, 'You mean because I've agreed with you?'

'What else? That's my definition of good thinking. So, now there's nothing to hold you back we can go tomorrow. I'll book two tickets.'

After booking the tickets Vittorio ordered a meal and a bottle of wine from room service.

'After this I must attend to some business matters. I suggest you relax for the rest of the afternoon, and then I think we should both get an early night,' he said, adding in a teasing voice, 'In our separate rooms, I promise.'

'Stop teasing,' she said cheerfully. 'I wasn't thinking that.'

'Good. Then we can both relax.'

'Of course. We agree to be friends. That's all.'

'Friends…' he mused. 'What kind of friends? Best friends?'

'We'll have to wait and see.'

She was right. Friendship was their only hope. Had she really feared lest he come to her door? After their argument the day before he could well believe that she didn't want him. His own feelings for her were less clear.

Officially they were enemies, and his instinct to protect her was troublesome.

She was becoming important to him in ways that confused him. Perhaps soon he would understand them. For the moment he preferred to wait and see what fate had in store.

He lifted his glass of wine in her direction.

'Here's to you,' he said. 'You don't know how much I'm going to rely on you.'

And it was true, he thought. She didn't.

It was a quiet meal, with very little talk. Instinctively

they both knew that for the moment enough had been said. Perhaps too much.

At the earliest moment they finished eating.

'And now I really must get on with some work. I'll head back to my room, but if you think of anything else you need today please call through.'

He bade her a polite good day, and left.

Returning to his room, he recalled something he'd meant to say to her, and hurried back to see her.

A surprise awaited him. He looked out into the corridor just in time to see her getting into the elevator and the doors closing.

Where on earth could she be going? he thought frantically. Surely not to talk to Rik?

There was no hope of catching up with the elevator. He went to his window and looked down. There she was, walking away along the road, and then turning through a large gate that he knew led to a church.

Every cautious instinct told him to stay where he was—not to follow her. But something about Jackie always overcame caution.

In a moment he was out of the door, hurrying until he reached the church gate.

Inside was a cemetery. As he watched she approached a tombstone and knelt before it. He was too far away to make out the name, but he could hear Jackie saying urgently, 'I'm sorry, Daddy. I really am.'

So this was Benton's grave, and she had come here to talk to him. Vittorio backed away, unwilling to invade her privacy, but he couldn't help hearing her next words.

'I don't really trust him. I'd like to, but he doesn't understand what a terrible thing was done to you, and that makes him almost as much of an enemy as his father. But I must go to Italy. I'll come back, I promise. Only forgive me. Please, *please* forgive me.'

As watched she pressed her lips to the stone, then leaned against it, sobbing.

Torn by the instinct to comfort her, he took a step closer—but stopped just in time. Whatever happened, she mustn't know he was there. He had an unnerving feeling… as though he'd been suddenly stranded on a desert island. He hadn't expected this, and the sensation of being caught unprepared was alarming.

He backed off and hurried away, haunted by her words— *I don't trust him… Almost as much of an enemy as his father…*

If that was how she thought of him he supposed he couldn't blame her. But it hurt more than he would have expected.

Back at the hotel, he returned to his room and went to the window, hoping to see her return. But hours passed with no sign of her and his heart sank. Where had she vanished to *now*? What trouble might she have fallen into? Had she changed her mind about accompanying him to Italy?

Then a noise from the corridor made him hurry outside. She was there, turning the key in her lock.

'There you are,' he said with relief.

'Were you looking for me? I'm sorry I vanished. I just had to— Well, never mind.'

He hesitated. All his cautious instincts warned him to keep the secret, but the need to be honest with her was greater.

At last he said, 'You just had to say goodbye to your father.'

She stared at him. 'How do you know?'

'I saw you.'

'But how?'

'I followed you to the cemetery.'

She gasped with outrage. 'You *followed* me? How *dare* you?'

She stormed into her room and tried to close the door, but he reached out to keep it open.

'Let me come in,' he said.

'I'd rather you didn't. In fact I'd rather you vanished off the face of the earth.'

'Well, I'm sure you'll eventually think of a way of making that happen. But for the moment we need to talk. Let me in, Jackie. *Please.*'

Furiously, she turned away. He followed her in, closing the door behind him.

'Don't judge me, Jackie—please. I'm not stalking you. I followed you because I'm concerned about you. You seemed so lonely, walking, and when you reached the grave...' He paused, feeling desperate. 'You cried so terribly. I wanted to take you in my arms and comfort you. I didn't because I knew you'd be angry that I was there. I went away. I wasn't sure that was the right thing to do, but I don't seem to get anything right these days. The more I try, the more wrong I get it. But I'm glad I was with you for a few minutes. I think I understand you better now.'

He saw a strange, slightly puzzled look come into her face.

'Yes, that surprises you, doesn't it?' he said. 'I'm the last person you'd expect to understand you.'

'People don't easily understand other people,' she murmured.

'But I think we manage it. We must talk about that another time. For now, please just tell me that you believe I meant no harm and you forgive me.'

'All right,' she said reluctantly. 'I realise you didn't mean it badly.'

'And I'm forgiven? Please Jackie. Let me hear you say it. *Please.*'

She drew a sharp breath, stunned by the desperation in

his voice and the intensity in his eyes. There was no way she could refuse this man anything he asked for.

'I forgive you,' she said.

'And you mean it?'

'Yes—*yes*—'

'As long as you *do* mean it. Things could so easily go wrong between us—but we won't let that happen. Best if you go to bed now and have a good night's sleep. Tomorrow will be a busy day. Goodnight.'

'Goodnight.'

Before leaving he turned to look back at her once more. Jackie tried to understand his expression, but there was something about it that confused her.

Nor was that the only thing about him so unexpected that she could hardly believe it. The way he'd almost begged her for forgiveness had startled her, revealing a side of him she'd never suspected.

She was glad to lie down. She needed sleep, but for some reason it didn't come. It was alarming that he'd been there while she spoke to her father. Had he heard her say that she didn't trust him?

She lay still, listening for the sound of his footsteps outside, wondering if they would return to her door. But nothing happened.

At last the silence seemed to overwhelm her and she fell asleep.

As Vittorio had said, they rose early next day and were soon ready to leave.

'You won't be insulted if I pay your bill, will you?' he asked as they went downstairs.

'Would it make any difference if I was?'

He grinned. 'Not the slightest.'

'Then I'd better give in—until I find a way to make you sorry.'

'I'll look forward to that,' he said ironically.

She watched as he went to the reception desk and paid. Then all was ready and they headed for the front door.

But as soon as it was open she saw something that made her stop, frozen with dismay.

'Oh, no!' she groaned.

'What is it?' Vittorio asked. 'Ah, I see. *Him!*'

Rik was standing there, barring their way, his face full of spiteful hilarity.

'So there you are!' he jeered. 'Just as I thought—you stupid woman!'

'You told me to leave so I went,' she said coldly.

'Yes, you went running to *him*. Think you're going to be a countess, do you? Don't kid yourself! He's playing a clever game to stop you suing him for the money his family stole. He'll use you, then throw you out.'

'The only one who's being thrown out is you,' Vittorio said coldly.

Rik gave contemptuous laugh. 'Don't tell me you're taken in by her—? *Argh!*'

The scream was dragged from him by the feel of Vittorio's hand about his neck.

'I know all I need to know about this lady,' Vittorio said harshly. 'But let me tell you something about myself. I'm a man who won't tolerate an insult to a friend, and who'll do anything necessary to make someone sorry they caused trouble. Do you understand me?'

'Yes…' Rik choked.

'Then get out of here while you still can. Otherwise I might do something we'd both regret.'

He released Rik, who staggered away, looking terrified. He gave one last appalled glance at Jackie. Then he fled.

'Are you all right?' Vittorio asked her.

'Yes—fine—thank you.'

In truth she was far from all right. She'd seen yet another

side of Vittorio—one that shocked her. The look in his eyes had been that of a man who would go to any lengths to punish someone who had defied him. She knew it had been in her defence, but that couldn't ease her horror.

'Would you really have hurt him?' she whispered.

'No, of course not. But I had to make him believe that I would. Scare someone enough and you don't need to do anything else to them. Being frank. Isn't that something you've tried yourself.'

'Now and then,' she admitted. 'Not violently, but—'

'But making him believe you know something he doesn't want you to know? I'd give a lot to know how often you've used *that* one.'

'You'll just have to wonder,' she said lightly.

'Congratulations. You're as bad as I am. Shake.'

He held out his hand.

Laughing, she took it. 'I'll never be as bad as you are,' she said. 'But I'm working on it.'

'Perhaps he was right about one thing. *Should* I be afraid of you suing me?'

'Of course not. How can I?'

'I've admitted the theft.'

'It was your father's theft, not yours. And there were no witnesses when you told me. You could just deny it and there'd be nothing I could do.'

'Maybe Rik overheard me?'

'Don't believe anything Rik says—especially that nonsense about me wanting to be a countess.'

'Of course. I know you wouldn't marry me in a million years. I heard you say so yourself, remember?'

'Look, about that… I really am sorry—'

'Don't be sorry. You're not the first woman who's said that about me.' He grinned wryly. 'As you can probably imagine.'

'I'm not going to be tricked into answering that!'

'Very shrewd. I can see you're a real discovery.'

'Because I'm not trying to trap you into marriage? Never fear. You're quite safe from me.'

Was he safe? he wondered. Despite the circumstances, and the fact that she wasn't beautiful, he found her fascinating. She was intriguingly clever and her sharp humour appealed to him.

But more than that was the intense emotion that seemed to reach out from her in a way he couldn't understand. They never spoke of it. There was just a feeling that their mysterious closeness was inevitable, and that it was bound to grow.

The thought made him cautious. Developing warmer feelings for her would put him in her power, and that was something he always strove to avoid.

As the son of a count, he was used to young women pursuing him for the sake of his title. He'd thought himself well protected until the girl who'd once won his heart had betrayed him with the son of a duke. He would never forget the moment he'd discovered them in bed together—or the look she'd bestowed upon him, as though she despised him for daring to hope for her.

That had been several years ago, but the memory stayed with him. Love was unsafe. It caused danger and pain, and a wise man kept his distance.

But life without love did not mean life without marriage. One day he would have to take wife for the sake of producing an heir. His father had spoken of it in the last moments of his life.

'Marisa,' he'd murmured. 'She's perfect for you.'

Marisa was the daughter of a *barone* and an ideal choice for Vittorio's wife—at least according to his father. For a year he'd made his wishes plain. But Vittorio had resisted. He was on good terms with Marisa, but only in a brotherly way. Despite her youth and beauty, she did not attract him. Nor did he want a wife he hadn't chosen for himself.

When he returned to Rome he knew that Marisa and various similar problems would be waiting. But with Jackie's friendship to support him he felt more at ease.

The taxi was waiting to take them to the airport.

'You'll like Rome. Your Italian is good enough to help you feel at home.'

'Do you spend a lot of time in the city?'

'Yes—plenty.'

'But isn't your time taken up with managing your estates?'

'I have to do that as well, of course, but I have an estate manager who handles the difficult stuff. Mostly my time is taken up with the department store.'

'You actually *work* there?'

'Does that surprise you? You think I'm useless for anything except lying around enjoying my title while others do the work?'

'After the way you've rescued me I'm not likely to think you useless.'

He gave her a teasing glance. 'Very tactfully said.'

'Yes, I've got to stay on your right side, haven't I? Why don't you tell me some more about the store so that I can flatter you further?'

'It sells a wide range of goods which I buy from all over the world. You're going to be very valuable to the business. But I've already told you that.'

'Yes, you grabbed me because I could be useful. Sheer cynical self-interest. Just what a businessman needs. Well done.'

They shared a laugh.

'Glad to see you're a realist,' he said. 'Would it be insulting to suggest that you too have some cynical self-interest?'

'No, I'd take it as a compliment.'

'Good for you.'

'Working for you is going to teach me a whole lot of

things that I can use in my future career.' She gave him a thumbs-up sign. 'Here's to cynical self-interest.'

'The most useful motive in the world,' he agreed, making the same gesture.

'Cheers!'

They shook hands.

At last the airport came into view. Soon they were queuing for their flight and boarding the plane.

Jackie was taken aback to discover that Vittorio had booked the most expensive first class seats. But then, why wouldn't he? He was a count and a successful businessman, wasn't he?

'Take the window seat,' he said. 'It's more interesting that way.'

'Is it a long flight?' she asked as the plane began to move slowly down the runway.

'Only two and a half hours.'

Never having flown before, she was nervous. But she managed to stay at ease until take-off, and then gazed out of the window as the ground fell away.

'What will happen when we get there?' she asked.

'We'll be met at the airport by my Aunt Tania. She lives with me and looks after the house. I called her this morning and asked her to prepare a room for you.'

Before she could reply, the plane quivered. She took a sharp, nervous breath and clenched her hands.

'It's all right,' Vittorio said. 'Planes always shake when they go through clouds. We're not going to crash.'

'No—I realise—it's just that—'

'It's just that you're afraid of flying.'

'I've never flown before.'

'Is there anything else bothering you?' he asked, regarding her with concern.

'Just a little headache. It's not too bad.'

He took her hand in his. 'Probably caused by nerves. Don't worry. We'll soon be there.'

CHAPTER FOUR

AT LAST THEY landed at Leonardo da Vinci Airport. They spent a few minutes collecting their bags and then they were able to make their way out. Jackie looked around, trying to come to terms with what was happening.

'Ah, there she is,' Vittorio said suddenly.

He began waving into the distance at a middle-aged woman who was waving back to him. The woman began to run forward and he hastened towards her until they were in each other's arms. Jackie reckoned this must be the Aunt Tania he had mentioned.

She moved a little closer, waiting for him to introduce them. But then his aunt turned aside, revealing a young woman who ran forward and threw herself into Vittorio's arms.

Jackie could see that he was tense. He embraced the girl formally, before standing back and turning to indicate Jackie. She couldn't make out exactly what he was saying, but she gathered it wasn't revealing.

'This is my Aunt Tania,' he told Jackie. 'And my friend Marisa. I've told them that we are planning a business arrangement that has made it necessary for you to see Rome.'

'Welcome to our city,' Aunt Tania said politely. 'Vittorio says you will be staying with us. That will be lovely.'

'Did you give her the best guest room?' Vittorio asked.

'Yes, just as you said. Now, let's go home.'

'Have you got a taxi waiting?'.

'No, Marisa drove me here.'

'And I can drive you home,' Marisa said quickly. 'This way.'

When they reached her car she pulled open the door next to the front passenger seat, indicating for Vittorio to get in beside her. He did so, leaving Jackie and Tania to sit together in the back.

It was a lengthy journey out of the city and through the countryside to the Martelli estate. Jackie studied the scenery, occasionally looking round to find Vittorio's aunt regarding her with curiosity.

'So you're here on business,' Tania said. 'What kind of business are you in?'

She took a sharp breath, caught off-guard, and felt troubled about how to answer.

Vittorio came to her rescue.

'Jackie's a specialist in merchandising,' he said, glancing back over his shoulder. 'What she doesn't know about display and point of sale isn't worth knowing.'

Jackie suppressed an ironic smile at his way of describing her work behind the counter in a little shop.

'So you're going to help my nephew run his business?' Tania queried.

'If I can. And I hope he can teach me something that will be useful,' she said.

To her relief, the subject was allowed to drop. Soon they reached the estate and the car swept through extensive grounds up to a great house.

'We're nearly there,' Vittorio said, pointing out of the car window. 'A little further and you'll see my home.'

As he spoke a large building came into view. Jackie gasped at its elegance and beauty.

'My goodness, it's like a palace!' she gasped.

'My ancestors had rather grandiose ideas. It was a matter of pride for them to live in a splendid home.'

And I bet it took a lot of money to maintain, she thought, forcing some of them into acts of dishonesty.

Perhaps the same thought had occurred to Vittorio, for he fell silent then.

'We only live in small part of it now,' Tania said. 'But we still relish the rest, which has a marvellous history.'

A woman whom Jackie took to be the housekeeper was waiting for them as they left the car and climbed the steps to the front door. Vittorio took the bags.

'I'll take these up to Jackie's room,' he said. 'Come along, Jackie.'

Inside, the building was just as luxurious. In a daze she followed him up the stairs and along a corridor until they reached her room. Like the rest of the house it was luxuriously appointed. A large bed took up most of the space, and the walls were lined with elegant wardrobes.

'The maid will be here to help you unpack,' he said. 'Are you all right? You look as though something's the matter.'

'I'm just confused. I can't get my head around everything that's happening. I've never been anywhere like this before.'

'Don't worry—you'll soon feel at home. I'll see to that.'

The words were kindly spoken, but it flashed across her mind that she could never feel at home in this place, surrounded by a luxury that haunted her with memories of her father's impoverished home.

Marisa appeared in the doorway, followed by a maid.

'This is Gina,' she said. 'She speaks English and she will help you.'

Vittorio patted her shoulder. 'I'll leave you to unpack now and I'll see you at supper.'

He followed Marisa out of the room.

Gina immediately got to work, unpacking the bags and putting things away.

Jackie watched her, trying to believe what was happening.

'Here you have a little bathroom,' Gina said. 'And through these windows you have a wonderful view.'

It was true. She was only one floor up, but looking out onto lawns that soon vanished into trees. The sun was setting, casting a glow ever everything.

'*No, no, no!*'

The cry from a female voice streamed upwards from below. Leaning out, Jackie was unable to see anyone, but she could tell the sound had come from behind a wall.

'Marisa—'

That was Vittorio. But after that one word he got no further for Marisa exploded again.

'*Perche,* Vittorio? *Perche?*'

Marisa was talking too fast for Jackie to understand much, but she knew that *perche* meant *why*. It was clear that Marisa was demanding an explanation and Vittorio was trying to make her be quiet.

Jackie recalled the suspicious glances Marisa had given her. Plainly her arrival was unwelcome.

The sound died and she turned back to the room. Gina was a skilled maid with a shrewd eye. She studied Jackie's appearance before casting her glance over several of the clothes.

'You are lucky, *signorina*,' she said. 'You have a slim figure. That is a blessing.'

'Slim?' Jackie brooded. 'That's one way of putting it. In England I've been called skinny—even scrawny.'

'*Scusami, signorina.* Scrawny?'

'In English it's a way of telling someone they're too thin.'

'No, no,' Gina protested passionately. 'You cannot be too thin for fashion. Rome is a city of great fashion. Everything will be fine for you here—especially when you've bought some new clothes.'

'Oh—well—I don't think I'll be buying new clothes,' Jackie said uneasily.

The maid's words were like a blow, reminding her how little cash she had.

'But you *must*. Everyone will want to meet you.'

'That's true,' said Vittorio from the doorway.

How long had he been standing there? Jackie wondered. How much had he seen and heard?

'My new business associate will make quite an entrance,' he said.

With a slight gesture of his head he dismissed Gina, who left the room.

'New clothes,' he said. 'You do need them. We can make arrangements tomorrow.'

'But I can't. I haven't got any money to buy clothes.'

'You crazy woman! I offered you a million pounds and you chucked it back in my face. Now you're complaining about poverty.'

'I'm not complaining,' she said defiantly. 'I'm being practical.'

'So be practical and accept my offer.'

'*No!* Not that. You don't understand, do you?'

'No—and I don't think you understand your own actions.'

He was wrong, she thought. She completely understood the reasons for her stubborn refusal to yield.

If she accepted the money he would consider the debt settled. And that idea was agony to her. For the sake of her father's memory she would never allow him to do that—however much she might need the money.

'Oh, you really *are* contrary, woman,' he growled.

'What's that supposed to mean?'

'You've hardly got a penny to your name but you turn down the best financial offer you'll ever have and treat me as a villain for making it. That's carrying illogicality to new heights.'

'Not illogicality. Pride. Memory of my father's suffering.'

'You think your father would want you to refuse?'

'Yes, because accepting would be like saying what happened to him doesn't matter.'

'I think he loved you too much for that. I think he'd have been glad to see things get better for you.'

'You— How dare you speak of him like that?'

'I only said he loved you. Didn't he?'

'Yes—with all his heart. But you have no right to make use of him like that.'

'All right, I'll say no more. But think about it, Jackie. What sort of future would he have wanted for you? Prosperous? Or living on the edge of poverty? If he was here now, listening to us, what do you think he'd say to you? *Take every penny and live well.* Or, *Tell him to keep his money and get stuffed. Give yourself the pleasure of kicking him in the teeth. Then live on the edge of poverty.*'

'Stop it!' she cried, backing away from him, hands over her ears. *'Stop it!'*

He reached out and for a moment she thought he would take hold of her. But then he dropped his hand, moving quickly away.

'I'll see you at supper,' he said, and left without another word.

As he closed the door she struggled with the desire to hurl something at it. It was shocking for him to put words into her father's mouth just to suit himself. But there was no doubt that he *was* baffled by her refusal to take his money, and she reckoned the reason was plain. A man so wealthy was used to being able to buy whatever he wanted.

Not just wealthy, she mused. He was handsome also. *Too*

handsome. He must be used to women collapsing at his feet and promising to do anything he wanted.

But not me, Vittorio. You've met the one woman who'll gladly tell you exactly where to go.

She wondered if she'd been wise to come here when their hostility was still acute. But he'd saved her from Rik. She would just have to cope as best she could.

To distract herself, she began going through her possessions.

She soon realised that Gina had put her finger on an unexpected problem when she'd spoken of Rome as being a city of great fashion. None of her clothes were fashionable. At best they might be described as serviceable, with several pairs of jeans and dresses that were plain.

Hurriedly she went through the clothes and found something that might do for the evening meal. It was pale grey, neat and slightly elegant. A few moments in front of the mirror gave her a chance to work on her hair, but she wasn't pleased with the result. Drawn back tightly it merely looked dreary. Left to fall around her face it seemed neglected.

There was a knock at the door and Gina appeared.

'Ah, *signorina*, I know what I can do for you. It will soon be time for supper, so I will take care of your hair.'

She had come prepared with hair tongs, and Jackie watched in awe as Gina turned her severe locks into a bundle of delightful curls.

'Thank you,' she said with feeling. 'It's so nice of you to take so much trouble for me.'

'Signor Vittorio said I was to do everything you needed to help you be at your best. He wants you to be happy.'

'How kind of him.'

Was he being kind, or did he just want to keep her quiet and uncomplaining? she wondered.

A moment later there came a knock on her door, and Vittorio entered.

'Excellent,' he said, regarding her. 'Our guests will be impressed.'

'Guests? Are there many coming?'

'Yes, we've had a few phone calls from friends who want to drop in. It's going to be quite a busy party. Shall we go?'

He held out his arm to her and she took it. Together they left the room and headed along the corridor to the top of the stairs. As they arrived she saw a little crowd gathered in the hall below. There were three middle-aged men and several young women. Most notable among them was Marisa, who stood looking up as they descended.

'Our guests are here already,' Vittorio observed.

When he began the introductions Jackie could hardly believe her ears. Every man seemed to have a title. She managed to pick up the words *duca, visconte, barone*… They exchanged greetings with them, their wives and their elegant young daughters.

Wow, she thought. Cinderella certainly had come to the ball tonight.

She wondered why they were all here. But when she saw how she was being regarded by the younger women a suspicion came over her. It was no accident that they were here. Marisa had clearly spread the word of her arrival, alarming all those who aimed to be the next Contessa.

'Let's go and have something to eat,' Tania said, leading the way into the dining room.

A long table dominated the centre of the room, with twenty places laid out. Vittorio escorted Jackie to a chair and sat beside her. She had the impression there was a faint disagreement on his other side, as two young women sought the chair beside him. But it was over in a moment.

The other seat beside Jackie was occupied by Aunt Tania, who was clearly still regarding her with interest. She had a thin, sharp face, which had a disconcerting habit of flashing into a brilliant smile.

'You must tell me all about yourself,' she said now. 'I'd never heard of you until Vittorio called me this morning to say he was bringing you. You're obviously a very significant business associate.'

'I'm afraid he makes me sound too important.'

'Jackie is too modest about her abilities,' Vittorio said. 'When I expand my English business in Rome I'll be doing everything she says.'

Tania raised her coffee cup in salute.

'Congratulations, *signorina*. If you knew how rarely he follows anyone else's advice—or even listens to it—you'd realise what a unique position you hold. Believe me, I'll do all I can to make you feel welcome here.' She smiled. 'My nephew would be very annoyed with me if I didn't.'

'Of course. I'm here to help him make a profit. That's what really matters.'

The two women shared a laugh. Vittorio noticed and nodded with pleasure.

Servants appeared with the supper. Between the excellent food and the friendly talk Jackie had an enjoyable evening.

At last the younger women began to leave the table and settle on sofas. Two of them seized Vittorio and playfully forced him to join them. He was immediately surrounded by admirers.

'I look forward to showing you our house,' Tania said. 'There has been much history here—many notable people. Sometimes we have even opened it to tourists.'

'That sound fascinating,' Jackie said. 'I love history. In England I used to like visiting great historical buildings where dramatic things had happened in the past.'

'Then you'll enjoy Castello Martelli. We've had our fair share of excitement there.'

'Lovely. I even—'

She was checked by a shriek of laughter that came from a nearby sofa.

Glancing over, she saw that Vittorio was deep in conversation with Marisa and the other young women who crowded round him. All of them were rocking with laughter.

'Some more wine?' Tania asked.

'No, thank you,' Jackie said. 'Would you mind if I went to bed? It's been a long day. It was my first flight and it's left me a bit shaken.'

'Yes. It can take it out of you, can't it? Especially if you're nervous.'

'That's very true.'

'You look as if you've got a headache. Go to bed now. I'll send Gina up with something to drink.'

'Thank you.'

At the door Jackie looked back to wave goodnight to Vittorio, but he was still enjoying himself with his female companions, managing to be enfolded in three pairs of arms at once. He seemed to have forgotten that she existed.

As she watched Marisa intervened, pulling the others away but doing it with laughter, as though claiming Vittorio as her property was no more than a joke to her.

Vittorio looked up, noticed Jackie in the doorway and waved. She gave him a slight wave back and departed.

As promised, Gina brought something up to her room.

'English tea,' she said. 'My mistress said you were to have the best.'

'She's being very kind to me.'

'She likes you. She doesn't like that other one, but if the Count marries her—well, what can we do? Goodnight, *signorina.*'

Gina slipped away, leaving Jackie to brood. And there was a great deal to brood about. However she had thought this visit would work out, it was happening very differently, and somehow she would need to find a way to deal with it.

She tensed suddenly, alerted by a noise from the corridor outside. There was the sound of a door being opened, and then Marisa's voice.

'Perché non si può solo ascoltare me?'

Jackie just managed to make out the meaning. 'Why can't you just listen to me?'

Vittorio's reply was also in Italian, but his meaning was blindingly clear. 'Because there's no point. We talk too much and it gets us nowhere. *You* won't listen to what *I* say.'

'Because I don't believe you really mean it. Listen to your *heart*, Vittorio—'

'I *am* listening to it, and it's saying no. There's nothing there. Goodbye, Marisa.'

Quietly Jackie looked out, just in time to see Marisa storming away down the corridor as the door opposite was closed.

So that was his room, she thought.

Glancing around to make sure Marisa was no longer there, she went and knocked at his door.

He opened it at once. 'Marisa, *per favore*— Oh, it's you.'

Looking shocked, he checked himself and drew back to let her in.

'Yes, it's only me,' she said, following him. 'I reckon it's time for you to come clean, Vittorio. You've concealed the truth for long enough.'

'What truth? What are you talking about?'

'I mean the reason you brought me here. You played the gallant knight, rescuing me from Rik, but it was actually about Marisa, wasn't it? You wanted to stop her troubling you and I'm a handy excuse.'

Vittorio closed his eyes like a man wondering how to cope with another disaster.

'It's a bit more than that…' He groaned. 'It's not just Marisa.'

'So it's all the others who hunted you down today?'

'I don't think it's an accident that so many people—women—turned up. They came to see *you*.'

'You think they're all competing for *you*? I've heard of conceit, but that takes the biscuit.'

'You're wrong. I'm not vain enough to think girls are after me for myself. It's the title they want, and they're not the only ones. My father tried to arrange a marriage between myself and Marisa. I told him I wasn't keen, but he wouldn't listen. He was so certain he could persuade me that he let her think it was all arranged. She reckons I'm her property, and if I so much as look at another woman she acts like a betrayed wife. It's getting more than I can stand. Why do you think they came today? Marisa spread the word that I'd arrived with you and they all descended on us to get a look at you. So, yes, I thought your presence here might help me, and I seized the chance because I'm going crazy with this situation.'

'But you didn't think to tell me?'

'I was going to but—well—I just lost my nerve. Suppose I *had* told you? What would you have done? Agreed to help me? I don't think so.'

'You're wrong. After the way you helped me deal with Rik I'll do anything I can for you.'

His eyes gleamed. 'Anything?'

'Anything at all.'

'You'll help save me from Marisa?'

She smiled. 'I'll go into battle against her and you'll be quite safe.'

'That would be wonderful. Just keeping her thinking we're an item. It may just work.'

'But why does it have to be me? Why couldn't you pick someone else?'

'Because you have one great advantage that makes you a better choice than anyone else.'

'What could that possibly be?'

'You've made it plain you don't like me or trust me. Another woman might take my attentions seriously, think I meant them, and then be hurt when she learned the truth. But *you* see me as a cold and arrogant—mercenary, even. That's fine. There's no danger that you'll ever fall in love with me. I know we've decided to be friends, but it's a cautious friendship with suspicion on both sides, and that makes us both safe.'

She regarded him ironically.

'So you chose me because you knew I'd never embarrass you by indulging in romantic thoughts about you? Oh, were you right about that!'

'That's what I reckoned. You'd sooner swoon over a slimy octopus than me.'

'I wouldn't go so far as to say *that*.'

'But you were thinking it?'

She regarded him with her head on one side. 'Maybe. Sometimes it's best to keep your thoughts to yourself. I'm sure you know all about that.'

'It's been useful. Let's shake on it.'

They clasped hands.

'Your aunt doesn't like Marisa, does she?' she observed.

'No, but she's my father's sister, and as such she feels bound by his wishes.'

'Nonsense. The only wishes that matter are yours.'

His face brightened. '*That's* what I like to hear a woman say.'

'Aha! You think it shows I have a submissive nature? She rubbed her hands. 'I could have a nasty shock waiting for you.'

'I'm sure you will. And I'm equally sure it will be interesting.'

From outside the building came the sound of voices. Vittorio opened the window and looked down.

'They're leaving,' he said. 'Come here.'

She went to stand beside him and he put his arm around her. Down below, Marisa was approaching her car while the other guests streamed out around her. Suddenly Marisa turned her head, gazing up at them.

'Shall we try to convince her now?' Vittorio murmured.

'Yes—what shall we do?'

'Rest your head on my shoulder.'

She did so, and he tightened his arm about her.

'Look up at me,' he murmured.

As soon as she did he leaned down and kissed her forehead.

Jackie drew a slow breath, waiting for him to drift lower until his lips touched hers. But he stayed as he was.

'She's there…watching us,' he said. Let's make this look good.'

His arms tightened, drawing her closer. His free hand caressed her cheek before drifting down, briefly touching her breasts. Jackie trembled, longing fiercely to take things further.

'You said you wanted me to help you…' she whispered.

'Yes—what are you going to do?'

'This,' she said, and reached up so that her arms went around his neck, drawing his head down so that she could caress his mouth with her own.

She could sense the surprise that shook him, then felt his grip on her tighten as he took control, moving his mouth against hers with growing urgency.

Caution told her that she shouldn't do this, but she couldn't make herself be cautious. Desire stormed through her, destroying everything but the need to be his and make him hers.

At last he spoke, his voice shaking. 'I think—I think we've done almost enough to convince her.'

'Yes—yes—'

'Just a few moments more...' His mouth brushed hers again.

Down below, Marisa got into her car. At the last moment she glanced up at them, made a sneering face, then started the car and drove away.

CHAPTER FIVE

'SHE'S GONE,' VITTORIO WHISPERED.

He could almost hear his own voice shaking. The last few minutes had affected him intensely, making him yearn to go further. But he struggled for control, fearful of driving Jackie away.

Reluctantly he released her. 'You did it. Marisa saw enough to get the message. Perhaps I should be grateful to you for taking command.'

'I didn't take command—'

'Didn't you?'

She thought she could guess his meaning. When she had reached up to draw his head down closer to hers, he'd known that her desire was as strong as his, and there was no way she could deny it. He had probably read the message in her eyes.

'You found the right way for both of us,' he said. 'You could say I followed your lead.'

'It was necessary for the performance,' she reminded him. 'Anything's worth doing for an effective performance.'

'Well said! A woman with efficient instincts.'

'And efficiency is everything,' she said lightly.

She met his gaze, both of them knowing that the real message was something quite different.

'Sometimes efficiency really *is* everything,' he said softly. 'But then—things change.'

'Well, they've changed for Marisa. I can't think why

she's worried about me. I'm no beauty. And don't bother to give me a polite answer or I'll thump you.'

'Right. You're no beauty. I heartily agree,' he said, trying to sound casual. He met her eyes. 'But you do have something else that's more than looks. You've got wit, and an intelligence that I find most appealing. In fact, since the day we met you've caught me out and tripped me up more than anyone's ever done before.'

'Then I'm surprised you brought me here.'

'Yes, I wonder what I was thinking of. I guess I don't mind being caught at a disadvantage—every now and then.'

'I'll remember that. I could have fun tripping you up.'

'I bet you will. There are women who conquer a man by their beauty, and those who conquer him by keeping him nervous, even scared.'

'And there's no doubt which one *I* am!' She laughed. 'But maybe I don't *want* to conquer you.'

'You won't make the effort? Then I'd feel insulted. Besides, you do it without meaning to.'

'You don't know that. I might have a fiendish plan going on.'

'I live in hope. But for the moment I'll say goodnight. We have a busy day tomorrow. You should beware. When we get to Rome I'm going to work you to death.'

'That's what I hoped. Anything else would be dull.'

'And let's not be *dull*, whatever we do.'

'No. Not that you could ever be dull here,' she murmured, glancing around at his bedroom. Like the rest of the house, it was lavishly decorated in a medieval style.

'This was my father's room,' he said.

'And now it's yours because you're the Count? Do you think you can be grandiose enough?'

'I'll try to be. I've never thought of myself as grandiose, but I suppose everything is going to be different now.'

'Yes,' she murmured. 'That's true. You won your battle

tonight. Marisa saw us, which is exactly what you wanted. From now on you'll be a free man.'

'A free man?' He looked into her eyes. 'I wonder just what that means?'

She met his gaze, suddenly confused. 'You'll find out gradually. I'm here to help you.' A sudden impulse made her say. 'It's getting late and I'm tired. I think I'll go to bed now. Goodnight.'

'Goodnight. And, Jackie—thank you for everything.'

She smiled and fled. It had suddenly become vital to escape him quickly and take refuge in her room.

Once there, she paced the floor, trying to understand the conflicting thoughts and feelings that struggled for supremacy inside her head.

It was madness to be upset, she told herself. Vittorio was a man of good looks and charm. Any woman would be thrilled to be taken into his arms. And for a brief moment she had known that delicious excitement. To feel his lips caressing hers, sense the tremors in his body—those pleasures had consumed her. He had wanted her, and the blissful knowledge had driven her to a response that had been almost beyond her control.

But then, like a warning blast, a voice in her mind had warned her to take care. To guard her feelings. He'd embraced her in order to deceive Marisa, then released her when Marisa had no longer been able to see them.

He was only pretending, she thought. He'd pretend for just long enough to get what he wanted and then she'd have outlived her usefulness to him. Just as if she fell in love with him he'd find it useful. And that was all he wanted of her—to be useful. Useful in the department store, useful about the money problem, useful about Marisa.

She'd do well to remember that falling for Vittorio would be extremely hazardous to her health. Mind you, he'd be as a big a fool to fall for *her*!

* * *

With Jackie gone Vittorio stood without moving for some moments, trying to cope with conflicting feelings. This had been his father's bedroom, and it still contained many memories.

Here they had spent their last few moments together, and Franco had revealed the secret that had set Vittorio on a new path. Putting right his father's wrongs had seemed like the right thing to do—and a simple thing.

But before that there had been other talks. Some of them about Vittorio's mother. He knew that both his parents had been unfaithful in their brief marriage. Adele, his mother, had married for the title—something which Franco, deeply in love, had not suspected until it was too late.

Looking at the surroundings where his father had made his last confession, he found that another scene came back to him. Then, too, Franco had lain there, dizzy with suffering, driving himself to tell the painful truth to his son, who had knelt beside the bed.

'I lost track of all the men she had…' He'd sighed.

Filled with fear, Vittorio had asked quickly, 'Do you mean that I'm not your son?'

'No, you're mine. When you were born I had a DNA test done to check, and the result was all I had hoped. But the fact that such a test was needed—' He had given a deep groan before adding wretchedly, 'And the other child…'

'What other child?'

'Do you remember how we lost your mother when you were twelve? She died giving birth. The baby also died. It wasn't mine. We hadn't made love for a long time, so I knew. She had never loved me as I loved her. I would have forgiven her, because I so much wanted her to stay with me, but then she was gone.'

'But how could you have kept her with you, knowing what you knew?' Vittorio had asked desperately.

'Yes, it's madness, isn't it? But love *is* a kind of madness. When you love a woman so much that you'll forgive her anything as long as she doesn't leave you, it's as though you cease to be yourself. I should have divorced her years before. I'd have been safer without her there to torment me. But I couldn't do it. I told myself I stayed with her for your sake, because you needed a mother. But the truth was I couldn't bear to let her go. So we stayed together…she kept living her riotous life. And then she died.'

Vittorio hadn't been able to reply. He'd dropped his head down into the bed, close to his father's, feeling only despair.

Franco had touched him. 'I pray that your life may be filled with more hope,' he'd said. 'Don't give your love to a woman who deceives you. Be cautious, my son. Don't trust too easily. Keep your love to yourself as long as you can.'

The advice had touched Vittorio's heart. Only recently he'd quarrelled with a young woman who'd briefly inspired his trust and affection before turning to another man. Everything in him had accepted that his father had been right, and that he must be cautious.

But then he'd met Jackie—frank, honest, different from any other women he'd met. Or so he'd thought until his growing attraction to her had begun to alarm him. Holding her in his arms, he'd felt a surge of feeling that was not merely desire, but also tenderness. And the awareness of her trembling in his arms, the fervour with which she'd kissed him, had left him feeling stunned.

She'd called it efficiency, claiming to have done no more than follow his lead. But the memory of her response lingered…delightful, alarming, warning him that the road ahead led into mystery.

It was unbearable not to know the answer. He went out into the corridor, looking to see if there was a light under her door. But there was none. Had she really gone to sleep?

Or was she lying in the darkness, facing a confusion as great as his own?

He stood outside her door, listening to the silence inside, trying to decide whether to call her or knock. But after hesitating a long time he backed away, sensing that this was not the right moment.

Next morning Jackie awoke early and took a shower. Standing under the water, she wondered what she would see in Vittorio's eyes this morning. She'd felt sure he would call on her the previous night, but nothing had happened.

She'd heard a faint sound, as though his footsteps had approached her room, but then there had been only silence. Unable to bear the tension, she'd leapt out of bed and pulled open her door. But the corridor outside had been dark and empty, with no sign of him. She had gone back to bed and lain there fretting until she'd managed to fall asleep.

This morning her thoughts were still troubled—even more so because her attraction towards Vittorio made her feel that she was failing her father again.

Somehow, somewhere, there must be a way to do the right thing. If only she could find it.

She dressed and went downstairs into the hall. Through an open door she could see Vittorio sitting at a desk.

He glanced up and waved to her. 'We'll be going in to breakfast in a moment,' he said. 'And then we can—'

The sound of the phone interrupted him, making him curse slightly and then answer it. Jackie went to stand by the window, gazing out at the grass and trees, entranced by their beauty. Clearly it was a magnificent estate, and she was curious to see more of it.

Glancing around, she saw that he had his back to her, absorbed in the call. Yielding to temptation, she slipped out of the door into the garden. For a few moments it was delightful to run across the lawn to where she could see a seat under one of the trees. She sat down on it and leaned back, closing her eyes and breathing in the cool air.

When at last she opened her eyes she found herself gazing at the building that reared up so magnificently, beautiful and luxurious. But the sight caused sorrow to fall over her heart, as it had done so often since she'd arrived here. This had been the home of the man who had cheated her beloved father, reducing him to poverty and despair.

In her mind's eye she saw her father again, his head sunk in misery when his wife had left him.

He had nothing, she thought. *And the man who lives here has everything.*

She could feel tears pouring down her cheeks and ducked her head, seizing a handkerchief to wipe them away. But there were more tears, followed by sobs. She sat there shaking, trying vainly to control her grief.

'Jackie— *Jackie?*'

The voice from overhead made her look up to see Vittorio standing there. At once he sat down beside her, reaching out to her.

'Come here,' he said.

'No!' She pulled sharply away. 'Go away. Leave me alone.'

'But I—'

'I said leave me alone. I don't want to talk to you.'

She jumped up, fleeing away from him until she plunged into the trees. When she felt safely out of sight she leaned against a tree trunk and abandoned the effort to control her tears.

Suddenly she felt a pair of strong arms go around her, pulling her against him.

'I'm sorry,' he said. 'I don't mean to crowd you, but stay with me a while. Let me help you.'

She couldn't answer. The feel of his chest was warm

and comforting, giving her a pleasure she hadn't thought to know. She trembled and felt him draw her even closer.

'Cry,' he said. 'You need to. Don't fight it.'

It felt incredible that she was letting this man, of all men, comfort her. But the feel of his arms about her was unlike anything that had ever happened to her before.

'Let's go inside,' he said. 'We'll have breakfast and then go into the city. We've got a lot to do.'

'Oh, yes,' she said wryly. 'I'm going to give you all that expert opinion—if I can think of anything. I really felt very awkward when you were telling your aunt how good I am.'

'You played your part beautifully.'

'But I don't even know what I'm supposed to be expert *about*.'

'That's why we're going into town. By the time we've finished you'll be able to give me your orders.'

She rubbed her hands. 'Roll on the day!'

'Well, I've been meaning to tell you—' He stopped, realising that he no longer had her attention. She was looking about her at the medieval beauty of her surroundings as though something had suddenly struck her, 'What's the matter?' he asked.

'Nothing. It's this place,' she said. 'I just have to keep looking at it. It's wonderful how history seems to live here all around us, as though your ancestors were still alive.'

'I know the feeling. I've felt them with me all my life, and if I want to meet them I go to the gallery, where their portraits hang. Would you like to see it?'

'I'd love to.'

He led her into a great room at the back of the house. Portraits hung all along the walls, of people dressed in clothes that spoke of past centuries.

'And *all* these are your ancestors?' Jackie mused in wonder.

'Not all. Have a look at this one.'

He drew her to a full-length picture showing a young woman in a horse-drawn chariot. With one hand she controlled the horses, in the other she held a sword. On her head she wore a military helmet.

'That's Bellona,' Vittorio told her. 'The Roman goddess of war.'

'You have a *female* deity of war? Surely—?'

'Surely it should be a man?' he said, grinning. 'In any other society it probably would be. But in Rome we like strong, powerful women.'

'Unless they happen to disagree with you?' she teased, her eyes challenging him.

'Ah, well, let's not go into that.'

'Very wise,' she said with mock solemnity. 'Just think of all the awkward things I could remind you of.'

'And how you'd enjoy doing it.'

Tania had slipped into the room behind them and was listening to them with pleasure.

'You'll have a chance to meet Bellona,' she said. 'We celebrate her festival every year. You'll probably enjoy that.'

'Yes, you two have a lot in common...' Vittorio observed.

'Vittorio!' Tania protested. 'I hope you're not being rude to our guest.'

'Don't worry, Aunt. Jackie's not offended. And here's someone else you should meet,' Vittorio said, turning her towards a picture of a man in a suit of armour. 'He was the very first Count Martelli. And the two men in the next picture are his sons. The elder one died and the younger one inherited the title.'

Along the walls they went, with Vittorio describing his ancestors one by one, introducing them as though they still lived with him.

One portrait especially seized Jackie's attention. It showed a man in the luscious garb of the seventeenth century, with long curling hair falling over his shoulders. But it was his face that claimed her attention. It was Vittorio's face that had come down the centuries.

'He was my great-great-great-great-grandfather,' Vittorio said.

'Yes, I can see. It's incredible. You're really one of them. Hey—what's that?'

Her attention had been seized by another picture, a few feet along. It showed two men dressed in the attire of ancient Rome. One of them also had a face similar to Vittorio's.

'He must be another ancestor of yours,' she said. 'Who's the man with him?'

'Julius Caesar—the Roman Emperor.'

'One of your family was a friend of *Julius Caesar*? They even had their portraits painted together?'

'Not at all. There's a common belief that one of my ancestors was part of Caesar's court, but that picture was painted hundreds of years later. It's just a fantasy. There are several fantasies like that in this gallery. Over here is Napoleon. When he was Emperor of France he annexed Rome, but when he was defeated we regained our freedom.'

The picture had been carefully designed to show Napoleon regarding his companion with admiration and respect. The companion's face also bore a notable resemblance to Vittorio's.

'It's marvellous, isn't it?' said Tania.

'That face—it's *him*!' Jackie exclaimed in wonder.

'Yes, you can't get away from me even a few hundred years later.' Vittorio laughed.

'Have you shown Jackie the picture of Lady Nanetta?' Tania asked.

'Not yet, but I'm looking forward to doing it.' He guided her across the room. 'Nanetta is a family legend,' he explained. 'She was a magnificent woman, but also an alarming one.'

He paused before a full-length picture of a tall, slender woman.

'She had dozens of suitors,' he said, 'but she rejected them all. Legend says that she was a witch. It's never been proved or disproved, but she inspired a lot of fear.'

'Why did she reject them all?' Jackie asked. 'Didn't she ever fall in love?'

'Never. She had a great fortune and she believed that was all men wanted of her. She said no man could be trusted, nor was ever worthy of love.'

'How sad to believe that,' Jackie murmured. 'How could anyone endure life with nothing to believe in?'

'Is love the *only* thing to believe in?' he asked wryly.

'Of course there's always money.'

'But you don't believe in that, having turned down so much.'

'If you mean your million pounds, I turned it down for love—of my father.' She saw tension come into his face and added, 'There's more than one kind of love.'

He hesitated before saying, 'You're right, of course.'

She went to stand before the woman's picture, trying to see if her face revealed anything. But Lady Nanetta stared into the distance, concealing her secrets.

'I wonder what taught her so much distrust?' Jackie said.

'She saw a lot of evidence to distrust in her life. She was hugely rich.'

'Which was why so many men wanted to marry her?'

'Probably. Of course they may have been attracted to her as well.'

'I doubt that,' Jackie said, studying the picture. 'She was no beauty.'

Vittorio considered the picture before glancing back at her. 'That matters little,' he said. 'A woman doesn't have to be a great beauty to intrigue men. Her moods, her wit, the hint of mystery she can carry—those can lure men as keenly as mere good looks.' After a thoughtful moment he added, 'Sometimes more so.'

He was giving her a look that might have been significant. She tried to be cautious about understanding it, but there was a glint in his eye she couldn't ignore.

She called common sense to her rescue. 'If you say so,' she said cheerfully.

'I *do* say so.'

'Then I'll have to believe it—however unconvincing.'

He chuckled and put his arm around her. 'Let's get going—we have a busy day ahead of us,' said Vittorio. 'But first we'll have breakfast.'

They ate quickly, and when breakfast was over he led Jackie out of the palace to a garage around the side. He regarded her curiously as she took out her purse and examined its contents.

'Need some money?' he asked.

'No. Thank you, but I'm quite independent. I can use my bank card to draw money from my English account, can't I?'

'If you've got the pin number, yes.'

In a few moments they were on their way to Rome.

'What are we going to see first?' she asked.

'My department store. I need to see how it's managing. And I'll be interested in your opinion. After that, I'd like to show you some of the city.'

At first the road wound through the estate, and Jackie watched from the window, charmed by the green fields and forests, until finally the estate was behind them and they were heading along the motorway that led to the city.

Once in Rome, Vittorio drove straight to an area where there were shops, restaurants and commercial buildings. He parked the car and led her through the streets, letting her absorb the atmosphere until it was time to visit his department store.

It was a huge place, selling goods from many different countries and a vast range of sources. There were departments for furniture, glass, hardware and jewellery.

Jackie walked through it in a daze of delight. Everywhere Vittorio introduced her to the staff as 'my expert from England'. In the glass and china department he explained that she was to be in charge, and she was treated with great respect.

When he was called away for a moment the staff crowded round her, full of eager questions. Their English was efficient, as was her Italian.

'There are some products I'd like to show you,' she said. 'I'll need a computer.'

One was immediately made available, and she went online to show them the many sites where she found products that made them exclaim with admiration. It was clear that her visit was a success.

At last she looked up to find Vittorio regarding her with amused satisfaction.

'Found me any new stock?' he asked.

'One or two things I think might go well.'

She indicated several choices. He nodded in agreement to all of them, and a staff member began making purchases.

'We'll leave him to it while we look around some more,' Vittorio said. When they were outside he said, 'I wish you could have seen your face while you were giving everyone instructions. I think that's your idea of heaven.'

'If you mean that I'm a bully—'

'Only the kind of bully that I need working for me,' he said with a grin. 'You promised to make profit for me, and I can see that you will. Well done!'

'Thank you. After all, you did promise me authority.'

'I must have known by instinct that authority is your default position.'

'You might have a point there,' she said with a brief laugh. 'I must admit I *do* enjoy being the one to give the orders.'

'After the way you had to put up with Rik, I'm not surprised.'

'Not just Rik. I used to annoy my father a lot by arguing.' She regarded him cheekily. 'I'm a very difficult character.'

'Well, I already knew *that*.' He took her hand in his and gave it a comforting squeeze. 'I can put up with you if you can put up with me.'

She squeezed back. 'I'll do my best—however hard it is.'

'I've got a feeling we're going to be a big success.'

Coming to Italy was proving to be everything she had dared to hope, thought Jackie. Here there were opportunities and a chance for the kind of new, more adventurous life that had once seemed impossible.

Suddenly she stopped.

'I didn't realise that your store stocked clothes.'

'Of course—it's our most popular department. Come and look.'

Jackie was soon in heaven! Vittorio introduced her to the staff and she watched, entranced, as boxes were opened to reveal costly gowns. She examined them, trying to imagine her dull self in any of the exquisite dresses.

'Perhaps—' she began, turning to Vittorio. 'Oh, where's he gone?'

'He was summoned to his office,' said Donna, the head assistant. 'Do you like our stock?

'Oh, yes, it's all so beautiful. Especially this one.' She gazed admiringly at a black satin evening gown.

'Yes, it's one of our new range. Would you like to try it on?'

'I'm not sure… It looks very sophisticated, and I'm not really like that.'

'But you might be if you saw yourself in it.'

'Oh, go on, then—let's try.'

Donna's advice was good. The dress was tight-fitting, and clung perfectly to Jackie's slender figure, giving it a drama and mystery she'd never been aware of before.

She turned back and forth, enjoying the sight of her new self in the mirror. Totally absorbed, she failed to notice the middle-aged woman who had arrived, and was watching her with pleasure.

'Is that dress for sale?' the woman asked Donna.

'Yes, Contessa. It's part of the stock that's just arrived.'

'It would suit my daughter perfectly. I'll buy it.' The shopper turned to the man who had just appeared beside her. 'You're really extending your talents in this store. Doesn't your model look lovely?'

'Yes,' Vittorio murmured, 'she does.'

He backed away quickly before Jackie could notice him. After a moment the Countess joined him. She was beaming.

'Now you have a satisfied customer,' she said. 'That dress looked so good on your model that I just *had* to buy it. Donna says it can be delivered tomorrow.'

He replied politely and escorted her away, before returning to the dress department. Jackie was still there, once more in her own clothes. For a moment Vittorio had a dizzying sensation that briefly she had become a different Jackie.

'It's time to move on, Jackie. We have a lot to fit in today.'

'Oh, that's a shame. I've had an amazing morning, and your store is magnificent.'

'No, no,' he said quickly. 'You mustn't say that. You're going to tell me how to bring it up to standard.'

'Suppose I think I can't?'

'Hush, don't say such a thing. Never admit failure.' He gave her a cheeky grin. 'You're here as an expert, giving me your lofty advice.'

'And you'll *take* my advice? I don't think so.'

'Then you can call me some suitable names. *Stupido, idiota, buffone.* You understand Italian well enough to take your pick.'

'I'll try to remember. Where to next, then?'

'I'd like to take you to my other shop. This one is much smaller. It could do with expansion, and I'd value your opinion.'

CHAPTER SIX

A SHORT STROLL brought them to the 'other shop', which she examined with interest, making notes. She was enjoying herself.

After a couple of hours they left.

Wherever they went Vittorio was instantly recognised. Even in the street people addressed him respectfully as 'Signor Conte', and regarded her with curiosity.

She could guess why she fascinated them. Word of her arrival had obviously spread fast, and she was clearly being regarded as the latest candidate for the position of Countess.

Me, she thought hilariously. *Plain, dreary me. Whatever next?*

'What's so funny?' Vittorio asked.

'Sorry—what?'

'You suddenly started laughing. People don't usually find Rome funny.'

'It's not Rome that's funny. It's me. Haven't you seen the way everybody is staring at me?'

'Sure—you've really got their attention.'

'And why? For the same reason Marisa is troubled by me. I'm seen as the latest candidate for your hand.'

'And that's funny, is it?'

'It is from the proper angle. Look.'

She pointed him towards the window of a shop they were passing. Turning, they looked at their reflections: Vittorio splendidly handsome, herself ordinary.

'Ever since the moment I came here,' she said, 'I've felt like Cinderella arriving at the ball.'

'Really? Does that make me Prince Charming?'

'Prince Charming or Prince Charm*less*. It depends on your mood.'

'You don't pull your punches, do you? Are you trying to lure me in or put me off?'

'What do *you* think?'

'I think you're trying to scare the life out of me. And succeeding.'

'That's all right, then. As long as you don't think I'm trying to lure you into marriage.'

'I promise never to think that.'

Vittorio wondered what he should have understood from her words. If she ever did set her sights on him he doubted he'd guess. She was too clever to be obvious. But the conversation had amused him too much to be troublesome.

'I'd better go into the bank while I'm here,' he said. 'The one across the road is the one I use.'

Inside the bank, she saw him treated with the same intense respect she had noticed before—which she guessed told her everything about the size of his bank balance.

'It would be easier if you banked here also, since you'll be living and working in Italy from now on,' he said. 'Tell them you want to transfer your London account.' He added lightly, 'Unless, of course, you're planning to dash back to the joys of working for Rik.'

'No chance!'

'Wise woman.'

He came to the counter with her and spoke in rapid Italian.

'There'll be bank cards for you in a couple of days,' he said at last. 'And now it's time for some lunch at last. This way.'

He led her to a little restaurant on the next corner.

As she looked through the menu he said, 'What would you like?'

'I don't know; I can't decide. I'll let you order for me.'

He regarded her with amused suspicion. 'You trust me to order for you? That's not like the Jackie I've come to know. Are you trying to catch me off-guard?'

'Well, I've got to do *something* to worry you, haven't I?'

'Don't bother. You worry me quite enough as it is.'

'In that case, please do your duty and order for me.'

He instructed the waitress, and in a few minutes a dish was set before her. It was a bowl filled with tiny lumps of meat and a few vegetables.

'It's called lamb *tagliata*,' he said. 'I remembered that you like lamb.'

'But that was the lunch we had in the hotel in London,' she said, astonished. 'You remembered from then?'

'Of course. I'm a businessman. I make efficient notes about my business associates and use them to my advantage.'

But he winked as he said it, and gave her a grin which she returned.

The food tasted magnificent. She devoured it with pleasure, aware that he was watching her closely.

'Mmm…lovely,' she said. 'You choose food well. I must put that in my own notes about *you*—along with a few other things.'

He nodded, implying that he understood her perfectly. 'Of course,' he said, 'my observations will have to include how careless you are about doing your job.'

'*What?*'

'You were supposed to be giving me an expert opinion of my store. So far all you've done is eat. I want to lodge a complaint.'

'I said it was magnificent!'

'But you were just being polite.'

'I'm *never* polite. Haven't you learned that yet? Hmm...
I'll have to give you a few lessons.'

'I'll look forward to it. But, in the meantime, you didn't
really *mean* magnificent, did you?'

'Suppose I say yes? Would that make me disappointing?'

'Come on, Jackie. Criticise. It's what you're here for.'

'Well, I *did* notice one thing missing. You have a huge
range of things from all over the world, but I saw nothing
from England.'

'That's because we've never had any real English expertise—until now. I did the right thing, kidnapping you.'

'You didn't exactly *kidnap* me,' she insisted. 'I wanted
to come.'

'Suppose you hadn't? Do you think that would have
made any difference?'

'No, I guess not.'

'You did a great job in the shop—especially when you
modelled that dress.'

'Modelled—? You saw me?'

'Yes, I keep turning up when I'm not wanted, don't I?
I was there with Contessa Valierse. She liked the sight of
you so much she bought the dress for her daughter. I seem
to gain from everything you do. As soon as I realised that,
I decided that you must belong to me.'

'And if I resist?' she teased.

'It won't make any difference. When an efficient businessman finds something that suits him he takes possession of it, ignoring all distractions.'

'And you think nobody can successfully fight you?'

'That's right. I always get my own way. Make a special
note of that.'

'Yes, I think I will.' She took out a scrap of paper, then
discovered a problem.

'Damn! I haven't got a pen.'

'Here.' He handed her a pen.

'I wonder if I should accept that…' she mused.

'You mean because you're about to write something critical about me? Go on. Be brave.'

'Thanks.' She took it and scribbled, *He always gets his own way*, adding a little swirl afterwards.

'What's that squiggle at the end?' Vittorio asked.

'It's code. It means, *That's what he thinks*.' Jackie chuckled.

'Hmm… At least you're honest.'

'Well, I'm not sure you get your own way as much as you think you do.'

'You will be. In time.'

Despite the seemingly harsh words, the atmosphere was teasing and friendly.

'Of course it doesn't do for a guy to be too self-confident around you,' he said. 'He'd pay a heavy price.'

'Or *I* would,' she said wryly.

He considered her. 'Is that the voice of experience?'

'There was a man I was once fond off. Just fond. His name was Peter. I wasn't passionately in love, but when he mentioned marriage I was interested.'

'What went wrong?'

'My father became ill. I was looking after him and Peter didn't like that. It made him feel that he came second.'

'*Did* he come second?'

'Yes, I suppose he did. He wanted me to put Daddy in a care home, but I couldn't do that. It would have broken his heart.'

'And Peter was angry about that?'

'We had a quarrel. I told him that he couldn't give me orders and that was that. In my admittedly limited experience I've discovered that men like to be in charge.'

'Surely that isn't aimed at *me*? You have as much control as I do.'

'Not as much. Maybe a bit.'

'We'll agree to disagree. So you sent him away with a flea in his ear?'

'Yes. He couldn't believe I meant it, but I wasn't going to change my mind. How about you? Have you never been tempted to settle down with any of the beautiful women who seem to throw themselves at you at any given opportunity?'

He made a face, but said nothing.

'I'm sorry,' she said. 'I didn't mean to pry. Your love life is none of my business.' She added cheekily, 'But perhaps you don't *have* one. Perhaps you live on a pinnacle of lofty indifference.'

'If only I did. There was one woman who taught me to be careful, and it was a strong lesson that I've never forgotten.'

'Was she after your title?'

'She was. But at first she played her role so convincingly that I didn't realise the truth. I was completely taken in—until the day I found her in bed with another man.'

'What? How *could* she?'

'The man was heir to a dukedom. His social standing and personal fortune were therefore much greater than my own. That told me everything I needed to know. Her fine words and loving behaviour towards me had been because she wanted my title. When a better title came along I ceased to exist as far as she was concerned.'

'She pretended to love you—?'

'It was a good act. Fooled me.'

'And you loved her?'

He hesitated, and she could tell that he found this hard to answer.

'I thought I did. But it was a useful lesson. I've never been deceived again. I keep my suspicious side working.'

His words were cool, but she had a sense that they concealed feelings he didn't want to admit. This deceitful woman had caused him a lot of pain—some of which had never completely abated.

'What a dreadful thing to happen,' she said. 'Can you ever trust anyone again?'

'Probably not. But it's safer that way. What about you? After this guy you sent away—has there been anyone since?'

'No, I've had too much to think about. First my father died, and after that I set my heart on saving up enough money to escape my miserable existence, start a new life.'

'But you could be doing that now, by taking the money I offered you. Why did you turn it down?'

'For Daddy's sake. It would have felt like insulting him—saying that his suffering didn't matter as long as I gained the money.'

'But he wouldn't know.'

'Maybe—maybe not. But I still value his opinion. What he would've thought about things is of paramount importance to me. What about you and *your* father's wishes? Don't you take *his* views into account when you make decisions? Isn't that what you were doing in trying to give me that money?'

Jackie was exactly right, he realised. His father was still there in his mind and his heart. At times it was as if he could hear his voice in his ear. And clearly the same was true of her. It was almost alarming.

'And do you feel that *he* would know whether you've managed it or not?' she asked.

'I don't know, of course,' he said quietly. 'But *I* will know.'

'And so will I. That's why I can't give in and take your money. I feel that it would break his heart.'

'And I have to keep my word to *my* father. If I don't, that would break *his* heart.'

'If only they could have talked to each other while they

were still alive,' she said wistfully. 'They could've sorted it out without us.'

He took her hand between his. 'Instead we must honour their memories and do right by them both.'

'Yes. I'm glad of that.'

He squeezed her hand. 'So am I.'

A waiter approached, making him release her quickly. When he'd ordered some coffee he said, 'Let's discuss the store. You said it needed more stuff from England. Tell me exactly what you mean…'

After lunch they were soon in the car, heading back through the country to the Castello Martelli. As darkness fell she saw the building's lights from a distance, and marvelled again at its magnificence and beauty.

Tania was waiting in the hall.

'Shall I get you some supper?' she asked.

'No need—we've enjoyed a late lunch,' Vittorio told her cheerfully. 'And now we have something to celebrate. This way, Jackie.'

His arm around her waist, he guided her into his office. Tania regarded them wryly. After a moment she went to the office door and stood watching while Jackie worked on the computer, accessing one English website after another while showing Vittorio her ideas for supplying his stores.

'Can you go back to the last one?' Vittorio said. 'I like those metal ornaments. Yes, that's it. Zoom in on that one. Great. Yes, I'll have that.'

He became aware of Tania stood in the doorway.

'Come and look, Aunt. Jackie's doing a wonderful job for us.'

'So I see,' Tania said, coming forward, smiling. 'You really seem very knowledgeable, *signorina*.'

'Please call me Jackie.'

'Jackie. Yes. Now, if my nephew is going to work you to death can I get you some coffee—or tea? A glass of wine?'

'I'm okay—thank you, Tania.'

'I will take a wine, please, Aunt Tania,' said Vittorio.

The other woman smiled at them both and headed to the kitchen. Jackie sensed that Tania was still undecided about her, but her manner was pleasant.

Once Tania was gone, Jackie's attention was brought back to the computer screen.

'I want to go back to town tomorrow,' announced Vittorio, 'but tonight I want to see some of those websites again.'

'I'll get started now,' Jackie said.

He sat with his attention fixed on what she was doing. Suddenly he said, 'Let me look at that.'

She enlarged the picture, which was of a metal vase with elaborate engraving.

He studied it for several minutes before saying, 'Fine. I'll buy some of those.'

He purchased the items online, studied more websites and purchased several more things. By the time they were finished he'd spent a thousand euros and was in good spirits.

'Fantastic job!' he said. I'd never have found that stuff without you. And tomorrow there'll be more. We must make an early start.'

'Then I'll have an early night,' Jackie said, rising.

He rose too, but she signalled for him to sit down. Tania had just returned to the office with Vittorio's drink, and Jackie got the sense that she wanted to talk with her nephew privately.

Vittorio nodded, gave her a gentle kiss on the cheek, and let her go.

When they were alone Tania poured him a glass of wine. 'It's been a good evening,' she said.

'Yes. I knew bringing Jackie here would be brilliant. She really knows her stuff.'

'And she makes sure you realise it,' Tania observed lightly.

'You sound suspicious. I thought you liked her?'

'In a way, I do. That's what makes it confusing. I want to believe in her but—' She sighed.

'But what?'

'What exactly is she *after*?'

'Nothing.'

'Oh, my dear boy, be realistic. Every young woman you meet is after something. Usually money.'

'No, that's one thing I can be sure of. She's not after my money. I offered her money and she refused it.'

'Obviously it wasn't enough.'

'I offered her in excess of a million English pounds.'

'A million—? Are you out of your mind?'

'In a way, yes. I've been partly out of my mind since Papà admitted on his deathbed that he'd cheated Jackie's father out of a million years ago.'

Tania gasped. 'No, that's not possible. You've imagined it.'

'It's true. He told me he and George Benton both placed a bet. Benton's paid off, but Papà stole the winnings before Benton knew. I've been desperate to put it right by paying back the money. I was going to give it to George Benton, but he's dead. So I offered it to Jackie and she turned me down.'

Tania gasped. 'She actually refused to take a sum like that? I don't believe it.'

'It's true. I'm not lying.'

'No, I mean I don't believe her refusal was genuine. She wants you to think her honest so that you'll be lured in further—perhaps even marry her.'

'I don't believe that.'

'No, because you've formed a high opinion of her—exactly as you were meant to.'

'So you don't really like her after all?'

Tania hesitated before saying carefully, 'I'm not sure. She makes me cautious. But she's so clever and sharp-witted I wonder if she might be the right woman for you, because *she* could be the one who could make you stop your nonsense.'

This seemed to strike him. He considered thoughtfully before saying, 'My *nonsense*? I think you two must be in cahoots.'

'Why? Has she called you out on your nonsense too?'

'Not outright, but she implies it every time she opens her mouth.'

'Good for her.'

'Today she called me Prince Charmless.'

'Indeed? She actually said that?'

'Without any hesitation.'

Tania chuckled. 'Now I'm *really* beginning to like her.'

'I like her too,' Vittorio admitted. 'In some ways. But not in others. It comes and goes, and the feelings get in-tertwined.'

'You mean you have opposite feelings at the same time?'

'Yes—it's hard to know what to think of a woman with several different aspects.'

'That can be the best kind of woman,' Tania observed.

'Certainly the most interesting,' Vittorio murmured. 'And now I think I'll have an early night myself.'

'I hope you're not going to go knocking on her door.'

'I wouldn't dream of it. She and I are just friends. We've both made that very plain.'

'As long as you're both realists.'

'Not a doubt of it. Goodnight, Aunt.' He gave her a friendly peck on the cheek and departed.

Despite retiring early, Vittorio found that his need for sleep deserted him as soon as he went to bed. After tossing and turning for a while he rose, pulled on some jeans and a T-shirt, and went downstairs, then out into the garden.

He couldn't be certain what had disturbed him. Although he knew his aunt's words had touched a nerve, he was unwilling to admit how that touch had agitated him.

We're just friends. We've both made that very plain.

Was that being realistic? Despite her lack of conventional beauty, Jackie held an attraction for him that was unsettling—all the more so because he doubted if she felt the same way.

He walked for a long time before returning to his room and going back to bed. But still sleep evaded him, and he lay there restlessly for several hours until he nodded off just before it was time to get up.

Bad news was waiting for him when he went down for breakfast. Leo, the permanent driver he employed, was feeling poorly.

'He can't drive you to Rome,' Tania told him. 'He isn't well enough.'

'No matter. I'll drive.' But he said it reluctantly. His disturbed night had left him feeling less than his best. But the trip was necessary, and he was sure he could be strong.

He reckoned it was the right decision as he observed Jackie on their journey. She had clearly done some research and knew where she wanted to visit.

'I'd like to see some more of the smaller shops,' she said after a few miles. 'The department stores are impressive, but a little shop can sometimes take you by surprise.'

'Yes, it can,' he said. 'I remember a little shop in London that took me *completely* by surprise. It was being run by a really prickly woman who trampled me underfoot, chucked me out and called me all kinds of names. And a few days later I was fool enough to bring her home with me. I can't think why…'

'I guess you just like being ill-treated,' she teased.

'That's right. And I'm sure she's got some more up her sleeve.'

'Never mind. If you fight back she'll probably make a run for it.'

'Don't you dare! Now I've got you here I'm going to keep you. You're my prisoner. Don't forget it.'

They laughed. And then they were in town, travelling the back streets where Vittorio discovered small businesses that impressed him in unfamiliar ways.

He watched as Jackie examined them, made notes, and drew his attention to things he hadn't noticed.

'You really *do* know your stuff,' he said at last as they got back into the car. 'I'm impressed.' He glanced around and said suddenly, 'Wait here, I'll be just a moment.'

On the far side of the road was a branch of the bank where he'd taken her the day before. He went in, stayed a few minutes, then returned to her.

'I've got something for you,' he said. 'Here.' He handed her a bundle of banknotes.

'But what—?'

'Now you're working for me, and that's your first commission.'

She flicked through the notes, astonished at the amount.

'It's more than I was expecting.'

'You're doing a good job. It's ten per cent of what I spent online under your advice.'

'We didn't actually agree my wages.'

'No, and if I was anything like the last man you worked for I'd cut the amount in half and defy you to challenge me. I wonder how far you'd get…'

'I never got anywhere arguing with Rik until you came and defended me,' she admitted.

'Right. But you're my employee now, and I don't expect you to work for nothing.'

'Well, if you put it like that—'

'You've *earned* that money, Jackie. Now, I'm starving,' Vittorio said. 'Just round that corner is a hotel with one of the best restaurants in Rome. Let's go. Unless you want to be difficult about that too?'

'No, I've had enough fun for today. Let's go.'

CHAPTER SEVEN

'YOU MEANT THAT about fun, didn't you? That's how you get your kicks—driving me mad.'

'Some people are more fun to drive mad than others.'

'You'd better watch out,' Vittorio said. 'It might be *my* turn to have fun.' He swung into a car park. 'Here we are.'

He escorted her inside the hotel and headed for the restaurant. When they were settled inside, Jackie's eyes widened at the sight of the menu.

'Best Roman cuisine,' Vittorio said. 'Does it tempt you?'

'Yes, it looks delicious.' He summoned the waiter and they ordered their food.

'Would you like wine?' he asked.

'Not really.'

'Me neither. I've got to drive us home. Let's have sparkling water.'

When the water arrived he filled both their glasses.

'To a successful business arrangement,' he said.

They clinked glasses.

'Here's the food,' he said with relief as the waiter approached them.

The dishes that were laid before her looked delicious, and tasted that way too.

'Lovely!' she said.

'Good.'

He paused, and she had a strange feeling that he was summoning up his courage. When he spoke again he sounded uneasy.

'The fact is I wanted us to spend a little time together. Because I feel we need to talk.'

Jackie stared at him, puzzled. 'Do we?' she asked softly. 'You might say that we're the last people to want to talk.'

'But that's wrong. We connect because I'm the only person who knows exactly how you feel.'

'I don't think you *do* know how I feel. You can't imagine how all your money and luxury depresses me.'

'Because of your father and what was done to him? I understand how that makes you feel, but I wasn't the man who did it.' He took a deep breath. 'Why do you hate me, Jackie?'

She gave a brief ironic laugh. 'I guess it's because you're the one who's available to me. I can't chastise your father, because he isn't here. But you are, so I can—' She gave a slight shrug.

'Well, that's honest, anyway. So when you kick me in the teeth you just pretend you're kicking him?'

'I guess you're right.' She sighed. 'I keep telling myself to be reasonable, but then I remember Daddy's face looking the way I saw it so often. His life was terrible at the end. He'd lost everything.'

'He hadn't lost you. He had a daughter who cared for him.'

'Yes, but I couldn't fill all the empty spaces in his life. Even now I'm still trying to do my best by him.'

Vittorio closed his eyes. 'I can't describe hearing how my father had cheated his friend, stolen from him—what that did to me. I'd always admired him, practically worshipped him as a man to be trusted and honoured. Suddenly to discover that there was another truth about him—that he was capable of such a terrible action—'

Jackie was dismayed to see that he was shaking. She reached out and took his hand. 'It's not your fault,' she said.

He opened his eyes, gazing straight at her. 'I never thought to hear you say something like that,' he said.

'Well, it's true. You didn't steal the money.'

'But I lived on it. I grew up in luxury that I had no right to. And when I started out in business my father supported me financially. He couldn't have done that if he hadn't had that stolen money. The knowledge tortured me, but I had to keep my feelings to myself. I couldn't let him know while he was dying. And there's been nobody else I could talk to. Until now.'

'And talking helps, doesn't it?' she murmured. 'I never thought to say this, but in a strange way your loss has been greater than mine. My father remains in my heart just as he always was—loving, gentle, sweet-natured. That will never change. But you've lost the father you loved and admired. He's vanished and been replaced by another father who horrifies you. I do understand how that must be a miserable loss to you.'

From the way he stared at her she could tell she'd taken him completely by surprise.

'How did you…?' he murmured. 'However did you…?'

How did she know? she wondered. Perhaps it was connected with the fierce sympathy for him that had risen in her so unexpectedly.

'You must have a gift for seeing into other people's hearts and minds,' he said.

She wasn't sure how to answer that. He was the last man in the world whose heart and mind she would have expected to see into.

'What is it?' he asked, looking at her face. 'Have I said something to disturb you?'

'No. I'm just thinking of the day we left England and Rik tried to stop me—the way you dealt with him. You said you'd do anything necessary to make him sorry he'd opened his big mouth, and that if he didn't get out you might do something you'd both regret. You were really scary.'

'And you thought that was the real me?'

'No—well, I did then. But now…'

He smiled. 'We all have different sides to our natures. I do have a side that's brutal, cruel, unforgiving, but I save it for creatures like him. Don't worry. You won't see it.'

'I'm not afraid,' she said, not entirely truthfully. 'As you say, we all have different sides. My own cruel, unforgiving side is lurking somewhere.'

'Hovering about *me* a lot recently, I guess?'

'I must admit I had it all geared up and ready for you. But now I know how different you are from what I expected…'

'You think perhaps I'm human and not an unfeeling robot?'

'I never thought you an unfeeling robot.'

'Liar.' But the word was said gently, and with a touch of humour.

'I guess I deserved that,' she said. 'If you were unfeeling you couldn't be suffering about your father as you do. You've really taken me by surprise.'

'I think we've taken each other by surprise.'

Vittorio rubbed a hand over his eyes, suddenly feeling wrung out by the emotions swirling in his head.

'Perhaps it's time we left,' he said.

His weariness was growing by the minute, and the tension of the evening was becoming more than he could cope with.

He signalled to the waiter, who approached with the bill.

Watching him, Jackie was struck by the heaviness in his manner, and the way he kept closing his eyes. Alarm began to grow in her.

At last the bill was paid.

'Time to go home,' he said.

'No.' She laid a hand on his arm. 'Vittorio, I don't think leaving is a good idea. You're in no fit state to drive.'

'But I haven't drunk any alcohol. You know that.'

'I know, but you're shattered. Your head's spinning.'

'You're right. I didn't sleep well last night.'

'You didn't sleep at *all*. You spent most of the night wandering in the grounds.'

'How the devil do you know that?'

'I saw you from my window—several times.'

'Yes, I suppose I was pretty obvious. I kept meaning to go inside and get some sleep, but somehow I couldn't make myself do it. I should have done. It's left me tired. But that's not the only thing. This evening—I've never talked about all this before.' He met her eyes. 'With you, it's different. You understand things that nobody else could, and I've said far more than I meant to say. It's hard to cope with what I… Things I said that I didn't mean to.'

She laid her hand over his. 'Can't I help you?'

'You've already helped by being you. At first the past seemed to make us enemies, but it's also—' Words seemed to fail him.

'It's also opened a door of fellow feeling that we never imagined,' she said softly.

'Yes. Suddenly everything in the world seems to be different—I'm confused, but I'm also glad.'

'Perhaps it means that we really have managed to become friends?' she suggested tentatively.

He gave a wry smile. 'My best friend. Who would ever have imagined that?'

'Friendship can come out of the strangest places.'

'They don't come much stranger than ours.'

'And now, because I'm your friend, I'm telling you not to try to drive home tonight. It wouldn't be safe.'

'Don't panic. It'll be all right.'

'I don't think so.'

'You think I can't be trusted to drive properly?'

'I think you're not well enough. I've seen how you keep closing your eyes the way people do when their head's aching. You're in a bad way, and you could collapse at the wheel.'

'I promise not to. Now, let's go.'

Jackie took a deep breath. What she was about to say was momentous. 'No. Vittorio, if you get into that car I'll call the police.'

He stared at her. 'Did I hear you right? That's the act of a *friend*, is it?'

'Yes. A friend who's trying to protect you from harm. I guess that's something you're not used to.'

'I'm certainly not used to people telling me what to do.'

'Don't worry. Now *I'm* here you'll get used to it.'

'So what's going to happen? Will *you* drive us home?

'No way. I'm not a confident driver, and I couldn't handle the Italian roads at night.'

'Then what are we going to do?'

'This is an hotel. We can stay the night and leave tomorrow. I'll go to Reception and book us two rooms.'

She tried to rise but his hand tightened on hers.

'I'll see to it,' he said.

He summoned the waiter and spoke in Italian. The waiter nodded and departed.

After a few moments he returned and addressed Vittorio, also in Italian.

'Oh, hell,' Vittorio groaned.

'What did he say?' Jackie asked. 'He spoke too fast for me to follow.'

'They don't have two rooms available. Just one. A double room.'

'Then take it,' she said. 'You need to go to bed. I can sleep in the car.'

'Why would you do that? Don't you trust me to behave decently?'

'Of course. It's just that— Well—'

'It's just that I'm on the point of collapse. I couldn't seduce you if I wanted to. You're quite safe.'

He rose to his feet.

Suddenly he staggered, reaching out to grasp at something. But there was nothing there. Jackie leapt to her feet, just managing to catch him in time to stop him falling.

She supported him to the reception desk, where he booked the double room. The receptionist cast curious glances back and forth between them, but said nothing.

'I wonder what he's thinking,' Jackie observed as they went up in the elevator.

'I imagine we can guess what he's thinking,' Vittorio growled. 'I planned to tell him you were my wife, but—'

'You're too well known around here to get away with that one,' she supplied. 'It wouldn't have worked. Much better for him to think I'm your latest lover.'

'That doesn't worry you?' he asked curiously.

'Why should it? Who cares about *my* reputation?' She gave a teasing chuckle. 'Yours is another matter. But I expect they're used to you appearing in this situation. All right—don't answer that.'

'You're enjoying this, aren't you?' he demanded.

'Well, I admit the sight of your face just now gave me a little cheeky pleasure.'

Cheeky, he thought wryly. If ever a word described someone that one described her. And she loved it.

Not for the first time he reminded himself to be on his guard. But his guard never really protected him against her.

At last the elevator reached their floor, stopping with a shudder that disturbed his balance again. Instinctively he seized hold of her. She clasped him in return, leading him out into the corridor.

'Room thirty-seven,' he gasped.

A notice on the wall gave her the direction of the room, which luckily wasn't far away. He reached into his pocket for the key and opened the door.

The room was large, dominated by a double bed. Slowly she led him across the floor so that he could slide onto it. He lay down with relief.

'Let me pull the duvet back so that you can lie underneath,' she said.

'No, I'm fine as I am. Thank you for getting me here.' He squeezed her hand. 'You're a life-saver. I'm sorry to do this to you.'

'No need to be sorry. Friends help each other.'

'I thought I'd be able to cope...'

'But what was there to cope with?'

Vittorio struggled to find the words to tell her about how his own thoughts and feelings had overcome him. But they were taking him over again.

'Forgive me...' was all he could say.

'There's nothing to forgive. We all have bad spells sometimes.'

'But I didn't handle it very well, did I?'

It was true, but she guessed he wasn't used to this kind of burden.

'Go to sleep,' she said. 'You need it.'

'I should call Tania first. She'll be expecting us home.'

'Yes, but tell her we can't come home because you've met a business associate and need to talk to him. We have to stay until your serious discussion is over. I'll be taking notes—like a secretary.'

'But where are we supposed to be sleeping?'

'You in here. Me in another room down the corridor.'

'But there isn't one.'

'Tania doesn't know that.'

He managed a smile. 'I guess you're right.'

She picked up the phone. 'Give me the number and I'll call her.'

Tania answered at once. Jackie immediately handed the phone to Vittorio, who managed to assume a vigorous, cheerful voice. Jackie couldn't follow every Italian word, but she could just about understand that he was doing as she'd advised.

'Thank you,' he said, hanging up at last. 'That's bought us a little time. You're a great organiser. Perhaps I really *should* go into business with you—not as an employee, but as a partner.'

'You never know. We might surprise each other.'

'I'm sure of it. Heavens, but my head is aching.' He closed his eyes and rubbed his hand over them.'

'Go to sleep,' she said. 'You'll feel better in the morning.'

'Where are you going to sleep?'

'There's a sofa over there.' She pointed to the sofa beneath the window.

Vittorio looked at it in concern. 'You'll never be comfortable there. It's too narrow and not long enough. Sleep here. This is a king-size bed. We can each take one side.'

'Not while you're lying diagonally on it,' she said. 'It doesn't leave me any room.'

He made some awkward movements to the side, but they seemed to tire him.

'It's no good,' she said. 'You need the whole bed. Stretch out and get comfortable.'

'But what about you? Who'll look after *you*?'

'I'm fine. You're the one who needs looking after. Shall I get something to cover you?'

'No, I'm warm enough. You go and lie down.'

He watched as she backed away and lay on the sofa. He felt as though he was sinking into a different world, overtaken by another self—one who was reaching out to her for safety. He frowned, trying to understand the mystery, but suddenly all thoughts vanished and a warm darkness descended on him.

Watching him, Jackie saw the exact moment when Vittorio fell into sleep. At last, she thought with relief. Now he could find a little peace.

But almost at once he began muttering in his sleep, then tossing and turning as though driven by some inner torment. It troubled her to see him floundering towards the very edge of the bed. At last one agitated movement brought him so near that he started to slide off, and she hurried across to hold him just in time.

'Steady,' she said.

'Mmm…' he murmured.

She couldn't tell if he'd heard her, or even knew she was there. His eyes were still closed but his hands grasped her, as if clinging to safety.

'Move back,' she urged him.

'Mmm?'

'Move back before you fall right off.'

He edged backwards, still holding her. She followed, joining him on the bed but not getting too close.

Suddenly he turned, throwing an arm over her. His eyes were closed, and from his deep breathing she sensed that he was still asleep. She tried to nudge him away gently, but his arm tightened, drawing her close until his head rested on her shoulder.

Instinctively she wrapped her arms about him completely. She was amazed at the feeling that swept over her. This man, who always seemed so strong and determined, had aroused in her an instinct to protect. She knew that he needed the safety she could give him.

'Goodnight,' she whispered. 'Sleep well.'

His answer was a soft murmur. She couldn't make out the words, but she felt the movement of his lips against her neck and tightened her arms at the sensation that went through her. At once she felt his arms tighten in response.

He lay still for a while, but soon his lips began to move again. She leaned closer, trying to hear what he was saying, but the words were indistinguishable.

She could make out only one.

'Elena,' he murmured. 'Elena— Elena—'

Then he was silent again, leaving her wondering.

Who was Elena? Was she the woman he'd spoken of? The one he'd found in bed with another man? Or was she some other ghost that haunted him?

He spoke again. 'Jackie— Jackie—'

'It's all right,' she said. 'I'm here.'

She wondered if he'd heard, and perhaps understood. Now he lay still. She listened intently for anything else he might say, but there was no more mention of Elena.

Who *was* she? And why was she with him in his head at this moment?

At last she felt her own body relax.

Her last thought before she drifted into sleep was that somehow this was perfect.

Vittorio had the sensation of being in another world. As time passed thoughts and impulses disturbed him more, driving sleep away, so that at last he opened his eyes.

He had no idea where he was. He only knew that he was being held in an embrace so comforting that blissful feelings streamed through him. But gradually everything became real and he discovered that he was lying in Jackie's arms.

At first he couldn't believe it. It was a dream. It must be. But her warmth against him, the feel of her breasts beneath his head, were sensations of such sweetness that he was filled briefly with pleasure—and then with alarm.

How could he have let this happen? With what crazy

lack of caution had he yielded to the desire to enfold her in his arms?

But at least she was asleep. If he was very cautious she might never know.

Moving with great care, he edged away, holding his breath lest she awake and discover how vulnerable he could be where she was concerned. That was something that must never happen. Inch by inch he drew back his arm and then his head, retreating to the safety of the far side of the bed.

There he lay tense and still, watching her for any sign of wakefulness. To his relief there was none. After a while he turned over and lay facing away from her, trying to get his thoughts and feelings in order. It wasn't easy...

Submerged in peaceful silence and sleep, Jackie was unaware of passing time until she felt herself returning to the world and opened her eyes. Memories were there of holding Vittorio in her arms, feeling him cling to her. But now she lay alone, and his back was turned to her.

A faint sense of disappointment was followed by a stronger feeling of relief.

He'd claimed her as his friend, but they didn't yet fully trust each other—and if he knew how she'd embraced him while he was unaware he might feel suspicious.

And he would not be pleased, she was sure. She remembered that he'd told her he wouldn't seduce her even if he wanted to.

He didn't want to. There was no doubt about that. If he'd woken to find himself in her arms he would have been embarrassed. Luckily fate had saved her from that disaster.

But then she remembered how she had enjoyed the sensation of holding him, the feel of his body against hers. And she knew there was another disaster that threatened her.

He stirred and turned to her. 'Ah, you're awake,' he said. 'Did you sleep well?'

'Perfectly, thank you.'

'No disturbing dreams?'

'Not a thing.'

'That's all right, then.'

She thought she detected relief in his voice. He couldn't have said more plainly that there was nothing between them but practical matters.

CHAPTER EIGHT

THE BEDSIDE PHONE RANG. Vittorio answered it and found himself talking to Tania, who sounded agitated.

'Are you *mad* to have that woman in your room?' Tania demanded.

'I told you we were both staying here.'

'But not in the same room. I just called the hotel to speak to her and they told me where she is. Have you *no* common sense?'

Vittorio ground his teeth and spoke quietly, hoping Jackie would hear little and understand less. 'There was only one room available. We had no choice.'

'Can you assure me you haven't lost control?'

'I'm not even tempted. She doesn't like me, and our relationship is strictly business.'

'So she hasn't even tried to put her arms around you?'

Vittorio ground his teeth. 'No,' he said. 'She hasn't. Goodbye, Aunt.'

He slammed down the phone.

'What's she so upset about?' Jackie demanded. 'I could hear her yelling even over the phone.'

'She's shocked because we're in the same room. She's concerned for your virtue.'

'Concerned for *yours*, you mean. Does she think I lured you into a double room because I have a scheme in mind?'

'We both know that you didn't want to share my room, disliking me as you do. I've reassured her that you don't want me.'

'But can she believe that *any* woman wouldn't seize the chance to seduce you and perhaps become a countess?'

'I guess not.'

Jackie began to chuckle. 'I can't believe this is happening. The idea of me acting the role of *femme fatale* is ludicrous.'

'Don't put yourself down,' he told her. 'You've got your attractions.'

'Not the kind likely to appeal to a man who can have any woman he wants,' she said cheerfully. 'I'm a realist. How much did you tell your aunt about what happened?'

'Nothing. She asked if you'd put your arms around me. I told her you hadn't.'

'Well, that's true. It was you who put your arms around *me*.'

He stared. 'Did I?'

'Don't worry. You didn't know what you were doing. I came over to the bed because you were close to the edge and I was afraid you'd fall. You were flailing wildly about and suddenly you grabbed hold of me. I couldn't get away.'

'Didn't you thump me hard enough?'

'Damn! I never thought of thumping you. Stupid of me.'

'Want to try now?'

'No, I'll save it and get some practice first. When I finally thump you—oh, boy, will you know you've been thumped!'

He grinned, but it soon faded.

'So we just lay there all night? Did I do anything? Say anything?'

She was tempted to ask him about Elena, but she backed away from the thought. Some deep instinct told her that she would be better not knowing.

'You muttered a load of nonsense,' she told him cheerfully.

'In other words typical me?'

'I didn't say that.'

'You didn't have to. What about you? Did you talk to me?'

'A little. You seemed so agitated that I told you it was all right.'

Suddenly he could hear exactly what she had said then. *'It's all right. I'm here.'* Again he felt the peaceful sensation that had overcome him earlier, as he'd lain in her arms. Everything had been all right because *she* was there.

So she knew that they had clung to each other by chance, but not how they had lain together so gently. It was a relief that she didn't recall the moment and blame him for it, but also disappointing that she didn't share the memory of it with him.

He rose and went to the door. 'I'll go and sort the bill downstairs,' he said. 'Then we can leave.'

'Let's have some breakfast first,' she said. 'We don't want you falling asleep at the wheel.'

Turning to leave, he gave her a wry grin. 'I'll forget you said that.'

He closed the door softly behind him.

Somehow she must banish from her mind the sweet memory of lying in his arms. A shared memory would have been lovely, but he seemed not to know everything that had happened between them. So it would be dangerous for her to brood on it lest her feelings riot out of control.

After that it seemed best to be businesslike. Downstairs they ate breakfast, discussed sensible matters and left the hotel.

Vittorio's headache had gone and he was relieved to find himself driving at the height of his ability. That was what a restful night did. It was a reason to thank Jackie, but he mustn't tell her, he warned himself wryly . She would be sure to turn it against him in a cheeky challenge. There was just no way of coping with this infuriating woman.

But she was more than infuriating. Alarming, trouble-some, teasing, tempting, alluring. And never more than one of them for five minutes at a time.

They were almost home before Vittorio broke the comfortable silence between them. 'I hope we haven't got another problem waiting for us.'

'What kind of problem?'

'Tania. How do we cope with her suspicions about last night?'

'That's easy,' Jackie said. 'We assume indifference.'

'You mean we don't speak to each other? As if we've quarrelled?'

'No, that would only convince her she's right. When we get there, just follow my lead.'

As he'd been doing for the last few days, he reflected ruefully.

At last the car drew up outside the castle—and there was Tania, standing by the door.

As they headed towards her Jackie said, loudly enough to be heard, 'You're quite wrong about this, Vittorio. It would be a very poor purchase and not worth the money.'

Catching on quickly, Vittorio enthusiastically joined the conversation. 'Of course I respect your opinion, Jackie, but I think that item would be a good buy.'

They continued this back and forth until they were at the front door, where Tania was still waiting to greet them.

'What are you two arguing about now?'

'Ask her—*she's* the expert,' Vittorio said. 'I don't even understand.'

'Do you *ever* understand?' Jackie demanded. 'That thing looked good, but you're too easily fooled.'

'What thing?' Tania asked.

'Let *her* tell you,' Vittorio said. 'I'm going to get a drink.'

He vanished, leaving the two women regarding each other.

'What thing are you arguing about?' Tania asked.

'I can't even remember. We've seen so many things that he might buy, but he's being awkward.'

'Has he been misbehaving?' Tania asked.

'Only in one sense. He thinks he knows everything about business, but he doesn't understand as much as he thinks he does. And if you dare tell him he's got it wrong he gets insulted.'

'Then perhaps you shouldn't tell him.'

'Oh, I think I should,' Jackie declared. 'It's not good to let a person think they're always right about everything. Of course, certain people are *always* going to be convinced of that, no matter what.'

'It's lucky he can't hear you saying that,' Tania observed.

'He's heard me say worse. He knows I'm not afraid to condemn him. Luckily he doesn't care about my opinion any more than I care about his.'

'I was rather worried about you two being in the same bedroom last night.'

'Don't be. Nothing happened.'

Tania still looked unconvinced.

'Look, Vittorio doesn't want anything from me except efficiency in business. And I don't want anything from him either. So don't worry. I'm not trying to drag him up the aisle.'

Tania gave her an amused look. 'Am I supposed to believe that?'

'Believe it. All the others may yearn to be a countess, but I don't. He's quite safe from me.'

'Has he told you about how lively things are going to get soon?'

'No. Why? What's going to happen?'

'Every June we give a ball. Everyone comes from miles around. It's a huge, exciting event. You'll have great fun choosing something to wear.'

'Do people wear fancy dress?

'Some of them. Some wear conventional ball gowns and some wear historical costumes. We even have a Lady Nanetta costume you could wear.'

'I'll really look forward to this ball.'

'And I want you to enjoy it. Ah, there's Gina. Please excuse me, Jackie, but I must get on.'

After Tania had left Jackie headed up to her room, intending to type up the notes she'd made in Rome. But after a few minutes there came a soft knock on the door. She found Vittorio standing there, and stood back to let him in.

'That was a brilliant idea of yours,' he said. 'If we're arguing about business there can't be anything else between us.'

'I promised her I wasn't trying to drag you up the aisle.'

'I know. I heard you.'

'You—? You were *listening*?'

'Of course. Just behind the door. You're more fun to eavesdrop on than anyone I know. Nobody else complains about me with as much imagination as you do. But I seem to have improved in your estimation. Saying I always think I'm right isn't as bad as saying I'm cold and arrogant.'

'All right—enjoy your laugh. I have to be tough on you in front of Aunt Tania so that she knows I'm not one of the crowd chasing you. That way you can use me as a defence.'

He nodded. 'And you're the perfect defence.' He hesitated before saying, 'Are you all right after what happened last night?'

'*Nothing* happened last night,' she said firmly.

'No—of course nothing did. I only meant— Well, it was nice to be in your arms.'

So he *did* know, she thought.

'Yes,' she agreed. 'It was nice and friendly.'

He regarded her for a moment before saying softly, 'Just friendly?'

'I don't know,' she murmured. 'It's hard to say.'

He didn't answer at first. Then he placed his fingers under her chin and raised it, before dropping his head to brush her lips with his own.

'I'm sorry,' he whispered. 'I shouldn't have done that. I just wanted to know—'

'Yes,' she said. 'But it's not possible. We *can't* know.'

'Can't we?'

'It's too soon.'

'Too soon can be the best time—when you're learning about each other and want to know more. Am I offending you? Do you want to push me away?'

'No—no—'

He lowered his head again, placing his mouth on hers more intensely than before, although not enough to alarm her. She responded with pleasure, moving her lips gently against his and relishing his instant reaction. She felt his arms tighten and a tremor go through his body.

Where was this leading? Control was slipping away from both of them.

And then— 'I'm sorry,' Vittorio said, releasing her. 'That was thoughtless and selfish of me.'

He stepped back, leaving a clear gap between them.

'Was it?' she asked, bewildered.

'You're vulnerable. I should have remembered—'

'But—'

'Forgive me, Jackie. I didn't mean to— Just forget it ever happened.'

'Forget what? How can I forget something that didn't happen?' she said in a freezing voice.

He backed further away. 'You're right—it didn't. It couldn't happen because we have to understand— I'd better go.'

He turned and abruptly left the room.

Jackie stood motionless, possessed by such a fury that

she was tempted to hurl something at the door. She restrained the impulse, lest he hear and realise how he had affected her.

She could hardly believe how intensely she had responded to him. The touch of his lips, the feel of his embrace had started an excitement that had spread swiftly through her, igniting a fierce response.

The best part of it had been her awareness of a response in *him*. In one blazing, beautiful moment she'd known that he wanted her as much as he'd managed to make her want him. But then, in an assertion of strength, he'd silenced his own desire, rejecting her with a pretence of chivalry that didn't fool her for a moment.

Did he *know* that he'd inflamed her passion before rejecting her? Or didn't he care about her feelings while he was protecting his own?

No, she thought bitterly. He didn't care. He didn't care about her at all. To yield to his own needs would have meant letting her know that she had a kind of power over him. And that was something that he wouldn't risk.

All the power had to be on *his* side. He'd left to protect himself, not her.

Well, two could play the power game!

The next morning Jackie went downstairs to find only Tania waiting for her in the breakfast room.

'Your argument must have been fiercer than it seemed,' she said. 'Vittorio's gone away on estate business.'

'Doesn't he often have to do that?'

'Sometimes. There's a tiny village on the far side of his land, and he needs to stay there for a couple of days.'

Before Jackie could reply her cell phone rang. Answering it, she found herself talking to Gary, a salesman who had frequently called in to the shop in London, usually with good products to offer. They were on friendly terms.

'Hello, Gary,' she said cheerfully.

'It was quite a shock to find you missing. Are you going to be over there long?'

'Hard to say.'

'Well if you return to England, don't forget me.'

'Not a chance. It'll be nice to see you again.'

She hung up.

Tania was arranging things on the breakfast table.

'That looks lovely,' Jackie said, regarding the food. 'When I've had breakfast it's time I started attending to some business.'

'What business?'

'Vittorio has left me in charge of a new department in his store. There's a lot to do, and I must go into Rome and get to work.'

'You don't have to if you don't want to,' Tania said.

'But I *do* want to. He's paying me well and I'm going to work hard and earn it. I'm really looking forward to it.'

It was true. Taking charge of the new department could be exactly the kind of pleasure she would most enjoy. But instinct warned her of another aspect.

After what had happened in the hotel Vittorio had gone away in order to avoid her. Well, if he thought she was going to play the rejected woman—watching for his return, wondering when he would find time for her—he was mistaken.

Tania called her a taxi and she was soon on her way to Rome. Entering the store, she wondered what reaction would greet her. Had Vittorio really declared her authority as definitely as she'd believed he had?

Her fears were eased at once. The staff in her department greeted her respectfully—especially Lisa, the chief assistant.

'We have some new stock just delivered,' she said eagerly. 'We were about to start unpacking it.'

'Splendid. Let's get going.'

The next few hours were delightful. The new arrivals were glass items, elegant and expensive, not just dishes but also small statues of animals.

'These are incredible,' Jackie said, lifting one up to study it. 'I think this is a lion…'

'Yes, and this one is a tiger,' Lisa said. 'Over here we have a horse and a bear.'

'All made of glass and *so* lovely. Where shall we put them?'

'I think we already have buyers,' Lisa said suddenly.

Jackie looked up to find a husband and wife descending on them. They were entranced by the statues and insisted on buying every one.

'I can't believe that really happened,' Jackie said in a daze. 'One minute we'd unpacked them—the next moment they were gone.'

'You must have bought the right thing,' Lisa said brightly. 'We'd better replace them quickly.'

In a moment Jackie was back on the computer, contacting the manufacturer and concluding another purchase.

'I've ordered three times as many,' she said. 'And they'll be delivered tomorrow.'

Her staff cheered. Jackie wondered if she had ever known a happier occasion in her life. To be in charge, to see everything work out so well, to know that she was more than capable of handling the situation—all this inspired a pleasure and a satisfaction that was almost beyond her understanding.

She plunged back into work, loving every moment. When the time came to leave she was almost reluctant.

'I know the store's closing, but I've got so much I want to do,' she said, indicating the computer.

'You could stay the night,' Lisa told her. 'Signor Vittorio has a place where he sleeps.'

'Then I'll use that.'

Jackie called Tania, wondering if Vittorio had arrived home yet. But she told her he wasn't expected for another day.

'I'm staying here at the store tonight,' she said.

'But are you sure?' Tania asked. 'I can arrange a taxi—'

'I must stay. There's so much work to do that I can't leave. Vittorio gave me this job so that I can make money for him, and I mustn't neglect it.'

'Very well. I'll explain to him when he returns.'

A tiny bedroom, almost as small as a cupboard, was attached to Vittorio's office. Clearly this was an emergency refuge, for use only when he was so submerged in work that nothing else mattered.

The bed was narrow, but comfortable. Jackie had worked late before retiring for the night. Now it felt good to brood over the success of the day. She looked forward to displaying everything to Vittorio.

She was up early next morning, greeting the staff, watching closely as their work got under way.

'The delivery is here,' Lisa said excitedly.

'Great. We'll get it displayed at once.'

'But there is so much!' Lisa protested. 'Where can we put it all?'

'Over there,' Jackie said, pointing to a large cabinet. 'Move the stuff out of that and we'll have room for everything.'

They got to work. Jackie watched, delighted at the way everything was changing for the better—not just in the store but in her life.

'It's going to look wonderful,' Lisa declared. 'We'll have to move some more things but—'

Lisa checked herself, clearly distracted by something she'd seen a few feet away.

Turning, Jackie saw Vittorio. After a glance at his grim face Lisa scuttled away.

'Tania told me I'd find you here,' he said. 'She says you stayed all night.'

He was scowling, and he sounded angry.

Jackie regarded him, puzzled. 'That's right,' she said. 'I got so involved in my work here that I wanted to concentrate on it, so I was here all night. I'm sure you're glad to know I've been working hard.'

'I'm not sure I'm *glad* about what I'm seeing. You've taken over and changed a great deal here. I don't remember us discussing it.'

'We didn't discuss it. There was a lucky chance—new stock that sold well. I've simply bought some more.'

'Which I can see is being delivered now. When did you order it?'

'Yesterday.'

'Surely not. It can hardly have been delivered so soon.'

'Let me show you.'

She accessed the computer, bringing up details of the order, which Vittorio regarded with growing shock.

'Look at the price of that stuff!' he breathed. 'You've bought so *much* of it, and paid all that extra money for a fast delivery. And you've done it without consulting me. Are you trying to make me bankrupt?'

'Are you saying you can't afford it? This from the man who tried to bribe me with a million pounds?'

'Don't dare say that. I didn't try to *bribe* you. I just want to pay you what you're entitled to. This is quite different. It isn't about money. It's about you trying to push me aside and take over.'

'I'm not *taking over*. I'm just exercising the authority you gave me.'

'I never meant it to be like *this*.'

Her temper rose. Everything had seemed so wonderful before, and now he was ruining it.

She faced him with blazing eyes. 'You said I'd be in

charge of my own department. That I'd have a team who would take my orders. I thought you meant it—but perhaps I should have understood you better.'

'What the devil do you mean by *that*?'

'I should have realised that you're a man who says what suits him but doesn't mean a word of it. When I ask you to live up to your promises, you object. When I stand up to you, you can't cope.'

His face tightened. 'We've made jokes about you being a bully,' he snapped, 'but it's *not* a joke. That's what you are.'

'I do *not* bully my staff.'

'No, but you're trying to bully *me*.'

'Then we're equal. We're both bullies. That's why we can never get things right between us.'

'Don't tempt me to fire you!' he snapped.

'You don't need to. I resign here and now. It's over. Finished.'

'No, wait— Jackie—'

'I mean it. I *won't* put up with you dictating to me. It's not what we agreed.'

'We didn't agree about you meeting men behind my back, but that didn't stop you.'

'What?'

'That's why you're here, isn't it? This guy named Gary called and you hurried here to meet him yesterday. And you stayed the night,'

'Did Tania—?'

'Yes, she heard you talking to him. Where is he?'

'In England.'

He paused to give her a bitter glance, before turning away and heading for his office, where he wrenched open the door to the tiny bedroom. He saw that it was empty.

'Where is he?'

'He's in England,' Jackie said furiously. 'He never came here and I haven't seen him. I came here to get on with some *work*. Vittorio, you're out of your mind. It was pure chance that he rang when he did.'

'And you said you looked forward to seeing him.'

'Only when I go back to England—which will now be soon. I'm finished here. I can't work for you any more. You're impossible.'

He took hold of her at once. 'I don't want you to go.'

'I didn't ask what you want. I'm going.'

'You're not.' His grip tightened. 'We made an agreement—'

'Which *you* have broken.'

'That's not true. I promised you status and authority—'

'And you didn't mean a word of it.'

'You think so? Let's see if I can change your mind.' He glanced out through the door, where Lisa could just be seen. *'Lisa!'*

Lisa entered the office, looking back and forth between them with a puzzled frown.

'I want to talk to the other staff,' Vittorio said. 'See how many of them you can get in here.'

'Some of them are busy serving.'

'Just get the ones who are free. I have an important announcement to make.'

When Lisa had gone Jackie asked, 'What are you going to tell them?'

'Wait and see.'

'But isn't it something I need to know?'

'You mean I need your *agreement*? No way. Listen to what I have to say, and then you'll know everything.'

'But you can't—'

'Don't tell me what I can and can't do. I'm your boss. Whatever I say, you'll have to accept it.'

She could have screamed with frustration. His meaning was all too clear.

Rather than let her embarrass him by resigning, he was

going to shame her by dismissing her in front of an audience. She'd thought him better, more generous than this.

The rest of the staff were coming into the room. Vittorio's grip on her arm remained firm as he greeted them.

'Gather round, everyone. I've got an announcement to make which will probably surprise you, but it's the inevitable result of Jackie's actions over the last two days.'

Jackie tensed in anguish. Could this *really* be happening?

'You've all seen how she's plunged herself into work,' Vittorio continued. 'Increasing the stock, changing the arrangements. I reckon there's only one response I can make to everything she's done…' He took a deep breath. 'So I've decided to promote her. From now on she'll have a place on the leadership team and a significant payrise.'

A friendly cheer broke out, backed up by the sound of applause.

Jackie barely heard. She was staring at Vittorio, trying to believe the words that were spinning in her head.

He met her eyes, his own gleaming with ironic humour and something else that she wasn't sure she could understand. He leaned down, murmuring, 'Now you know what I wanted to say. Do you have any objections?'

'I don't know.'

Everyone crowded round her, patting her, congratulating her.

'I don't *think* I have any objections,' she said.

He leaned down again and whispered in her ear. 'Think about it and tell me later.'

'Yes,' she agreed.

Like everything else between them, it would have to be decided on later.

CHAPTER NINE

'WE'LL SETTLE THE details later,' Vittorio told his employees. 'For the moment all you need to know is that Jackie is a great power.'

He took Jackie's hand so that she had no choice but to follow him out of the building to a small restaurant nearby. 'Now for something to eat,' he said. 'After that I need something to boost my strength,' he added when they were settled at the table.

'So do I. You really enjoyed catching me on the wrong foot, didn't you?'

He turned, regarding her with an indignation that amazed her.

'*What* did you say?' he demanded. 'You think I caught you on the wrong foot? No way. You threatened to leave and I responded by improving your position. Who won? I'd say *you* did.'

'Oh, come on—'

'*You* come on. You've transformed the department to suit your own ideas. When I ventured to protest you reduced me to silence. Let's be clear who's the strong one—and it's not me.'

His tone was almost light, yet she detected a hint of definite annoyance.

She smiled at him. 'For a moment I thought you were really angry,' she said.

'No, I know how to accept defeat.'

'I wasn't trying to defeat you—'

'We'll have to disagree about that. But the sight of your face when I said you were promoted is something I'll always remember.'

'Did you really mean it?' she asked. 'It sounds so incredible.'

'Then you'll have to prove I got it right, won't you?'

'I'll try. And, however it may seem, I really *am* grateful. I thought you were going to dismiss me—'

'No way. You're far too valuable for me to risk throwing you away. You're going to make me a big profit.'

'But think of the money you've risked by doubling my salary.'

'True. I shall have to work you twice as hard.' He grinned. 'Perhaps you should be afraid.'

'The one thing I *can't* imagine is being afraid of you.'

'Is that true?' he asked ironically.

It wasn't, but just now it seemed better to be tactful.

'True enough,' she said. 'Thank you for what you did today. I'm really grateful.'

'So we're friends again?' he asked.

'I guess we are.'

He smiled and began to lean towards her. For a moment she thought he meant to kiss her, but suddenly his face lit up.

'Stefano!' he cried. 'Fancy finding you here!'

Looking around, Jackie saw a good-looking man in his thirties standing a few feet away. The man approached the table and sat down in the chair that Vittorio had pulled out for him.

When they had clapped each other on the shoulder Vittorio said, 'Jackie, let me introduce you to my great friend—Barone Stefano Fedele.'

She shook his hand. 'Signor Barone.'

'Call me Stefano,' he said, kissing her hand theatrically. 'A friend of Vittorio's is a friend of mine.'

'Come and eat with us,' Vittorio said.

'I would love to, but I'm in a hurry. I'll see you at the ball.' He grinned cheekily. '*If* I'm invited.'

'You know you are. Always!'

'It'll be a great evening. As always. Now, I must go, but I look forward to seeing you.'

He hurried away.

'What a nice man,' Jackie said.

'Yes, he's got a lot of charm. Too much sometimes.'

'Too much?'

'A bit of a flirt. Did you notice how he kissed your hand?'

'Yes. Charming…'

'His name means "faithful". And never did a man have a less appropriate name. He's what is politely known as a playboy. The impolite version you can probably imagine.'

'Okay, you've warned me. I won't go falling for him.'

'Do you *ever* fall for any man?' he asked with a touch of humour.

'That depends on the man. Sometimes I have to be wary of a man because he's nice enough to tempt me. Others don't fit the bill.'

'How long does it take you to decide which category a guy fits into?'

'It varies. Sometimes ten seconds is enough, and sometimes I have to give him a chance.'

She sounded well experienced in dealing with unwanted men, Vittorio thought. He wondered in which of the two categories she would place himself, and was briefly tempted to ask her—in a jokey manner. But caution made him resist the temptation.

He was still troubled by the memory of the kiss he had ventured to give her two days ago, and how it had affected him so intensely that he'd backed off in fear—rejecting her and rejecting his own inner self that had started to make him aware of things that troubled him.

He longed to know if the memory haunted her too. But he had an uneasy feeling that perhaps it amused her.

They barely spoke on the journey home. Once there, he returned to work in his office and she joined Tania, who was deep in planning for the ball.

'Things are building up,' she said. 'We've started receiving replies to the invitations. All acceptances. Nobody ever refuses.'

She showed Jackie the guest list, on which some names had been marked with a tick to indicate acceptance.

'You can tick Baron Stefano Fedele,' Jackie said. 'We met him this afternoon and he's looking forward to it.'

'You met him? Tell me more.'

Beaming, Tania listened as Jackie described the meeting.

'He's a good friend,' Tania said. 'And we need some of those to counterbalance the crowd of women who'll turn up and flaunt themselves. I wish we could keep them out, but they come from notable families and we have to invite them all out of good manners. We can't tell them to leave their daughters behind!' Tania sighed. 'By far the worst woman we will be forced to endure is the woman who betrayed my nephew in the past.'

'She's actually *invited*?' Jackie gasped. 'After what she did?'

'Her husband is the Duke of Revendo. His family have always been part of high society, invited to all notable occasions. If they were left out everyone would know why. And the gossip would be terrible. Vittorio simply can't risk having people giggle about how he was rejected by the Duchess because he wasn't noble enough.'

Jackie was stunned. In her mind Vittorio was the stern, determined man who had rescued her from Rik and used his strength to defend her. They had shared occasional jokes, and the night he had collapsed in the Rome hotel had shown her a gentler side to him. But never for a moment had he seemed as vulnerable as Tania's words now suggested.

Had something changed for him that night? Had there been a moment when he'd dreamed the woman lying beside him was the beloved he'd lost? Had she, Jackie, looked different to him ever since?

She couldn't tell. But suddenly, with all her heart, she longed to know.

Tania hesitated before asking quietly, 'Is everything all right between you and Vittorio—about that other man?'

'There isn't another man. I know you heard me talk to Gary on the phone, but I didn't go into town to meet him. He's in England.'

'Oh, dear. I'm afraid I told Vittorio about his call and…' She sighed helplessly.

'And he thought the worst because he thinks no woman can be trusted. Why is he so sure of that? I know about this woman who deceived him with another man, but surely he's had time to grow out of that?'

'You're right. It's not just her. It was his mother too. He adored her. They were very close, and he felt he was the centre of her life until she deserted him.'

'She ran away with another man?'

'No, she died in childbirth—but the baby came from an affair with another man. The baby died too. They're buried together. I once saw Vittorio looking at that grave, and what I read in his face was heartbreaking. He loved her so much, and had always felt she loved him, and yet she lay there with another son in hers arms for ever.'

'But that's terrible,' Jackie said. 'How could he bear it?'

'It still causes him great pain. To be fair, I can't entirely blame his mother. His father was never faithful. He slept with dozens of other women and she took refuge in affairs of her own. They did it to get back at each other, but it was their child who suffered.'

'And it's still with him, even now?'

'Yes. If even his *mother* couldn't be trusted, then he believes no woman can be trusted.'

'And then there was this girl who betrayed him?'

'Worst of all is our being forced to receive her at the ball. But now I suggest an early night,' Tania said. 'From now on we will have a mountain of work to do.'

As they left the room Jackie and Tania continued to discuss the ball for a while longer before Vittorio joined them. Tania was talking enthusiastically about the costume she planned to wear before turning to Jackie.

'Jackie, I really think you should wear Lady Nanetta's gown. What about you Vittorio? Modern evening dress?'

'No, if Jackie agrees I will be taking my costume from the guy in the picture next to Lady Nanetta. Let's have a look at him now.'

Vittorio and Jackie went to the gallery to find the picture he was talking about. Jackie studied it with fascination. He was a tall man in Regency attire. The trousers were white, the jacket dark blue.

'You're going to wear *that*?' Jackie asked.

'If I can get into it. I think I probably can.'

'All the women who want to be in your harem will love it.'

'If I wanted a harem I'd be flattered by that remark. As it is, I'll remind you that you're here to protect me.'

Tania appeared in the doorway of the gallery then, beckoning Vittorio over. He went to talk to her and Jackie went up to her room. She wanted to be alone to get her thoughts together.

She had been troubled before by a guilty feeling that she was enjoying this luxury at the expense of her father's suffering.

She reached into her bag. After few moments she found what she was seeking and took it out to study it. It was a photograph that she had taken of her father ten years ago. There was George's face, gazing back at her, his eyes as gentle and warm as she remembered them.

'That's a nice picture,' said a deep voice.

Turning, she saw Vittorio standing close. He had slipped in through the half-open door and come over to her without her realising.

'It's my father,' she said.

'I know. I recognise him from the picture my father had of him.'

'You have a picture of my father? Oh, please, let me see it.'

'I'll get it.'

He left her room, heading across the corridor to his own. Impulsively she followed him, and saw him going through a drawer, turning out papers. He handed a photograph to her, and she stared at it in astonishment.

'Yes, that's Daddy. And the other man is your father.'

'You say that as though you've seen him before.'

'The day after we met I went online to look up the Counts of Martelli. I was curious about you.'

'And you wanted to know if I was who I'd said I was, or whether I'd been telling you a pack of lies?'

He spoke cheerfully, without resentment, but she felt self-conscious enough to say, 'I didn't know you so well in those days.'

'And now you know me better you trust me even less?' he said, in the same light-hearted voice.

'It depends on the circumstances. Sometimes I think you're the biggest fraudster ever. At other times our minds seem to connect so well that...' She paused.

'That you don't believe me to be so bad after all?'

'You probably knew that already.'

'Well, whatever you think of me it's pretty obvious that our fathers got on well. This picture says a lot, don't you agree? It was taken in Italy. You can see that they were good friends.'

The two men faced the camera, grinning, arms raised exuberantly, clearly rejoicing in each other's company.

'They *do* look happy together,' she murmured.

'Yes, they do. There's no hint there of what was to happen later.'

'No. I don't think I ever saw Daddy enjoy himself so much.'

'Nor me. My father was a serious man, and an honourable one—or so I once thought. I don't recall ever seeing him bouncing with glee like this.'

In silence they met each other's eyes. Each knew what the other was thinking, but neither spoke. No words were necessary.

At last she said, 'Do you have any more pictures of your father?'

He rummaged in the drawer and produced a head shot. It depicted what Vittorio had described—a serious, honourable man, who looked incapable of any shameful action.

Jackie gazed at him, hoping her desperate emotion couldn't be seen on her face.

You did it, she thought. *You ruined my lovely father's life and got away with it. And your son thinks he can put it right with money because he can't understand that nothing can ever put it right.*

She handed the picture back.

Vittorio put it aside and clasped his hand over hers. 'I'm sorry,' he said.

'Don't be. He did it. Not you.'

'If only there was something you would let me do—'

'Stop it. *Stop it!*' she said quickly. 'Don't talk about it again.'

'Yes, it's dangerous ground, isn't it? Jackie, will we ever be able to risk treading that ground?'

'I don't know. Sometimes I think not—but how can we know?'

'We can't know,' he said. 'We can only hope.'

'Yes,' she murmured. 'But for the moment hope will take time.'

She hurried away, escaping to her own room and locking the door. She seized her father's picture again and looked at it for a long moment.

'Oh, Daddy,' she whispered, 'what shall I do? Please tell me?'

But if his loving eyes were sending her a message she could not understand it.

The next morning Tania departed to visit friends overnight. Jackie and Vittorio returned to Rome. She had noticed a small empty shop on a corner, and become fascinated by the idea of taking it over.

'It might be useful as a showcase for people who don't want to go to a huge store,' she said.

'That's an interesting idea,' Vittorio replied.

They spent some hours in the shop, which belonged to the man who lived above it. Vittorio made an offer that he accepted and the deal was quickly settled.

He finished the day by taking her into a nearby jeweller's shop and buying her a diamond necklace.

'That's—that's very generous of you,' she stammered.

'You've more than earned it. And if anyone asks you, tell them it was a gift from me.'

Thus supporting their pretence of being a couple, she thought. It was a severely calculated act, and there was nothing emotional about the gift, but she had to admit that it was beautiful and looked lovely about her neck.

'I need to call in to the bank,' he said. 'I won't be long.'

He was back in a moment, with an unusual, slightly mischievous look on his face that puzzled her.

'What's happened?' she asked.

'It'll tell you when we get home.'

'Why do you have to make a mystery of everything?'

'Because when a man knows he's doing the right thing he has to make sure nothing can get in the way.'

'Am I *likely* to get in the way of the right thing?'

'Let's say we don't always see eye to eye about what the right thing is.'

She longed to press him further, but felt it would be wise to wait until their journey was over.

At last they arrived home and he followed her to her room.

'Tell me,' she said, smiling with anticipation.

He produced a piece of paper from his pocket and handed it to her.

'You'll find the answer there,' he said.

Eyes wide, she opened it. In a moment she was overtaken by shock.

'What—what is this?'

'It's your bank statement.'

'But—how come—?'

The statement clearly indicated receipt of over a million British pounds converted to euros.

'How does that money come to be there?' she demanded.

'I put it there. You're entitled to it.'

'But I told you I wouldn't take it. You have no right to force it on me.'

'And you have no right to refuse it. It was something I *had* to do, Jackie.'

'Why? So that you can feel better about your thief of a father? I told you *no!* If you could have given it to Daddy that would have been right, but he's dead and it's too late. You can't ease his suffering now and you can't buy me off.' She looked at the statement again. 'When did you do this?'

'Yesterday. I called the bank and instructed them on the phone.'

'You dared to—?'

'I told them to take that money out of my account and transfer it to yours.'

'But I've told you a dozen times not to do anything like that,' she snapped.

'Don't *my* wishes count for anything?'

'Not when they make so little sense.

'No, it doesn't make any sense to you that I loved my father and can't forgive what was done to him. If he was alive and could accept the money himself, that would be fine. But he can't. And now it's your own feelings that matter to you. And your father's.'

'Jackie—'

'Listen to me, Vittorio, and try to understand. The only thing that would ever make things right would be if you gave back the money not to me but directly to Daddy.'

'But that's impossible!'

'Yes. It's impossible. And that's why we'll never agree about this. When you put that money in my account you did something bad and arrogant.'

She came to stand before him, regarding him with a cynical face.

'What trick did you play to get a copy of my bank statement? Do people obey you in everything?'

He seemed uneasy. 'Not everything, but they do know me at the bank. I told them that you're my fiancée.'

'You told them what?'

'I said we were going to be married.'

'And what happens when they find out you were lying?'

'I wasn't lying. Marriage would be the best thing for us, and I count on your good sense to make you see it.'

'Are you out of your *mind*? We're the last people in the world who should think of marriage.'

'On the contrary. We're the first. From the moment we met we've understood each other—'

'*No*. It's seemed like that sometimes, but all you understand is wanting your own way. This isn't about *my* father's suffering—it's about *your* father. You want to restore your image of him as a decent and honourable man. And I can't let you do that because of how guilty it would make me feel to let you buy me off. You don't understand how I could actually turn down your money. Tell me, Vittorio, has anyone in your whole life actually refused to let you buy them?'

'No,' he said, white-faced. 'People are sensible about money.'

'But I'm not sensible and hard-hearted. I'm human. I've got feelings. What would you know about that?'

'And what would *you* know about feelings?' he raged. 'The only one you have is hatred.'

'Just for you.'

'All this because I asked you to marry me?'

'But you *didn't* ask me. You told me that the decision had been taken—after you'd informed the rest of the world. Well, now you'll have to tell them that you got it wrong, because I'd sooner die than marry you. I want nothing from you—not your money *or* this.'

She seized the box containing the diamond necklace.

'Take it,' she said.

But he backed away, holding up his hands to ward her off. 'Jackie, please don't do this.'

'*I said take it.*'

She wrenched open the box, tore out the necklace and hurled it at him. He managed to seize it in time to stop it hitting his face, and tossed it back into the box.

'We won't talk about this now,' he said. 'Not while you're in such a state. When you've calmed down you'll see matters more rationally.'

'Don't fool yourself. I know what you mean by "rationally". It means me seeing things from your point of view. Well, that will never happen. I can't stand the sight of you, I can't bear to be in the same room as you, and I never want to be with you again, you monstrous bully. Now, get out. I'm leaving.'

He left at once, anxious to get away from the hate-filled atmosphere.

Jackie watched him go and locked the door. At all costs he must not be allowed to return.

Oh, how she hated him. Once she might have loved him, but not any longer. Not now that he'd insulted her with an offer of marriage and money. It might seem crazily illogical, but this man had inflamed her feelings and then tried to take possession of her as a business venture.

Now there was only one thing left that she could do.

She had to get out of here. To get away from him and fast.

She threw her things into her suitcase and checked to be sure she had her passport and purse.

It would be a long walk to Rome, and briefly she considered asking Leo, the chauffeur, to drive her. But she abandoned the idea as risky. She must walk.

Before leaving, she wrote a note to Vittorio.

I'm sure you realise why I have to go. It wasn't working between us and it never would.

She slipped it under his bedroom door. Then she went to the back staircase, where she could descend unseen. At the bottom she found herself near the back door. She would be able to slip out unnoticed.

She began to walk. Her best hope lay in reaching the main road, where she might get a bus or a taxi the rest of the way. But her walk went on and on with no sign of hope.

The light was fading, and when a hut appeared in the

distance ahead of her she could only just make it out. It had started to rain. Just a soft drizzle at first, but it had swiftly become a downpour. She began to run, heading for the hut, hoping to reach it quickly, but she was already soaked when she got there.

Opening the door, she saw that it was shabby. In the poor light she could see little else, but there was at least a bed where she would be able to rest until light broke next morning.

She stripped off her clothes, seizing the small towel she'd brought with her, and drying herself as well as she could. She put on some basic items from her suitcase and lay down.

Gazing into the darkness, she wondered at herself for choosing this way out.

Might she not have stayed in the *castello* with the man who had once seemed to be winning her heart? Did she *really* have no chance of winning his?

Maybe she was being cowardly, running away, but what choice did she have? How could she stay with Vittorio knowing she could never win his love when he was so determined not to let her? No, she'd served her purpose. He'd paid the debt, assuaged his guilt, and now he'd surely be relieved to see her gone. Besides, she was glad to get away from him—wasn't she?

CHAPTER TEN

FOR WHAT FELT like hours Vittorio sat at his desk, trying to concentrate. At last he threw down his pen and faced facts. As so often before, the infuriating woman had wiped everything except herself from his mind.

If they were to have a future together she'd have to learn that he must sometimes think of other things. And the sooner they sorted it out the better.

He went to her bedroom and opened the door.

But she wasn't there.

Downstairs, he searched room after room without finding her. Tearing his hair, he went to the kitchen to find Gina.

'Do you know where Jackie is?' he asked.

'I saw her go out an hour ago.'

'Go out? Where?'

'For a walk, I think. She was carrying a case, but she couldn't have been going far or she'd have asked Leo to drive her.'

'Did she leave a message?'

'No, Signor Conte.'

So now Gina knew he'd been deserted, and suddenly it was unbearable that she should see him at such a moment.

In fury and despair he ran upstairs to his bedroom. There on the floor he found Jackie's note, and read it with mounting disbelief.

Downstairs he confronted Gina again. 'Which direction did she go?'

'In that direction.' She pointed through the window.

The path she indicated led to the main road and ulti-mately to Rome. Given the note Jackie had left him, the meaning was obvious.

'Poor Jackie,' Gina said. 'It's raining so hard now. How terrible for her. Shall I tell Leo to go after her?'

'No need,' Vittorio said through gritted teeth. 'I'll go myself.'

The rain seemed to get heavier as he headed for the car. What on earth had possessed her to do this?

The only possible answer appalled him.

She was heading for Rome—perhaps the railway sta-tion, perhaps the airport. Whichever it was, she was on her way back to England, leaving him with her cruel message and nothing to hope for.

Through the darkness the car's headlights flooded the road ahead, showing no sign of her. But she *must* be some-where near here, he thought frantically. In the time she'd had to walk she couldn't have got much further than this.

Then he saw the hut, and pulled up quickly.

There were no lights on inside, but he had a torch in the car and took it with him.

He opened the door tentatively, unable to see much. 'Is anybody there?' he called.

The response was a choking sound. Turning his torch to the far wall, he saw Jackie lying on a bed.

'Jackie!'

He rushed forward and knelt beside the bed.

'What the hell are you doing, leaving like this?' he de-manded. 'Are you mad?'

'Yes,' she murmured. 'I had to get away from you.'

'Because I'm a monstrous bully. That's what you called me, and you were right. I'm a bully and I'm about to prove it. I'm taking you home with me. Don't argue. You're com-ing with me whether you want to or not—because you're soaking wet and I'm not leaving you here to get pneumonia. If you refuse then I'll be forced to carry you.'

'You think I'm just going to give in to your bullying?'

'Why not? When we were in that hotel you bullied *me* to stop me driving home and I gave in, didn't I?'

She rubbed a hand over her eyes. 'Then I guess I can't say no...' She sighed.

'Wise woman.'

He helped her to her feet. At once she swayed, making him seize her urgently.

'I'd better carry you anyway,' he said.

'No, I can manage.'

'Jackie, please—'

'I said I can manage. Let me go. I don't need your help.'

He released her, but stayed close, keeping his hands only a few inches away, so that she could cling to him if necessary. She managed to get to the door without needing him, but then let him support her the last few yards.

She had insisted that she didn't need his help, but as he eased her into the car she had to admit that she wasn't sorry to be returning to warmth and comfort.

Ten minutes brought them back to the house, where Vittorio parked the car before helping Jackie out.

'Go up to bed,' Vittorio said. 'I'll send Gina to dry you off and make sure you're well.'

It was lovely to snuggle down in the comfortable bed, and even lovelier to reflect on what had just happened. True, Vittorio had shown his authoritative side, insisting that she return. But he'd also shown his kinder side, looking after her carefully as he'd driven home.

It was the same old confusion. Which man *was* he? The coldly authoritative one who would tolerate no disagreement? Or the gentle, concerned one who kept a kind eye on her needs?

He was both, she decided.

There was a tap at the door.

'Can I come in?' he asked.

'Yes, come in.'

'I had to see how you were.'

'I'm very sleepy, but I don't feel too bad.'

'Then you must have a nice long sleep.'

He reached out for the blanket and drew it up over her shoulders. She snuggled down blissfully.

'I'm sorry if I caused you a lot of trouble,' she said. 'It was just—'

'I think I know what it was.' He sat down on the bed. 'When you're better we must have a talk to see if we can sort out all the ways we misunderstand each other. It's strange when you remember how many times we've noticed how well our minds connect. Yet sometimes the connection fails.'

'It comes and goes,' she mused, 'but will we ever really understand each other? We're so different.'

'*Are* we different? Haven't we found a hundred ways in which we're the same?'

'Yes,' she murmured, 'I guess so…'

As she spoke her eyes closed. Vittorio watched as her breathing grew deeper, more peaceful. When he was sure she was asleep he took a gentle hold of her hand.

'It's been a lesson for both of us,' he said. 'And there's still some way to go. But we'll get there, won't we?'

When she didn't reply he leaned down and whispered in her ear.

'We will, because we must. We really must, Jackie.'

He laid his lips softly against her cheek and left the room quickly, before she could wake.

Jackie slept well that night, and the next morning went downstairs to find Vittorio already eating breakfast.

'How are you this morning?' he asked.

'Fine.'

'Good. We must get things sorted out.'

'What things?' she asked cautiously.

'We've got the ball to think about. It wasn't very kind to Tania, the way you dashed off. Hate *me*, if you want to, but don't take it out on her.'

'I don't hate you.'

'Really? You could have fooled me.'

'That was because you'd forced that money on me. You're so sure you can buy me off, aren't you? But you can't. I want you to take it back.'

'No way.'

'If you don't take it back I'll be out of here tomorrow.'

'You'll—? After all we—? Surely we agreed on that?'

'No, you *thought* I'd agreed because I shut up about it. But I still feel the same. If I accept that money I'll be saying that my father's suffering doesn't matter. But it *does* matter. It matters more than anything in my life. It would be an insult to him that I couldn't endure. Why do you want to make me suffer?'

'The last thing I want is for you to suffer,' he said, speaking the truth.

'Then what are you going to do?'

He picked up the phone, dialled a number and engaged in a sharp-sounding conversation in Italian.

When he'd put the phone down he said, 'I've told the bank that transferring that money to you was a mistake and they're to transfer it back.'

'Will it work? Won't they say that since it's in my account I have to tell them myself?'

'Perhaps they should—but they'll do what I tell them. Let me show you.'

In his office he switched on a computer, logged in to his bank and showed her that the money had immediately been transferred.

He stared at the screen, feeling blank despair at what it told him. He'd promised his father to return the money to Jackie, and felt glad when he'd managed to do so. But now he'd yielded, taken it back, and in his heart he'd betrayed his beloved father.

Jackie was also staring at the screen, trying to take in the incredible sight that she could see.

'They just obeyed you,' she murmured. 'However did you persuade them?'

'I've got a place on the board.'

'Of course. Why didn't I think of that? Is there anywhere you *don't* have power?'

Suddenly his temper rose. 'Are you out of your mind to say that? You just told me what to do and I did it. Who obeyed whom? And you dare to accuse *me* of having all the power.'

'I'm—I'm sorry,' she stammered. 'I didn't think—'

'Do you *ever* think? You've got it so firmly fixed in your mind that I'm a controlling bully that you never look at our relationship closely enough to see how often it's the other way around. You told me to get on to the bank and transfer the money, and I did it straight away!'

'Yes, I'm sorry. I didn't see it that way—'

'No, because it doesn't fit your convenient picture of me. Heaven help me if I do something that doesn't fit your expectations. You'll wipe it out of your mind the way you tried to wipe *me* out.'

'Stop it,' she cried, suddenly weeping. 'Please stop.'

Tears had come without warning. She turned her head but it was too late. He'd already seen them.

'Hey, come on, there's no need for that.' His rage vanished and he took her into his arms, resting her head on his shoulder. 'Don't cry,' he said kindly.

She pulled herself together and drew back.

'You're wrong,' she said huskily. 'I *do* know you can be nice.'

'However hard it is for you to admit it?' he said, smiling. 'I'm sorry.'

'Enough of that. It's good that we're talking. We can sort everything.'

'Can we? There's so much to be sorted.'

'I know. But we can do anything if we try. Come here.'

He drew her close and placed a kiss on her mouth. It was gentle rather than passionate, and it warmed her heart.

'Sit down and have some coffee with me. Then we can plan what we're going to tell Tania.'

'She doesn't know about what happened yesterday?'

'Nothing happened. As far as she's concerned you didn't dash off and banish me into the wilderness.'

'I certainly didn't banish you into the wilderness!'

He regarded her wryly. 'That depends on what you mean by "wilderness".'

He guessed she had no idea of the bleak desert in which he'd found himself when he had found her gone. It had felt like the worst kind of wilderness. And that had alarmed him because clearly there was no wilderness for her.

'We'll have to get to work on the ball,' he said. 'Tania's counting on our help.'

'Yes. You're right. I should have thought of that before I left. I was selfish.'

He touched her face. 'You're not selfish. You just panicked at the thought of being stuck with me for life. We all panic.'

'You? Surely not. I can't believe you *ever* panic.'

Briefly he recalled the wild churning of his stomach when he'd found her goodbye note.

'You're right,' he said quickly. 'Not me. Ever. Now, let's—'

He was interrupted by a beep from the computer.

'It's an email I've been waiting for,' he said.

He did a quick check and opened the new message.

'It's from the store,' he said. 'Some stuff we ordered has started to arrive. I need to be there.'

'I'm coming with you. We'll go to the store and then on to the railway station to meet Tania.'

They drove into town, straight to the store, where they found a mountain of new arrivals. Jackie was briefly nervous, lest they be more of the glass statues that had caused their row, but these were different items. They had come from England and they pleased Vittorio.

'Great,' he said, looking at them. 'Well done, Jackie. I did the right thing promoting you and doubling your salary. You're really benefitting the store.'

She smiled and thanked him, but at the back of her mind was a sense that his action was rooted in their disagreement over money that constantly haunted them. It was always there. When he couldn't give her money one way he found another way to lavish it upon her. Would this nightmare ever go away?

Another thought troubled her. She knew the need to fulfil his father's wishes was so vital to Vittorio that he would seek to keep her close to him until he'd achieved what he sought. Was it anything but that? When he had eased his pain would he feel able to dismiss her?

For another half-hour they worked in his office. Then a knock on the door made him look up to see Donna from the clothes department.

'I've brought what you ordered, Signor Conte.'

Carrying a large parcel, she advanced into the room, laid it on his desk, and departed.

'Have a look,' he said to Jackie. 'It's yours.'

Puzzled, she opened the parcel—and stared at what she found there.

'The dress!' she gasped. 'The one—'

It was the black satin dress she'd tried on when she'd first visited the store.

'It's a gift,' he said.

'You're *giving* this to me? You mean that?'

'You can wear it at the ball.'

'But Tania says I'm supposed to be Lady Nanetta.'

'That's up to you. You *can* be Lady Nanetta—severe, rigorous, terrifying every man she meets. Or you can be a different woman...the one I saw in this gown the other day.'

'And what is *she* like?'

'I'm not quite sure. I'm still waiting to find out.'

In truth, he felt he already knew. When he'd chanced upon her wearing the seductive gown, its satin clinging to her figure, he had discovered something startling about her and how she could affect him. The time had not yet come when he could speak of it, but the moment *would* come. He promised himself that.

'I'll wear it with the diamond necklace you gave me,' she murmured.

'And you'll be the belle of the ball.' He paused. 'You know, it would help me if we could seem like we're even more of an item. Maybe engaged? And it will help you look the part. I don't want Marisa and the others to think I'm in need of a wife!'

'Okay, I'll do my best,' she agreed simply, knowing if she said much more she would start grilling him about exactly what he was looking for.

And she didn't even know what she wanted as the answer. Did he want a bride—just not Marisa? Or did he not want a bride *ever*?

'Come now,' he said, interrupting her thoughts. 'Let's take this with us and go to meet Aunt Tania at the station.'

When the train drew in an hour later they were there, waiting for Tania.

'Lovely to see you both,' she declared when they had

all embraced. 'How are you getting on? Not strangled each other yet?'

'We're saving that until after the ball.' Jackie chuckled.

'Splendid. Nice to know that you can put important things first. We've got a mass of things to do…'

From the moment the next day dawned it was clear that Tania had been right. The castle was buzzing with preparations.

Over the next few days quantities of extra food were delivered and temporary staff were hired. A television company had even made contact.

At last the great day arrived. In her room, Jackie donned the black satin gown.

'Can I come in?' Vittorio called.

'Yes.'

He entered the room. 'How's this?' he said.

He was wearing the historical costume of the man in the portrait of Lady Nanetta. Jackie stood back to survey him, hardly able to believe her eyes. As had been fashionable at the time, the white trousers were tight-fitting, emphasising the fact that Vittorio's legs were long, slim and attractive.

And sexy, she thought, against her will.

'What do you think?' he asked, turning to give her a better view.

'I think that costume is very…efficient,' she said coolly.

'Yes. Luckily it fits me. And I think *you* chose the right dress. That one will lure every man in the room.'

'*Every* man?' she teased. 'Every single man?'

'Well, you can't ignore me tonight, can you? Not when everyone's expecting to hear that we're engaged.'

'No, I promise to do whatever you want.'

'Do you *know* what I want from you?'

She looked up at him with shining eyes. 'I'm sure you'll let me know.'

'You can count on it. Now, we must make everything perfect. Why aren't you wearing the necklace I gave you?'

'I've tried to put it on but I can't fasten it. It's too difficult.'

'Give it to me.'

He took the necklace and moved behind her, reaching around her neck to position the jewels. She tensed at the feeling of his fingers brushing her flesh.

At last he turned her so that he could look at her face. 'Are you all right?' he asked. 'Nervous?'

'I'm fine.'

From outside they heard the noise growing.

'People are beginning to arrive. Let's take a look.'

Going to her window, they looked out. They could see cars arriving, discharging their passengers. Wide-eyed, Jackie looked at the costumes that were appearing.

Some were obvious fancy dress—clowns, animals—others were historical costumes.

Tania appeared behind them.

'You look very fine,' she told Jackie. 'You'll be a big success. *Oh!*'

The exclamation was drawn from her by the sight of a splendidly attired couple whose arrival had caused others to stare in admiration.

'Whoever are *they*?' Jackie asked in astonishment.

'The Duke and Duchess of Revendo. I must go down and welcome them in.'

Tania vanished, leaving Jackie staring down at the couple.

So *that* was the woman who had broken Vittorio's heart by dumping him for a loftier man. She turned her head to look at Vittorio. He was looking down at the Revendos but his face revealed nothing at all.

It never does, she thought. *Whatever he's feeling, he*

doesn't want anyone to know. It's almost as though he's afraid of the world.

She gave a brief gasp of laughter.

Afraid of the world. He'd be so mad at me if he knew I was thinking that.

But it was true. Vittorio didn't trust anyone. Even her.

'What's funny?' Vittorio asked sharply.

'Nothing. Why?'

'You laughed. Why? Is the crowd below so funny?'

'Some of them.'

'Meaning Elena Revendo? I expect Tania's told you about her, hasn't she?'

'Yes,' she said reluctantly. 'But you told me about her first. How can you bear to invite her?'

'Why not? She did me a great favour. Because of her I know things about female deceit, ambition and greed I might not have learned soon enough to be useful. As it is—'

'As it is you learned that lesson in time to distrust every woman you ever meet. Good for you. What would life be like if you made the mistake of *trusting* a woman?'

He regarded her wryly. 'There *is* one woman I trust,' he said. 'One who isn't greedy for money or a title, who's intelligent, honest, and brave enough to express her opinion even when it annoys people.'

The gleam in his eyes made it obvious that he meant her. It might be unwise to feel flattered by such ironic praise, but she couldn't help it.

'You mean when she annoys *you*,' she said. 'Does she annoy anyone else as much as you?'

'I doubt it. Infuriating me is something she's brought to an art form.'

'She sounds like a nightmare,' she observed lightly. 'For safety's sake you should avoid her like the plague.'

'I try, but she has a habit of popping up in my mind when I'm not expecting her.'

'Then the answer's obvious. Expect her all the time. She's so awkward that it'll make her stay away just to confuse you.'

He grinned. 'Yes, she enjoys confusing me.'

From below, they could hear the orchestra start to play. 'It's time we went down,' he said.

Offering her his arm, he walked with her, out and along the corridor to the top of the stairs.

As soon as they appeared there was a squeal from below. Everyone looked up to enjoy the sight of their elegant entrance. Some of them laughed, some cheered, some applauded.

Jackie had no difficulty seeing Marisa's face. She was at the front, staring up at them with an expression that could not hide her dismay.

Wondering if Vittorio had noticed, she gave him a sideways glance. He returned it, smiling. She smiled back, happy to know they were in this together.

Marisa, watching them from below, scowled.

Most of the guests had heard about Jackie, and eagerly crowded forward to be introduced to her. It was clear she was the star of the evening, and every guest, male and female alike, seemed to be charmed by her.

Vittorio revelled in the attention Jackie was receiving, but soon enough was enough. He wanted her to himself for a while.

'Shall we dance?' he asked.

Together they proceeded to the ballroom, where the orchestra had just started a waltz.

'We've fooled them,' he said, turning her gently around and around. 'Let's give them a bit more.'

'By doing what?'

'Can't you smile at me as though I'm your heaven on earth?'

'But what would that prove?' she asked. 'Only that I'm

one of the crowd chasing you. Now, if *you* smiled at me that would be better. But don't worry. I understand why you don't want to.'

'Don't I?'

'Heaven on earth? *Me?* More like purgatory, driving you mad.'

'Which is just how you like it.'

'I can't deny that.'

They laughed together. Those dancing near them observed them and assumed that they were in perfect accord and exchanged significant glances.

'Now we've *really* given them something,' she teased.

'And if they were to hear me tell you that you look wonderful tonight they'd enjoy that even more.'

'No, don't say that. Some of them already want to murder me.'

'But I *want* to say it.' He raised his voice. 'You're lovelier than I've ever seen you.'

'Hush, don't overdo it.'

They laughed again. Then he whirled her around and around until the music came to an end.

'That was a great dance,' he said. 'I hope we can have another one before the night is over.'

'I'm sure we can. But now you have your duty to do with every hopeful woman here.'

'Yes, ma'am.'

Turning away, she found herself facing Vittorio's Baron friend—the one she had recently met in the city.

'Stefano,' she said happily. 'How lovely to see you.'

'And you, *signorina*. I remember our meeting with great pleasure. Since then I've hoped to meet you again. Shall we dance?'

'That would be lovely.'

He put his arm around her waist, drew her close, and began to spin her into the dance.

CHAPTER ELEVEN

STEFANO WAS AN expert dancer, and Jackie found her own moderate skills rising to meet his. It was an exhilarating experience. With his help she discovered her feet could move faster and in more complex movements than she had ever dreamed.

'That was great,' he said as the music ended. 'Now let's waltz together.'

'Yes, let's,' she said, moving into his open arms.

The gentle movements of the waltz made it easier for her to look around at the other dancers. One couple stood out. Vittorio was dancing with the Duchess of Revendo.

'Oh—' she gasped.

'What is it?' Stefano asked. 'Are you feeling unwell?'

'No, I'm fine. Everything's fine.'

'I'm not sure I believe you. When people say it like that things are never really fine.'

'Yes, they are,' she said quickly.

This was something she couldn't bear to talk about. She tried to catch a glimpse of Vittorio's face, to see if it revealed any emotion. But as he whirled around with the woman who had once meant everything to him there was only a blankness in his face that might have meant indifference, or an emotion too strong to reveal.

But then he smiled. And his partner smiled back at him. And suddenly they seemed magically connected.

It lasted only a moment before they turned away, out of

Jackie's sight. She took a deep, troubled breath, wondering what life was doing to her and what it would do next.

'You're not going to have any trouble finding partners,' Stefano said as the dance came to an end. 'Look at them all, watching you.'

He was right. There was another offer for her to dance, and then another. She accepted two partners, and then Stefano came forward and claimed her again.

'You're the belle of the ball,' he said as they twirled.

'Only because I'm dancing with the best dancer in the room!' she said. 'I gather you've got quite a reputation.'

'For dancing?'

'Only partly,' she teased.

She recalled what Vittorio had said about Stefano and his reputation as a playboy.

He was handsome, delightful, and he could make her laugh. Many women would have fallen for him, but these days Jackie was too wise. All sorts of new feelings had grown within her now, protecting her from a man as obvious as this.

But to spend a few minutes dancing with him was an innocent pleasure.

'How are you coping with Vittorio?' he said.

'He's not easy, but I don't manage too badly.'

'Everyone knows he's in love with you and heading for the altar.'

'Nonsense,' she said firmly, remembering Vittorio's face as he'd danced with the Duchess.

'Apparently he told someone at the bank that you were engaged.'

'Oh, that—oh, no. That was just a careless mistake.'

He chuckled. 'Who do you think you're kidding? If there's one man who would never make that kind of mistake it's Vittorio.'

'Yes, but—I'm not one of those women chasing him.'

'Of course you're not. That's why you've caught him.'

'Oh, nonsense. I haven't.' She thought for a moment. '*Have* I?'

'Don't you think you have? Or didn't you want to?'

'I haven't quite decided about that yet.'

A burst of laughter overcame him and Jackie joined in, unable to help herself.

Feeling her shake in his arms, Stefano grasped her more firmly. 'Steady,' he said. 'Don't lose your balance. Hold on to me.'

She did so, and felt herself once more whirled dramatically across the floor,'

Standing near the door with Vittorio, Tania was regarding them with her head on one side.

'The man Jackie's dancing with,' she said. 'Isn't that Stefano?'

'Yes.'

'I hope you warned her about him. Women lose their hearts to him so easily.'

'Not Jackie,' Vittorio observed. 'She never loses her heart to *anyone*.'

'Is that personal experience talking?' asked Tania curiously.

'It could be.'

'But you haven't decided yet? Perhaps you should take your own advice.'

'What advice is that?'

'You once told me that a shrewd businessman never lets a good deal escape him. Seize it while it's going, you said. Perhaps *there's* your deal.'

'A businessman?' he murmured. 'Is that all I am?'

'At one time you'd never have doubted it.'

'At one time I was a different man.'

As they watched the dance ended. At once another man appeared to claim Jackie, who went happily into his arms.

The two of them waltzed contentedly until the music ended, at which moment two more young men approached her, both trying to claim her. All around them the other dancers paused to enjoy the sight.

'Don't let a good deal escape,' Tania urged.

'You're right,' he said. 'Time I acted.'

He strode out onto the floor, arriving just as the two hopeful men were getting deep into argument.

'Sorry to break up the party,' he growled. As he spoke he put his arms around Jackie, drawing her close in a clasp too firm for her to resist. 'But the lady belongs to *me*.'

'Do I?' she asked lightly.

'You do. And if you don't know it now you soon will.'

Vittorio knew a strange feeling as he took her into his arms. Only a few minutes ago she'd been dancing with a well-known charmer, gazing up into his face, collapsing with delighted laughter, and then whirling away with him as though aiming for another world.

Now she was in his own arms, looking coolly up into his eyes and thinking—

Just what *was* she thinking? What lurked behind her gaze?

'I warned you not to fall for Stefano,' he said.

'I didn't. I was just being polite.'

'Polite to him *and* every other man in the room—thus making me look an idiot.'

'Why should it affect you?' she asked lightly.

'Because there's a rumour that we're engaged.'

'A rumour *you* started, for your own convenience. You just wanted to get the better of me about our disagreement.'

'And yet somehow you're the one who always finishes on top,' he observed. 'Isn't that strange?'

'Not strange at all, seeing that I've got right on my side,' she said.

'You *always* think that, don't you?'

'Sure—it's something I learned from you. Oh, boy, the things you've taught me! Get your own way at all costs. Never ask anyone else's opinion, and if they dare to offer one tell them to shut up.'

'I didn't ever tell you to shut up,' he protested.

'Not in words, but you don't need words. Why are you complaining? I had a few dances…enjoyed some innocent fun. It didn't do you any harm. We're not really a couple. We just made a bargain.'

He didn't answer. He had an uneasy feeling that the bargain was slipping away.

'Vittorio, listen to me. You claim that all women are deceitful liars, playing one man off against another. So what are you saying now—that I'm just one of them? Am I no better than the Duchess?'

'Leave her out of this.'

'How can I when you made such a point of dancing with her?'

'That was a courtesy. I danced with her to show that she doesn't trouble me. She did once, but now when we meet things are different.'

'Different? That could mean anything.'

'It means that my heart no longer belongs to her. It belongs to someone else—but I shouldn't have to tell you that. You should know without words.'

'Perhaps,' she whispered. 'But sometimes words can help.'

'Or they can make things worse—which they often do with us. Why are you so determined to quarrel with me, Jackie?'

'*I'm* determined to quarrel?'

'You know how badly I want to sort things out between us. Maybe I was clumsy about the money, but I was desperate to put things right between us, to make you stop hating me because of your father. You can see that, but you won't yield an inch.'

'Why *should* I? Stop this, Vittorio. You talk of putting it right, but nothing will *ever* put it right for my father because he isn't here any longer. If I took the money from you his tragedy would still be the same as it always was. The only difference would be my conscience, tormenting me because I'd benefitted from his suffering, knowing that after all his lovely treatment of me I'd just shrugged my shoulders and said it didn't matter.'

'Would he have blamed you for that?'

'No, he'd have told me to put myself first.'

'Then *listen* to him.'

'I can't take advantage of his sweet nature. I owe him better. But, Vittorio, this is no time to venture over such dangerous ground.'

'You could be wrong.' His arms tightened, drawing her closer. 'Perhaps the best way to tread on dangerous ground is in each other's arms.'

'Perhaps,' she agreed.

'Sometimes I think "perhaps" is the most troublesome word in the world. *Perhaps* I have feelings for you that frighten me. *Perhaps* you have the same, but you fight them off.'

'Perhaps…' she said, giving him a challenging look.

They were dancing slowly past a large open door. Suddenly he whirled her through it and into a dark corridor.

'What are you *doing*?' she demanded.

'Finding out what "perhaps" means.' His voice became intense. 'There's something I need to know. Jackie.'

'What?'

'This.'

He dropped his head so that his mouth covered hers. For an instant she tried to resist, remembering their last kiss which had ended in rejection. But the feel of his mouth was thrilling, devastating. Her mind sought to reject him, but her flesh warmed and trembled with pleasure.

Her arms seemed to go about him of their own accord, drawing him closer, seeking something that only he could give her. She moved her lips against his, revelling in the excitement of his response. She had the sudden devastating conviction that he was hers. He belonged to her because that was what he had chosen.

And with shattering conviction she knew that if she weakened she would belong to him. But how weak did she dare to be?

He raised his head a little. Her mouth was free but she could still feel the whisper of his breath against it.

'Well?' she murmured. 'Did you find the answer you wanted?'

'Perhaps…perhaps…' he said softly. 'There was just a hint. But you're not going to let me guess too soon, are you?'

Her smile teased and challenged him. 'If it's true you shouldn't need to guess. You should *know*.'

'Only if you'll *let* me know. You like to keep me wondering, don't you?'

'It can be fun,' she said.

'There's more in this for us than fun, Jackie. Can't you feel that?'

'I'm not sure *what* I feel. I'm still waiting for you to teach me.'

'Devil! Witch! Stop playing games with me.'

'All right,' she whispered, and drew his head down again until his lips touched hers.

She knew at once that she'd taken him by surprise, and a sudden determined impulse made her embrace him with greater fervour, enveloping him with her desire and rejoicing in his responding passion.

'Vittorio—'

'Jackie— Jackie—'

There was something in his voice that made her heart soar. But suddenly it was all over. He released himself from her and stepped back.

'Why do you torment me, Jackie?'

'I don't—'

'Don't deny it. You knew what you were doing tonight would drive me mad. That's how you get your pleasure, isn't it?'

'I've told you—'

'Did you enjoy dancing with them knowing what the sight of you was doing to me?'

'But I *didn't* know. How was I supposed to know you cared either way? You don't care about me. You pretend to for the sake of our audience, but it's all an act—'

'And *that's* why you hate me? Oh, yes, you've made yourself very plain about that. You hate me because I gained from what my father did to yours. You say all those polite things about how *he* did it, not me. But I see the truth in your eyes every time you look around this place. You see him, don't you? You see your father standing there. And he tells you to hate everything—including me.'

'Yes, he's here for me, but he doesn't tell me to hate. Hatred was never his way. All I feel is his love, which will always be with me.'

Before he could answer there was a shriek of laughter from further along the corridor. Instinctively they both backed off.

'Do you want to go back to the ball?' he asked.

'Not yet—I'm not quite ready.'

'Nor I. Let's stay away together for a while.'

'I'd like to go and have a cup of tea.'

'Tea? Not coffee? Ah, yes, you're English aren't you? Come along.'

Smiling, he offered his arm and they went along the corridor to the kitchen together.

But a surprise was waiting for them. There were already several young women in the kitchen, and as they neared she heard one of them say, 'What a shock Jackie must have given you all!'

The reply came in Italian, causing the first woman to say, 'I don't understand Italian. You know I don't.'

'*Scusami*. In English you would say Signorina Jackie is fooling herself. She thinks she can win Vittorio, but she doesn't know him. Jackie hasn't got a chance, but she's too stupid to realise that. Vittorio will take her to his bed, have what he wants, then throw her out. And *we'll* all have a good laugh.'

Jackie began to shake. To hear all this with Vittorio standing there, hearing it as well, was a nightmare.

'Are you sure he'd do that?' someone asked. 'He might really be in love with her.'

'Get real. Vittorio's *never* really in love with anyone. I've seen the way he looks at her,'

'So have I,' said a voice that sounded like Marisa's.

Jackie tensed as the voice continued.

'And *I've* seen the way he looks at any woman he's trying to seduce. That special expression he can put in his eyes—he's brilliant at that. Fools them every time.'

'I shouldn't think Jackie's easily fooled. I reckon she's tougher than that.'

'That just makes her more of a challenge. It'll make it all the funnier when she realises what a fool he's made of her.'

'But there's a rumour that they're engaged. Apparently he told someone at the bank.'

'I'll bet *he* didn't tell anyone. *She* told someone, trying to back him into a corner.'

'Wasn't he supposed to be engaged to *you*, Marisa? I remember when everyone was talking about it.'

'People talk about everything,' came Marisa's voice. 'What does it matter?'

'Perhaps you should think about Dino Norese,' said someone else. 'He's mad about you.'

'Dino's all right. Nothing special.' Marisa's reply was cool and lofty.

'Let's get out of here fast,' Vittorio murmured in Jackie's ear. 'We don't want them to see us.'

He drew her along the corridor until they were out of danger.

Her head was whirling with what she had heard. The world saw her as a woman foolishly trying to enjoy an impossible conquest and making herself absurd. And Marisa was trying to gain from this too, seeking to reclaim Vittorio.

Some of her words came back to her.

'I've seen the way he looks at any woman he's trying to seduce. That special expression he can put in his eyes...'

That special expression. She had seen that expression in his eyes, and it had pleased her more than she cared to admit.

He wanted her. She wanted him to want her. And there lay danger.

Suddenly Vittorio stopped, taking hold of her shoulders and looking determinedly into her face.

'You're not taking any notice of that nonsense, are you?' he demanded. 'Do you *really* believe I'm trying to lure you into bed for the pleasure of dumping you afterwards? Is that what you think? *Is it?*'

'No,' she protested. 'But obviously it's what everyone else thinks. It makes me look like the biggest fool on earth. I've got to get out of this place—and this time I'm going to leave for good.'

'Jackie, please think straight. If you leave again you'll make *me* look like the biggest fool on earth.'

'Can't you understand? They think I'm so desperate to marry you that *I* spread the rumour we're engaged.'

'And if I know one thing about you it's that you're *not* desperate to marry me. This is my fault, for what I said at the bank. And I have to put it right.'

'Fine. Go back there and tell them the truth.'

'What truth?' he demanded. 'We have so many truths, and some of them contradict each other.'

'The truth that we fight all the time—that we don't trust each other and can't talk without hurling accusations.'

'That won't convince them that we're not going to marry. Quite the reverse. Some of the most successful couples I know keep up their battle from morning till night. I'm beginning to think we're perfectly suited to each other.'

'Very funny.'

'True—it *is* funny. I like a laugh. The thought of laughing with you for the rest of my life has a certain appeal.'

'But laughter fades after a while,' she said. 'We've got to be sensible.'

'Sensible? Us?'

'Yes, it doesn't sound likely, does it? But I think it's time to put things right.'

'How do you want to do that?'

'We return to the ball separately. We're very polite to each other—'

'You mean with the kind of frigid politeness people use when they actually want to murder each other?'

'Yes. But I've had that temptation often enough to know how to overcome it.'

'Okay, I'll obey your orders. We act indifferent, but I think we should have a polite dance with each other.'

'To confirm the indifference,' she said.

'Right. Let's make a start.'

'You go first.'

He went in ahead of her. Jackie waited several minutes

and then she too returned to the ballroom, going at once to where coffee was being served, and talking politely to the guests she found there.

On the far side of the room she could see Vittorio dancing again, talking cheerfully to his partner. He seemed oblivious to her presence—but that was the polite distance they had promised each other.

'Will you dance with me, *signorina*?'

The man standing before her was a duke. Extending his hand, he led her onto the floor, silently announcing to the world that he had heard the rumour of their engagement and she was accepted in Vittorio's high society.

After him she was claimed again and again. There was no doubt that she was a success.

Across the floor she could just make out Marisa, approaching Vittorio, speaking to him intensely. From her expression she seemed displeased, and clearly his reply did not improve her mood.

So he'd made her understand that she had no hope, Jackie thought. But what had he told her about their imaginary engagement?

Her mind was spinning with everything that had happened that evening. Between herself and Vittorio things seemed to change from moment to moment, leaving her permanently confused.

And now came the moment for which she had been waiting. Vittorio advanced towards her, hand outstretched, and asked theatrically, 'Will you do me the honour, *signorina*?'

She went into his arms, feeling them close around her as they went spinning across the floor. Even as they whirled she was acutely aware of the curious faces following their every movement.

'They've heard the rumours of our engagement,' he said. 'They're trying to decide how true it is. Time to tell them.'

As the music ended he raised his voice.

'Can I have your attention?'

All around them couples slowed to a halt, staring at him curiously.

'I think you know Jackie,' he said. 'Ever since we came here as a couple everyone has wondered about her. Are we lovers? Are we going to announce our engagement soon? Guess what. We've wondered that ourselves. We have our disagreements—sometimes too often. And we've told ourselves—and each other—that these troubles made it impossible for us to be together.'

Jackie turned wild eyes on him. What was he thinking of, to let strangers into their private lives? This way he would make her look more foolish than ever.

'But there's something more important than troubles,' Vittorio declared, still speaking loudly to the crowd. 'And this is it.'

Before Jackie realised what he was doing he pulled her into his arms and laid his mouth passionately over hers. At first she was too stunned to react, but the feel of his lips caressing hers soon took possession of her mind, her heart and her flesh.

From all about them came cheers and applause. Everyone was delighted.

'It's time we gave them the message finally,' he whispered.

'How do you mean?'

Suddenly his arms released her and he dropped down to one knee.

'Jackie, will you marry me?' he called, loud enough for everyone to hear. 'Will you make me the luckiest man on earth? Will you make me unbelievably happy?'

He looked up at her.

'Do I get an answer?' he said.

'Do you really want one? Aren't you just fooling?'

'No, I'm not fooling. Will you marry me?'

'Then my answer…' she took a deep breath '…is yes.'

The cheers were riotous.

She had the dizzying sensation of having won a triumphant victory for the first time in her life. Plain, dull Cinderella had won Prince Charming.

Well, perhaps Prince Charmless, she thought. But she wasn't complaining.

Tania came forward, arms outstretched to embrace her.

'What a lovely thing to happen!' she declared, loud enough for everyone to hear. 'I'm so glad.'

Everyone got the message that despite her low birth Jackie was being welcomed into the Count's family. It was all settled happily and the ball could continue to the end of the evening.

Together Jackie, Vittorio and Tania bade the guests farewell, and at last the castle was empty.

Tania kissed them both.

'He has made the right choice,' she told Jackie. 'It's so lovely to see that just for once he's got it right.'

'Just for once?' Jackie queried comically. 'Surely he gets things right more often than not?'

'You'll find out about that—but hopefully not too soon. Wait until after the wedding before you discover what a clown he can be. Then it'll be too late for you to escape.'

'Thanks a lot, Aunt.' Vittorio said wryly. 'What would I do without you?'

'You'd have married one of those stupid debutantes. As it is, you've got a woman who'll keep your feet on the ground and make you act sensibly.'

'Hush,' said Jackie urgently. 'He doesn't *want* to act sensibly.'

'That's what I like to hear,' Vittorio said, slipping his arm around Jackie's waist. 'A woman who understands me.' He laughed. 'And now I think I'll go to bed. It's been a heavy day. Jackie—we'll celebrate tomorrow. I'll buy you a ring.'

'Lovely,' she said, smiling.

She doubted if he was really tired. He simply wanted to get away from her to sort out his thoughts. She understood, because it was the same with her.

They left the ballroom together. As they went upstairs she waited for him to say something about that devastating scene, but he was silent.

At her door he said, 'We'll talk tomorrow. We have much to say.'

In her room she stripped off the black satin dress, hanging it up with great care. From now on she would treasure it as a sign of the new Jackie.

But who *was* Jackie now? she wondered.

Suddenly she no longer knew.

Was Jackie the woman whose heart reached out to Vittorio despite her sensible resolutions?

Tonight should have been a delight. He had declared his longing for her before the world.

Yet deep within her there was still the suspicion that he wanted to marry her not for love but to silence the troubles that still disturbed him. He longed to make things right with his father's memory. Other people would have found that strange and incredible, but to Jackie, also intent on keeping her father's memory alive, it made sense.

Suddenly there was a slight sound from outside, followed by a click as the door was opened.

'Can I come in?' Vittorio asked.

'Yes.'

'I thought I should come and apologise,' he said. 'It must have been a shock when I sprang that proposal on you. I just got a bit carried away.'

'It's all right. Don't worry. I'm not actually expecting you to marry me.'

'Everyone else is.'

'Meaning Marisa and the other women? Soon she'll grab herself a husband and we can pretend until then.'

Vittorio gazed at her incredulously. 'I said you were a woman who understands me, and I was more right than even *I* knew.'

'I understand you well enough to know you don't want to get married—so don't worry.'

He gave a brief, wry laugh. 'You're only half right about that. Sometimes I'm not keen on marriage, but sometimes I feel that you're the one person who could tempt me.'

She regarded him with her head on one side. 'Temptation is there to be resisted,' she said. 'Be sensible.'

'According to you, I always resist being sensible. Maybe I'm right. Perhaps it's something we should think of.'

'Think of *marriage*?'

'Unless this is your way of rejecting me. Is your answer no, Jackie?'

'I don't know,' she said slowly. 'Everything is so confused between us. We're often friends, but we hover on the verge of being enemies.'

'I know. But somehow enmity just doesn't work. We always return to being—well—'

'Friends?'

'That too, but friendship is too simple.'

'Don't you feel friendship for me?'

'I feel all sorts of things for you that I don't want to feel. I try to fight them, but they fight me back.'

She nodded. 'I know what you mean.'

'Do you remember that night we spent together in Rome?'

She considered. 'I'm not sure we actually spent it *together*. We were on the same bed, but in different worlds.'

'There were some very close moments. I can remember lying in your arms. I wasn't sure how I got there, but it felt wonderful—warm and safe, and as though the whole world had changed and become kinder.'

His gentle tone revived her memory of waking with him, looking into his face and seeing it vulnerable as it had never seemed before. The sight had touched her heart, arousing a feeling of protectiveness towards him that had never entirely faded.

'Yes,' she murmured. 'The world was different.'

'We can make it different, if that's what we want.'

'If we want it badly enough.'

He stroked her face with tender fingers. 'I know what I want, and how badly I want it. But is it what *you* want?'

'Perhaps,' she whispered.

'Ah, yes—perhaps. The word that we said could decide everything. Perhaps we need to know more.'

He drew her closer, placing his mouth over hers.

He was right. They needed to know more. They needed this.

She moved her mouth against his, telling herself that she was merely seeking information, and what she learned sent shivers of delight through her.

But then she was invaded by a thought that made her draw back.

'What is it?' he asked. 'Am I doing something wrong? Don't you want me?'

'Perhaps…' she said, echoing their significant word.

'Is that your way of keeping me doubtful?'

'No, it's my way of saying I want to be sure if you really want me. Have you forgotten that time when you began to kiss me and then backed off, saying I was too vulnerable? You might be going to do that again.'

He groaned, and dropped his head so that she could no longer see his face.

'Why did you do that, Vittorio? Why did you reject me?'

'I didn't reject you. Believe me, Jackie, I didn't. I *forced* myself to let you go. I wanted you so much that I didn't dare go on any more.'

'But why? What would have happened if you'd gone on?'

'We would have made love, and then you would have known—everything.'

'Would I? Do we ever know what "everything" is?'

'Not really. We think we do, but there's always something—' He gave a sigh. 'I meant everything about *me*—how I feel, the power you have—'

'What power? I don't have *any* power. You could turn your back on me and leave at any minute.'

'Could I?'

'Go on—prove it. Reject me.'

He regarded her for a moment with a curious expression, as though he was trying to be quite certain of how she was manipulating him. At last a knowing smile took over his face.

'You know I can't reject you. You're just demonstrating your control and my weakness.'

'Then prove me wrong. Go on. Toss me aside.'

'If I could, I would. But I can't. You have me. I'm yours. Now you can crow with triumph.'

'I don't think I'll do that,' she said, sliding her hands around his face. 'I think I'd rather enjoy exercising my control.' She smiled. 'Kiss me. That's an order.'

He obeyed at once, touching his lips to hers. She waited for the kiss to grow more forceful, but that didn't happen. The soft touch continued, filling her with a sensation of sweetness that made her want to weep with pleasure.

Then he increased the pressure, and suddenly the kiss was as forceful as she could possibly have desired. She responded joyfully, urging him on further, and felt his embrace grow more intense as he moved towards the bed and drew her down beside him.

His hands began to explore her body, pulling away her

clothes. Her heart beat more strongly as things progressed to their inevitable conclusion.

When it was over peace descended on her as they lay together.

'Are you all right?' he asked, gazing anxiously down into her face. 'Did I do wrong?'

'Do you *think* you did?'

He shook his head. 'Having you in my arms feels more right than anything has ever felt before. Do you mind if I stay?'

'For as long as you like.'

He gave a sigh of pleasure and eased down so that his head lay on her breast.

She enfolded him with an instinctive protectiveness that overcame her to her own surprise.

Who would ever have thought this man would need her protection? Yet instinct told her that he did, for reasons that he himself had never suspected.

'Go to sleep, my love,' she whispered. 'I'm here. I'll always be here for you, as long as you need me.'

He didn't move, but she felt his breathing grow deeper.

'And you *do* need me,' she murmured.

He slept almost motionless for the rest of the night, and awoke looking lively.

'That was a great night's sleep.' he said. 'No bad dreams. What about you? Did I keep you awake, lying on you in that position?'

'Not at all,' she said cheerfully.

In truth she was feeling slightly stiff, but the pleasure of giving him a peaceful night was stronger than anything else.

'I'd better go before anyone sees me here,' he said, rising quickly.

At the door he turned to look at her anxiously.

'Jackie, things *are* all right between us, aren't they?'

'Perhaps,' she said.

'Perhaps?' He laughed. 'You know, that's a perfect answer. Bye, now. See you later.'

He vanished, closing the door behind him. Jackie lay back, closing her eyes, relishing memories of the night before, wondering where they would lead.

CHAPTER TWELVE

SHE WENT BACK to sleep and overslept, and was late going downstairs. Vittorio wasn't there, and only arrived half an hour later. From the frown on his face it was clear that he was displeased.

'I need a word with you,' he said.

'Has something happened?'

'Yes. I've been in touch with the bank. I wanted to return your money, but I can't. It seems you've put a block on your account so that nothing can be put in it. Did you do that?'

'Yes.'

'Why?'

'Why did *you* try to put the money in again, against my will? You *know* how I feel about it, yet you've tried to force it on me again.'

'So you fought back by blocking your account against me?' he snapped.

'I didn't fight—'

'Didn't you? Isn't that we do?'

'Only when there's no choice!' she cried. 'Why did you try to make me accept that money again?'

'Because it's the right thing to do.'

'The right thing? To ignore my feelings and make me accept something that hurts me? That's the *right thing* to do?'

'I didn't mean to hurt you—'

'No, you just don't care whether you hurt me or not.'

'I'd hoped to help you understand that you're making a fuss about something that doesn't matter.'

'My feelings don't *matter*? Thanks. I was beginning to understand that anyway.'

'Jackie, please talk sense. Why has this issue of money become so important to us?'

'It's not the money itself. It's what it *means*. You want me to take it for your father's sake, and to comfort you, but it wouldn't comfort *me*. The pain would stay with me. And if you had any feeling for me you would understand that. But you don't, and if we stayed together this would be with us all our lives, spoiling everything we might have had. I love you, but I'm beginning to think I could never be happy with you, and I could never make you happy.'

'How can you *say* that? How would you know what makes me happy?'

'Look ahead down the years, Vittorio. Can you really see happiness when we feel so differently about the things that matter?'

'We can make it happen. We don't have to give in just because we have a disagreement.'

'This isn't just a disagreement. It's more important than that. It's a difference that could last all our lives, poisoning everything. It was only because of a disaster that we met in the first place. Perhaps we were never meant to.'

'Stop it!' he said savagely. 'Don't talk like that. *Stop it.*'

'Yes. There's no point in talking, is there?' she said.

She fled the room, desperate to get away from a conversation that was breaking her heart. Against all likelihood Vittorio had claimed her love. Now, before her loomed a vision of a future without him.

He still didn't understand. He thought it was about money, but it wasn't. How could they ever be united as one when they saw life so differently?

In her own room she switched on her laptop, seeking

the distraction it could sometimes give. She forced herself to concentrate on the emotionless screen, hoping to control all feeling before she yielded helplessly.

An email had arrived. Opening it, she read it.

Things are chaos at the shop without you. Rik has managed to sell it and the new owner is desperate for staff who understands the place. Gary.

This was it. The sign she'd been waiting for—her chance to put the past behind her. Vittorio, Rome—everything she wanted to forget.

It had to happen. They weren't right together. She'd thought she could make it work because she loved him, but maybe sometimes love wasn't enough.

Going downstairs, she found Vittorio, as she'd expected, in his office, buried in paperwork.

'I have something to tell you,' she said. 'I'm going back to England.'

'Will you be away long?'

'I'll be away for ever. I'm saying goodbye, Vittorio.'

'Goodbye? So you really think we no longer have a chance?'

'Did we ever have a chance? We thought we'd got things right at last, but it was an illusion. Let's be honest. We need to forget that we met—and especially forget *how* we met. That has always been a kind of poison between us. Now it's time for us to face the truth and part. And you need never worry that I'll start any legal action. I promise I never will.'

'Is that what you imagine has been troubling me all this time?' he demanded angrily.

'I don't know *what's* been troubling you. I don't think I'll ever understand you any more than you will understand me. It's best that we say goodbye now.'

He gave a bitter laugh. 'Perhaps I should have expected this. You've meant more to me than any other woman because the others were after my title and my money. I valued you because I thought you wanted only me. But you don't want me. So you're right. Let's call it a day.'

His words were like a blow to her heart. If he had said he loved her everything would have changed. But he wanted her only for reasons of pride.

'Yes, let's,' she said. 'I'll call the airport now.'

'Let me do it for you.'

He immediately got on the phone.

After making a few notes he said, 'There's a flight at midday tomorrow. I'll book you on it.'

A few minutes were enough to do the job. Then all was settled.

'I'll print your ticket off for you,' Vittorio said. 'And I'll arrange a taxi to get you there in good time.'

'Will you see me off?'

'Yes, I'll come to the airport and make sure you get on the right plane. We don't want you to get lost, do we? Don't worry. Everything will go well.'

But nothing was going well, she thought sadly. They were parting, and all he cared about was arranging things properly. His insistence that she'd meant more to him than any other woman had been just empty words. She meant nothing to him.

But as she lay in bed that night she managed to find a little hope. There had been times when he'd treated her with something that might have been affection. Perhaps when they were at the airport tomorrow he might show some feeling. Perhaps he'd ask her to change her mind and come back. She would kiss him goodbye and then— *oh, please*—let him kiss her back. Let him discover that they really loved each other. Surely she could make him want her?

Still clinging to hope, she finally fell asleep.

She awoke early, dressed quickly and hurried downstairs, full of hope and determination. She would not give in. Today she would open her heart to Vittorio and persuade him to open his heart to her. It would be a day of victory.

She was smiling as she went into the kitchen.

But there a shock awaited her. There was no sign of Vittorio.

Tania was sitting alone at the table. She looked up and smiled at Jackie.

'Have a good breakfast,' she said. 'Vittorio said you'd be leaving early for the airport. He asked me to tell you goodbye for him.'

'He—what?'

'He got called away to an important meeting. He says he's sorry, but he couldn't help it.'

Jackie drew a sharp breath, fighting back the desire to cry out.

It was over.

He had abandoned her without a word of goodbye, and in doing so he'd made plain his indifference to her.

'I'll leave at once,' she said. 'Goodbye.'

'Must you go?' Tania asked. 'I've so liked having you here.'

'Thank you, but the sooner I go the better. I've turned into a different person here—one I'd better get rid of.'

'But why? It's true you've become another person, but she's very attractive. She's bright and witty, always ready to join in the fun.' Tania smiled fondly, adding, 'She's a true Roman.'

'That's very kind, but my *other* self is actually rather stupid. She's easily taken in because she believes what she wants to believe. Now it's time for her to face facts.'

'But does she know which are the right facts to face?'

Tania asked, regarding her curiously. 'Sometimes one makes mistakes about these things.'

'Not this time,' Jackie said with a sigh. 'I got it wrong at first, but now I've seen the light and—well, that's all that matters.'

'But there might still be things you should know.'

Jackie managed a smile. 'If there are, I think I'll discover them at the right moment. Now, I must go and finish my packing.'

She made a quick escape. Tania's unease told its own story. Vittorio's aunt knew that he was up to something that would hurt Jackie badly, and she was unsure what to reveal.

But Tania didn't need to tell her, Jackie thought. Vittorio was angry with her for daring to leave him.

Jackie hurried upstairs. The sooner she was out of here the better.

Tania waited until she was out of earshot, then picked up the phone and dialled a number.

'Vittorio? Is that you? Oh, good. Listen—she's just been down here. I told her that you'd been called away early— no, I didn't tell here where you've really gone. I kept quiet about that, as we agreed. My dear boy, are you sure you're going about this the right way? I know she's an attractive young woman, but she can also be very difficult— All right, I suppose you're right to take the chance, but you might have to duck for safety when she finds out what you've actually been up to today.'

The flight to London seemed to take for ever. Jackie tried to tell herself that one stage in her life was finished and she must prepare for the next. But no common sense thoughts could heal the pain in her heart.

Her love was over—which meant that her life was effectively over. And she didn't know how she would endure it.

Arriving in London, she headed straight for the shop. It seemed strange when she arrived—more restricted, less interesting.

Perhaps she could find a job here. The place apparently needed her.

Going inside, she saw nobody—until a man appeared from the back.

'Can I help you?'

'I'm looking for a job,' she said. 'Are you short-staffed? Do you need anyone?'

He shook his head.

'I'm afraid I can't give you a job. Only the owner can do that.'

'Then can I talk to the owner?'

'I'll fetch him.'

He went deep into the back of the shop and she heard him call, 'Can you come here, sir?'

After a moment a man appeared, the sight of whom made Jackie gasp.

'Vittorio!'

Smiling, he came towards her and laid his hands gently on her shoulders.

'But what are you—?' she gasped. 'How did you get here?'

'I booked you on the midday flight, but I booked myself on the flight at six in the morning. That's why I'd already gone when you woke up. I needed to get here well ahead of you.'

'So *you're* the new owner?' she said, stunned.

'No. You'll find the owner's name here.'

He drew out a piece of paper bearing the owner's name, and showed it to her.

'But that—it's *my* name there.'

'That's because you're the owner,' he said simply. 'Just as your father would have wanted.'

'But Rik—'

'I contacted Rik from Italy and persuaded him to sell to me. A lawyer here finished the formalities, and when I arrived I went straight to the lawyer and transferred the property to you. That's why I needed to get here well ahead of you.'

'But—how am I going to run this place? Are you telling me that it's all right for me to move back to London?'

'No, I'm telling you that you're coming home with me, because I'm not letting you go—now or ever. I hope you agree to that, or I'll be forced to bring my bullying side to the surface.'

There was a gleam of humour in his eyes, but also something else that might have been an anxious plea.

She gave him a warm smile, saying, 'Perhaps you should beware. I might have to bring my bullying side to the surface.'

'And we both know I don't cope with that very well. But it's lucky you're a great businesswoman, because you can organise this place while living with me in Rome. Please, Jackie. *Please.*'

She touched his face. 'I guess it would be heartless of me to refuse. We'll do it your way.'

He smiled and kissed her hand.

'I've taken over the apartment upstairs, where you used to live. Come up with me. I've got something to show you.'

It felt strange to be climbing the stairs to her old home—like moving back in time. Inside she found it much the same as she remembered: plain and basic.

While he made her a cup of tea she studied the papers that made her the owner of the shop.

'However did you do this? And how can I accept it?'

'You can because I've got something else for you—something that will solve the great problem that has always come between us. I mean the money. We will never be at peace over that until we find a final decision that feels good to us both.'

'But is there such a thing? How could there be?'

'I think I've found it. Look at this.'

He handed her a letter that she read with mounting astonishment. It came from a charity and was addressed to her father.

'It says he's donated a quarter of a million pounds,' she gasped. 'But how could he?'

'Easily—with a little help.' Vittorio handed her several more letters. 'Look at these.'

The letters were from three more of her father's favourite charities, each one thanking him for the gift of a quarter of a million pounds.

'*You* did this?' she breathed.

'Let's say I was your father's messenger boy. I told you I'd find a way of handing over the money in a manner that you couldn't resist, and I've done it. It's really just a way of forcing you to do what I want, selfish bully that I am. You said I couldn't understand why this was so important to you, and at first you were right. But then I started to fall for you and the more I came to love you the more I saw it through your eyes.'

'You can *do* that?' she cried joyfully. 'You really understand now?'

'I knew you didn't want the money yourself, but it was painful to you to know that I had it. You told me that we needed a way to return it to him without involving you, but that didn't seem possible.'

'You found one,' she breathed. 'You found it. Look what it says about him.'

She read from one of the letters. '"After his magnificent gift George Benton will be celebrated as one of our greatest benefactors—a man whose generosity knew no bounds and for whom no admiration and respect would be enough."' She looked quickly through the other letters. 'All four of them say something like that. Look!'

He took the papers from her, gazing with a pleasure that matched her own.

'They do him justice,' he said. 'That's the best we could hope for.'

We. The joyful word echoed through her brain. They were together in this.

'We,' she breathed. 'You said "we".'

'It's "we" because now everything matters the same to both of us. We're a team, and we always will be. Forgive me, my darling, for taking so long to see the light, but now I have seen it. I was desperate for a way to reach out to you and prove that my heart understood yours. I knew nothing else would ever make you love me.'

'And you're right,' she breathed. 'I thought you'd never understand the truth about what was keeping us apart, but you do. And now you've actually found a way—' She seized the letters. 'This is brilliant. I've never been so happy in my life.'

'Then why are you crying?' he asked anxiously, for tears had begun to pour down her cheeks.

'I can't help it,' she wept. 'Suddenly—'

Suddenly she was invaded by an emotion more powerful than any she had ever known.

Vittorio put his arms around her. 'Hold on to me,' he said. 'You're safe now. I'll never let you go.'

'Never? Promise me?'

'I promise. What greater tribute could I pay to your late father than by promising to love, protect and care for his daughter for the rest of her life?'

He kissed her. She returned the kiss joyfully, then rested against him, feeling the warmth and sweetness of knowing he was hers for ever.

'Did you always mean to give me the shop?'

'Of course. A man should give his bride a wedding gift. And this is mine to you.'

'A wedding gift?'

'We're getting married. You promised to marry me ages ago and I'm holding you to that promise. I won't take no for an answer. Say yes. Say you'll marry me and accept the shop.'

The words sounded forceful, but he said them with a gentle smile that ended all her fears. Now she could only do what her heart urged.

'All right,' she said softly. 'I'll marry you. *And* I'll accept the shop.'

Now that they understood each other perfectly she could sense that everything was different. They had reached their destination at last and there was no more to fear.

They spent the night together—not making love, but lying peacefully in each other's arms.

In the darkness of the night Jackie awoke to find Vittorio standing at the open window, looking up into the sky.

She went to stand beside him. 'I think our fathers would be overjoyed that we've found each other. They'd be even more delighted that we've finally begun to love and understand each other in the way they always wanted.'

He put an arm around her. With the other he reached up to the heavens. She followed his gaze to where the stars glittered and the moon glowed.

'They're up there too,' he said. 'Can't you tell?'

'Yes,' she breathed. 'And I think—I think they're shaking hands to congratulate each other.'

'That's what I think too,' Vittorio said.

Then he drew her closer, enfolding her in an embrace that would protect them all their lives.

* * * * *

SNOWBOUND WITH HIS INNOCENT TEMPTATION

CATHY WILLIAMS

To my three wonderful daughters

CHAPTER ONE

'HONESTLY, ALI, I'M FINE!' Complete lie. Becky Shaw was far from fine.

Her job was on the line. The veterinary practice where she had been working for the last three years was in the process of being sold—and being turned into yet another quaint coffee shop to attract the onslaught of tourists who arrived punctually every spring and summer, snapping the gorgeous Cotswold scenery with their expensive cameras and buying up all the local art in a flurry of enthusiasm to take away a little bit of local flavour with them. Her friends Sarah and Delilah had got it right when they had decided to turn their cottage into a gallery and workshop. Not that they had had to in the end, considering they had both been swept off their feet by billionaires.

And then there was the roof, which had decided that it was no longer going to play ball and she was sure that right now, if she listened hard enough, she would be able to hear the unnerving sound of the steady leak drip-dripping its way into the bucket she had strategically placed in the corridor upstairs.

'I keep telling you that you're too young to be buried out there in the middle of nowhere! Why don't you come out to France? Visit us for a couple of weeks? Surely the practice can spare you for a fortnight...'

In three months' time, Becky thought glumly, the practice would be able to spare her for approximately the rest of her life.

Though there was no way that she was going to tell her sister this. Nor did she have any intention of going out to the south of France to see Alice and her husband, Freddy. Her heart squeezed tightly as it did every time she thought of Freddy and she forced herself to answer her sister lightly, voice betraying nothing.

'I'm hardly *buried out here*, Alice.'

'I've seen the weather reports, Becks. I always check what the weather's doing on my phone and the Cotswolds is due heavy snow by the weekend. You're going to be trapped there in the middle of March, when the rest of the country is looking forward to spring, for goodness' sake! *I worry about you.*'

'You mustn't.' She glanced out of the window and wondered how it was that she was still here, still in the family home, when this was supposed to have been a temporary retreat, somewhere to lick her wounds before carrying on with her life. That had been three years ago. Since then, in a fit of lethargy, she had accepted the job offer at the local vet's and persuaded her parents to put all plans to sell the cottage on hold. Just for a little while. Just until she got her act together. She would pay them a monthly rent and, once she'd got herself on a career ladder, she would leave the Cotswolds and head down to London.

And now here she was, with unemployment staring her in the face and a house that would have to be sold sooner rather than later because, with each day that passed, it became just a little more run down. How long before the small leak in the roof expanded into a full scale, no-holds-barred deluge? Did she really want to wake up in the middle of the night with her bed floating?

So far, she hadn't mentioned the problems with the house to her parents, who had left for France five years previously, shortly having been joined by Alice and her husband. She knew that if she did the entire family would up sticks and arrive on her doorstep with tea, sympathy and rescue plans afoot.

She didn't need rescuing.

She was an excellent vet. She would have a brilliant recommendation from Norman, the elderly family man who owned the practice and was now selling to emigrate to the other side of the world. She would be able to find work somewhere else without any problem at all.

And besides, twenty-seven-year-old women did not need rescuing. Least of all by their younger sibling and two frantically worried parents.

'Shouldn't *I* be the one worrying about *you*?'

'Because you're three years older?'

Becky heard that wonderful, tinkling laugh and pictured her beautiful, charming sister sitting in their glamorous French gîte with her legs tucked under her and her long, blonde hair tumbling over one shoulder.

Freddy would be doing something useful in the kitchen. Despite the fact that he, like her, was a hardworking vet, he enjoyed nothing more than getting back from the practice in which he was a partner, kicking off his shoes and relaxing with Alice in the kitchen, where he would usually be the one concocting the meals, because he was an excellent cook.

And he adored Alice. He had been swept off his feet from the very first second he had been introduced to her. At the time, she had been a high-flying model on the way to greatness and, whilst Becky would never have believed that Freddy—earnest and usually knee-deep in text books—could ever be attracted to her sister—who was cheerfully proud of her lack of academic success and hadn't read a book cover to cover in years—she had been proved wrong.

They were the most happily married couple anyone could have hoped to find.

'I'll be fine.' Becky decided to put off all awkward conversations about job losses and collapsing roofs for another day. 'I won't venture out in the middle of a snow-storm in my pyjamas, and if anyone out there is stupid enough to brave this weather on the lookout for what they can nick then they won't be heading for Lavender Cottage.' She eyed the tired décor in the kitchen and couldn't help grinning. 'Everyone in the village knows that I keep all my valuables in a bank vault.'

Old clothes, mud-stained wellies, tool kit for the hundreds of things that kept going wrong in the house, enviable selection of winter-woolly hats…just the sort of stuff any robber worth his salt would want to steal.

'I just thought, Becks, that you might venture out here and have a little fun for a while before summer comes and all those ghastly crowds. I know you came over for Christmas, but it was all so busy out here, what with Mum and Dad inviting every single friend over for drinks every single evening. I…I feel like I haven't seen you for absolutely ages! I mean, just the two of us, the way it used to be when we were younger and…well… Freddy and I…'

'I'm incredibly busy just at the moment, Ali. You know how it is around this time of year with the lambing season nearly on us, pregnant sheep in distress everywhere you look… But I'll come out as soon as I can. I promise.'

She didn't want to talk about Freddy, the guy she had

met at university, the guy she had fallen head over heels in love with, had he only known, the guy who had turned her into a good friend, who had met Alice, been smitten in the space of seconds and proposed in record time.

The guy who had broken her heart.

'Darling, Freddy and I have something to tell you and we would much rather tell you face to face...'

'What? What is it?' Filled with sudden consternation, Becky sat up, mind crash-banging into worst case scenarios.

'We're going to have a baby! Isn't it exciting?'

Yes, it was. Exciting, thrilling and something her sister had been talking about from the moment she had said *I do* and glided up the aisle with a band of gold on her finger.

Becky was thrilled for her. She really was. But, as she settled down for one of the rare Saturday nights when she wasn't going to be on call, she suddenly felt the weight of the choices she had made over the years bearing down on her.

Where were the clubs she should be enjoying? Where was the breathless falling in and out of love? The men in pursuit? The thrilling text messages? When Freddy had hitched his wagon to her sister, Becky had turned her back on love. Unlike Alice, she had spent her teens with her head in books. She'd always known what she'd wanted to be and her parents had encouraged her in her studies. Both were teachers, her father a lecturer, her mother a maths teacher at the local secondary school. She had always been the good girl who worked hard. Beautiful, leggy Alice had decided from an early age that academics were not for her and of course her parents—liberal, left wing and proud of their political correctness—had not batted an eyelid.

And so, while Becky had studied, Alice had partied.

'Everyone should be free to express themselves without being boxed into trying to live up or live down to other people's expectations!' had been her mother's motto.

At the age of eighteen, Becky had surfaced, startled and blinking, to university life with all its glorious freedom and had realised that a life of study had not prepared her for late-night drinking, skipping lectures and sleeping around.

She had not been conditioned to enjoy the freedom at her disposal, and had almost immediately developed a crush on Freddy, who had been in her year, studying veterinary science like her.

He, too, had spent his adolescence working hard. He, too, had had his head buried in text books between the ages of twelve and eighteen. He had been her soul mate and she had enjoyed his company, but had been far too shy to take it to another level, and had been prepared to bide her time until the inevitable happened.

Only ever having watched her sister from the sidelines, laughing and amused at the way Alice fell in and out of love, she had lacked the confidence to make the first move.

And in the end, thank goodness, because, had she done so, then she would have been roundly rejected. The boy she had considered her soul mate, the boy she had fancied herself spending her life with, had not been interested in her as anything but a pal. She had thought him perfect for her. Steady, hard-working, considerate, feet planted firmly on the ground...

He, on the other hand, had not been looking for a woman who shared those qualities.

He had wanted frothy and vivacious. He had wanted someone who shoved his books aside and sat on his lap.

He had wanted tall and blonde and beautiful, not small, dark-haired and plump. He hadn't wanted earnest.

As the dark night began to shed its first flurries of snow, Becky wondered whether retreating to the Cotswolds had been a good idea. She could see herself in the same place, doing the same thing, in ten years' time. Her kid sister felt sorry for her. Without even realising it, she was becoming a charity case, the sort of person the world *pitied*.

The house was falling down.

She was going to be jobless in a matter of months.

She would be forced to do something about her life, leave the security of the countryside, join the busy tide of bright young things in a city somewhere.

She would have to climb back on the horse and start dating again.

She felt giddy when she thought about it.

But think about it she did, and she only stopped when she heard the sharp buzz of the doorbell, and for once didn't mind having her precious downtime invaded by someone needing her help with a sick animal. In fact, she would have welcomed just about anything that promised to divert her thoughts from the grim road they were hell-bent on travelling.

She headed for the door, grabbing her vet's bag on the way, as well as her thick, warm, waterproof jacket, which was essential in this part of the world.

She pulled open the door with one foot in a boot, woolly hat yanked down over her ears and her car keys shoved in her coat pocket.

Eyes down as she reached for her bag, the first things she noticed were the shoes. They didn't belong to a farmer. They were made of soft, tan leather, which was already beginning to show the discolouration from the snow collecting outside.

Then she took in the trousers.

Expensive. Pale grey, wool. Utterly impractical. She was barely aware of her eyes travelling upwards, doing an unconscious inventory of her unexpected caller, registering the expensive black cashmere coat, the way it fell open, unbuttoned, revealing a fine woollen jumper that encased a body that was…so unashamedly *masculine* that for a few seconds her breath hitched in her throat.

'Plan on finishing the visual inspection any time soon? Because I'm getting soaked out here.'

Becky's eyes flicked up and all at once she was gripped by the most unusual sensation, a mixture of dry-mouthed speechlessness and heated embarrassment.

For a few seconds, she literally couldn't speak as she stared, wide-eyed, at the most staggeringly good-looking guy she had ever seen in her life.

Black hair, slightly long, had been blown back from a face that was pure, chiselled perfection. Silver-grey eyes, fringed with dramatically long, thick, dark lashes, were staring right back at her.

Mortified, Becky leapt into action. 'Give me two seconds,' she said breathlessly. She crammed her foot into wellie number two and wondered whether she would need her handbag. Probably not. She didn't recognise the man and, from the way he was dressed, he wasn't into livestock so there would be no sheep having trouble giving birth.

Which probably meant that he was one of those rich townies who had second homes somewhere in one of the picturesque villages. He'd probably descended for a weekend with a party of similarly poorly equipped friends, domestic pets in tow, and one of the pets had got itself into a spot of bother.

It happened. These people never seemed to realise that dogs and cats, accustomed to feather beds and grooming parlours, went crazy the second they were introduced to the big, bad world of the real countryside.

Then when their precious little pets returned to base camp, limping and bleeding, their owners didn't have a clue what to do. Becky couldn't count the number of times she had been called out to deal with weeping and wailing owners of some poor cat or dog that had suffered nothing more tragic than a cut on its paw.

In fairness, *this* man didn't strike Becky as the sort to indulge in dramatics, not judging from the cool, impatient look in those silver-grey eyes that had swept dismissively over her, but who knew?

'Right!' She stepped back, putting some distance between herself and the disconcerting presence by the door. The flurries of snow were turning into a blizzard. 'If we don't leave in five seconds, then it's going to be all hell getting back here! Where's your car? I'll follow you.'

'Follow me? Why would you want to follow me?'

His voice, Becky thought distractedly, matched his face. Deep, seductive, disturbing and very, very bad for one's peace of mind.

'Who *are* you?' She looked at him narrowly and her heart picked up pace. He absolutely towered over her.

'Ah. Introductions. Now we're getting somewhere. You only have to invite me in and normality can be resumed without further delay.'

Because this sure as hell wasn't normal.

Theo Rushing had just spent the past four-and-a-half hours in second gear, manoeuvring ridiculously narrow streets in increasingly inhospitable weather conditions, and cursing himself for actually thinking that it would be a good idea to get in his car and deal with this mission himself, instead of doing the sensible thing and handing it over to one of his employees to sort out.

But this trip had been a personal matter and he hadn't wanted to delegate.

In fact, what he wanted was very simple. The cottage into which he had yet to be invited.

He anticipated getting it without too much effort. After all, he had money and, from what his sources had told him, the cottage—deep in the heart of the Cotswolds and far from anything anyone could loosely describe as civilisation—was still owned by the couple who had originally bought it, which, as far as Theo was concerned, was a miracle in itself. How long could one family live somewhere where the only view was of uninterrupted countryside and the only possible downtime activity would be tramping over open fields? It worked for him, though, because said couple would surely be contemplating retirement to somewhere less remote…

The only matter for debate would be the price.

But he wanted the cottage, and he was going to get it, because it was the only thing he could think of that would put some of the vitality back into his mother's life.

Of course, on the list of priorities, the cottage was way down below her overriding ambition to see him married off, an ambition that had reached an all-time high ever since her stroke several months ago.

But that was never going to happen. He had seen firsthand the way love could destroy. He had watched his mother retreat from life when her husband, his father, had been killed suddenly and without warning when they should have been enjoying the bliss of looking towards their future, the young, energetic couple with their only child. Theo had only been seven at the time but he'd been sharp enough to work out that, had his mother not invested her entire life, the whole essence of her being, in that fragile thing called love, then she wouldn't have spent the following decades living half a life.

So the magic and power of love was something he could quite happily do without, thanks very much. It was a slice of realism his mother stoutly refused to contemplate and Theo had given up trying to persuade her into seeing his point of view. If she wanted to cling to unrealistic fantasies about him bumping into the perfect woman, then so be it. His only concession was that he would no longer introduce her to any of his imperfect women who, he knew from experience, never managed to pull away from the starting block as far as his mother was concerned.

Which just left the cottage.

Lavender Cottage...his parents' first home...the place where he had been conceived...and the house his mother had fled when his father had had his fatal accident. Fog...a lorry going over the speed limit... His father on his bicycle hadn't stood a chance...

Marita Rushing had been turned into a youthful widow and she had never recovered. No one had ever stood a chance against the perfect ghost of his father. She was still a beautiful woman but when you looked at her you didn't see the huge dark eyes or the dramatic black hair... When you looked at her all you saw was the sadness of a life dedicated to memories.

And recently she had wanted to return to the place where those memories resided.

Nostalgia, in the wake of her premature stroke, had become her faithful companion and she wanted finally to come to terms with the past and embrace it. Returning to the cottage, he had gathered, was an essential part of that therapy.

Right now, she was in Italy, and had been for the past six weeks, visiting her sister. Reminiscing about the cottage, about her desire to return there to live out her final days, had been replaced by disturbing insinuations that she might just return to Italy and call it quits with England.

'You're barely ever in the country,' she had grumbled a couple of weeks earlier, which was something Theo had not been able to refute. 'And when you are, well, what am I but the ageing mother you are duty-bound to visit? It's not as though there will ever be a daughter-in-law for me, or grandchildren, or any of those things a woman of my age should be looking forward to. What is the point of my being in London, Theo? I would see the same amount of you if I lived in Timbuktu.'

Theo loved his mother, but he could not promise a wife he had no intention of acquiring or grandchildren that didn't feature in his future.

If he honestly thought that she would be happy in Italy, then he would have encouraged her to stay on at the villa he had bought for her six years previously, but she had lived far too long away from the small village in which she had grown up and where her sister now lived. After two weeks, she would always return to London, relieved to be back and full of tales of Flora's exasperating bossiness.

Right now, she was recuperating, so Flora was full of tender, loving care. However, should his mother decide to turn her stay there into a permanent situation, then Flora would soon become the chivvying older sister who drove his mother crazy.

'Why are you getting dressed?' Theo asked the cottage's present resident in bemusement. She was small and round but he still found himself being distracted by the pure clarity of her turquoise eyes and her flawless complexion. Healthy living, he thought absently, staring down at her. 'And you still haven't told me who you are.'

'I don't think this is the time to start making chit chat.' Becky blinked and made a concerted effort to gather her wits because he was just another hapless tourist in need of her services. It was getting colder and colder in the little hallway and the snow was becoming thicker and thicker. 'I'll come with you but you'll have to drive me back.' She swerved past him, out into the little gravelled circular courtyard, and gaped at the racing-red Ferrari parked at a jaunty angle, as though he had swung recklessly into her drive and screeched to a racing driver's halt. 'Don't tell me that you came here in *that*!'

Theo swung round. She had zipped past him like a pocket rocket and now she was glaring, hands on her hips, woolly hat almost covering her eyes.

And he had no idea what the hell was going on. He felt like he needed to rewind the conversation and start again in a more normal fashion, because he'd obviously missed a few crucial links in the chain.

'Come again?' was all he could find to say, the man who was never lost for words, the man who could speak volumes with a single glance, a man who could close impossible deals with the right vocabulary.

'Are you *completely mad*?' Becky breathed an inward sigh of relief because she felt safer being the angry, disapproving vet, concerned for her safety in nasty weather conditions, and impatient with some expensive, arrogant guy who was clueless about the Cotswolds. 'There's no way I'm getting into that thing with you! And I can't believe you actually thought that driving all the way out here to get me was a good idea! Don't you people know anything *at all*? Not that you have to be a genius to work out that these un-gritted roads are *lethal* for silly little cars like that!'

'Silly little car?'

'*I'd* find the roads difficult and *I* drive a *sensible* car!'

'That *silly little car* happens to be a top-end Ferrari that cost more than you probably earn in a year!' Theo raked fingers frustratedly through his hair. 'And I have no bloody idea why we're standing out here in a blizzard having a chat about cars!'

'Well, how the heck are we supposed to get to your animal if we don't drive there? Unless you've got a helicopter stashed away somewhere? Have you?'

'Animal? What animal?'

'Your *cat*!'

'I don't have a cat! Why would I have a cat? Why would I have any sort of animal, and what would lead you to think that I had?'

'You mean you haven't come to get me out to tend to an animal?'

'You're a vet.' The weathered bag, the layers of warm, outdoor clothing, the wellies for tramping through mud. All made sense now.

Theo had come to the cottage to have a look, to stake his claim and to ascertain how much he would pay for the place. As little as possible, had been his way of thinking. It had been bought at a bargain-basement price from his mother, who had been so desperate to flee that she had taken the first offer on the place. He had intended to do the same, to assess the state of disrepair and put in the lowest possible offer, at least to start with.

'That's right—and if you don't have an animal, and don't need my services, then why the heck are you here?'

'This is ridiculous. It's freezing out here. I refuse to have a conversation in sub-zero temperatures.'

'I'm afraid I don't feel comfortable letting you into my house.' Becky squinted up at him. She was a mere five-foot-four and he absolutely towered over her. He was a tall, powerfully built stranger who had arrived in a frivolous boy-racer car out of the blue and she was on her own out here. No one would hear her scream for help. Should she *need* help.

Theo was outraged. No one, but no one, had ever had the temerity to say anything like that to him in his life before, least of all a woman. 'Exactly *what* are you suggesting?' he asked with withering cool, and Becky reddened but stoutly stood her ground.

'I don't know you.' She tilted her chin at a mutinous angle, challenging him to disagree with her. Every pore and fibre of her being was alert to him. It was as though, for the first time in her life, she was *aware* of her body, *aware* of her femininity, aware of her breasts—heavy and pushing against her bra—aware of her stiff and sensitive nipples, aware of her nakedness beneath her thick layer of clothes. Her discomfort was intense and bewildering.

'You could be *anyone*. I thought you were here because you needed my help with an animal, but you don't, so who the heck are you and why do you think I would let you into *my* house?'

'*Your* house?' Cool grey eyes skirted the rambling building and its surrounding fields. 'You're a little young to be the proud owner of a house this size, aren't you?'

'I'm older than you think.' Becky rushed into self-defence mode. 'And, not that it's any of your business, but yes, this house is mine. Or at least, I'm in charge while my parents are abroad and, that being the case, I won't be letting you inside. I don't even know your name.'

'Theo Rushing.' Some of the jigsaw immediately fell into place. He had expected to descend on the owners of the property. He hadn't known what, precisely, he would find but he had not been predisposed to be charitable to anyone who could have taken advantage of a distraught young woman, as his mother had been at the time.

At any rate, he had come with his cheque book, but without the actual owners at hand his cheque book was as useful as a three-pound note, because the belligerent little ball in front of him would not be able to make any decisions about anything.

Furthermore, she struck him as just the sort who *would* bite off the hand clutching the bank notes, or at least try and persuade her parents to...

He was accustomed to women wanting to please him. Faced with narrowed, suspicious eyes and the body language of a guard dog about to attack, he was forced to concede that announcing the purpose for his visit might not be such a good idea.

'I'm here to buy this cottage so you'll find yourself without a roof over your head in roughly a month and a half' wasn't going to win him brownie points.

He wanted the cottage and he was going to get it but he would have to be a little creative in how he handled the situation now.

He felt an unusual rush of adrenaline.

Theo had attained such meteoric heights over the years that the thrill of the challenge had been lost. When you could have anything you wanted, you increasingly lost interest in the things that should excite. Nothing was exciting if you didn't have to work to get it and that, he thought suddenly, included women.

Getting this cottage would be a challenge and he liked the thought of that.

'And I'm here...' He looked around him at the thick black sky. He had planned to arrive early afternoon but the extraordinary delays had dumped him here as darkness was beginning to fall. It had fallen completely now and there were no street lights to alleviate the unlit sky or to illuminate the fast falling snow.

His eyes returned to the woman in front of him. She was so heavily bundled up that he reckoned they could spend the next five hours out here and she would be immune to the freezing cold. He, on the other hand, having not expected to leave London and end up in a tundra, could not have been less well-prepared for the silent but deadly onslaught of the weather. Cashmere coats were all well and good in London but out here...

Waiting for an answer before she dispatched him without further ado, Becky could not help but stare. He was so beautiful that it almost hurt to tear her eyes away. In those crazy, faraway days, when she had been consumed by Freddy, she had enjoyed looking at him, had liked his regular, kind features, the gentleness of his expression and the warmth of his brown, puppy-dog eyes.

But she had never felt like this. There was something fascinating, *mesmerising*, about the play of shadow and darkness on his angular, powerful face. He was the last word in everything that *wasn't* gentle or kind and yet the pull she felt was overwhelming.

'Yes?' She clenched her gloved fists in the capacious pockets of her waterproof, knee-length, fleece-lined anorak. 'You're here because...?'

'Lost.' Theo spread his arm wide to encompass the lonely wilderness around him. 'Lost, and you're right—in a car that's not very clever when it comes to ice and snow. I'm not...accustomed to country roads and my satnav has had a field day trying to navigate its way to where I was planning on ending up.'

Lost. It made sense. Once you left the main roads behind—and that was remarkably easy to do—you could easily find yourself in a honeycomb of winding, unlit country lanes that would puzzle the best cartographer.

But that didn't change the fact that she was out here on her own in this house and he was still a stranger.

He read her mind. 'Look, I understand that you might feel vulnerable out here if you're on your own…' And she was, because there was no rush to jump in and warn him of an avenging boyfriend or husband wending his weary way back. 'But you will be perfectly safe if you let me in. The only reason I'm asking to be let in at all is because the weather's getting worse, and if I get into that car and try and make my way back to the bright lights I have no idea where I'll end up.'

Becky glanced at the racy, impractical sports car turning white as the snow gathered on it. *In a ditch*, was written all over its impractical bonnet.

Would her conscience allow her to send him off into the night, knowing that he would probably end up having an accident? What if the skittish car skidded off the road into one of the many trees and there was a fatality?

What if he ended up trapped in wreckage somewhere on an isolated country lane? If nothing else, he would perish from hypothermia, because his choice of clothing was as impractical for the weather as his choice of car.

'One night,' she said. 'And then I get someone to come and fetch you, first thing in the morning. I don't care if you have to leave the car here or not.'

'One night,' Theo murmured in agreement.

Becky felt the race of something dangerous slither through her.

She would give him shelter for one night and one night only…

What harm could come from that?

CHAPTER TWO

THE HOUSE SEEMED to shrink in size the minute he walked in. He'd fetched his computer from his car but that was all and Becky looked at him with a frown.

'Is that all you brought with you?'

'You still haven't told me your name.' The house was clearly on its last legs. Theo was no surveyor but that much was obvious. He now looked directly at her as he slowly removed his coat.

'Rebecca. Becky.' She watched as he carelessly slung his coat over one of the hooks by the front door. She could really appreciate his lean muscularity, now he was down to the jumper and trousers, and her mouth went dry.

This was as far out of her comfort zone as it was possible to get. Ever since Freddy, she had retreated into herself, content to go out as part of a group, to mingle with old friends—some of whom, like her, had returned to the beautiful Cotswolds, but to raise families. She hadn't actively chosen to discourage men but, as it happened, they had been few and far between. Twice she had been asked out on dates and twice she had decided that friendship was more valuable than the possibility of romance.

Truthfully, when she tried to think about relationships, she drew a blank. She wanted someone thoughtful and caring and those sorts of guys were already snapped up.

The guys who had asked her out had known her since for ever, and she knew for a fact that one of them was still recovering from a broken heart and had only asked her out on the rebound.

The other, the son of one of the farmers whom she had visited on call-out on several occasions, was nice enough, but nice enough just wasn't sufficient.

Or maybe she was being too fussy. That thought had occurred to her. When you were on your own for long enough, you grew careful, wary of letting anyone into your world, protective of your space. Was that what was happening to her?

At any rate, her comfort zone was on the verge of disappearing permanently unless she chose to stay where she was and travel long distances to another job.

She decided that inviting Theo in was good practice for what lay in store for her. She had opened her door to a complete stranger and she knew, with some weird gut instinct, that he was no physical threat to her.

In fact, seeing him in the unforgiving light in the hall did nothing to lessen the impact of his intense, sexual vitality. It was laughable to think that he would have any interest in her as anything other than someone offering refuge from the gathering snow storm.

'I can show you to one of the spare rooms.' Becky flushed because she could feel herself staring again. 'I don't keep them heated, but I'll turn the radiator on, and it shouldn't take too long to warm up. You might want to…freshen up.'

'I would love nothing more,' Theo drawled. 'Unfortunately, no change of clothing. Would you happen to have anything I could borrow? Husband's old gardening clothes? Boyfriend's…?' He wondered whether she intended to spend the rest of the evening in the shapeless anorak and mud-stained boots. She had to be the least fashion-conscious woman he had ever met in his entire life, yet for the life of him he was still captivated by something about her.

The eyes, the unruly hair still stuffed under the woolly hat, the lack of war paint...what was it?

He had no idea but he hadn't felt this alive in a woman's presence for a while.

Then again, it had been a while since he had been in the presence of any woman who wasn't desperate to attract his attention. There was a lot to be said for novelty.

'I can let you borrow something.' Becky shifted from foot to foot. She was boiling in the coat but somehow she didn't like the thought of stripping down to her jeans and top in front of him. Those sharp, lazy eyes of his made her feel all hot and bothered. 'My dad left some of his stuff in the wardrobe in the room you'll be in. You can have a look and see what might be able to work for you. And if you leave your stuff outside the bedroom door, then I guess I can stick it in the washing machine.'

'You needn't do that.'

'You're soaked,' Becky said flatly. 'Your clothes will smell if you leave them to dry without washing them first.'

'In that case, I won't refuse your charming offer,' Theo said drily and Becky flushed.

Very conscious of his eyes on her, she preceded him up the stairs, pointedly ignoring the bucket gathering water on the ground from the leaking roof, and flung open the door to one of the spare bedrooms. Had she actually thought things through when she had fled back to the family home, she would have realised that the 'cottage' was a cottage in name only. In reality, it was reasonably large, with five bedrooms and outbuildings in the acres outside. It was far too big for her and she wondered, suddenly, whether her parents had felt sorry for her and offered to allow her to stay there through pity. They hadn't known about Freddy and her broken heart but what must they have felt when she had dug her heels in and insisted on returning to the family home while Alice, already far flown from the nest, was busily making marriage plans so that the next phase of her life could begin?

Becky cringed.

Her parents would never, ever have denied her the cottage but they weren't rich. They had bought somewhere tiny in France when her grandmother had died, and they had both continued working part-time, teaching in the local school.

Becky had always thought it a brilliant way of integrating into life in the French town, but what if they'd only done that because they needed the money?

While she stayed here, paying a peppercorn rent and watching the place gradually fall apart at the seams…

She was struck by her own selfishness and it was something that had never occurred to her until now.

She would phone, she decided. Feel out the ground. After all, whether she liked it or not, her lifestyle was going to change dramatically once she was out of a job.

Theo looked at her and wondered what was going through her mind. He hadn't failed to notice the way she had neatly stepped past a bucket in the corridor which was quarter-full from the leaking roof.

It was startling enough that a woman of her age would choose to live out in the sticks, however rewarding her job might be, but it was even more startling that, having chosen to live out in the sticks, she continued to live in a house that was clearly on the verge of giving up the fight.

When he bought this cottage, he would be doing her a favour by forcing her out into the real world.

Where life happened.

Rather than her staying here…hiding away…which surely was what she was doing…?

Hiding from what? he wondered. He was a little amused at how involved he temporarily was in mentally providing an answer to that ridiculous question.

But if he had to get her onside, manoeuvre her into a position where she might see the sense of not standing in his way when it came to buying the cottage, then wouldn't it help to get to know her a little?

Of course, there was no absolute necessity to get anyone onside. He could simply bypass her and head directly to the parents. Make them an offer they couldn't refuse. But for once he wasn't quite ruthless enough to go down that road. There was something strangely alluring underneath the guard-dog belligerence. And he was not forgetting that there were times when money *didn't* open the door you wanted opening. If he bypassed her and leant on the parents, there was a real risk of them uniting with their daughter to shut him out permanently, whatever sums of money he chose to throw at them. Family loyalty could be a powerful wild card, and he should know… Wasn't family loyalty the very thing that had brought him to this semi-derelict cottage?

She was switching on the ancient heating, opening the wardrobe so that she could show him where the clothes were kept, fetching a towel from the corridor, dumping it on the bed and then informing him that the bathroom was just down the corridor, but that he would have to make sure that the toilet wasn't flushed before he turned on the shower or else he might end up with third-degree burns.

Theo walked slowly towards her and then stopped a few inches away.

When Becky breathed, she could breathe him in, masculinity mixed with the cold winter air, a heady, heady mix. Leaning against the doorframe, she blinked, suddenly unsteady on her feet.

He had amazing lashes, long, dark and thick. She wanted to ask him where he was from, because there was an exotic strain running through him that was quite… captivating.

He had shoved up the sleeves of his jumper and, even though she wasn't actually looking, she was very much aware of his forearms, the fine, dark hair on them, the flex of muscle and sinew…

Her breathing was so sluggish that it crossed her mind… *was it actually physically possible to forget how to breathe?*

'I don't get why you live here.' Theo was genuinely curious.

'Wh-what do you mean?' Becky stammered.

'The house needs a lot of work doing to it. I could understand if your parents wanted you in situ while work was being done but…can I call you Becky?…there's a bucket out in the corridor. And how long do you intend emptying it before you face the unpalatable fact that the roof probably needs replacing?'

Hard on the heels of the uncomfortable thoughts that had been preying on her mind, Theo's remarks struck home with deadly accuracy.

'I don't see that the state of this house is any of your business!' Bright patches of colour stained her cheeks. 'You're here for a night, *one night*, and only because I wouldn't have been able to live with myself if I had sent you on your way in this weather. But that doesn't give you the right to…to…'

'Talk?'

'You're not *talking*, you're—'

'I'm probably saying things that have previously oc-curred to you, things you may have chosen to ignore.' He shrugged, unwillingly intrigued by the way she was so patently uninterested in trying to impress him. 'If you'd rather I didn't, then that's fine. I have some work to do when I get downstairs and then we can pretend to have an invigorating conversation about the weather.'

'I'll be downstairs.' This for want of anything more coherent to say when she was so...*angry*...that he had had the nerve to shoot his mouth off! He was rude be-yond words!

But he wasn't wrong.

And this impertinent stranger had provided the impe-tus she needed to make that call to her parents. As soon as she was in the kitchen, with the door firmly shut, be-cause the man was as stealthy as a panther and obviously didn't wait for invitations to speak his mind. There was some beating around the bush but, yes, it *would* be rather lovely if the house *was* sold, not that they would ever dream of asking her to leave.

But...but...but...but.

Lots of *buts*, so that by the time Becky hung up fif-teen minutes later she was in no doubt that not only was she heading for unemployment but the leaking roof over her head would not be hers for longer than it took for the local estate agent to come along and offer a valuation.

Mind still whirring busily away, she headed back up the stairs. She wished she could think more clearly and see a way forward but the path ahead was murky. What if she couldn't get a job? It should be easy but, then again, she was in a highly specialised field. What if she did manage to find a posting but it was in an even more remote spot than this? Did she really want the years ahead to be spent in a practice in the wilds of Scotland? But weren't the more desirable posts in London, Manchester or Birmingham going to be the first to be filled?

And underneath all those questions was the dissatisfaction that had swamped her after she had spoken to her sister.

Her life had been put into harsh perspective. The time she had spent here now seemed to have been wasted. Instead of moving forward, she had stayed in the same place, pedalling furiously and getting nowhere.

She surfaced from her disquieting thoughts to find that, annoyingly, the clothes she had asked to be placed outside the bedroom door were not there.

Did the man think that he was staying in a hotel?

Did he imagine that it was okay for her to hang around like a chambermaid until he decided that he could be bothered to hand over his dirty laundry for her to do? She didn't even have to wash his clothes! She could have sent him on his way in musty, semi-damp trousers and a jumper that smelled of pond water.

He obviously thought that he was so important that he could do as he pleased. Speak to her as he pleased. Accept her hospitality whilst antagonising her because he found it entertaining.

She had no idea how important or unimportant he was but, quite aside from the snazzy little racing-red number and the designer clothing, there was something about him that screamed *wealth*.

Or maybe it was *power*.

Well, none of that impressed *her*. She'd never had time for anyone who thought that money was the be all and end all. It just wasn't the way she had been brought up.

It was what was inside that counted. It was why, although Freddy had not been the one for her, there was a guy out there who was, a guy who had the sterling qualities of kindness, quiet intelligence and self-deprecating humour.

And, having ducked the dating scene for years, she would get back out there…because if she didn't then this was the person she would be in the years to come, entrenched in her singledom, godmother to all and sundry and maid of honour to her friends as they tied the knot and moved on with their fulfilling lives.

Swamped by sudden self-pity, she absently shoved open the door to the spare room, which was ajar, and… stopped. Her legs stopped moving, her hand froze on the door knob and her brain went into instant shutdown.

She didn't know where to look and somewhere inside she knew that it didn't matter because wherever she looked she would still end up seeing him. Tall, broad-shouldered, his body an amazing burnished bronze. She would still see the hardness of his six pack and the length of his muscular legs, the legs of an athlete.

Aside from a pair of low-slung boxers, he was completely naked.

Becky cleared her throat and opened her mouth and nothing emerged but an inarticulate noise.

'I was just about to stick the clothes outside…'

Without the woollen hat pulled down over her head, her hair was long, tumbling down her back in a cascade of unruly, dark curls, and without the layers upon layers of shriekingly unfashionable arctic gear…

She wasn't the round little beach ball he had imagined. Even with the loose-fitting striped rugby shirt, he could see that she had the perfect hourglass figure. News obviously hadn't reached this part of the world that the fashionable trend these days leaned towards long, thin and toned to athletic perfection, even if the exercise involved to get there never saw the outside of an expensive gym.

He could feel his whole body reacting to the sight of her lush curves and he hurriedly turned away, because a pair of boxers was no protection against an erection.

He was staring. Becky stood stock-still, conscious of herself and her body in ways she had never been before. Why was he staring at her like that? Was he even aware that he was doing it?

She couldn't believe that he was staring at her because she was the most glamorous woman he had ever set eyes on. She wasn't born yesterday and she knew that when it came to looks, well, a career could not be made out of hers. Alice had got the looks and she, Becky, had got the brains and it had always seemed like a fair enough deal to her.

He'd turned away now, thankfully putting on some ancient track pants her father had left behind and an even more ancient jumper, and by the time he turned back around to face her she wondered whether she had imagined those cool, grey eyes on her, skirting over her body.

Yes, she thought a little shakily. Of course she had. *She* had stared at *him* because he looked like a Greek god. *She* on the other hand was as average as they came.

Should she feel threatened? She was alone in this house…

She didn't feel threatened. She felt…excited. Something wicked and daring stirred inside her and she promptly knocked it back.

'The clothes.' She found her voice, one hand outstretched, watching as he gathered items of clothing and strolled towards her. 'I'll make sure they're washed and ready for you tomorrow morning.'

'First thing…before I'm sent on my way,' Theo murmured, still startled at the fierce grip of his libido that had struck from nowhere.

She couldn't wait to escape, he thought with a certain amount of disbelief.

Something had passed between them just then. Had she even been aware of it? A charge of electricity had shaken him and she hadn't been unaffected. He'd seen the reaction in the widening of her eyes as she had looked at him, and the stillness of her body language, as though one false move might have led her to do something…rash.

Did *rash* happen out here? he wondered. Or was she out here because she was escaping from something rash? Was the awkward, blushing, argumentative vet plagued by guilt over a misspent past? Had she thrown herself into a one-way relationship to nowhere with a con man? A married man? A rampant womaniser who had used her and tossed her aside? The possibilities were endless.

She certainly wasn't out here for the money. That bucket on the landing said it all. She might be living rent free at the place but she certainly wasn't earning enough to keep it maintained. Old houses consumed money with the greed of a gold-digger on the make.

'What if it's still snowing in the morning?'

She was clutching the bundle of clothes like a talisman and staring up at him with those amazing bright blue eyes. Her lips were parted. When she circled a nervous tongue over them, Theo had to fight down an urge to reach out and pull her against him.

'It won't be.'

'If you weren't prepared to risk my life by sending me on my way, then will you be prepared to risk someone else's life by asking them to come and collect me and take me away?'

'I could drive you myself. I have a four-wheel drive. It's okay in conditions like this.'

'When I knocked on your door…' Theo leant against the door frame '…I never expected someone like you to open it'

'What do you mean *someone like me*?' Becky stiffened, primed for some kind of thinly veiled insult.

Theo didn't say anything for a couple of seconds. Instead, he watched her, head tilted to one side, until she looked away, blushing. Very gently, he tilted her face back to his.

'You're on the defensive. Why?'

'Why do you think? I…I don't know you.' The feel of his cool finger resting lightly on her chin was as scorching-hot as the imprint from a branding iron.

'What do you think I'm going to do? When I said *someone like you*, I meant someone young. I expected someone much older to be living this far out in the countryside.'

'I told you, the house belongs to my parents. I'm just here… Look, I'm going to head downstairs, wash these things…' Her feet and brain were not communicating because, instead of spinning around and backing out of the room, she remained where she was, glued to the spot.

She wanted him to remove his hand…she wanted him to do more with it, wanted him to curve it over her face and then slide it across her shoulders, wanted him to find the bare flesh of her stomach and then the swell of her breasts… She didn't want to hear anything he had to say, yet he was making her think, and how could that be a bad thing?

She barely recognised her voice and she certainly didn't know what was going on with her body.

'Okay.' He stepped back, hand dropping to his side.

For a few seconds, Becky hovered, then she cleared her throat and stepped out of the room backwards.

By the time he joined her in the kitchen, the clothes were in the washing machine and she had regained her composure.

Theo looked at her for a few seconds from the doorway. She had her back to him and was busy chopping vegetables, while as background noise the television was giving an in-depth report of the various areas besieged by snow when spring should have sprung. He felt that her house would shortly be featured because there was no sign of the snow letting up.

Before he had come down, he had done his homework, nosed into a few of the rooms and seen for himself what he had suspected from the bucket on the landing catching water from the leaking roof.

The house was on its last legs. Did he think that he was doing anything underhand in checking out the property before he made an offer? No. He'd come here to conduct a business deal and, if things had been slightly thrown off course, nothing had fundamentally changed. The key thing remained the business deal.

And was the woman peeling the vegetables an unexpected part of acquiring what he wanted? Was she now part of the business deal that had to be secured?

In a way, yes.

And he was not in the slightest ashamed of taking this pragmatic view. Why should he be? This was the man he was and it was how he had succeeded beyond even his own wildest expectations.

If you allowed your emotions to guide you, you ended up a victim of whatever circumstances came along to blow you off course.

He had no intention of ever being one of life's victims.

His mother had so much to give, but she had allowed her damaged heart to take control of her entire future, so that, in the end, whatever she'd had to give to anyone else had dried up. Wasn't that one reason why she was so consumed with the thought of having grandchildren? Of seeing him married off?

Because her ability to give had to go somewhere and he was the only recipient.

That was what emotions did to a person. They stripped you of your ability to think. That was why he had never done commitment and never would. Commitment led to relationships and relationships were almost always train wrecks waiting to happen. Lawyers were kept permanently busy sorting out those train wrecks and making lots of money in the process.

He had his life utterly in control and that was the way he liked it.

He had no doubt that whatever had brought Becky to this place was a story that might tug on someone else's heartstrings. *His* heartstrings would be blessedly immune to any tugging. He would be able to find out about her and persuade her to accept that this was no place for her to be. When, inevitably, the house was sold from under her feet, she would not try and put up a fight, wouldn't try and coax her parents into letting her stay on.

He would have long disappeared from her life. He would have been nothing more than a stranger who had landed for a night and then moved on. But she would remember what he had said and she would end up thanking him.

Because, frankly, this was no place for her to be. It wasn't healthy. She was far too young.

He looked at the rounded swell of her derrière…

Far too young and far too sexy.

'What are you cooking?'

Becky swung round to see him lounging against the door frame. Her father was a little shorter and reedier than Theo. Theo looked as though he had been squashed into clothes a couple of sizes too small. And he was barefoot. Her eyes shot back to his face to find that he was staring right back at her with a little smile.

'Pasta. Nothing special. And you can help.' She turned her back on him and felt him close the distance between them until he was standing next to her, at which point she pointed to some onions and slid a small, sharp knife towards him. 'You've asked me a lot of questions,' she said, eyes sliding across to his hands and then hurriedly sliding back to focus on what she was doing. 'But I don't know anything about you.'

'Ask away.'

'Where do you live?'

'London.' Theo couldn't remember the last time he'd chopped an onion. Were they always this fiddly?

'And what were you doing in this part of the world? Aside from getting lost?'

Theo felt a passing twinge of guilt. 'Taking my car for some exercise,' he said smoothly. 'And visiting one or two…familiar spots en route.'

'Seems an odd thing to do at this time of year,' Becky mused. 'On your own.'

'Does it?' Theo dumped the half-peeled onion. 'Is there anything to drink in this house or do vets not indulge just in case they get a midnight call and need to be in their car within minutes, tackling the dangerous country lanes in search of a sick animal somewhere?'

Becky stopped what she was doing and looked at him, and at the poor job he had made of peeling an onion.

'I'm not really into domestic chores.' Theo shrugged.

'There's wine in the fridge. I'm not on call this evening and, as it happens, I don't get hundreds of emergency calls at night. I'm not a doctor. Most of my patients can wait a few hours and, if they can't, everyone around here knows where the nearest animal hospital is. And you haven't answered my question. Isn't it a bit strange for you to be here on your own…just driving around?'

Theo took his time pouring the wine, then he handed her a glass and settled into a chair at the kitchen table.

His own penthouse was vast and ultra-modern. He didn't care for cosy, although he had to admit that there was something to be said for it in the middle of a blizzard with the snow turning everything white outside. This was a cosy kitchen. Big cream Aga…worn pine table with mismatched chairs…flagstone floor that had obviously had underfloor heating installed at some point, possibly before the house had begun buckling under the effect of old age, because it wasn't bloody freezing underfoot…

'Just driving around,' he said slowly, truthfully, 'is a luxury I can rarely afford.' He thought about his life— high-voltage, adrenaline-charged, pressurised, the life of someone who made millions. There was no time for standing still. 'I seldom stop, and even when I do, I am permanently on call.' He smiled crookedly, at odds with himself for giving in to the unheard of temptation to confide.

'What on earth do you do?' Becky leant against the counter and stared at him with interest.

'I…buy things, do them up and sell them on. Some of them I keep for myself because I'm greedy.'

'What sorts of things?'

'Companies.'

Becky stared at him thoughtfully. The sauce was simmering nicely on the Aga. She went to sit opposite him, nursing her glass of wine.

Looking at her, Theo wondered if she had any idea of just how wealthy he was. She would now be getting the picture that he wasn't your average two-up, two-down, one holiday a year, nine-to-five kind of guy and he wondered whether, like every other single woman he had ever met, she was doing the maths and working out how profitable it might be to get to know him better.

'Poor you,' Becky said at last and he frowned.

'Come again?'

'It must be awful never having time to yourself. I don't have much but what I do have I really appreciate. I'd hate it if I had to get in my car and drive out into the middle of nowhere just to have some uninterrupted peace.'

She laughed, relaxed for the first time since he had landed on her doorstep. 'Our parents always made a big thing about money not being the most important thing in life.' Her bright turquoise eyes glinted with sudden humour. 'Alice and I used to roll our eyes but they were right. That's why...' she looked around her at the kitchen, where, as a family, they had spent countless hours together '...I can appreciate all this quiet, which I know you don't understand.'

The prospect of saying goodbye to the family house made her eyes mist over. 'There's something wonderfully peaceful about being here. I don't need the crowds of a city. I never have or I never would have returned here after... Well, this is where I belong.' And the thought of finding somewhere else to call home felt like such a huge mountain to climb that she blinked back a bout of severe self-pity. Her parents had moved on as had Alice. So could she.

Theo, watching her, felt a stab of alarm. A pep talk

wasn't going to get her packing her belongings and moving on and a wad of cash, by all accounts, wasn't going to cut it with her parents.

When was the last time he had met someone who wasn't impressed by money and what it could buy?

His mother, of course, who had never subscribed to his single-minded approach to making money, even though, as he had explained on countless occasions, making money per se was a technicality. The only point to having money was the security it afforded and that was worth its weight in gold. Surely, he had argued, she could see that—especially considering her life had been one of making ends meet whilst trying to bring up a child on her own?

He moved in circles where money talked, where people were impressed by it. The women he met enjoyed what he could give them. His was the sort of vast, bottomless wealth that opened doors, that conferred absolute freedom.

And what, he wondered, was wrong with that?

'Touching,' he said coolly. 'Clearly none of your family members are in agreement, considering they're nowhere to be seen. The opposite, in fact. They've done a runner and cleared off to a different country.'

'Do you know what?' Becky said with heartfelt sincerity. 'You may think you're qualified to look down your nose at other people who don't share your…your… materialism, but I feel sorry for anyone who thinks it's worth spending every minute of every day working! I feel sorry for someone who never has time off to just *do nothing*. Do you ever relax? Put your feet up? Listen to music? Or just watch television?' Becky's voice rang with self-righteous sincerity but she was guiltily aware that she was far from being the perfectly content person she was making herself out to be.

She hadn't rushed back to the cottage because she couldn't be without the vast, open peaceful spaces a second longer. She'd rushed back because her heart had been broken. And she hadn't stayed here because she'd been seduced by all the wonderful, tranquil downtime during which she listened to music or watched television with her feet up. She'd stayed because she'd fallen into a job and had then been too apathetic to do anything else about moving on with her life in a more dynamic way.

And it wasn't fun listening out for leaks. It wasn't fun waiting for the heating to pack up. And it certainly wasn't fun to know that, in another country, the rest of her family was busy feeling sorry for her and waiting for her to up sticks so that the house could be sold and valuable capital released.

'I relax,' Theo said softly.

'Huh?' She focused on a sharply indrawn breath, blinking like a rabbit caught in the headlights at the lazy, sexy smile curving his mouth.

'In between the work, I actually do manage to take time off to relax. It's just that my form of relaxation doesn't happen to include watching television or listening to music... But I can assure you that it's every bit as satisfying, if somewhat more energetic...'

CHAPTER THREE

'WHAT DO *YOU* do here?'

'What do you mean?' Becky asked in sudden confusion.

'To relax.' Theo sprawled back, angling the chair so that he could loosely cross his legs, ankle resting on thigh, one arm slung over the back of the chair, the other toying with the wine glass, twirling it slowly between his long fingers as he continued to look at her.

'I mean,' he continued pensively, 'it's all well and good killing time in front of the television with your feet up, while you congratulate yourself on how peaceful it is, but what else do you get up to when you've had your fill of the great open spaces and the lack of noise?'

'I grew up here' was all Becky could find to say.

'University must have been a very different change of scenery for you,' Theo mused. 'Which university did you go to?'

He could see her reluctance to divulge any personal details. It made him want to pry harder, to extract as much information as he could from her. Her dewy skin was pink and flushed. In a minute, she would briskly stand up and dodge his personal attack on her by busying herself in front of the Aga.

'Cambridge.'

'Impressive. And then you decided, after going to one of the top universities on the planet, that you would return here so that you could get a job at a small practice in the middle of nowhere?'

'Like I said, you wouldn't understand.'

'You're right. I don't. And you still haven't told me what you do for relaxation around here.'

'I barely have time to relax.' Becky stood up abruptly, uncomfortable with his questioning. She rarely found her motives questioned.

'But I thought you said…' A smile quirked at the corner of Theo's mouth.

'Yes, well,' snapped Becky, turning her back to him, more than a little flustered.

'But when you do…?' Theo followed her to where she was standing, clearing an already tidy counter.

He gently relieved her of the cloth and looked down at her.

Becky had no idea what was happening. Was this flirting? She had successfully convinced herself that there was no way the man could have any interest in her, aside from polite interest towards someone who had agreed to let him stay for the night because of the poor weather conditions. But when he looked at her the way he was looking at her now…

Her mind broke its leash and raced off in all sorts of crazy directions.

He was obnoxious. Of course he was, with his generalisations, his patronising assertions and that typical rich man's belief that money was the only thing that mattered.

He was just the sort of guy she had no time for.

But he was so outrageously beautiful and that was what gripped her imagination and held it. That was what was making her body react with such treacherous heat to his smoky grey eyes.

He'd painted a picture for her when he'd told her how he relaxed. *He hadn't had to go into details because in a few sentences she had pictured him naked...aroused... focusing all that glorious, masculine attention on one woman...*

'You surely must get a little lonely out here?' Theo murmured softly. 'However much you love the peace and isolation.'

'I...'

Her eyelids fluttered and her lips parted on an automatic denial of any such thing.

Theo drew in a sharp breath, riveted by the sight of those full, plump lips. She had no idea how alluring that mixture of apprehension and innocence was. It made him want to touch, even though he knew that it would be a mistake. This wasn't one of those women who'd stopped being green round the ears when they were sixteen. Whatever experiences this woman had had, whatever had driven her back to this house—and he was certain that something had—she was innocent.

He stepped back and raked his fingers through his hair, breaking the electric connection between them.

Becky was trembling. She could feel the tremor running through her body, as though she had had a shock and was still feeling the aftermath of it, even though he had returned to the table to sit back down. She couldn't look at him as he picked up the conversation, making sure to steer clear of anything personal.

He asked her about the sort of situations she had to deal with out in the country... How many were in the practice? Had she always wanted to be a vet? Why had she chosen that over a conventional medicine course?

He didn't ask her again whether she was lonely.

He didn't ask her why she had chosen to retreat to the country to live when she could have had a job anywhere in the country.

When he looked at her, it was without that lazy, assessing speculation that made her blood thicken and made her break out in a cold sweat.

He complimented her on the meal and asked her about her diet, about how she managed to fit in her meals with the hours she worked.

He could not have been more meticulously polite if he had been obeying orders with a gun held to his head and she hated it.

His arrival at the house was the most exciting thing that had happened to her in a long time and it had occurred just when she had been questioning her whole life, putting it into perspective, trying to figure out a way forward. It had occurred hard on the heels of her sister's phone call, which had stirred up a grey, sludgy mix of emotion in her, some of which she didn't like.

It also felt as though fate had sent him along to challenge her.

And how was she going to respond to that challenge? By running away? By retreating? She was going to be challenged a lot more when her job came to an end and the roof over her head was sold, and what was she going to do then? Dive for cover, close her eyes and hope for the best?

Where was the harm in getting into some practice now when it came to dealing with the unexpected? It wasn't as though there would be any repercussions, was it? You could bare your soul to a stranger on a plane and then walk away when the plane landed, safe in the knowledge that you wouldn't clap eyes on that person again, so if they happened to be a receptacle for all your secrets, what difference would that make?

She felt as though she had been on standby for someone just like him to come along and shake her world up a little because things had settled in a way that frightened her.

'It does get lonely,' she said, putting down her fork and spoon and cupping her chin in the palm of her hand to look at him. She cleared her throat, realising that this was something she had never said aloud to anyone. 'I mean, I'm busy most of the time, and of course I have friends here. It's a small place. Everyone knows everyone else and, since I returned, I've caught up with friends who went to school with me. It's nice enough but…' She took a deep breath. 'You're right. Sometimes, it gets a little lonely…'

Theo sat back to look at her narrowly. He had angled to find out more about her. He had reasoned that knowledge was power. To find out about her would help him when it came to buying the house. But, more than that, he had been strangely curious, curious to find out what had brought her and kept her here.

Now she was telling him—was it a good idea to encourage her in her confidences?

She wasn't the confiding sort. He could see that in the soft, embarrassed flush in her cheeks, as though she was doing something against her better judgement.

'Why are you telling me this?' he asked softly and Becky looked at him from under her lashes.

'Why not?'

'Because you've been resisting my questions ever since I turned up here and started asking them.'

Becky's flush deepened.

'I don't know you,' she said honestly, shrugging. 'And

once you leave my house I'll never see you again. You're not my type—you're not the sort of person I would ever want to continue having any sort of friendship with, despite the weird way we've happened to meet.'

'Such irresistible charm...' he murmured, catching her eye and countering her sheepishness with raised eyebrows.

Becky laughed and then warmed when he smiled back, a watchful, assessing smile. 'A girl doesn't get much chance to be irresistibly charming out here in the sticks,' she said. 'The livestock don't appreciate it.'

'But there's more than livestock out here, isn't there?' Theo prodded.

'Not much,' Becky confessed. She grimaced and then looked away, down to the wine glass which appeared to be empty. He had brought the bottle to the table and now he reached across to top her up. 'I say that I'm not on call-out twenty-four seven,' she laughed. 'Let's hope I don't get an emergency call tonight because I might just end up with my car in a ditch.'

'Surely no one would expect you to go out in weather like this?' Theo looked at her, startled, and she laughed again.

She had a lovely laugh, soft, ever so slightly self-conscious, the sort of laugh that automatically made you want to smile.

'No. Although I *have* had emergencies in snow before where I've had no choice but to get into my car, head out and hope for the best. Sheep. They sometimes have poor timing when it comes to lambing. They don't usually care whether it's snowing or whether it's three in the morning.'

'So just the demanding sheep to get your attention...' He considered that, in the absence of a significant other, she would be as free as a bird should she find herself having to leave the house at short notice.

To somewhere—he mentally justified the inevitable—where there might be more for a girl of her age than sheep and livestock.

'I don't suppose someone like you ever feels…like you're not too sure where you're going or what the next step might be.'

The question caught him by surprise because it wasn't often anyone ignored his 'no trespass' signs to ask anything as outrageously personal, and for a few seconds he contemplated not answering. But, then again, why not? Like she had so aptly said, they were ships passing in the night.

And besides, he liked that shy, tentative look on her face. It was so different from the feisty little minx who had first greeted him at the front door. He liked the fact that she was opening up to him. Normally uninterested in most women's predictable back stories—which were always spun as a prelude to someone trying to get to him—he had to admit that he was keen to hear hers.

She wanted nothing from him and that was liberating. He thought that it allowed him actually to *be himself.*

Of course, within certain limits, considering he had chosen to keep her in the dark about his real reasons for descending on her like a bolt from the blue, but there was no such thing as absolute truth between people, was there?

'No,' he drawled. 'I make it my business to always know where I'm going and I certainly have never been wrong-footed when it comes to the future.'

'Never?' Becky laughed uncertainly. He was so overwhelming, so blindingly self-assured. Those were character traits that should have left her cold but in him they were sexy, seductive, almost endearing. 'Nothing has ever happened in your life that you haven't been able to control?'

Theo frowned. Outside, through the kitchen window, he could see the driving fall of white, as fine and fierce as a dust storm, lit up and dazzling in the little patch outside the window where a light had been switched on.

Inside was warm and mellow. He hadn't felt so un-stressed in a while and he recalled why he had been stressed for the past several months. Nothing to do with work. The stress of work was something he enjoyed, something he needed to survive, the way a plant needs rain or sun. He had been stressed out by his mother. This was the first time he could think about her without his gut tightening up.

'My mother has been ill,' he heard himself say abruptly. 'A stroke. Out of the blue. No one saw it coming, least of all me. So, yes, that could be categorised as something that has happened that has been out of my control.'

Becky wanted to reach across and squeeze his hand because he looked awkward with the confession. She wasn't accustomed to pouring her heart out to anyone and, clearly, neither was he. Not that she wouldn't have been able to see that for herself after five minutes in his company.

'I'm sorry. How is she now? How is your father dealing with it? And the rest of your family? Sometimes, it's almost harder for the family members.'

Theo wondered how he had managed to end up here, with a virtual stranger leaning towards him, face wreathed with sympathy.

'There's just me,' he said shortly. 'My father died…a long time ago and I'm an only child.'

'That's tough.' Becky thought of her own family arrangements.

'Do you feel sorry for me?' he prompted with silky smoothness. He smiled slowly, very slowly, and watched as the blood crept up to her hairline. She wanted to look away, but she couldn't, and that gave him a heady kick because the oldest game in the book was being played now and he liked that.

He liked it a lot more than spilling his guts like one of those emotional, touchy-feely types he had never had time for.

This was safe ground and known territory. When it came to sex, Theo was at home, and this was about sex. Why bother to beat about the bush? She wanted him and the feeling was mutual. He didn't understand why he found her so appealing, because she was not his type, but he did, and he wondered whether that had to do with the fact that for once there was no pressure. He wasn't even certain that she would take his hand if he offered it and allow herself to be led up to that bedroom of hers.

The uncertainty just lent another layer to the thrill of a chase he hadn't yet decided to embark upon.

Though she was so unknowingly sexy…

He wondered what she would look like without clothes on. He had to guess at a figure she was hell-bent on concealing and he was desperate to see what was there. He flexed his fingers and shifted.

'Of course I feel sorry for you,' Becky was saying with heartfelt sincerity. 'I'd be devastated if anything happened to one of my family.' She watched as he slowly eased his big body out of the chair. Her heart began to beat fast and it was beating even faster when he leaned over her to support himself on either side of her chair, caging her in.

She wanted to touch him. She wanted him to touch her. In no way did she feel in the slightest threatened by this tall, lean, powerful man physically dominating her with his presence.

She felt...feminine.

It was an unfamiliar feeling because femininity was something she had always presumed herself lacking. It went with good looks and both of those were the domain of her sister.

'How sorry?' Theo murmured huskily. Her excitement was contagious. He could feel it roaring through his veins, making him act in this unexpected way, because the caveman approach was just not his thing. He didn't sling women over his shoulder or rip their clothes off. That would have been on a par with beating his chest and swinging from tree to tree on a vine. But he wanted to sling this one over his shoulder, especially when she sat there, staring at him with those incredible eyes, chewing on her lower lip, refusing flippantly to give in to the massive charge of attraction between them.

'I...' Becky offered weakly. 'What's going on here?'

'Sorry?' Theo wondered whether he had misheard.

'I'm not sure I understand what's going on...'

'What do you think is going on? We're two adults and we're attracted to one another and what's going on is me making a pass at you...'

'Why?'

Theo straightened. He shot her a crooked smile and then perched on the edge of the table. 'This is a first for me.'

'What is?' Startled, Becky stared at him. She was so turned on that she could barely speak and she couldn't quite believe that this was happening. Not to her. Stuff like this never happened to her. She had always been the bookworm who attracted fellow bookworms. Face it, even Freddy had been a bookworm just like her. Guys like Theo didn't go for girls like her. They went for hot blondes in tight dresses who batted their eyelashes and knew what to do when it came to sex.

What did she know about sex? Nerves gripped her but the promise of that ride, with its speed, its thrills and its unbearable excitement, was much, much greater than any attack of nerves.

She wanted this.

'Never mind,' she said softly, eyes dipped. Her innate seriousness wanted to be reassured, wanted to be told that this was more than just sex, but of course it wasn't. It was purely about sex and that was part of its dragging appeal. This went against everything inside her and yet she couldn't resist its ferocious tug on all her senses.

'Look at me, Becky.'

She obeyed and waited with halted breath for him to say what he had to say.

'If you have any doubts at all, then say so right now and we both walk away from this.'

She shook her head and smiled, and Theo nodded. 'And Becky...' He leaned over her once again, his dark, lean face utterly serious. 'There's something I should tell you from the outset, just so that there are no mis-understandings. Don't invest in me and don't think that this is going to be the start of something big. It won't. I don't do relationships and, even if I did, we're from different worlds.'

He didn't do relationships and, even if he did, they were from different worlds...

He was giving her an out and he wasn't beating about the bush. This would be a one-night stand. She was going to hand her virginity over to someone who had made it clear that there was nothing between them bar physical attraction The one thing on which she had never placed any emphasis. Yet this was more than longing on her part. Her virginity felt like an albatross around her neck and she wanted to set herself free from it more than anything in the world.

'Message received and understood,' Becky murmured and blushed as he delivered her a slashing smile. 'You're not from my world either and, although I *do* do relationships, it would never, ever be with someone like you. So we're on the same page.' The dynamics of what happened next was making her perspire. Should she tell him that she was a virgin? No. Chances were he would never guess anyway…and she didn't want him to take fright and pull back.

'I've wanted you the minute I saw you,' Theo confessed unsteadily, fingers hooking under the waistband of the jogging bottoms he had borrowed.

'Even though I'm from a different world?' She tilted her chin up and stared at him.

'You've admitted the same about me' was his gruff response.

'I don't know why I find you attractive at all,' she muttered to herself and Theo laughed.

'Don't spare my ego, whatever you do.'

Their eyes tangled and she felt an affinity with him, this inappropriate stranger, that was so powerful it took her breath away. It was as if they were on exactly the same page, united, thinking as one, mixed up with one another as though they belonged.

Shaken, she stared at him.

Turned on beyond belief, Theo stayed her as she made to stand. 'Not yet,' he murmured. He stood in front of her and then he knelt and parted her legs, big hands on her inner thighs. Becky held her breath and then released it in a series of little gasps and sighs. She wanted to squirm. She wasn't naked but the way he was holding her, his position between her legs, made her feel exposed and daringly, recklessly wanton.

She flung back her head and half-closed her eyes. She felt his fingers dip under the waistband of her jeans and then the soft pop of the button being released, followed by the sound of the zipper being pulled down.

Everything was heightened.

She could hear the hammering of her heart against her rib cage, the raspy sound of her jerky breathing, the soft fluttering of her eyelids. She wriggled as he began to pull down her jeans.

This was surreal. The girl who had always thought that sex would be with someone she had given her heart to was desperate for a man who was just passing through. The girl who had quietly assumed that she'd *know* when love struck was being floored by something she had never anticipated—unbridled, hot, heady, sweat-inducing lust.

Cool air hit her legs. She half-opened her eyes and groaned softly, reaching out to curl her fingers in Theo's hair. He looked up and their eyes met.

'Enjoying yourself?' he asked in a wickedly soft voice and Becky nodded.

'Then why don't you get vocal and tell me?'

'I can't!'

'Of course you can. And you can tell me what you want me to do as well…' Her panties were still on. He could breathe in her musky scent through them and see the dampness of her desire, a patch of moisture against the pale pink cotton. He didn't pull them down. Instead, he gently peeled them to one side, exposing her, and blew softly against the mound.

'What should I do next?' he enquired.

'Theo…' Becky gasped in a strangled voice. She'd slipped a little down the chair.

'Tell me,' he ordered softly. 'Want me to lick you down there? Want to feel my tongue sliding in and teasing you?'

'Yes,' Becky whispered.

'Then give me some orders…' He was so hot for her, turned on by her shyness, which was so different from what he was accustomed to.

He had to shed his clothes. Urgently. The top, then the jogging bottoms, taking his boxer shorts with them. She was looking at him, eyes wide.

'Lick me…' Just saying that made her whole body burn. 'I'm so wet for you…' He was so beautiful that he took her breath away. Her mind had always drawn a convenient line at the bedroom door. In her head, the act of making love stopped with kissing, fumbling and whispering of sweet nothings.

She had never pictured the reality of the naked male, not really. This surpassed all her fantasies and she knew, somewhere deep down inside, that the benchmark he had set would never be reached by any other man. He was so gloriously masculine, his body so lean and exquisitely perfect, the burnished gold of his colouring so impossibly sexy.

Theo pulled off the panties, wanting to take his time, and knowing that it would require super-human control to do that, because he was so hard he was hurting. She was wonderfully wet and she shuddered as he slid his questing tongue against her, seeking out the little throbbing bud and then teasing it, feeling it swell and tighten.

Becky was on fire, burning up. Two of his fingers joined his tongue in its devastating assault on her senses.

She pushed his head harder against her. She felt so ready to take him into her. 'Come in me,' she begged.

'All in good time.' Theo barely recognised his voice. Having boasted about his formidable talent for exercising control all the time in all areas of his life, he was finding out what it felt like to lose it. He was free-falling, his body doing its own thing, refusing to listen to his head…

Head buried between her legs, he sucked hard and felt her come against his mouth, her body arching up, stiffening, her breath sucked in as her orgasm ripped through her, long and shuddering.

He rose up, watching her brightly flushed face and her feverish twisting as her orgasm subsided.

His good intentions to hang onto his self-control had disappeared faster than water being sucked down a plug hole.

'Hold me,' he commanded, legs straddled over her.

Dazed, Becky took him in her hand. Nothing had ever felt so good. Every inhibition she had ever had when she had thought about making love to a man for the first time disappeared the minute he touched her.

It felt *so right*.

He made her feel special, made it feel natural for her to open herself up to him in the most intimate way imaginable.

Touching him now, she was no longer apprehensive, even though her mind skittered away from the physical dynamics of having someone as big as he was inside her. She was so wet and so giddy for him that it wasn't going to be a problem…

She delicately traced her tongue along his rigid shaft then took him into her mouth and felt a surge of heady power as he groaned and arched back.

Instinct came naturally. She even knew when he was

nearing his orgasm…and she sensed that this was not how he had planned things to go.

Looking down at her, Theo could scarcely believe that his control had slipped so completely that he couldn't contain the orgasm he knew was a whisper away. Her mouth circling him was mind-blowingly erotic, as was the focused expression on her face and the slight trembling of her fingers cupping him.

Intent on not coming like *this*, he pulled away, and for a second he thought that he had succeeded, thought that he could hold himself in check for the length of time it would take them both to get upstairs. He was mistaken. He could no more control the inexorable orgasm that had been building from the moment she had looked at him with those turquoise eyes…the moment he had known that they would end up in bed together, whether it made sense or not, whether it was a good idea or not…than he could have controlled a fast approaching tsunami.

For Becky, still transported to another planet, this was inexplicably satisfying because it was proof positive that he was as out of control as she was.

Watching him come over her had rendered her almost faint with excitement. Her heated gaze met his and his mouth quirked crookedly.

'Would you believe me if I told you that this has never happened in my life before?' Theo was still breathing thickly and still shocked at his body's unexpected rebellion. 'I'm taking you upstairs before it happens again.' He lifted her up in one easy movement and took the stairs quickly. She could have been as light as a feather. Her hair was all over the place, her cheeks were bright with hectic colour and her eyes drowsy with desire.

The curtains hadn't been drawn and weak moonlight seeped into her bedroom. It was still snowing, a steady, silent fall of white that somehow enhanced the peculiar dream-like feel to what was going on.

Theo took a few seconds to look at her on the bed. Her dark hair was spread across the pillows and her pale, rounded body was a work of art. Her breasts were big, bigger than a generous handful, her nipples cherry-pink discs.

He was going to take his time.

He'd acted the horny teenager once and it wasn't going to happen again. He still couldn't compute how it had happened in the first place.

He joined her on the bed, pinned her hands to her side and straddled her.

'This time,' he said roughly, 'I'm going to take my time enjoying you...' He started with her breasts, working his way to them via her soft shoulders, down to the generous dip of her cleavage, nuzzling the heavy crease beneath her breasts until he settled on a nipple, and there he stayed, lathing it with his mouth, suckling, teasing and tasting, drawing the throbbing, stiffened bud into his mouth, greedy for her.

Becky writhed and groaned. She spread her legs and wrapped them around him, desperate to press herself against the hardness of his thigh so that she could relieve some of the sensitivity between them. But he wasn't having that and he manoeuvred her so that she was lying flat, enduring the sweet torment of his mouth all over her breasts.

He reached back to rub between her legs with the flat of his hand but not too much, not too hard and not for long.

He needed more than this erotic foreplay. He needed to be inside her, to feel that wetness all around him.

'My wallet's in my bedroom,' he whispered hoarsely. 'I need it to get protection. Don't go anywhere...'

Where was she going to go? Her body physically missed his for the half a minute it took for him to return and, during that time, she thought again about whether she should tell him the truth, tell him that she was a virgin…and, just as before, she quailed at the thought.

But as he applied the condom, looking directly at her as his fingers slid expertly along his huge shaft, she felt a twinge of nerves.

Theo settled between her legs and nudged her, pushing against her wetness gently. He wasn't going to go hard and fast. He was going to take his time and enjoy every second of her. He felt her momentarily tense but thought nothing of it. He was so fired up he could barely think at all and he certainly couldn't read anything from her response until he pushed into her, sinking deep and moving faster than he wanted but knowing that he just had to.

He heard her soft grunt of discomfort and stilled. 'I'm a big boy…tell me if I'm hurting you because you're really tight. Deliciously tight…' He sank deep into her and then it clicked.

Her blushing shyness, the way he had felt, as though everything he was doing was being done for the first time, that momentary wince…

'Bloody hell, Becky—tell me you're not a virgin…?'

'Take me, Theo. Please don't stop…'

He should have withdrawn but he couldn't. *A virgin.* His body was aflame at the thought. He'd never wanted any woman the way he wanted this one. Every sensation running through his body felt primitive. He was the caveman he never thought he could be, and the fact of her virginity made him feel even more primal, even more like a caveman.

Their bodies were slick with perspiration. With a groan, he thrust hard, deep into her tightness, and the feeling was indescribable as she rocked with him, wrapping her legs around his waist and coming seconds before he did, crying out as she raked her fingers along his back, the rhythm of her body matching his.

'You should have said.' He fell onto his back, disposing of the condom and thinking that he should be feeling a lot more alarmed that he had slept with someone as innocent as she was. So much for her escape to the country in the wake of some dastardly affair with a married man, or whoever it had been.

He was her first.

He'd never been more turned on.

'It doesn't make any difference.' She rolled so that she was half-balancing on his chest and staring down at him. 'Like I said, Theo, this isn't the beginning of anything for me. One night and then we exit one another's lives for ever...' She traced her finger around his flat, brown nipple. Why did it hurt when she said that?

'In that case...' Theo wasn't going to play mind games with himself as to whether he had done the right thing or not. 'Let's make the most of the night...'

CHAPTER FOUR

THEO STROLLED THROUGH into the kitchen of his sprawling four-bedroom penthouse and ignored the food that had been lavishly prepared by his personal chef, who kept him fed when he was in the country and actually in his apartment. The dish, with its silver dome, was on the counter, alongside a selection of condiments and some basic instructions on heating.

Instead, he headed straight for the cupboard, took down a squat whisky glass and proceeded to pour himself a stiff drink.

He needed it.

His mother, still in Italy, was back in hospital.

'A fall,' her sister Flora had told him when she had called less than an hour ago. 'She was on her way to get something to drink.' She had sounded vague and unsettled. 'And she tripped. You know those tiles, Theo, they can be very smooth and slippery. And I have told your mother a thousand times never to wear those stupid bedroom slippers when she is in the house! Those slippers with the fur and the suede are for your little box houses in England with lots of carpet! Not for nice tiles!'

'On her way to get something to drink?' Theo had picked up on the uneasy tone of his aunt's voice, and he had been right to, even though it had taken some prodding and nudging in the right direction to get answers out of her.

Now he sank into the long cream leather sofa and stared, frowning, past the stunning art originals on either side of the marble fireplace at nothing in particular. His mind was consumed by the very fundamental question…

What was he going to do?

His mother had not been on the way to fetch herself a glass of orange juice at a little after three-thirty in the afternoon. Nor had she tripped in her haste to make herself a fortifying cup of tea.

'She has been a little depressed,' Flora had admitted reluctantly. 'You know how it is, Theo. She likes it out here but she sees me…my grandchildren…I cannot hide any of this from Marita! I cannot put my children and my grandchildren in a cupboard and lock them away because my sister might find it upsetting!'

Theo had gritted his teeth and moved the grudging conversation along, to discover that depression was linked with drinking. His mother had gradually, over the weeks, become fond of a tipple or two before dinner and it seemed that the tipple or two had crept earlier and earlier up the day until she was having a drink with lunch and after lunch.

'Why haven't you told me this before?' he had asked coldly, but that had produced a flurry of indignant protests and Theo had been forced to concede that Flora had had a point. She didn't share the villa with his mother. She would not really have seen the steady progression of the problem until something happened to bring it to her notice.

Such as the fall.

'She's due out of hospital in a week's time,' Flora had said. 'But she doesn't want to return to London. She says that she has nothing there. She enjoys my grandchildren, Theo, even though it pains her to know that...'

There had been no need for his aunt to complete the sentence with all its barely concealed criticism.

Getting married and having hordes of children was the Italian way.

Going out with legions of unsuitable women, remaining stubbornly single and promising no grandchildren whatsoever was not.

And it wasn't as though he had siblings who could provide for his mother what he was unwilling to.

But he had to do *something*...

He glanced at his computer, lodged on the gleaming glass table on which he had stuck his feet. For a few seconds, he stopped thinking about the predicament with his mother and returned to what he had spent the last fortnight thinking about.

Becky.

The woman had occupied his mind so much that he hadn't been able to focus at work. The one night, as it happened, had turned into three because the snow had continued to fall, a wall of white locking them into a little bubble where, for a window in time, he had been someone else.

He had stopped being the powerhouse in charge of his own personal empire. He had stopped being responsible for all those people who depended on him for a livelihood. There'd been no fawning women trying to get his attention wherever he went or heads of companies trying to woo him into a deal of some sort or another. He was untroubled by the constant ringing of his mobile phone because service had been so limited that, after informing his PA that he couldn't get adequate reception, he had done the unthinkable and switched the phone off.

He had shed the billionaire persona just as he had shed the expensive clothes he had travelled in.

He had chopped wood, did his best to clear snow and fixed things around the house that had needed fixing.

And of course he had noted all the flaws with the cottage, which were not limited to the leaking roof. Everywhere he'd looked, things needed doing, and those things would only get worse as time went on.

He knew that if he played his cards right he would be able to get the place at a knockdown price. He could bypass her altogether. He had found out where her parents lived, even knew what they did for a living. He could simply have returned to London, picked up the phone and made them an offer they couldn't refuse. Judging from the state of the cottage, it wouldn't have had to be a high offer.

But that thought had not even occurred to him. He had played fast and loose with the truth when Becky had first asked him what had brought him to the Cotswolds and, like all good lies, it had been impossible to disconnect from it.

Maybe he had kidded himself that once he returned to London his usual ruthlessness would supplant his momentary lapse in character when he had been living with her. It hadn't worked that way and he had spent the past fortnight wondering what his next step was to be.

And, worse, wondering why he couldn't stop thinking about her. Thinking about her body, warm, soft and welcoming. Thinking about the way she laughed, the way she slid her eyes over to him, still shy even though they had touched each other everywhere. She haunted his dreams and wreaked havoc with his levels of concentration but he knew that there was no point picking up the phone and calling her because what they had enjoyed had not been destined to last.

They had both recognised that.

She had laughed when he had stood by her front door, back in his expensive cashmere, which was a little worse for wear thanks to the weather.

'Who *are* you?' she had teased, with a catch in her voice. 'I don't recognise the person standing in front of me!'

'It's been fun,' he had returned with a crooked smile but that about summed it up.

Back in the clothes she usually didn't step out of, she was the country vet, already thickly bundled up to go to the practice where she worked. He could no more have transported her to his world than he could have continued in her father's old clothes clearing snow and chopping wood for the fire.

But he'd felt something, something brief and piercing tugging deep inside him, a sharp ache that had taken him by surprise.

He focused now and looked around him at the fabulous penthouse, the very best that money could buy. He'd bought it three years previously and since then it had more than quadrupled in price. It sat at the top of an impressive converted glass and red brick government building which was formidably austere on the outside but outstandingly modern and well-appointed on the inside. Theo liked that. It gave him the pleasant illusion of living in a building of historic interest without having to endure any of the physical inconveniences that came with buildings of historic interest.

He wondered how Becky would fit in here. Not well. He wondered how she would fit into his lifestyle. Likewise, not well. He moved in circles where the women were either clothes horses, draped on the arms of very, very rich men, or else older, at ease with their wealth, often condescending to those without but in a terribly well-mannered and polite way.

And the women all dripped gold and diamonds, and were either chauffeured to and from their luxury destinations or else drove natty little sports cars.

But his mother...would like her. She was just the sort of natural girl his mother approved of. There was even something vaguely Italian about the way she looked, with her long, dark hair and her rounded, hourglass figure.

His mother would approve and so...

For the first time since he had returned to London after his sojourn in the back of beyond, Theo felt a weight lift from his shoulders.

Trying to deal with the annoying business of Becky playing on his mind when she should have been relegated to the past had interrupted the smooth running of his life and he could see now that he had been looking at things from the wrong angle.

He should have realised that there was only one reason why he hadn't been able to get her out of his mind. She was unfinished business. The time to cut short their sexual liaison had not yet come to its natural conclusion, hence he was still wrapped up with her and with thoughts of making love to her again.

He would make contact with her and see her again and he would take her to see his mother in Italy. She would be a tonic for his mother, who would be able at least to contemplate her son going out with a woman who wasn't completely and utterly inappropriate.

She would find her mojo once again and, when she was back to full strength, he would break the news that he and Becky were finished, but by then Marita

Rushing would be back on her feet and able to see a way forward.

And, he thought with even greater satisfaction, she would have the cottage to look forward to, the cottage she had wanted. Would Becky agree to speak to her parents about selling it to him? Yes. She would because it made financial sense and he had no doubt that he would be able to persuade her to see that. The house was falling down and would be beyond the point of reasonable sale in under a year, at which point the family home would either collapse into the ground or else be picked apart and sold to some developer with his eye on a housing estate.

Would she agree to this little game of pretend for the sake of his mother's health? Yes, she would, because that was the sort of girl she was. Caring, empathetic. When she had spoken about some of the animals she had treated in the course of her career, her eyes had welled up.

The various loose strands of this scheme began to weave and mesh in his mind.

And he felt good about all of it. He was solution-oriented and he felt good at seeing a way forward to solving the situation with his mother, or at least dealing with it in a way that could conceivably have a positive outcome.

And he felt great about seeing Becky again. In fact, he felt on top of the world.

He nudged his mobile phone into life and dialled…

Becky heard the buzz of her phone as she was about to climb into bed, and she literally couldn't believe her bad luck, because she had had two call-outs the past two nights and she really, *really* needed to get some sleep.

But then she drowsily glanced at the screen, saw who was calling and her heart instantly accelerated into fifth gear.

He had her number. He had taken it when he had been leaving on that last day because the roads had still been treacherous, even though the snow had lightened considerably, and she had been worried about him driving to London in his *silly little boy-racer car.*

'I'll call you if I end up in a ditch somewhere,' he had drawled, and then he had taken her number.

Noticeably, he hadn't given her his, and that had stung, even though she had made it perfectly clear that what they'd had was a done deal—there for the duration of the snow, and going just as the snow would go, disappearing into nothing until you couldn't even remember what it had been like to have it there.

Of course he hadn't called but for her the memory of him hadn't disappeared like the snow. Where white fields had faded from her mind, the memory of him was still as powerful after two weeks as it had been after two hours.

It didn't help either that, with the practice winding down, work was thinning out as the farmers, dog-owners, cat-owners and even one parrot-owner began transferring business to the nearest practice fifteen miles away. She had the feeling of being the last person at the party, hanging around after the crowd had dispersed when the lights were being switched on and the workers were beginning to clear the tables. The same sad, redundant feeling of someone who has outstayed their welcome.

And the house…

Becky had decided that she wouldn't think about the house until she had found herself a new job because there were only so many things one person could worry about.

But neither of those massive anxieties could eclipse the thoughts of Theo, which had lodged in her head and continued to occupy far too much space. She found herself regularly drifting off into dreamland. She wondered what he was doing. She longed to hear his voice. She checked her phone obsessively and then gave herself little lectures about being stupid because they had both agreed that theirs would only be a passing fling. She rehearsed fictional conversations with him, should they ever accidentally bump into one another, which was so unlikely it was frankly laughable.

She wondered why he had managed to get to her the way he had. Was it because he had come along at a point in time when she had been feeling especially vulnerable? With her job about to disappear and her sister finally achieving the picture-postcard life with her much-wanted baby on the way? Or was it because she had been starved of male attention for way too long? Or maybe it had been neither of those things.

Maybe she had never stood a chance because he was just so unbelievably good-looking and unbelievably sexy and she had just not had the arsenal to deal with his impact.

When she caught herself thinking that, she always and inevitably started thinking about the women he might now be seeing. She hadn't even asked him whether he had a girlfriend! He had seemed, for all his good looks, as the honourable sort of guy who would never have cheated on any woman he might have been seeing, but of course she could have been wrong.

He could have returned to London in his fancy car and immediately picked back up where he had left off with some gorgeous model type.

Realistically she had never expected him to get in touch so she stared open-mouthed at the buzzing mobile phone in her hand, too dumbstruck to do anything.

'Hello?'

Theo heard the hesitancy in her voice and immediately

knew that he had done the right thing in contacting her, had made the right decision. When he had driven away from her house two weeks ago, he had told himself that he had had a good time, but at the end of the day she had been a virgin and he'd been driving away from a potential problem. She had laughed off the fact that he had been the first man she had slept with, had told him that she was attracted to him, and why not?

'You're not the right guy for me,' she had said seriously. 'But, if I carry on waiting for Mr Right to come along, I might be waiting for a very long time.'

'In other words, you're using me!' he had laughed, amused, and she had laughed back.

'Are you hurt?' she had teased.

'I'll survive…'

And she hadn't been lying. There had been no clinging when the time had come for him to go. She hadn't tried to entice him into carrying on what they'd had. There had been no awkward questions asked about whether he would miss her. Her eyes hadn't misted over, her lips hadn't trembled and she hadn't clung to the lapels of his coat or given him one final, lingering kiss. She had smiled, waved goodbye and shut the door before he had had time to fire up the engine.

He might have been her first but he certainly wasn't going to be her last. Maybe that was another reason why he hadn't been able to get her out of his head. He'd effectively been dumped, and he'd never been dumped in his life before, simple as that.

'Becky…'

Becky heard that wonderful lazy drawl and the hairs on the back of her neck stood on end. She steeled herself to feel nothing, but curiosity was eating her up. Had he missed her? Had he been thinking about her every second of every minute, which was what it had felt like for her? Thinking about him all the time...

'How are you?'

'Been better.' They could spend time going around in polite circles before she asked him the obvious question—*why have you called?*—and Theo decided that he would skip the foreplay and get down to the main event. 'Becky, I could beat around the bush here, but the fact is I've called to ask you for...a favour. This would be a favour better asked face to face but...time is of the essence, I'm afraid. I just haven't got enough of it to woo you into helping me out.'

'A favour?' Of course he hadn't called because he'd missed her. Disappointment coursed through her, as bitter as bile.

'Do you remember I spoke to you about my mother? It would appear that...' He sighed heavily. 'Perhaps it would have been better to be having this conversation face to face after all. I know that this is asking a lot, Becky, but there have been some...unfortunate problems with my mother—problems that do not appear to have a straightforward solution.' The direct approach was failing. He stood up, paced and sat back down. 'I need you, Becky,' he said heavily.

'Need me to do what?' Her voice had cooled.

'Need you to come to London so that I can talk to you in person. I can send my driver for you.'

'Are you crazy, Theo? I don't know what's going on with your mother. I'm sorry if she's having problems but you can't just call me up out of the blue and expect me to jump to your summons.'

'I understand that what we had was... Look, I get it that, when you closed your front door, you didn't anticipate me getting in touch with you again.' Theo seriously found it hard to believe that this could actually be the case because the shoe was always on the other foot. Women were the ones desperate for him to make contact and he had always been the one keen to avoid doing any such thing.

He instinctively paused, waiting to hear whether she would refute that statement. She didn't.

Becky thought that he was certainly right on that count—she hadn't anticipated it—but she had hoped. It hadn't crossed her mind that she would indeed hear from him and he would be asking a favour of her!

That certainly put paid to any girlish illusions she might have had that their very brief fling had meant anything at all for him. She was thankful that she had waved him a cheery goodbye and not made any mention of hoping that they might meet again.

'You're right—I didn't—and I don't see how I could possibly do you any favours in connection with your mother. I don't even know her.'

'She fell,' Theo said bluntly. 'I've just come off the telephone with her sister. She apparently...' He paused, dealing with the unpalatable realisation that he was actually going to have to open up about a situation which felt intensely personal and which he instinctively thought should be kept to himself.

'Apparently what...?' Becky could feel vulnerability in his hesitation. He was so strong, so proud, so much the archetypal alpha male that any sort of personal confession would seem like an act of weakness to him.

Despite herself, she felt her heart go out to him, and then banked down that unwelcome tide of empathy.

'She's been depressed. The recovery we had all hoped for has been a physical success but...'

Again, that telling pause. She had a vivid picture of

him trying to find difficult words. She felt she knew him, and then she wondered how that was possible, considering they had spent a scant three days in one another's company. *Knowing* someone took a long time. It had taken her nearly two years before she had felt that she *knew* Freddy, and then it had turned out that she hadn't known him at all, so how likely was it that this sensation of being able to *sense* what Theo was feeling from down the end of a telephone was anything other than wishful thinking?

She wasn't going to give in to any misplaced feelings of sympathy. By nature, she was soft. It was why she had chosen to study veterinary science. Caring for sick and wounded animals was straight up her alley. But Theo was neither sick nor a wounded animal. He was a guy she had slept with who hadn't bothered to get in touch with her until now, when he obviously wanted something from her.

'She fell because she was drinking,' he said abruptly.

'Drinking?'

'No one knows how long it's been going on but it's reached a stage where she's drinking during the day and…a danger to herself. God knows what might have happened if she had been behind the wheel of a car…'

'I'm so sorry to hear that,' Becky said sincerely. 'You must be worried sick…'

'Which is why I called you. If my mother's problems are alcohol related, then it's obvious that she's slipping into a depressed frame of mind. There were signs of that happening before she left for Italy…' He sighed heavily. 'Perhaps I should have insisted that she go for therapy, for counselling of some sort, but of course I thought it was a straightforward case of being down because she had had a stroke, because she had had a brush with her own mortality.'

'That's understandable, Theo.' Becky automatically consoled him. 'I wouldn't beat myself up over it if I were you. Besides, there's nothing you can do about that now. Weren't you the person who made a big deal about telling me how important it was to live in the present because you can't worry over things that happened in the past which you can't change?'

'I told you that?'

'Over that tuna casserole you told me you hated.'

'Oh, yes. I remember…'

Becky's skin warmed. His voice had dropped to a husky drawl with just the ghost of a satisfied smile in it and she knew exactly what was going through his head.

He had pushed the dish of tuna bake to one side, pulled her towards him and they had made love in the kitchen. He had laid her on the table, her legs dangling, the dishes balanced in a heap that could have crashed to the floor at any given moment. He had parted her legs and had licked, sucked and nuzzled between them until she had been crying and whimpering for him to stop, for him to come inside her—and come inside her he had, with urgent, hungry, greedy force that had sent her soaring to an orgasm that had gone on and on and had left her shattered afterwards.

'So,' she said hurriedly, 'you couldn't have foreseen. Anyway, I'm sure everything will be fine when you bring her back to London, where you can keep an eye on her. You could even employ someone…'

She wondered whether that was the little favour he had phoned about. Perhaps he had returned to his busy tycoon lifestyle and was too preoccupied with making money to make time, so he'd decided that she might be able to see her way to helping him out. She'd been short-sighted enough to mention to him that the practice was going to close. Maybe he thought she'd have lots of free time on her hands.

'She's refusing to return to London.'

'Yes, well...'

'Nothing to come back here for, were, apparently— her words.'

'I still don't see why you've called me, Theo. I don't see how I could possibly help. Maybe you should...'

'Needs something to live for.'

'Yes, but...'

'She's old-fashioned, my mother. She wants what her sister has. She wants...a daughter-in-law.'

Becky thought she had misheard and then she figured that, even if she hadn't, she *still* had no idea what that had to do with her.

'Then you should get married,' she said crisply. 'I'm sure there would be hundreds of women falling over their feet to drag you up the altar.'

'But only one that fits the bill. You.'

Becky burst out laughing, manic, disbelieving laughter. 'You've telephoned out of the blue so that you can ask me to marry you because your mother's depressed?'

Theo's mouth compressed. He hadn't *asked her to marry him*. He loved his mother but even he could see a limit to the lengths he would go to in order to appease her. But, if he had, hysterical laughter would not have been the expected response.

'I'm asking you to go along with a fake engagement,' he gritted. 'A harmless pretence that would do wonders for my mother. We go to Italy...an all-expenses-paid holiday for you...and you smile a lot and then we leave. My mother will be delighted. She will have something to live for. Her depression will lift.'

'Until she discovers that it's all been a complete lie and there won't be any fairy-tale white wedding.'

'By which time two things will have been achieved. She will no longer be so depressed that she's dependent on a bottle to help her through, and she will realise that I'm capable of having a relationship with someone who isn't a bimbo.'

'So let me get this straight,' Becky said coldly. 'I'm the one for this *harmless pretence* because I have a brain and because—I'm reading between the lines here—I'm not tall, blonde and beautiful. I'm just an ordinary girl with an ordinary job so your mother will like me. Is that it?'

'You're not exactly what I would call *ordinary*,' Theo mused.

'No.' She was shaking with outrage and, underneath the outrage, hurt.

'Why not?'

'Why do you think, Theo? Because I'm not into deceiving people. Because I have some morals—'

'You're also heading for the unemployment line,' he said, cutting her off before she could carry on with her list of high-minded virtues. He was still scowling at her roar of laughter when she had thought he might have called to ask her to marry him. 'Not to mention living in a house that's falling apart at the seams.'

'Where are you going with this?'

'I could get you up and running with a practice of your own. You name the place and I'll provide the financial backing and cover all the advertising. In fact, I can do better than that—I'll set my team on it. And I'll get all those nasty little things that are wrong with your house repaired…'

'Are you trying to *buy* me so I do what you want?' And the weird thing was…she had thought about him so much, wanted him so much, would have picked up where they had left off if he had made the first move and called her. But this…

Theo wondered how his brilliant idea had managed to get derailed so easily. 'Not buying you, no,' he said heavily, shaking off the nasty feeling that yet again with this woman his self-control was not quite what it should be. 'Business transaction. You give me what I want and I give you…a great deal in return. Becky, that aside…' his voice dropped a notch or two '… I'm asking you from the bottom of my heart to do this for me. Please. You told me that you loved your parents. Put yourself in my shoes—I only want my mother to regain her strength.'

'It's not right, Theo.'

He heard the hesitation in her voice and breathed a heartfelt sigh of relief.

'I am begging you,' he told her seriously. 'And be assured that begging is something I never do.'

Becky closed her eyes tightly and took a deep breath. 'Okay. I'll do it, but on one condition…'

'Name it.'

'No sex. You want a business transaction, then a business transaction is what you'll get.'

CHAPTER FIVE

BECKY HAD WONDERED whether she would be given the fortnight off. She was owed it, had worked unpaid over-time for the past few months, but leaving someone in the lurch was not something she liked to do.

She had half-wished that she would be firmly told that she couldn't be spared, because as soon as she had agreed to Theo's crazy plan she had begun to see all the holes in it. On the contrary, her request was met with just the sort of kind-hearted sympathy that had made her realise how much she would miss working for the small practice.

'You come and go as you please until the place closes,' Norman had said warmly. 'Can't be nice for you, work-ing here, knowing that it's winding down and that you won't be seeing our regulars again. Besides, you need to start thinking about your next job—and don't you worry about anything, Rebecca, you'll get a glowing reference from me.'

'The faster you can make it to London, the better, Becky,' Theo had said as soon as those fateful words—*okay, I agree*—had left her mouth, and he hadn't allowed her to sit on her decision and have any sort of rethink.

She'd needed a bit of time to get things sorted with her job and her house before she just breezed off abroad for two weeks.

'What things?' he had demanded.

She could practically hear him vibrating with impatience down the end of the line. He'd called her several times over the two-day period she'd taken to pack some stuff, check the house for incipient problems that might erupt the minute her back was turned and anxiously leave copious notes on some of the animals that had been booked in to have routine procedures done over the two-week period.

Already regretting her hasty decision, she'd plied him with questions about his mother.

She'd repeatedly told him that it was a crazy idea. He'd listened in polite silence and carried on as though she hadn't spoken, but he *had* talked about Marita Rushing and about the health problems that had afflicted her. He'd only closed up when she'd tried to unearth information prior to the stroke, to life before she had started worrying that her son might never marry and might never make her the grandmother she longed to be.

'Not relevant.' He swept aside her curiosity with the sort of arrogant dismissiveness that she recognised as part and parcel of his vibrant, restless personality.

'She won't believe that we have any kind of relationship,' Becky told him the night before she was due to leave for London. Ever since she had laid down the 'no sex' ground rules, he had been silent on the subject. He hadn't objected and she'd thought that he was probably glad that she had spared him the necessity of trying to resurrect an attraction that hadn't lasted beyond her front door.

That hurt but she told herself that it simplified things. He had suggested that she treat his proposition as a business transaction, and there was no reputable business transaction on the planet that included sex on tap. They'd had their fling and now this was something else. This was his way of doing the best he could to try and get his mother back on her feet and her way of trying to sort out her future.

In a way, accepting his generosity almost turned it into a job—an extremely well-paid job, but a job nevertheless—which meant she could distance herself from that flux of muddled emotions she still seemed to have for him.

It helped her to pretend to herself that there wasn't a big part of her that was excited at the prospect of seeing him again.

'People always believe what they want to believe, but we'll talk about that when you come,' he eventually said.

Becky had accepted that. She'd had too much on her mind to pay attention to whatever story line he might think up. He insisted on sending a driver for her, even though she had told him that the train was perfectly okay.

Now, sitting in the back seat of his chauffeur-driven black Range Rover, she felt the doubts and hesitations begin to pile up.

Along with a suffocating sense of heightened tension, which she valiantly tried to ignore. She told herself that he was not going to be as she remembered. She was looking back at that small window in time through rose-tinted specs. He wouldn't be as striking or as addictive as she had found him when he had stayed with her. Locked away in the cottage with the snow falling outside, she had built their brief fling into an impossibly romantic tryst.

The fact that they were so unsuitable for one another had only intensified the thrill. It was like putting the prissy, well-behaved head girl in the company of the bad boy who had roared into town on his motorbike. No matter how much the sparks might fly, it would all come crashing down because it wasn't reality.

When she went to London, reality would assert itself and she would see him as he really was. Not some tall, dark, dangerously sexy stranger who had burst into her humdrum life like an unexploded bomb, but a nice-looking businessman who wore suits and ties and carried a briefcase.

He would be hassled-looking, with worry lines on his face that she hadn't noticed because she had been swept away on a tide of novelty and adventure.

He hadn't been lying about his wealth. He'd never boasted, but he hadn't tried to hide it. She'd briefly wondered whether he had been enticing her by exaggerating just how much punch he packed, but any such vague doubts were put to rest as the silent, über-luxurious car pushed through the London traffic to glide into a part of the city that was so quiet it *breathed* wealth.

The tree-lined street announced its pedigree with the cars neatly parked outside fabulous, very pristine mansions. Some had driveways, most didn't. At the end of the street, a severe, imposing building dominated the cul-de-sac. It was gated, with a guard in a booth acting as sentry just within the ornate black wrought-iron gates. The very fact that the place was secured against anyone uninvited was an indication of the sort of people who lived there and her mouth fell open as the car drove through, directly to an underground car park.

Becky tugged her coat around her and thought about the two worn, battered cases she had brought with her. She hoped no one would see her on her way to his apartment because she would probably be evicted on the spot.

He had come into her world and he had slotted in, had replaced his city garb with her dad's country clothes and had mucked in as though he had spent his entire life in a shambolic cottage in the middle of nowhere.

But that was not his world. This was. And there was no way that she was going to fit in with the sort of seamless ease with which he had fitted into her world.

'I'll show you to the underground lift.' The chauffeur turned to glance at her. It was the first thing he had said since a polite 'Good morning' earlier when he had greeted her at the front door and taken her cases from her to stick them in the car trunk.

Becky nodded and they walked, in silence, through some glass doors into a reception area which housed a bank of four gleaming lifts, comfortable furniture for several people to relax and two very big, very well-cared-for plants that formed a feature on either side of the row of lifts. Yet another guard in uniform was sitting behind a circular desk and he nodded and exchanged a few pleasantries with Theo's driver, who had brought her bags out with him from the car.

This had all been a very bad idea. She should never have come. She didn't belong here. Their worlds had collided and then flown off in different directions. She should have left it there, just an exciting memory to draw upon now and again, something to put a smile on her face as her life, temporarily upset, carried on along its prescribed route.

Instead, she was here, listening to the porter tell her where to locate Theo, who would be waiting for her. Her battered bags were by her feet. She felt cumbersome and ungainly in her big coat, with all its useful pockets, and underneath the big coat there was nothing more glamorous. Her usual jeans, layers and baggy jumper. She wondered what the chauffeur had thought of her, and now she wondered what the porter was making of her, but she refused to give in to all the insecurities nudging at the door.

This was a business deal. She was doing him a favour and he was doing her one. There was no necessity for her to fit in or not fit in.

But her stomach was knotted with nerves as she was whooshed up in the mirrored lift to the fourteenth floor.

The lift opened out onto a plush carpeted landing. She stared straight ahead into an oversized mirror, on either side of which were two grand abstract paintings.

'Turn right,' the porter told her with a kindly smile, 'and you can't miss Mr Rushing's apartment.'

She turned right and saw the porter had not been kidding. The entire floor was clearly occupied by just one apartment. The corridor was more of an outside landing, with a glass and metal sideboard against the wall over which was another abstract work of art. It was very light and airy. She looked around her and just then, just as she was torn between moving forward and fleeing back to the sanctuary of the lift, a door opened and there he was.

Her heart fluttered erratically and her mouth went dry. He hadn't changed and it had been absurd wishful thinking to have hoped that he might. If anything, he was taller, more aggressively masculine and more sinfully sexy than she remembered. Wearing loafers, a pair of black jeans and a black, fitted short-sleeved polo, he was lounging against the doorframe, watching her as she tried to get herself together and present a composed image.

Theo looked at her. His mind, coolly analytical, recognised what he had known would present itself to him and that was a woman who, quite simply, didn't fit into the world of sophistication and glamour he occupied. He had known that she wouldn't have dressed for the occasion, and anyway, he doubted she had the sort of clothes that would allow her to blend in. She looked ill at ease, with her ancient suitcases on either side of her, and in the exceptionally practical sort of outfit that worked when she was tearing off to see to a sick animal but offered nothing more than functionality.

But then there was that other part of him…the part that remained uncontrolled by his coolly analytical mind… the part that had made him lose concentration at work because he hadn't been able to get her out of his mind…

The part that looked at her standing metres away from him and felt a surge in his libido that took his breath away. It didn't matter what she wore, how unfashionable her clothes were or how awkward she looked as she hovered suspiciously by her cases… She still turned him on.

But no sex.

Those had been her ground rules, and of course they made sense. It didn't matter whether he still wanted her or not. It had been short-sighted to imagine furthering what they had had by a fortnight so that he could somehow get her out of his system.

Perhaps if she had jumped at the opportunity to get back into bed with him again…

If she had greeted his phone call with the sort of breathless pleasure with which any other woman would have responded…

Well, under those circumstances, he would have had no problem in stepping up to the plate and taking what was on offer. But, if she had been the sort of woman to agree to two weeks of abandoned sex, then she wouldn't have been the woman he had gone to bed with.

She might have fancied him, she might have lost her virginity to him because she had been unable to fight the attraction and at that point in her life had chosen to allow the physical side of her to overrule the intellectual side of her, but essentially he wasn't the type of man she was interested in—hence the 'no sex' stipulation.

Common sense had reasserted itself. Of course, she was right. She was far too serious to indulge in a no-strings-attached liaison, especially when she would be going against the grain and faking a relationship with him for the sake of his mother.

The most important thing was his mother's health and he didn't want Becky to start questioning what she was doing because they were sleeping together, because she was having an affair with the wrong guy.

Besides, he had never chased any woman, and he wasn't about to start now.

Annoyed with himself because his libido wasn't playing ball, he pushed off from the doorframe and walked towards her. She looked as though, given half a chance, she would turn tail and scarper.

But of course she wouldn't do that, would she? She was being paid for the favour she was doing him. It didn't matter how morally high-minded you were, money always ruled the day.

She'd only been persuaded into this escapade because of the money. He had thought her different from all the other women he had ever dated in the past, women who had been impressed by his bank balance and the things he was capable of buying for them, but was she really?

His mouth thinned. At least the cards were on the table with no grey areas for misunderstandings. This was a business transaction and focusing on that would get his wayward libido back on the straight and narrow...

'You're here.' He picked up her bags and stood back, silver-grey eyes skirting over her. 'I wondered if you'd get cold feet at the last minute.'

Becky heard the cool in his voice and interpreted it as

what it was—the voice of a man who no longer had any physical interest in her. He needed her help and he was willing to pay a high price for it. This wasn't about any lingering attraction or affection on his part. This was about business and she shouldn't be surprised because, when it came to business, he was clearly at the top of the field and you didn't get there without ruthlessly being able to take advantage of opportunities.

He wanted to do what he felt was the best thing for his mother and she was an opportunity he had taken advantage of.

'I was tempted.' Becky fell into step alongside him and decided right there and then that she would have to be as cool and as detached as he was. 'But then I thought about what was on the table and I realised that I would be a fool to turn down your offer.'

'You mean the money.' His voice hardened as he stood back, allowing her to brush past him into the apartment.

Becky slipped past and was frozen to the spot. This wasn't an *apartment*…this was a *penthouse complex*. It was very open plan. Staring ahead, she looked at the wall of raw brick interrupted by a series of modern paintings that she knew, without being clued up on art, were priceless originals. Curving to the left was a short, twisting spiral staircase that led to an arrangement of rooms which she assumed to be bedrooms, although she could be wrong. But there were living spaces in front and on either side, from the glorious, huge sitting area with its white arrangement of leather sofas to a spacious kitchen in shades of grey and a dining area that was cool and contemporary. There were almost no walls, so the spaces all ebbed and flowed into one another in a beguiling mix of brick, wood and marble.

And it was vast. High ceilings, limitless space and

cool, subdued colours that always seemed to character-
ise immensely expensive houses. This was the sort of
place where too much colour would be a rude intrusion
and clutter was to be discouraged at all costs.

'Impressed?' Against his will, Theo felt a kick of pride
at her awed expression. Other women had been awed.
Frankly, all of them. This one was different.

'It's beautiful.' Becky turned to him, her glorious eyes
sincere. 'You must feel very privileged living here...'

Theo shrugged. 'I've stopped noticing my surroundings,' he said, sweeping up the cases and striding off towards the staircase. 'Just as you, doubtless, have stopped
noticing the leaking roof in your cottage.' Part of the deal
had been to do repair work on the cottage, and Theo intended to do a damn good job so that the basics could
be covered before he bought the place, because he had
no doubt that it would be his in due course, especially
now that setting her up in a practice of her own was part
of the deal.

He wondered what it would be like to set her up with
a practice in London...

Then he shook free the ridiculous notion.

'I'm not allowed to forget the leaking roof,' Becky said
coldly, 'considering I have to avoid stepping in a bucket
of water every other day.'

'Had it fixed yet?' He paused outside a bedroom door
to look down at her.

Becky stared back up at him, angry with herself for the
way he could still make her feel like this—hot, bothered
and unsteady—when obviously everything had changed
between them. She had to get a grip. She couldn't spend
the next two weeks in a state of heightened awareness.

'One of my friends has offered to oversee the repair

work. I didn't think I could leave it leaking and unsupervised for two weeks.'

'I'll cover the costs.'

'There's no need.'

Theo pushed open the bedroom door but then stood in front of her, barring her path. 'Let's not skirt away from the base line here, Becky. There's a deal on the table and I intend to stick to it. You're doing me a great favour, and in return you get repair work done to your house and I set you up in a practice of your own so that you don't have to worry about whether you'll be able to get another job easily or not.'

Becky reddened. Put like that, without all the frilly business of helping him out to soften the *base line*, she couldn't quite believe what she was doing here. The practical side of this had not been the real reason she had ended up here, had it? It appalled and frightened her, if she was being brutally honest with herself, but she knew that the bigger part of her reason for standing right here, in front of a bedroom in this marvellous penthouse suite of rooms, was because she had nurtured the tiniest slither of hope that he might still find her as attractive now as he had a fortnight ago. She had broken all her rules when she had slept with him. It hadn't mattered how inappropriate he was for any kind of relationship, she had wanted to keep on breaking those rules for a little bit longer.

Now that she was here, it seemed like a ridiculous thing ever to have thought. She stuck out like a sore thumb and she wouldn't be surprised if he made sure to hide her away until they disappeared off to Italy, just in case he was spotted by anyone he knew.

Of course he wouldn't fancy her. Of course she had been a blip for him, just as he had been a blip for her. He would never have got in touch had the unfortunate situation with his mother not arisen. Thank goodness she had not shown her hand but instead had gone on the defensive the minute she had realised that he wanted her to do him a favour, and had laid down her 'no sex' ground rules. She knew that if he had chosen to break them, declared that he had missed her after all, then she would have cracked. She knew that if he had looked at her when she had stood there in that plush landing and then swept her up into his arms, her 'no sex' stipulation would have crumbled.

It hadn't happened and she had been an idiot to think that it might have.

'Fine.' She smiled brightly and peered around him to the bedroom which, like the rest of the place, was the last word in fabulous. 'Would you mind very much if I… er…had a shower? It's been a long drive down here…'

She risked a quick glance. She wanted to ask him why he was in a mood with her when he had been the one to ask her down here in the first place, but she didn't, because she needed to be as cool as he was. She wasn't going to start pleading with him to be *friendly*. Maybe he resented having her here in the first place. Maybe he felt as though he had been cornered into doing the only thing he could think of for his mother but, really, he didn't want to. He just didn't have a choice. Perhaps he had wanted to get back to his normal life of playing with beautiful, glamorous models but suddenly he had had to rummage up a feasible girlfriend to produce to his mother and she had been the only woman he knew plain enough to pass muster.

'And then,' she carried on, 'we could hammer out the details? If I'm supposed to be involved with you, we should at least get our stories straight.'

Theo marvelled at the speed with which she had abandoned her scruples about deceiving his mother and fallen in line now that there was a financial incentive dangling on the horizon.

'Quite,' he drawled. Her bags looked lost and out of place where he had placed them and he clenched his jaw, toughening up against any weakness inside him to imagine that those bags were a reflection of their owner, who must also be feeling lost and out of place.

'I...' She turned to him, burying her hands in her pockets so that she didn't impulsively and foolishly reach out to touch him. 'I've never done anything like this before...' She shuffled and then made herself stop, reminded herself that she was a qualified vet who dealt with far more important situations than this and handled herself competently and efficiently.

'Which is why we have to discuss what's going to happen. It's not going to be believable if you're a bag of nerves whenever you're around me. My mother will want to believe that I'm actually capable of being attracted to a woman with a brain, but even she is going to start having doubts if you act as though you're terrified of slipping up. Anyway, take your time, I'll be downstairs in the kitchen. We can...discuss how we proceed when you join me.'

He felt he needed a stiff drink.

By the time she emerged forty-five minutes later, he was wondering what exactly the details of his little ill-conceived adventure might be. His mother knew that he was bringing a girl to meet her and had already perked up because this was the first time in nearly two years he had done that.

There was no going back now.

His cool eyes swept over her as she slowly walked into the kitchen. She had changed into jeans and yet another baggy jumper and was wearing a pair of bedroom slippers.

Becky didn't miss the way he had given her the once-over and yet again she was burningly conscious of just not fitting in to the surroundings, a bit like a cheap souvenir from a package holiday amidst a collection of priceless pieces of china.

You didn't seem to mind this look when you were in my cottage, she thought with sudden resentment.

'You're doing it again,' Theo drawled, strolling to get a glass from the cupboard and pouring her some wine.

'Doing what?'

'Looking as though you'd rather be anywhere else but where you actually happen to be.'

'This is just such a stupid idea.'

'I suggest you move on from that. It's too late to get cold feet now and, besides, you have nothing to worry about.' He drained his glass and poured another. It was a little after seven and food had been prepared by his chef. From nowhere came the memory of her little kitchen and the way he would sit at her kitchen table, watching her as she cooked, anticipating touching her.

'What do you mean *I have nothing to worry about*?' She gulped down some wine and looked at him cautiously. He was just so beautiful. Why couldn't her imagination have been playing tricks on her?

'It's going to be two weeks,' Theo said drily. 'Two weeks for which you will be richly rewarded. In return, all you have to do is smile prettily and chat now and again. I will be with you at all times. I'm not asking you to turn into my mother's best friend. Your main purpose will be to...' he sighed heavily '...give her a purpose, make her see the future as something to look forward to.

It's a short-term plan,' he continued with a hint of dissatisfaction, 'but it's the only plan I have.'

'Why don't you just take someone you actually want to have a proper relationship with?' Becky suggested, frowning. 'Instead of this great big charade?'

Theo burst out laughing. 'If I had one of those stashed up my sleeve,' he mused, 'then don't you think I would have pulled her out by now? No, if I were to present my mother with any of the women from my little black book, she would run screaming in horror. She's had her fill of my women over the years. I honestly don't think her heart could take any more.'

'Why do you go out with them if they're so unsuitable?'

'Whoever said that they were unsuitable *for me*?' Theo answered smoothly. 'At any rate, it's irrelevant. Even if there was someone whose services I could avail myself of, it would be an unworkable arrangement.'

'Why?' Becky wondered whether he was actually aware of how insulting his remarks were.

'Because it would lead to all sorts of complications.' He thought of some of his girlfriends who had started daydreaming about rings and white dresses even though he had always made it clear from the outset that neither would be on the agenda. 'They might start blurring the line between fact and fiction.'

'How do you know that *I* won't do that?' Becky surprised herself by asking the question but this was a level playing field. He could say what he wanted, without any regard for her feelings, so why should she tiptoe round what she had to say to *him*?

'Because,' he countered silkily, 'you made it clear from the start that I wasn't your type and I don't see you getting any unfortunate ideas into your head.' She'd never told him what had driven her into the Cotswolds, what heartbreak had made her want to bury herself in the middle of nowhere. He wondered what the guy had been like. Nice, he concluded. So *nice* that he hadn't had the balls to entice her between the sheets. He couldn't stop a swell of pure, masculine satisfaction that *not nice* had done the trick.

'You're here because I offered you a deal you couldn't refuse and that suits me fine. No misunderstandings, no demands springing from nowhere, no unrealistic ambitions.'

And no sex… That could only be a good thing when it came to those nasty misunderstandings… Besides, if he had been having uninvited fantasies about her, then surely seeing her out of context, awkward and ill at ease in his territory as she was now, would slowly prove to him that her novelty value had been her only powerful draw…?

At the moment, he was still finding it difficult to look at her without mentally stripping her of her clothes, which was infuriating.

'But cutting to the chase…' He looked at the food which had been prepared earlier and was neatly in copper pans on the hob. He switched on the hob and had a quick think to ascertain the location of the plates. 'We met…?'

Becky shrugged. 'Why lie? Tell your mother where I live and that we met at my cottage. Tell her that you got lost because of the snow and ended up staying over for a few days.'

'That won't work,' Theo said sharply. He flushed and cursed the lie that could not now be retracted. 'Love at first sight might be a bit improbable.'

'Why?'

'Because it's not in my psyche, and anyone who knows me at all would know that.'

'So what *is* in your psyche?' Somehow, she had been so engrossed talking to him, that food had found its way to a plate and was now in front of her. Delicious, simple food, a fish casserole and some broad beans. With her nerves all over the place, her appetite should have deserted her, but it hadn't. The food was divine and she dug in with gusto.

Theo watched her, absently enjoying her lack of restraint. 'We met one another. After a diet of tall, thin models, beautiful but intellectually unchallenging, I fell, without even realising it, in love with someone who had a brain and made me jump through hoops to get her.'

Becky felt slow, hot colour invade her cheeks because, in that low, sexy, husky voice, it could have truly been a declaration of love. 'You mean you went for someone short and fat.' She covered over her embarrassment with a high-pitched, self-deprecating laugh and Theo frowned.

'Don't run yourself down,' he said gruffly. For a moment, he was weirdly disconcerted, but he recovered quickly and continued with cool speculation, 'There's no way I would ever have gone for someone who didn't like herself…'

'I like myself,' Becky muttered, glaring.

Theo grinned. 'Good. You should. Tall, thin and glamorous is definitely not all it's cracked up to be.'

Becky blushed, confused, because there was a flirtatious undercurrent to his voice, which she must have misheard because there had certainly been nothing flirtatious in his manner since she had arrived.

'And there's something else my mother would never buy,' he said slowly, pushing his plate to one side and relaxing back in the chair, his hands clasped behind his head so that he was looking down at her.

'What?'

'Your wardrobe.'

'I beg your pardon?'

'You can't show up in clothes you would wear on a house visit to see to a sick dog. You're going to have to lose the jeans and practical footwear. We're going to be staying on the coast, anyway. Much warmer than it is over here. You'll have to bid farewell to the jumpers, Becky, and the layers.'

'This is *me*,' she protested furiously. 'Aren't you sup-posed to have fallen for completely the opposite of the models you've always gone out with?'

'I'm not asking you to buy clothes that could be folded to the size of handkerchiefs but, if we're going to do this, then we're going to do it right. You'll have an unlimited budget to buy whatever you want…but it's time to kiss sweet goodbye to what you've brought with you…'

CHAPTER SIX

THEO GLANCED AT his watch and eyed the suite of rooms which Becky had been inhabiting with a hint of impatience.

His driver was waiting to take them to his private jet and he'd now been waiting for twenty minutes. Theo was all in favour of a woman's right to be late, except Becky wasn't that type, so what the hell was keeping her?

The vague dissatisfaction that had been plaguing him for the past forty-eight hours kicked in with a vengeance and he scowled, debating whether he should go and bang on her door to hurry her along.

The fact was that he had seen precious little of her since she had arrived at his apartment. They had discussed the nuts and bolts of what they would be doing but she had firmly rejected his offer to accompany her to the shops to buy a replacement wardrobe. She didn't want to do it in the first place, she had mutinously maintained, and she certainly wasn't going to have him traipsing around in her wake telling her what she could or couldn't wear. It was bad enough that he wanted her to try and project a persona she didn't have.

She'd made it quite clear that her decision to go along with the charade was one she had almost immediately regretted, and he'd been left in no doubt that only the prospect of having an uncertain future sorted out was the impetus behind her act of generosity. In other words, she'd been drawn by the offer of financial assistance. He was, above all else, practical. He could appreciate her sensible approach. He was grateful for the fact that there were absolutely no misplaced feelings of wanting more than the lucrative deal he had offered her. So, sex was off the agenda? He certainly wouldn't be chasing her although it was highly ironic that they were no longer physically intimate when they were going to have to convince his mother that they were.

He caught himself thinking that it would have been a damned sight more convenient if they had just fallen into bed with one another, for they were supposed to be a loved-up item, and then was furious with himself because he knew that he was simply trying to justify his own weakness.

If he'd thought that seeing her out of her comfort zone, an awkward visitor to *his* world, would cure him of his galloping, unrestrained libido, then he had been mistaken.

He still felt that he had unfinished business with her and for once his cool, detached, analytical brain refused to master the more primitive side of him that *wanted her*.

Had she brought a uniform of shapeless jumpers and faded jeans in a targeted attempt to ensure that he didn't try and make a pass?

Had she honestly thought that he would have forgotten what that body had felt like under his fingers?

He had become a victim of intense sexual frustration and he loathed it.

He wondered what she had bought to take to Italy and had already resigned himself to the possibility that she had just added to her supply of woefully unfashionable clothes as a protest against being told by him what to do.

Yet he had meant what he had told her…his mother knew him well enough to know that he liked well-dressed women. Or at least, she knew that the well-dressed woman was the sort of woman he was accustomed to dating. She'd certainly met enough of them over the years to have had that opinion well and truly cemented in her head. He might be able to sell her an intelligent woman as the woman who had finally won through but, intelligent or not, she'd never be convinced by a woman who couldn't give a damn about her appearance.

So how would she react if Becky decided to turn up in jeans and a baggy tee shirt? Trainers? Or, worse, sturdy, flat, laced-up shoes suitable for tramping through fields?

And yet, as he had told her, no other woman could possibly do for the role. And he couldn't think of a single one who would have held his interest long enough for his mother or anyone with two eyes in their head to believe that he was actually *serious*.

He smiled wryly because his mother would have been very amused if she could only see him here now, hovering by the door, glancing at his watch, prisoner of an unpredictable woman who wasn't interested in impressing him.

He was scrolling through messages on his phone when he became aware that she had emerged into the open-plan living area where he had now been tapping his feet for the past forty minutes.

He didn't have to look up.

He was as aware of her stealthy approach just as a tiger was aware of the soft tread of a gazelle.

He glanced up.

The battered bags, which he had insisted she replaced, were, of course, still there.

But everything else…

His eyes travelled the length of her, did a double take and then travelled the length of her all over again. He had been slouching against the wall. He now straightened. He knew that his mouth was hanging open but he had to make a big effort to close it because his entire nervous system seemed to have been rewired and had stopped obeying the commands from his brain.

Becky had had doubts about her drastic change of wardrobe. It had taken her far longer than necessary to get ready because she had wavered between wearing what she had bought and wearing what she was accustomed to wearing.

But he had got to her with those jibes about her clothes.

They had spent their glorious snatched time in the cottage snowed in, hanging around in old, comfy clothes. Because that was what the situation had demanded. But just how drab did he think she was? She had actually packed all of her summer wardrobe to take to Italy with her. She wasn't an idiot. She had known that thick layers would be inappropriate. How could he imagine that she would have presented herself as his so-called girlfriend dressed like a tramp?

She had never been more grateful for her decision to make sure he knew that the status of their relationship was purely business. If she had thought him not her type, then his stupid remarks about her having to change her appearance had consolidated that realisation.

How superficial was it to measure a woman's attractiveness by the type of clothes she wore?

But some devil inside her had decided to take him at his word. He wanted her to dress up like a doll? Then she would do it! She'd never been the sort to enjoying shopping. Buying clothes had always been a necessity rather than a source of pleasure. And in her line of work there was certainly no need to invest in anything other than purely functional wear. Durability over frivolity. She was all too aware that even the summer items she had packed were of a sensible nature. Flat sandals for proper walking in the countryside, sneakers, lightweight jeans and tee shirts in block colours, grey and navy, because bright colours had never been her thing. Her sister had always pulled off reds and yellows far more successfully.

But that was what Theo would be expecting. Perhaps even *dreading*. The fake girlfriend letting her side down by appearing like a pigeon to all the peacocks he had dated in the past. Maybe he had envisioned having to sit his mother down and persuade her to believe that he could actually fall for someone who didn't own a single mini-skirt and wouldn't have been caught dead wearing anything with sequins or glitter. Or lace, for that matter. And that included her underwear.

She had been timid in shop number one. Indeed, she had wondered what the point of being daring and rebellious was for a so-called liaison that wasn't destined to last longer than a fortnight.

But she had made herself go in and, by the time she had hit Harrods, she had found herself thoroughly enjoying the experience. How was it, she thought, that she had never sampled the carefree joy of trying on clothes, seeing herself as another person in a different light? How had she never realised that shedding her vet uniform could be downright liberating? She had retreated from trying to compete with her sister on the looks front and had pigeon-holed herself into the brainy bookworm with no time for playing silly dressing-up games. She had failed to see that there was a very healthy and very enjoyable middle ground.

In a vague way, as she had stood in one of the changing rooms, marvelling at the swirl of colour she had actually dared to try on, she had acknowledged that Theo was somehow responsible for this shift in her thinking. Just as he had been responsible, in a way, for hauling her out of her comfort zone, for taking her virginity, for being the one to make her enjoy the physical side of her.

Then she'd wondered what he would make of her change of wardrobe and that had spurred her on to be more daring than she might otherwise have been in colours, in styles, in shapes…

She'd even overhauled her lingerie, not that there had been any need, but why not?

And right now, in this breathless silence as he stood watching her with those amazing, brooding eyes, she thought that it had been worth every second of laborious trying on.

'I see you've gone for *barely there*…' Theo managed to get his legs working and his runaway brain back into gear.

The skirt was apricot and the top was dove-grey, and both fitted her like a glove, accentuating an hourglass figure that was the last word in sexy. The body that had driven him wild was on full display. Her tiny waist was clinched in, her full breasts were stunningly and lovingly outlined in the tight, stretchy top and even the grey trench-coat, which was as conventional as could be, seemed vaguely sensual because of the body it was incapable of covering up.

He'd told her that his mother would never have bought a girlfriend who dressed like a country vet, but he hadn't expected to be taken at his word.

And he didn't like it.

He scowled as he headed for her bags. 'I see you stuck to the ancient suitcases.'

'I thought it might be taking things a bit too far if I showed up with Louis Vuitton luggage considering I'm a working vet,' she snapped, stung by his lack of response to her outfit.

Would it be asking too much for him at least to acknowledge that she had done as asked and bought herself some peacock clothes?

Theo stood back and looked at her. 'No one would guess your profession from what you've got on.'

'Is that why you were staring at me?' she asked daringly. 'Because you think I should have bought stuff more in keeping with what a working vet on holiday would wear?'

They were outside and a driver was springing to open the passenger door for her.

Theo shot him a look of grim warning because he hadn't missed the man's eyes sliding surreptitiously over her, taking in her body in a quick sweep.

Harry had worked for him for two years and, as far as Theo could recall, had never so much as glanced at any of the women he had ferried from his apartment.

Theo flushed darkly. He turned to her as the car began purring away from the flash apartment block, through the impressive gates and in the direction of the airfield which, she had been told the day before, was an hour's drive away.

'When I suggested a change of wardrobe might be a good idea, I didn't think you'd go from one extreme to the other.'

'You said your mother would never find it credible that you would go out with someone who dressed the way I did. In other words, someone who looked like a bag lady.'

'That's quite the exaggeration.' But he had the grace to flush because she wasn't that far from the truth.

'You wanted me to be more like the kind of women you'd go out with so...' She shrugged.

Theo looked at her averted profile, the defensive tilt of her head, the way the skirt was riding provocatively up one thigh... He wondered whether she was wearing stockings or tights and his body responded enthusiastically to the direction of his thoughts.

'The women I'm accustomed to dating are...built a little differently to you,' he muttered truthfully. He had to shift to ease the pain of his sudden erection.

Becky's defences were instantly on red-hot alert but, before she could launch a counter attack, he continued, clearing his throat.

'They wouldn't be able to pull off an outfit like that quite like you're doing right now...'

'What do you mean?' Becky heard the husky breathlessness in her voice with dismay. This was a guy who had only got in touch because he had wanted something from her. A guy who had been happy to press on with his life after a couple of days. Even though she'd made a big deal of assuring him that there was no way he could ever have stayed the course with her, no way that she would want any more than the couple of days on offer, she'd be an idiot if she were to kid herself that she hadn't hoped for some sort of follow-up. Even a text to tell her that he missed her just a bit.

Because *she'd* missed *him* and thought about him a lot more after he'd gone than she should have.

She might not have played on his mind, but *he'd* played on *her* mind.

That had been part of the reason why she'd put down the 'no sex' rule when she'd agreed to his outrageous proposition.

If he thought that he could come to her for a favour,

tell her that she was the only one who fitted the bill because she was credibly average enough to convince his mother that he was serious about her, and then expect sex as some kind of bonus just because they'd been there before, then he was in for a shock!

But then, beneath that very sensible way of thinking was something she hardly dared admit even to herself. That *thing* she had felt for him and still felt for him after he'd disappeared back down to London frightened her. The power of his attraction had been so overwhelming that it had blitzed all her dearly held principles. In the face of it, she had had no choice but to throw herself into bed with him.

She was terrified that if she allowed herself to be weak, if she allowed herself to be overwhelmed by him again, then she would end up hurt and broken. She wasn't sure how she knew that but she just did.

So the last thing she should be doing right now was straying from the 'business arrangement' agenda and letting herself get side-tracked by personal asides.

'I mean…' he leaned towards her, his voice low '…my driver has never looked twice at any of the models who have stalked into this car over the years but he couldn't take his eyes off you.'

Becky went bright red. She wanted to put her hands to her cheeks to cool them. She glanced towards his driver, but the partition between the seats had been closed. Even so…

'If you think the stuff I bought is inappropriate, then I can easily, er, replace them…'

'Depends.'

'On what?'

'What else is in those suitcases of yours? Maybe I should have had a look before we left,' he continued in a low, thoughtful voice. 'Made sure you hadn't bought anything that would make my mother's hair curl...'

'You're being ridiculous,' Becky told him briskly. 'I doubt I've bought anything that any girl of my age wouldn't feel comfortable wearing, and your mother certainly wouldn't blink an eye at this outfit or any of the others if she's met any of your past girlfriends. I know, if they were all models, then what I'm wearing now would have been their idea of over-dressing.' Her skin was tingling all over and, although she wasn't looking at him, she was very much aware of his eyes on her, lazy and speculative.

Gazing at her pointedly averted profile, Theo had never felt such a surge of rampant desire. If this was what unfinished business felt like, then he wondered how he was going to cope for the next fortnight when he would be condemned to look without touching.

'At any rate, you've bought what you've bought,' Theo said roughly, dragging his mind off the prospect of trying to entice her into bed, because that would be a show of weakness he would never allow.

With the conversation abruptly closed down, Becky lapsed into nervous silence, while next to her Theo worked on his phone. When she glanced across, she could see him sending emails and scrolling through what appeared to be a mammoth report. He was completely oblivious to her. One minute it had felt so weird, so intimate...the next, she could have been invisible.

When she thought about the next fortnight, her stomach twisted into anxious knots, so instead she projected beyond that to where her life would be after they returned from Italy. He had told her that he would set her up in business, she only had to pick the spot, and she busied herself thinking about a possible location.

She wondered when the cottage would be sold. Her parents were unaware of the state of gradual disrepair into which it had fallen and that was something she had decided she would keep to herself. When it eventually sold—and there was no guarantee that would be soon, because the property market was hardly booming at the moment—it would get a far bigger price now that work was being done to fix the broken-down bits and she was pleased that her parents would reap the rewards from that. They had let her stay there for practically nothing.

Looking back at it, Becky could scarcely remember why she had felt so driven to run away when her sister and Freddy had tied the knot. She could scarcely remember what it had felt like to have a crush on Freddy or when, exactly, he had turned into just a pleasant guy who was perfect for her sister. She couldn't believe that some silly infatuation gone wrong had dictated her behaviour for years. If she hadn't allowed herself to lazily take the route of least resistance, she would not be here now, because she wouldn't have been at the cottage, pottering through life doing something she loved but without the necessary interaction with guys her own age.

She would never have met Theo. He had blasted into her life and galvanised her into really looking at the direction she had been taking. It just went to show how a series of coincidences could result in major life changes.

'Penny for them.'

Becky blinked and focused on him. He was leaning back against the door, his big body relaxed, legs spread slightly apart. Even like this, in repose, relaxed, he was the very image of the powerful alpha male and her heart gave a treacherous little leap.

'I was thinking about coincidences,' she said truthfully and Theo inclined his head.

'Explain.'

Becky hesitated. She knew that she needed to go on the defensive. She also knew that, if they were supposed to be *an item*, then for the duration of a fortnight she would have to stop treating him like the enemy.

He wasn't the enemy, she thought. Although he was... *dangerous*. Horribly, wonderfully, thrillingly, excitingly *dangerous*. And *that* was something she would never let on, because if there was one guy on the planet who would be tickled pink at being considered *dangerous* it was Theo Rushing. The more she agonised over the impact he still had on her, the more power she gave him over her state of mind.

He'd made those lazy little remarks to her about the way she looked and she'd practically gone into meltdown.

Well, it was going to be a nightmare if she went into a meltdown every time he turned his attention to her, especially considering they would have to pretend to be in love in front of his mother.

'I was thinking,' she ploughed on, determined to level the playing field between them so that she could be as cool as he was, 'that if you hadn't shown up out of the blue at the cottage, if it hadn't been snowing and you hadn't have ended up being stuck with me...'

'"Stuck" takes all the fun out of the memory.' Keen grey eyes noted the delicate colour that stained her cheeks and the way her eyelids fluttered as she breathed in sharply. Little giveaway signals that her 'no sex' rule had more holes in it than she probably would want to admit.

She'd made a big deal about how unsuited they were to one another and she was right. He could no more fall for someone as intensely romantic as she was than he could have climbed a mountain on roller skates. And, yet, the physical attraction was so strong that you could almost reach out and touch the electric charge between them.

She'd slept with him because she hadn't been able to fight that physical attraction. He hadn't been able to fight it either and he itched to touch her again.

Even though he knew that it probably wasn't a very good idea. He certainly wouldn't dream of going down the road of actively chasing her when a rebuff was waiting directly round the corner but…

He looked at her, eyes brooding and hooded.

There was no law against flirting, or pushing the barrier she had hastily erected, just to check and see how flimsy it was…was there…? Some might maintain that that would be a perfectly understandable response given that he was a red-blooded male with a more than healthy libido that just so happened to be fully operational when it came to her.

It would be a delicate compromise between maintaining his pride, holding on to his self-control and tipping his hat at common sense whilst testing the waters…and then playing a 'wait and see' game.

It would certainly enliven the next two weeks.

'I was drifting.' She ignored his little jibe. 'And you were a wake-up call.'

'Am I supposed to see a compliment in that?' he drawled. 'I don't think I've ever been described as any woman's *wake-up call*.'

'When this is over and done with, I feel that life can really start again for me.'

'I suggest we just get through the next couple of weeks before you start planning the rest of your life.'

'What if your mother doesn't like me?' Becky suddenly asked. 'I mean, you've taken it for granted that, because she hasn't approved of the women you've dated in the past, somehow she'll approve of me because I'm different from them—but she may not like me and, if she doesn't, then this whole charade will be a waste of time.'

Businesslike though this arrangement was, Theo was still irked to think that uppermost in her mind were worries about the financial side of things. 'Are you afraid,' he enquired coolly, 'That you might not get your money if things don't go according to plan?'

That had not occurred to Becky but she didn't refute it. She was going to be as cool about this as he was. She wasn't going to get bogged down in her own emotional issues. This was an exchange of favours and, the more she recognised that important aspect of their so-called relationship, the happier and more relaxed she would be. Their eyes met and she kept her stare as steady and as level as his.

'Well, nothing's been signed,' she pointed out with what she thought was an admirable amount of reasonable calm.

Theo gritted his teeth. One thing his mother was guaranteed to like about her was her honesty, he thought grimly. Marita Rushing had complained often and loudly that the bimbos she had met would have done whatever he asked because of his money.

'It must get boring for you,' she had declared a couple of years previously, after she had met one of the last of his leggy blondes before he had decided that introductions, always at his mother's insistence, were no longer a very good idea, however much she insisted.

His mother had never bought into the argument that having a woman do whatever he wanted was just what the doctor ordered for someone who had far too much stress on the work front to tolerate it on the home front. What he saw as soothing, she saw as unchallenging.

Becky took *challenging* to another level. If she didn't like anything else about his brand-new love interest, then that was something she would love. She would have first-hand insight into how frustrating the honest and challenging woman was capable of being.

By the end of the fortnight, he surmised that there was a good chance that his mother would be only too keen to concur when he'd say that there was a lot to be said for the eager-to-please lingerie model.

Instead of the woman who hadn't shied away from telling him that he wasn't her type, who had been frank about using him to please her, to teach her about making love, presumably so that she could implement the lessons learnt with a man more suitable… A woman who had agreed to help him out because of what she could get out of it in return and who, now, was worried that she might not reach the promised land if things did not go according to plan with his mother.

His lips thinned. 'Are you implying that I'm not a man of my word? That because I didn't get a lawyer to draw up an agreement for both parties to sign, that I would renege on what I promised to deliver?'

Becky sighed and lay back, eyes half-closed. 'You're the one who raised the subject.'

'Whatever the outcome of the next two weeks, you will get exactly what I have promised. In fact, name the place and I will get my people to start checking out suitable sites for a practice. Presumably you would want to go in with someone?'

She angled her head so that she was looking at him, and as always she had to fight not to respond outwardly to his masculine beauty.

'Maybe I'll go to France,' she thought aloud. 'Join the family. I'm going to be an aunt in a few months' time.'

And she wouldn't have a problem with Freddy. She could now, for the first time, fully admit what she had suspected for years. That, whilst she had been upset when he had chosen Alice over her, she hadn't been devastated. Whilst she had told herself that she needed to return to the family home, to be surrounded by what was familiar so that she could put heartbreak behind her, she had just given in to the indulgence of licking her wounds and then had stayed put because it had been easy. In truth, on the occasions when she had seen Freddy, she had secretly found him a little bland and boring—although to have admitted that, even to herself, would have opened up a Pandora's box of questions about the sort of man she was looking for.

She had always assumed that her soul mate would come in a package very much like Freddy's.

But Freddy was dull and so, she thought slowly, would be all those thoughtful, caring types she had held up as the perfect match for her.

She had allowed herself to assume, from a young age, that because Alice was the beautiful one in the family she would automatically be suited to guys as beautiful as she was. And for her, Becky, would come the steadier, more grounded, less beautiful types. But life had proved her very wrong, for her sister had fallen madly in love with the ordinary guy while she...

Her heart began to race. She felt nauseous, and suddenly she just couldn't look at the man next to her, even though she knew that she would still be able to see him with her eyes shut because he was so vividly remembered in her head. Like a diligent, top-of-the class student, the sort of student she had always been, she had filed away every single thing about him into her memory banks and all that information would now stay there a lifetime. She knew every small detail of his face, from the tiny lines that formed at the corners of his eyes when he smiled, to the slight dimple on just one side of his cheek when he laughed…from the way those silver-grey eyes could darken when he was roused, to the feel of his muscular shoulders under her fingertips.

She'd thought she was immune to him touching her heart because he hadn't ticked the right 'suitable for re-lationship' boxes in her head. She'd assumed that she hadn't been able to get him out of her mind after he had left for London because he had shaken her out of her com-fort zone, so it was only natural that he had left behind a certain ache. What she hadn't done was ask herself the more fundamental question: why had she allowed him to break into her comfort zone in the first place?

Physical attraction was one thing but, of course, there had been much more to what she had felt for him, even after a day, two days…three days…

He had touched something deep inside her, stirred something into life. Why had no one warned her that love at first sight actually existed? Rather, why on earth hadn't she learnt from Alice and Freddy, both of whom had fallen head over heels in love from the very second their eyes had met?

And now here she was.

Panic and confusion tore through her. She felt she might faint. He was saying something about France, in that lazy, sexy voice of his but she barely heard him over the thundering of her heart. She wasn't aware of the car moving or didn't even know whether they were close to where his private jet would be waiting for them.

After a while, she heard herself responding to whatever he was saying. For the life of her, she had no idea what.

The only thing running through her head was the next two weeks and how she would survive them.

She could never let him suspect how she felt. She had her pride. If she had to live with memories, then she didn't want to add to the tally of difficult ones—the memory of him laughing incredulously at her or, maybe worse, backing away as if she were carrying a deadly infection.

The next two weeks weren't going to be a business arrangement to be endured as best as possible.

The next two weeks were going to be an assault course.

CHAPTER SEVEN

BECKY HAD GRUDGINGLY accepted Theo's advice that she change her wardrobe or risk not being a credible girlfriend. He was rich and he was accustomed to dating women for whom shopping for clothes was a career choice. Even if he liked women who didn't care, his definition of 'not caring' would be designer jeans and designer silk blouses and designer high heels, accompanied by lots of gold and diamond jewellery. Dressing down in a no-expense-spared kind of way.

There was no way cheap, durable, all-weather clothing would have passed muster.

One glance at his fabulous apartment had told her that. Her old, tired suitcases had stuck out in the midst of all the luxurious splendour of his penthouse apartment like an elephant in a china shop.

But his private jet—which, he explained with an indifferent wave of his hand, was useful to his CEOs for whom time was usually a great deal of money—was a sharp reminder not only why he had pushed her to buy a new wardrobe but of the huge chasm between them.

Even in her fancy, expensive clothes, she was horribly conscious of *not quite fitting in*. She knew that she was gaping. Gaping at the pale, soft, butter-cream leather seats and the gleaming chestnut interior. It was a small plane, fast and light, and capable of seating only a dozen people, but it was truly exquisite inside, with a long sideboard, on which was a basket heaped with fresh fruit, and a marble bathroom that included a shower and thick, fluffy towels.

Looking at her, Theo knew that he should have been put off by her obvious open-mouthed awe. She didn't pretend to be blasé about flying in a private jet. She was impressed and it was written all over her face. There was no need for her to say *wow* for him to notice that.

He wasn't put off. He was as pleased as the cat that had just got the cream. He dumped all intentions of working on the short flight and instead gave her an amused, verbal, in-depth description of the plane, what it was capable of doing and where he'd flown on business.

'You must have really felt as though you were slumming it when you got stuck in my cottage,' Becky said ruefully and Theo looked away.

The thought of admitting at this late stage that he had hardly found himself *stuck* in her cottage by pure chance was unthinkable. It hardly made a difference, because what did it matter whether she eventually found out or not that he had appeared there by design? But something inside him twisted, an uneasy tug on his conscience, which was usually unassailable.

'But you just fitted in,' she pondered absently.

'I didn't always have money at my disposal,' he said abruptly and she looked at him, surprised, because this was the first time he had ever come right out and said anything at all about his past. During all that concentrated time when they had been trapped in the cottage, held prisoner by the weather, he had talked about what he did, various situations he had encountered…he had amused her and held her spellbound with stories of the places he had been to…

But he had not once reminisced about his past.

'You act as though you were born with a silver spoon in your mouth,' Becky said encouragingly.

This was just *small talk*, she told herself. But deep down she already knew she had fallen in love with the man. She had recognised that awful, awful truth just as she had recognised that falling in love with him had not been part of the deal. But the deal was for her to keep up the act of being the woman he had recruited to play this role, the woman who wouldn't be stupid enough to try and blur fact with fiction, so shouldn't she be as natural and as chatty as she possibly could be?

And, if she learnt a little more about him, then where was the harm in that? She preferred not to think of it as furtively feeding her greedy desire to know as much about him as she could, to take as much as she was capable of taking with her, so that in the long weeks and months ahead she could pull all those little details out of their hiding places and dwell on them at her leisure.

'Do I?' Theo didn't know whether to be taken aback or amused at her blunt honesty.

'You don't pay any attention at all to your surroundings,' Becky explained. 'You barely notice all those wonderful paintings in your apartment and you hardly looked around you when you stepped aboard this jet.'

'It's easy to become accustomed to what you know. The novelty wears off after a while.'

'When did that happen?' Becky asked with lively interest. 'I'm only asking,' she hurried on, 'because, if we're supposed to be an item, it's only natural that I would know a little bit about you…'

'You know a great deal about me,' Theo drawled.

'But I don't know anything about your...past.'

'The past is irrelevant.'

'No, it's not,' Becky disagreed stoutly. 'The past makes us the people we are. What if your mother says something about you, expecting me to know what she's talking about, and I look at her blankly and have to admit that I haven't got a clue what she's talking about?'

'I doubt she'd die of shock,' Theo responded drily. 'I'm a private person and my mother is all too aware of that.'

'You wouldn't be private with someone you're supposedly serious about.'

'I think you're confusing me with someone else,' Theo responded wryly. 'You're mixing me up with one of those touchy-feely types who think that relationships are all about outpourings of emotion and the high drama sharing of confidences.'

'You're so sarcastic, Theo,' Becky muttered.

'Realistic,' Theo contradicted calmly. 'I don't do emotional drama and I wouldn't expect any woman I was serious about to do it either.'

Becky stared at him. 'You mean you'd want someone to be as cold and detached as you?'

'I wouldn't say that I'm *cold and detached*, and if you think hard about it, Becky, I'm pretty sure you'd agree.' He shot her a wolfish smile, enjoying the hectic colour that flooded her cheeks as she clocked what he was saying and bristled.

'That remark is inappropriate,' Becky spat, all hot and bothered. She had laid down her ground rules, and it was even more important now that he obey them, because how was she going to keep a clear head if he did again what he had just done? Got under her skin like that, with a few words and a sexy little smile?

'Why? Because you've told me that you're not interested in going to bed with me?'

Becky went from pink to scarlet. 'This—this isn't what this is about,' she stuttered, her voice letting her down because it was high-pitched and cracked, not at all the voice of someone cool, confident and in control.

'You shouldn't dress like that if you want me to stay focused,' Theo told her bluntly.

Becky hated the stab of pleasure that raced through her. She'd made the fatal error of thinking that sex was just an act that could be performed without the emotions coming into play. She wasn't built like that.

But Theo was.

He'd said so himself. He took women to bed and then dispatched them when they began to outstay their welcome. He never involved his emotions because he had no emotions to involve.

Emotional drama. That was what most normal people would call *falling in love* and it was what she had stupidly gone and done with the last man on the planet who deserved it. At least Freddy had been a worthwhile candidate when it came to feelings, even if she hadn't been the one for him nor, as it turned out, he for her. At least he was capable of *feeling*.

'If you recall,' Becky told him coldly, 'I was told that none of my clothes were going to cut the mustard...'

Theo grunted. He thought that it was a good thing that they would be staying at his villa. Fewer men crashing into lamp posts as they turned around to stare. His blood boiled when he thought of young Italian boys looking at her with that open, avid interest that they never bothered to hide. Salivating.

'Anyway.' She was keen to get away from the topic of her clothes, keen to get away from anything that could make her skin prickle and tease her body into remembering what it had felt like to be touched by him. 'You were filling me in on your background.' She smiled and cleared her throat. 'You were going to try and convince me that you remember what it's like to have no money when you act as though you were born to the high life. I can't believe you've ever been anything but rich...'

It occurred to Theo that it had been a long, long time since he had let his guard down with any woman. She was looking at him, her bright blue eyes soft and questioning, her full lips parted on a smile, her body language so damned appealing that he couldn't tear his eyes away from her.

'You're not trying to turn me into a touchy-feely guy, are you?' he murmured, but returned her smile.

'I wouldn't dream of trying,' Becky said honestly.

'Are you going to feel sorry for me if I tell you my sob story?'

'I don't believe you have a sob story.' Her heart was beating so fast and so hard, she could actually feel it knocking against her rib cage. This definitely wasn't flirting, they were having a proper conversation, but it still felt like flirting. There was still something charged in the atmosphere that made her tingle.

'My mother...had her heart broken when she was a young woman.' Theo was startled that he was telling her this because it was an intensely private part of his past that he had never revealed to anyone. 'I was very young at the time.'

'What happened?' Becky asked breathlessly.

'My father was killed. Quite suddenly. One of those freak accidents you read about sometimes. Wrong place, wrong time. My mother was inconsolable. She...' This was skating on thin ice, and he paused, but then decided to push on. Again, that tug on his conscience. Again, he swept it uncomfortably aside. 'Packed her bags overnight, from what I understand, sold for a song the house they had shared and went as far away as she could. Of course, there was no money. Or very little. She worked in all manner of jobs so that she could give me whatever she felt I wanted...or needed. She instilled in me the importance of education and made sure I got the best on offer. She worked her fingers to the bone because, in the midst of her own personal heartbreak, I was the only person in the world who mattered to her.'

And she'd never moved on. Until she'd started talking about the cottage, talking wistfully about her desire to return there after her hasty departure over two decades ago. Coming to terms with the tragedy that had broken her had, to Theo, been a signal of her moving on at long last because, if she could reconcile herself to the past, then she would be free of the vice-like grip it had had over her.

He'd preferred that *moving on* solution to the other, which was moving on to become a mother-in-law and eventually a grandmother, moving on to a different and more rewarding phase in her life.

'I can see why this is so important to you,' Becky said simply and it took Theo a couple of minutes to drag his mind away from the surprise of his confession so that he could properly focus on her.

'Have you been moved by my heart-breaking tale?'

'Don't be so cynical.' Did he feel that his duty from a young age had been to fulfil the role of man of the family? Had their lack of money made him thirsty for financial security? Her liberal-minded parents had prided themselves on their lack of absorption when it came to money. Was that why they had never told her that they might have liked the cottage to be sold so that they could have more of a financial comfort blanket? Having boxed themselves into the position of people who didn't place any value on money, had they then been too embarrassed to tell her to move out? Had that sentiment been there alongside the sympathy they had felt for her as the daughter with the non-existent love life?

She felt as though Theo had burst into her life and opened a Pandora's box of feelings and realisations she had never been aware of before.

'My mother will probably be a little subdued when we get to Italy,' Theo said, changing the conversation with a slight frown. 'My aunt will not have told her that she's made me aware of the reason for her hospital visit, which is good, but my mother is a proud woman, and I think she'll be nursing a certain amount of…shame that she has become reliant on alcohol to help her get through the day.'

'I get that,' Becky murmured.

There was nothing cloying about her sympathy and Theo slanted an appreciative glance across at her. She was matter-of-fact about the circumstances for this charade—a result of working in a profession where she was alert to all sorts of vulnerability in people, he guessed, who harboured deep feelings about the pets she was called upon to treat. A tough man might shed tears if his dog had to be put down but Theo guessed that those tears would only be shed in the presence of the vet who administered the final injection.

Becky decided that it was better not to dwell on Theo's surprising show of confidence-sharing. This wasn't some side of him he was unexpectedly revealing to her. This was necessary information he felt he had to impart and he had done so dispassionately.

Some gut instinct also made her realise that, if she

tried to reach out to him and prolong the moment, he would retreat faster than a speeding bullet and resent her for being the one with whom this very private information had had to be imparted.

She had never met a man more proud or more guarded. She could understand why the thought of having any one else do what she was doing had been out of the question as far as he was concerned. Any woman who was in the slightest bit interested in the sort of relationship he clearly had no interest in would have seized the opportunity to take advantage of his need to confide, would have seen it as an opportunity to go beyond the skin-deep experience he was willing to have.

Becky shuddered when she thought of the irony of sitting here, in love with him, if only he knew it.

Deliberately, she changed the subject, and it wasn't very long before the jet was dipping down to the landing strip and then gliding to a smooth stop.

They had left behind a cold and grey London—not freezing, as it had been in the Cotswolds, but nevertheless miserable and dank.

They landed here to blue skies and a crispness in the air that felt like the touch of perfect spring.

A car was waiting for them.

Theo might have had hard times growing up but he had certainly not been tainted by the memory. He had made his fortune and had no qualms in spending his money with lavish extravagance. No expense was spared when it came to creature comforts.

He led her to the waiting car and ushered her into the back seat, moving round to the opposite side so that he could slide in next to her.

'My mother grew up in Tuscany,' Theo told her as she stared out at the mouth-watering scenery flashing past them. Lush green mountains were the backdrop to picturesque, colourful houses nestled into the greenery like a child's painting of match boxes in different, flamboyant colours.

'But,' he continued, 'she moved to England when she met and married my father. When her own mother died six years ago, I decided to invest in a villa near Portofino, because that's where her sister lives. Of course, that was before the place became flooded with A-listers. I, personally, think they should have both moved back to Tuscany when Flora's husband died three years ago, but they like the weather on the peninsula.'

'Shh!'

'Come again?'

'Don't talk,' Becky breathed. 'It's interrupting my looking.'

Theo laughed and then gazed at her rapt expression as she took in the outstandingly postcard-pretty harbour dotted with fishing boats and luxury yachts and lined with tall, graceful, colour-washed houses.

A tantalising view before the car swept up into the hills, curving and turning so that flashes of the harbour appeared and disappeared, getting smaller and smaller with each brief glimpse.

Becky had forgotten all her doubts, her apprehension, even the stark, dangerous reality of her feelings for the man sitting next to her. All had been swept aside by the sumptuous glamour of her surroundings. She realised that she hadn't actually had a proper holiday in ages and certainly nothing along these lines. This was a one-off. She was dipping her toes into another world and it wouldn't happen again.

She caught her breath as the car glided smoothly through some impressive gates, up a tree-lined drive and then into a little courtyard, in front of which was a lovely two-storeyed house, gaily painted a bright shade of salmon, with deep-green shutters which had been flung back.

There were tall trees everywhere, casting patterns of shade across the walls of the house, and on the leafy grass and clusters of flowers, and bushes were pressed against the walls, seemingly trying to clamber upwards to the roof.

The porch on the ground floor was broad enough to house a cluster of chairs and its replica was a balcony on the first floor, the white railings of which were laced with foliage that spilled over the sides, bursting with colourful flowers that stretched down to reach the bushes and flowers that were clambering up.

It was enchanting and Becky stood still for a minute as the chauffeur and Theo, with the cases, walked towards the front door.

'Is this another *shh* moment?' Theo asked, strolling back for her and leading her gently to the door.

'I think I'm in love.' She looked up at him, face flushed, poised wickedly on a perilous ledge where she was telling him nothing but the complete truth, just for this heartbeat moment. 'With this beautiful house…' she completed with the thrill of someone who had just managed a narrow escape from the jaws of untold danger.

She was unaware of being observed until she heard some delighted clapping and, when she blinked and turned round, it was to see a small, very pretty middle-aged woman standing in the doorway of the house with a broad smile on her face. She was propped up and leaning heavily on a cane.

And in that split instant Becky saw with her own eyes the depth of love that had driven Theo to take the drastic measure of setting up this charade for the benefit of his mother.

For he had walked quickly to the door to sweep his mother into a hug that was uncharacteristically gentle and very, very loving.

'Enough of you!' Marita Rushing was tenderly pushing her way out of his bear hug to beam around him at Becky, who had remained in the background, dithering, acutely self-conscious and not quite knowing what to do.

'At last, he brings a *real* woman for me to meet! Come here and let me see you, child!'

'I haven't seen her this happy in a long time' was the first thing Theo said to her hours later, after Marita Rushing had retired for the evening to her quarters, which were on the ground floor—a very happy situation, considering her mobility was not yet back up to speed after the accident. It also meant that there was no concerned surprise that a bedroom wasn't being shared by the love birds. Marita Rushing might have been traditional but Becky didn't think that she was so traditional that she wouldn't have been suspicious to discover that her vastly experienced son was sleeping in a different bedroom from the love of his life.

Becky turned to him, half-wanting to continue the conversation, half-wanting him to leave, because he was in the room she had been allocated and she had yet to recover from all the touching that had gone on throughout the course of the evening.

'Don't forget,' he had whispered at one point, his breath warm against her ear, sending all sorts of forbidden tingles up and down her spine, 'that you're the light of my life, that I can't keep my hands off you...'

At that point, he had been sitting next to her on the

sofa whilst opposite them his mother had been chatter-
ing away, excitement stamped into every fluttering gesture and every thrilled smile. His hand had been on her
thigh, casually resting there with the heavy weight of
ownership. She had tried to snap her legs together but
the insistent slide of his thumb at the very acceptable
point just above her knee had prohibited any such display of prudishness.

They were an item and he had had no qualms about
running away with the concept.

At every turn, she had felt those lazy grey eyes on
her. When he had touched her, he had managed to touch
her in places that provoked the greatest physical arousal,
even though you'd never have guessed if you'd been
looking from the outside, because every touch was as
light as a feather and as soft as a whisper, lingering just
a little too long and in places that were just a little too
intimate.

'I'm surprised your mother wasn't a bit more curious
as to the circumstances of our meeting.' She walked towards the window and looked outside to a moonlit night
and the soft glow the moon cast on the silent, gently
swaying trees and bushes. The window was open and
she could breathe in the cool, salty tang of sea breeze.
Beyond the lawns, trees and shrubbery, she could see the
black, unmoving stillness of the sea, a different shade of
darkness from the darkness of the sky. She could have
gazed out at the scenery for ever, were it not for the presence of Theo, lounging by the door, sending ripples of
awareness zinging through her body as lightning-fast
as quicksilver.

She turned back around, perching against the window ledge, hands gripping the sill on either side of her.
'I mean…you happened upon an injured dog at the side

of the road, whilst out driving in the country? And, concerned citizen that you are, you took it to the nearest vet who just happened to be me?'

Theo flushed darkly and frowned. Deceiving his mother did not come naturally to him. In fact, he had never deceived her about anything, not even about the unsuitable women who had liberally littered his life in the past. But the physical change he had seen in her was worth it. He hadn't been lying when he had said that it was the happiest he had ever seen her.

He wasn't about to let anyone climb on the moral high ground and start lecturing him about the rights and wrongs of the decision he had made when all that mattered, as far as he was concerned, was the end result. Least of all when that *someone* was a woman who was only in it for the money.

He quietly shut the door and walked towards her. She had changed from one sexy-as-hell outfit into another sexy-as-hell outfit. What surprised him wasn't his mother's lack of suspicion at the story he had told her, but her lack of suspicion at just how damned sexy a country vet could look.

But it wasn't just the way the soft, straight elbow-length dress in pale coral outlined the curves of her body. In itself, the dress hardly shrieked *sexy*…on anyone else it would just have looked like a pleasant, relatively expensive silk dress. But on *her*… Something about the shape of her body, the slightness of her waist, the soft flare of her hips, the shapeliness of her legs, combined with an air of startled innocence…

Just looking at her now was doing all sorts of things to his body. She was wearing a strapless bra. She was too generously endowed to go braless but, bra or no bra, it didn't take much for him to recall the sight of those cherry-tipped breasts and the way those cherry tips had tasted.

He raked his fingers through his hair and stopped abruptly in front of her, glaring into narrowed, bright blue eyes.

'Why would my mother question how we met?' he asked roughly, looking away, but then looking at her again and trying hard to resist the temptation to stare down at the contour of her body under the wispy dress.

'It just seemed a very unlikely story,' Becky muttered, folding her arms and sliding her eyes away from him.

'No more unlikely than some of my other introductions to women,' Theo muttered.

'Like what?'

'Three years ago I did a charity parachute jump from my jet and landed in a field where there was a shoot going on. Some butter advert. She was tall, blonde, Swedish and almost ended up flattened by me when I landed. We went out for nearly three months. Ingrid was her name.'

'And now here you are. With a country vet.'

'Like I said, I've never seen my mother happier.'

'Because she thinks that we're going to give her a happy-ever-after story,' Becky murmured, eyes cast down. She shuffled and then glanced up at him.

'I know what's going through your head, Becky. You think I'm being cruel because sooner or later she will discover that there will be no happy-ever-after...'

'Aren't you?' Before she had met his mother, Marita Rushing had been a name. Now she was a delightful, living, breathing woman, shrouded in sadness, but still ready to smile at the prospect of her son settling down. Deceit had never felt so immediate and yet she could still recall the way they had hugged and that feeling she had had that he was simply doing something he hoped would be for the best in the long run. 'Forget I said that.' She sighed. 'Do you have any plans as to how we fill our time while we're here?'

Theo had planned to work, whilst ensuring he cast a constant supervisory eye on Becky to make sure she kept her distance. He wanted his mother to like her, wanted her truly to believe that he was capable of forming relationships with girls who weren't five-minute visitors to his life because they were so utterly unsuitable. He wanted Marita to regain her strength so that he could bring her back to London. But he didn't want Becky to bond too firmly with his mother. After all, she wasn't going to be a permanent fixture in his life.

He also planned to have a word with his aunt to establish just what his mother's frame of mind was whilst she was recuperating at the villa.

And, lastly, he wanted to probe her about any potential interests his mother might have mentioned which he could weave into her life once she was in London.

There was still the matter of the cottage which, once bought, would be a welcome distraction from any brooding thoughts.

He frowned, recognising that the whole cottage-purchase scenario was mired in all sorts of ethical tangleweed. Something else he would see to when the time came.

For now…

'One step at a time' seemed the best way forward. First thing in the morning, he would check the cupboards to see what alcohol there was lurking. His mother had been restrained that evening, with just the one glass of wine. He needed to make sure that any drinking had been a temporary blip and not something that might require an intervention.

Work would have to take a back seat.

Between all the things he knew he would have to do, all the necessary obligations he would have to see to, a sudden thought threaded its way through, curving, cornering and bypassing duty, obligation and necessity, like a tenacious weed pushing past the well-laid rose bushes in search of light and air…

Time out.

Two weeks.

'There's a lot to see here,' he told her huskily. 'It's to be expected that we do some exploring.'

Becky looked at him in some alarm. 'Exploring?'

'That's what couples sometimes get up to when they go on holiday together,' Theo inserted.

'But we're not a couple,' Becky pointed out uneasily.

'Go with the flow, Becky.'

'That's easy for you to say.'

'Meaning?'

'Nothing.' She sighed, very nearly trapped by her own treacherous thoughts. It was easy for him to treat this like just some situation that could be enjoyed while it lasted. His emotions weren't involved. Hers were. A spot of sightseeing would be, for him, just a *spot of sightseeing*. Whilst, for her, it would be more sinking into the quagmire that was already engulfing her, making it almost impossible for her to stand back and take an objective view of what they were doing.

'And you're going to have to stop all that touching stuff,' she heard herself say in a burst of defiance.

She'd been thinking of how vulnerable it made her feel just being in his company. She'd been imagining what it would be like for them to be out and about, like a normal couple, doing something normal like sightseeing. Then she'd thought about him holding her hand and how that would feel, the sparks that would run through her—the stolen sensation of it *actually* being true, that they *actually* weren't playing a part...

She'd never thought that it would be possible to project so many scenarios into such a small space of time. Ten seconds and she had seen her life flash past straight into a black void of a future where every minute snatching stolen moments in the present would be weeks spent trying to find a way back to the light in the future.

And then she'd thought of him touching her, those devastating little touches that had meant nothing to him...

Now she just couldn't meet his eyes, because he would be wondering where that cool, collected woman had gone, the one who had agreed to go through with this because of the tangible rewards at the end of it. The one who had chatted to his mother as though the charade were no more difficult than anything else she had ever been called upon to do.

'What *touching stuff*?' Theo murmured in a low, husky voice.

'You know what I mean...' She looked at him with sullen defiance and he smiled, a slow, utterly mesmerising smile that made the breath hitch in her throat and brought her out in a panicked cold sweat.

'I haven't been touching you,' he said softly. 'This...' He trailed one long finger along her collar bone and then allowed it to dip under the neckline of the dress, before pausing at the dip between her breasts, in that shadowy cleavage that was rising and falling as though she were recovering from running a marathon. '*This* is touching you. I haven't been doing that, have I?'

'Theo, please...'

'I like that. I like it when you beg for me...'

'This isn't what it's about. This is...is...' His finger

had slipped deeper, was now trailing over the top of her strapless bra, making gentle inroads underneath, and she could feel her nipples poking painfully against the bra, wanting the thing he was teasing her with. 'This is a business arrangement,' she finished in a breathless whisper, shifting her body, but not nearly firmly or fast enough to avoid his devastating caress.

'I know, but I can't seem to take my eyes off you, Becky. And where my eyes go, my hands itch to follow...'

'You promised.'

'I did no such thing.' He stepped back with an obvious show of reluctance. 'If you don't want *that* kind of touching, then I'll refrain, but Becky—if you look at me with those hot little stolen looks, and you lick your lips like you'd love nothing better than to taste me, you can't expect me to keep my hands to myself.'

'I don't mean to do that!'

Theo dropped his eyes, appreciating the subtle message that way of phrasing her words had given him. She 'didn't mean to do that' implied that she was fighting to uphold the 'no sex' stipulation she had put on this little game of theirs, if it could be called a game. Which meant that she still wanted him as much as he still wanted her, but she was a good girl whose innate moral code could not permit random sex with a man with whom there would and never could be any future. She had succumbed once, and had probably used every argument under the sun to justify that weakness, but she was determined not to succumb again.

And he itched to touch her. He'd wanted it the second he'd decided to get in touch with her again and he hadn't stopped, even though he had his own inner voices urging caution.

Or at least urging him to pay some attention to his

pride…irritating little voices reminding him that he had never chased a woman in his life before and that there was no reason to start now. But he'd spent the entire evening fighting a war with a libido that was out of control…

'But you do it anyway,' he drawled softly. He held his hands up in a gesture of phoney surrender before shoving them into the pockets of his trousers. 'And, while you do that, don't expect me to play ball…'

CHAPTER EIGHT

TEN DAYS AFTER they arrived, Becky woke to the crippling pain of a headache, aching bones and the first, nasty taste of fever in her mouth.

And, for the first time in living memory, she thought that she might actually be *pleased* that she was about to come down with a cold. Or flu. Or any other virus that would give her an excuse to stick to her bed for twenty-four hours because the past few days had been the sweetest of tortures.

Theo had laid his cards on the table. He wasn't going to play ball. She'd set her rules down and he'd coolly and calmly told her that he was going to ignore them.

So she had expected a full-on attack and had been bracing herself to deal with that. She had, as ammunition, plentiful supplies of simmering anger, self-righteous moral preaching and offended outrage that he should dare to ignore *her* wishes.

If he wanted to stage an assault, then she would be more than ready for the fight, and she knew she would fight like a cornered rat, because her defences were fragile and her determination was weak and full of holes.

She was utterly and completely vulnerable to him and that, in itself, gave her the strength to cast him in the role of veritable enemy, which she felt was something she could deal with.

But there was no assault.

If anything, some of that intimate touching stopped. She would feel his eyes on her, a lazy, brooding caress that did all sorts of things to her senses, but those intrusive fingers on her skin when there was nothing she could do about it were no more. Indeed, after dinner, when they had fallen into the habit of sitting in one of the downstairs sitting rooms—an airy space where, with the windows flung open, the sound of the distant sea was a steady background roll—he would often sit opposite her, legs loosely spread, arms resting on his thighs, leaning forward in a way that was relaxed whilst still being aggressively alert.

Peeling her eyes away from him was proving a problem.

And, without her armour to fall back on, she had been reduced to playing a waiting game of her own which meant that she was always on full alert.

Several times she had asked him whether he might not like to escape and do some work.

'I'm perfectly happy to find a quiet corner somewhere and read,' she had told him. There were lots of those in the villa, although her favourite space was outside, curled up in a swinging chair on the veranda, from where she could see the stretch of front lawn with its shady trees and foliage and beyond that the flat ocean, a distant band of varying shades of blue.

'Don't you go worrying about me,' he had delivered in a soothing tone, although his eyes had been amused. 'It's delightful that you're concerned but, in actual fact, I'm managing to keep on top of my work very well at night.'

Which meant that the long days were spent in one another's company. They had had two trips into Portofino, where he had shown her around the picturesque harbour with its rows upon rows of colourful houses nestled in the embrace of the lush hills rising behind them. They had lunched at an exquisite and very quaint restaurant and she had had far too much ice-cold Chablis for her own good.

But his self-restraint had turned her into a bag of nerves and she had a sneaking suspicion that he knew that, which in turn made him all the more restrained.

For much of the time they were together, however, his mother was chaperone and companion.

For that, Becky was relieved because it afforded her a certain amount of distance from Marita Rushing. Becky knew, without a shadow of a doubt, that if she and the older woman were alone together for long enough they would become firm friends and the deceit in which she was engaged would feel even more uncomfortable than it already did.

She also suspected that Theo was deliberately making sure that he worked late at night, when everyone was asleep, so that he could keep a watchful eye on his mother, to ascertain her levels of alcohol intake.

'I honestly don't think she has a problem,' Becky had told him quietly the evening before, as they had been about to head off to their separate quarters.

'How would you know?' he had said roughly, but then had shaken his head, as though physically trying to clear it of negative thoughts. 'Are you a doctor?'

'Are you?' she had responded with alacrity. 'And, in actual fact, I have a great deal more training in medicine than you—and I'm telling you that there's no need to watch over your mother like a hawk. She hasn't said a word to you about the drinking situation because it was a blip on her horizon, and she's probably ashamed when she thinks about it now. If you keep following her around, she's going to begin to suspect that Flora has said something to you and she'll never live it down. She's a very proud woman.'

He had glowered but she had stood her ground and eventually he had laughed shortly and shrugged, which she had taken as a sign that he had at least listened to what she'd had to say.

But being with him all the time...was exhausting. She felt as though she couldn't drop her guard, even though she was beginning to wonder whether he hadn't lost complete interest in her after his cocky assertion that her defences were there to be knocked down should he so choose.

He might have wanted her to begin with but he wasn't a man who pursued and, in the end, old habits had died hard. She'd stuck her hands out to ward him away and he'd decided to back off because he couldn't be bothered to do otherwise.

And what really troubled her was the fact that *she cared*.

Instead of basking in the relief that she didn't have to keep swatting him away, she found herself missing that brief window when he had looked at her as though she still mattered to him, at least on a physical level.

She caught herself, on more than one occasion, leaning forward to get something, knowing that one glimpse and he would be able to see down her flimsy, lacy bra to her barely contained breasts.

So now she felt miserable with the start of a cold and she couldn't have been happier because she needed the time out to try and regroup.

An internal line had been installed in his mother's

room, connecting her to the kitchen and the sitting room, should she ever need to be connected, but in the absence of any such convenience Becky did the next best thing and dialled through to Theo's mobile.

She looked around her at the beautiful suite of rooms into which she had been put. Marita Rushing couldn't handle the stairs up, and there was no reason for her to venture up, but every day a housekeeper came and cleaned the house from top to bottom, as well as making sure that food was cooked, if that was necessary.

The housekeeper was a very quiet young girl who barely spoke a word of English and had been mortified, on day one, when Becky had helpfully tried to join her in tidying the bedroom.

At first Becky had wondered whether the girl would report back to Theo's mother that the loved-up couple slept in separate quarters, but then she very quickly realised that that would never happen.

Now, she wondered what it might have been like if that half-formulated, barely realised fear, which had been there when this whole charade had first been suggested, had actually come to pass. When Theo had first contacted her, she had quailed at the thought of having to share a bedroom with him, after the initial biting disappointment that the only reason he had picked the phone up had been to ask a favour of her.

For surely, in this day and age, that would be a given? If his mother was expected to fall for them being a couple, then she would likewise expect them to share a bed.

And what if they had?

Would her 'no sex' stipulation have been swept aside under the overwhelming surge of her physical attraction, combined with the power of knowing that she had fallen in love with him? Would common sense have been obliterated by the deadly combination of love and lust? Between those twin emotions, would there have been any room left for her head to prevail?

And would she have been worse off than she was now? Because she was a wreck. Which was probably why she had succumbed to a bug. Her body was telling her that she needed to rest.

Theo picked up on the third ring and, even though it wasn't yet six thirty in the morning, he sounded as bright-eyed and bushy-tailed as if he had been awake for hours.

'Why are you up so early?' were his opening words, and Becky nearly smiled, because for all the frustration he engendered in her she had become accustomed to certain traits of his. A complete lack of social niceties was one of those traits.

'Why are you?' she countered.

'Why do you think?' In the outer room, which had been converted into an office years previously—indeed as soon as the villa had been bought and the prospect of going there, even for a couple of days at a time, had become inevitable—Theo pushed himself away from the sleek, metal-and-wood desk and swivelled his chair so that he was staring out of the floor-to-ceiling window.

She hadn't come to him.

He'd really and honestly believed that she would have cracked. After all, he had seen the flare of mutual attraction in those luminous eyes, and he hadn't banked on her resistance, whatever she might have said to the contrary.

Why would he have? Since when had he ever been prepared to withstand any woman's resistance? He didn't know the rules of that particular game but he had felt his way and decided that he'd said what he had to say, but he wasn't going to push things with her. If she wanted to huff and puff and flounce around with maidenly virtue wrapped round her like a security blanket, then sooner or later she would drop the act.

He knew women, after all.

He also knew the power of good sex. It was more than a worthy adversary for any amount of doubts, hesitations or last minute qualms.

And they'd had good sex. The best.

Unfortunately he'd misread the situation and, having taken up a certain stance, he was condemned to dig his heels in or risk being a complete loser by being the first to crack.

It was beginning to do his head in. They were both bloody adults! They'd already slept together! It wasn't as though they were tiptoeing around one another in some kind of slow burn of a courtship game! Plus his mother was living the dream life, loving every second of seeing her son with a woman of whom she seriously approved.

Throw hot attraction into the mix and he just couldn't work out why it was that he was barely able to focus on his work and was having to take cold showers twice a day when it all should have been so simple.

And now, hearing her voice down the end of the line, he couldn't stop his imagination from doing all sorts of weird and wonderful things to his body as he pictured her, sleep-rumpled, in only her birthday suit.

Or else covered from top to toe in a Victorian maiden's nightie, to match her crazy 'no sex' rules...

Either image worked for him.

'I'm working.' He shifted, trying to release some of the sudden painful pressure.

'Do you *ever*,' she was distracted enough to ask, 'get any sleep at all, Theo?'

'I try and avoid sleep. It's a waste of valuable time.

Is that why you've called at…six forty in the morning? To check and see whether I'm getting my essential fix of beauty sleep?'

'I've called because…I'm afraid today is going to be a bit of a write-off for me.'

'Why? What are you talking about?'

'I've woken up with a crashing headache and all sorts of aches and pains. I think I may have a cold. It won't last but I'm going to stay in bed today.'

'My mother will be disappointed.' Theo stood up, brow furrowed. 'She had planned on introducing you to her favourite tea shop…'

'I'm sorry, Theo. I could venture downstairs but I feel absolutely rotten and I wouldn't want to…pass anything on to your mother. She's had a pretty poor year and a half and the last thing she needs is to catch germs from her house guest. In fact, if you don't mind, I'm going to grab some more sleep and hopefully I'll be fighting fit by tomorrow…'

'What have you taken?'

'Are you concerned?' Becky couldn't resist asking. 'Do you think that you won't be getting value for money if I take a day off?' As soon as the words had left her mouth, she wished that she could snatch them and stuff them back in.

'Are you offering to stay an extra day, Becky? I know you have a very strong work ethic.'

'I'm sorry. I shouldn't have… Well, I'm sorry…'

'Go back to sleep, Becky. I'll get Ana to bring you up some food when she gets here.'

He cut the connection, mouth thin as he contemplated the due reminder of why she was in this villa, mutual attraction or no mutual attraction. There was nothing like a sudden sucker-punch to remind a person of priorities.

* * *

Becky struggled up, reluctantly rising from a disturbed, fever-ridden sleep. She had taken a couple of tablets two hours previously and she could feel the effects of the tablets beginning to wear a little thin.

In fairness, she felt better than she had two hours before, but she still needed a day off, a day during which she could gather herself.

She didn't see Theo immediately. The curtains were drawn, thick, heavy-duty curtains designed to plunge the room into darkness so that if you wanted to lie in you weren't wakened by the stealthy creep of dawn's fingers infiltrating the room.

Sleepy eyes rested on the now familiar pieces of furniture, then shifted to the glass of water, now empty, on the side table, then…

'You're up.'

Becky's heart sped up and her mouth fell open, before a wash of misplaced propriety had her yank the sheet over her bare arms.

She had bought a complete new wardrobe and that complete new wardrobe included lingerie that she would never have dreamed of buying before. Little wisps of lace and not much else. Her nightwear was along those lines. It left next to nothing to the imagination. It couldn't have been more different from the homely, comfy, warm, practical nightwear she had made her own for the past twenty-seven years. She had thrown caution to the winds when she had gone on her shopping spree and had robustly decided, *in for a penny, in for a pound…*

'What are you doing here?' She was acutely conscious of her nipples scraping against the lacy top and the brevity of the matching knickers.

'Doctor's orders. Breakfast. I'm on a mission of mercy for the invalid. What would you like to eat?'

'Please don't put Ana to any trouble,' Becky begged. 'She has enough to do around here without bringing me up breakfast in bed as though I'm Lady Muck. I just need to spend the day in bed sleeping and I'll be back on my feet by tomorrow.'

'And, while you're in bed, the diet of choice for returning to full health is starvation? Because you don't want to put the housekeeper out?'

Becky flushed. Theo's attitude to the hired help was very different from hers. He was pleasant and polite but, as far as he was concerned, they were paid handsomely to do their jobs and were no different from any of the other employees in his service working at any of the companies he owned. A business transaction. Simple.

'Doesn't matter.' He waved one hand in nonchalant dismissal. 'Ana is off sick. Probably has the same bug that you have.'

'How awful!' Becky was stricken.

'And please,' Theo interjected with wry amusement, 'don't start beating yourself up about being the carrier of germs. I expect Ana brought it to the house with her. She has five siblings—a lot of scope for bugs to find places to set up camp.'

'And your mother? Don't tell me she has it as well...?'

'Fortunately not but I've shipped her off to Flora's for two days. Her health is fragile and the last thing she needs is a dose of the flu.'

'You're probably going to be next,' Becky said glumly.

'I'm never ill.'

'Have you told those germs that have set up camp with Ana's siblings? Because they might not know. They might have already decided that you'd make an excellent playground for them to have some fun on.'

'I'm as strong as an ox. Right. Food order.'

So it was just Theo in the house. There was no need for apprehension because, had he wanted to keep touching her and provoking her, he could have. All that had bitten the dust. His declaration of intent had been empty.

And now the poor guy felt obliged to put himself out for her when he would probably rather be working on a day off from supervising his mother and chaperoning his so-called girlfriend in the guise of enthusiastic lover.

'I guess…' she allowed her voice to linger thoughtfully before tailing off. 'I *guess* I should really have something to eat. I mean, I *have* had a pretty restless night, to be honest.'

Theo raised his eyebrows. The duvet had slipped a little and, if he wasn't mistaken, she didn't seem to be clad in the all-encompassing Victorian meringue he would have imagined. In fact, those thin spaghetti straps, as wispy as strands of pale cotton, pointed to a completely different get-up underneath the duvet.

'So what will it be?' he asked gruffly, clearing his throat and concentrating one hundred percent on her flushed face.

'Perhaps a poached egg,' Becky murmured. 'And some toast. Maybe a bit of fried ham as well, but not fried in oil, maybe fried in a little butter, just a dash. Protein. Important for my recovery, I imagine. And if there's juice… that would be nice. I noticed Ana squeezing oranges with an electric juicer… And perhaps some tea as well…'

'You've done a complete turnaround from not being hungry and not wanting to put anyone out,' Theo complained in a voice that told her that he knew very well what that turnaround was all about, and Becky smiled sweetly and apologetically at him.

'I'd understand if you didn't want to make me breakfast, Theo. I don't suppose it's the sort of thing you've ever done for any woman in your life before. In fact, I'm guessing that no woman would ever have been brave enough to have fallen ill when you were around to see it. They'd probably have known that they would get short shrift from you.'

'And that,' Theo countered smoothly, 'shows just how special you are, doesn't it? Because here I am, offering to be your slave while you're bedridden...'

Becky reddened. She knew why he was here. His mother would probably have told him to make sure he took care of her. Marita was like that. She had had a brief but idyllic married life with a man she had fallen desperately in love with at a very young age. Her concept of love was romantic and idealised because that was what she had had. She actually had no idea how jaded her son was when it came to the concept of love and romance. In her heart, she truly believed that he was capable of falling in love and finding the happiness she had found with her partner and soul mate.

Becky had come to understand exactly what Theo had meant when he had told her that, introduced to a girl deemed suitable, she would happily believe the fiction played out for her benefit.

She had also come to understand why he had done what he had because, however uncomfortable she was with the deceit, she could see improvements in his mother practically from one hour to the next. Flora, in a quiet aside two evenings previously, had confirmed how much Marita Rushing's frame of mind had improved since Theo had come to visit with Becky on his arm.

'She's a different woman,' Flora had confided. 'She is my sister again and not this poor, frail woman who felt she had nothing to live for... It was different when Theo was young and needed her, but since all those heart problems...and realising that he had no interest in settling down... Well, it is good that you are here.'

'I'm fine with just toast' was all she could find to say, mouth downturned at his coolness.

'I wouldn't dream of depriving you of essential sustenance to overcome your cold.' Theo grinned and gave her a mock salute. 'Anything else to add to the order? Or should I exit while the going's good?'

Becky allowed herself a smile once he'd left the room.

He got to her on so many fronts and one of those was his sense of humour. He could be as ironic as he could be cheeky and those two strands, woven together, was a killer package.

Reminding herself of the reality of their situation and the reality of what he felt for her was a daily challenge.

Lying back against the pillows, she wondered whether she should quickly change into something more suitable, but then realised that in her haste to replace her entire wardrobe for the two week period she had recklessly omitted anything that remotely resembled sensible clothing. Even the shorts she had packed had been knee-length linen. A small but exquisitely inappropriate wardrobe for someone who was now bedridden with a severe cold.

Theo returned less than twenty minutes later with a tray. He nudged the bedroom door open with his shoulder, half-expecting to find her sitting primly on the chair by the window, clad in anything but whatever sexy nightwear she had been wearing. However, she was still in bed, with the duvet sternly pressed flat under both arms, a step away from encasing her completely like a mummy.

'Your breakfast...' He dragged a chair over to the bed, deposited the tray on her lap and proceeded to sit down next to her.

'There's no need for you to stay.' Becky looked at the muddle of food on her plate and was puzzled as to how her poached egg and ham had been translated into something that was unidentifiable.

'The poached egg,' Theo pointed out with an elegant shrug, 'didn't quite go according to plan. I'm afraid I had to be creative...'

How could she keep the duvet in place while she ate? She tried, but gradually it slipped a little lower.

From his advantageous position next to the bed, Theo felt like a voyeur as he looked at the soft, silky smoothness of her shoulders and back. He talked to distract himself from falling into a trance because there was something hypnotic about the movement of her shoulder blades as she tucked into the breakfast.

Becky could feel those brooding, silver-grey eyes on her. Even though she wasn't looking at him, wasn't even sneaking sidelong glances in his direction...

Hot little looks, as he had called them...

The fever-induced weakness had been overtaken by a thrilling edge-of-precipice feeling as she finished the last morsel of food on the plate and dutifully put down her knife and fork.

When she glanced down, she could see how the duvet had slipped and how the lacy top was peeking open ever so slightly, allowing a fine view of her pale skin underneath.

This was playing with fire and she didn't know why she was doing that. She had spent so long being strong. She had accepted that he had lost interest in her. She had beaten herself up over her stupidity in falling in love with the man and had been extra careful to make sure that she wasn't exposed.

But now she could feel his eyes on her and that little voice that she had listened to right at the very beginning—that stupid little voice that had lured her to touch the flame, to climb into bed with him—was once again doing its thing and getting under her skin to wreak havoc with the defences she had meticulously been building up.

So, she'd fallen in love with him... So it had to be the most stupid thing she could ever have done...not that she had been able to stop herself... But here she was, fighting hard and being a martyr, making sure he didn't come near her. She'd given him her best 'hands off' stance, had told him that sex wouldn't be on the agenda, but, aside from feeling morally smug, what good had it done her? Was she happy and content with her decision? Had it made him any less tempting?

She was so desperate to read into the future and protect herself against further hurt—so keen to make sure he didn't add to the tally of pain she would suffer at a later date should she repeat her original mistake and get into bed again—that she was in danger of having a complete nervous meltdown.

'That was very nice. Thank you.' She heard the telltale throaty nervousness in her voice and glanced across at him as he removed the tray. When she leaned back against the pillows, she didn't rush to yank the duvet back up into position.

She feigned innocence, half-closing her eyes with a sigh of contentment at being well fed. She'd been hungrier than she'd thought and the eggy stuff he'd served up had been a lot tastier than she had expected.

She half-opened one eye to find him towering over her, arms folded, his dark features inscrutable.

He'd pulled back the curtains but not all the way and the sun penetrated the room in a band of light, leaving the remainder of the room in shadow. The light caught him at an angle, defining the sharp jut of his cheekbones and the curve of his sensuous mouth. He wasn't smiling. Nor was he scowling. He was…just looking, and adding things up in his head, and that sent a frisson of awareness racing up and down her spine, because she knew what things he was adding up and she liked that.

She'd missed him. He'd gone AWOL on her and she hadn't liked it. Her brain might have patted itself on the back and thought it'd won the battle but her body was staging a rebellion and common sense didn't stand a chance.

'You wouldn't happen to be playing any games with me, would you?' Theo asked softly.

'Don't know what you mean…'

'Oh, really, Becky,' Theo said drily. 'Would that be because you're just a poor invalid who's feeling too under the weather to be thinking straight?'

'I feel a bit better now that I've had something to eat.'

'And that would account for the suddenly relaxed body language?'

Becky didn't say anything but their eyes tangled and neither could look away—neither wanted to break the electric charge zapping between them. She could hear her breathing slowing up and could almost feel the rush of hot blood through her veins. Her skin prickled and her nipples were tightening, pinching, hard, throbbing buds poking against the flesh-coloured lace.

For Theo, things seemed to be happening in slow motion, from the darkening of her turquoise eyes to the raspy unsteadiness of his breathing.

His erection was a sheath of steel and would be outlined against his lightweight tan khakis. *Dip your eyes a bit lower, baby,* he thought, *and you'll have more than your fill of exactly how turned on I am right now.*

She did.

And that, too, seemed to happen in slow motion, as did the way the tip of her tongue erotically wetted her full lips. Her hair was everywhere, spread against the white pillows and over her shoulders, wild and tangled and utterly provocative.

'No sex,' he reminded her in a rough, shaky undertone and Becky looked at him, eyes lacking all guile as she considered what he had just pointed out.

'You stopped touching,' she heard herself say in a breathy voice—because suddenly it seemed very important for him to tell her that he still fancied her, even though she could read that he did in his eyes, and in the very still, controlled way he was standing. And in the erection he was not bothering to hide. She just needed him to say it…

'As per your instructions.'

'I know, but…'

'Are you fishing for me to tell you that I wanted to keep touching you? Because you won't have to throw your line very far to hear me say it. I wanted to keep touching you…' He raked his fingers through his hair. This was what he wanted and it was what he had wanted all along. When he thought about her body and what it could do to him, he had to suck his breath in sharply just to control his wayward libido from doing what it shouldn't. 'I wanted you after I left the Cotswolds and I haven't stopped. It's been hell looking and not being able to touch. Is that more or less what you wanted to hear…?'

Becky thought that she would like to hear much, much more. But *want* was all she was going to hear and she was sick of pretending to herself that she could keep pushing that aside because it didn't come with *love*.

She was too weak.

She had a few days left here and she was too weak to keep trying to be strong.

Whatever capacity Theo had to love, it was never going to be her. Privately, she didn't think he would ever love anyone.

'He never saw me in love,' his mother had whispered sadly to her only the evening before when he had been called away on one of the rare emergency conference calls he had allowed through. 'He just saw me when I was sad and alone. That's made him the man he is today. Afraid of love… Until now…until he found you…'

Becky had ignored the bit about Theo being afraid of love until he found her, which was a joke, and analysed and analysed and analysed the rest of what his mother had said. It might have been an over-simplification, but it was probably grounded in truth. His background had made him what he was when it came to love. He would never trust anything that had the power to destroy and, in his mind, his mother had been destroyed by love. He couldn't see beyond that and never would.

What he had to give and all he had to give was…his touch.

'More or less,' Becky agreed on a broken sigh. She pushed down the duvet, revealing the lacy nonsense she was wearing, which concealed nothing. Her pink nipples were visible through the lace, as was the shadowy dark down between her thighs.

She rested her hand on the mound between her legs, wanting badly to squeeze her legs together to relieve the fierce burning between them. His eyes were practically black with unconcealed lust and a heady sense of power raced through her veins, obliterating everything in its path.

'Becky.' Theo barely recognised his voice. 'There's something you should know…' All those half-truths were coming home to roost but she needed to know, needed to know that in life there was no such thing as coincidence, needed to know the truth about her cottage. What had seemed a good idea at the time, concealing the purpose of his arrival there so that he could feel out the terrain, was now an unthinkable error of judgement.

'Don't say a word,' Becky rushed in before he could say what she knew he was going to, another one of those warnings that what they were about to do was meaningless. She just didn't want to hear it. She didn't need to have that rammed home to her. Again.

'We have a few more days and after that we go our separate ways. We won't see one another again, so nothing has to be explained. We can…just enjoy this window…and then tomorrow is another day…'

CHAPTER NINE

HE WOULD TELL HER. Of course he would. Instead of being an anonymous buyer in three months' time, he would show his hand. He would also pay over the odds for the cottage he had originally intended to buy at a knockdown price, poetic justice for the people who had bought it at a knock-down price from his mother.

In three months' time, what they had now would all be water under the bridge. They'd probably chuckle as they exchanged contracts because, face it, she would have emerged a winner. She would be in a brand-new job in a brand-new location, renting a brand-new apartment. Work would have been done on the cottage so that the time left spent there would be comfortable. No buckets collecting water from a leaking roof!

She wasn't interested in hearing long stories now about his appearance at the cottage and the reasons behind it.

And he wasn't that interested in killing the moment by telling her either, although, in fairness, he would have done had she not waved aside his interruption.

She was fired up.

He was fired up.

Talk was just something taking up too much time when there was so much they both wanted to do.

Becky watched Theo's momentary flicker of hesitation and found that she was holding her breath. This was as proactive as she was capable of being. She knew that if he decided to back away now…if he thought that he wasn't prepared to step back into the water, even though she had assured him that these last few days would simply be about giving in to lust and closing that door between them once and for all…then she would retreat.

She would have lost her pride but, even so, she would retreat without regret because she was no longer prepared to turn her back on what could be hers for a few days more.

She was sick to the back teeth of being a noble martyr.

In the heat of the moment and with surrender in her mind, she couldn't, for the life of her, remember what had propelled her to fling down that 'no sex' addendum to the proposal he had put forward. She'd been so strident and sure of herself.

'You're not well,' Theo said gruffly.

'Why are you being so thoughtful?' Becky teased, not quite certain of the response she would get, but he grinned rakishly at her.

'Because I'm a gentleman.'

'Maybe I don't want you to be a gentleman right now,' Becky murmured, wriggling slightly to make room for him on the double bed. 'Are you sure you're not scared of getting into bed with me because you might catch my germs? I know you said that germs would never dare attack you but…'

'You're a witch.' Theo half-groaned. He walked towards the window and drew the curtains, plunging the room into instant darkness. He had to adjust his trousers, had to control his erection, which was throbbing under the zipper. He took a few seconds to stand by the window and look at her.

Very slowly he began undressing. This was more for his benefit than it was for hers. Move too fast and he would have to take her quick and hard, and he didn't want that. He wanted to enjoy every second of this—he wanted to savour her body and remember the feel of it under his exploring mouth and hands.

He wanted to take his time.

Becky fell back against the pillows as he began to stroll towards her. Shirt discarded, trousers unzipped. He was physical perfection. He was lean and muscular and looked *strong*. The sort of man who would always emerge the winner in any street brawl. She could have kept looking at him for ever.

She had no idea where her cold had gone. She had woken up feeling rotten, and thinking that she could do with a day off to recover from the impact daily contact with him was having on her state of mind, and now here she was, cold forgotten, as though it had never existed.

She was on fire but not with fever. She was burning up for the man now staring down at her, his hand resting lightly on his zipper. She could see the prominent bulge of his erection underneath the trousers. He was well endowed and he was massively turned on. It showed. It thrilled her.

She reached forward and lightly touched that bulge and the soft sound of his indrawn hiss was as powerful as any drug, sending her already drugged senses into frantic overdrive.

She sat up while he remained standing next to the bed.

The duvet had been shrugged off. Theo looked down at her soft shoulders, her riotous hair and all the luscious places exposed by the very revealing, and for her very risqué, nightwear. He greedily took in the heaviness of her breasts, lovingly outlined by the lace, two shades of flesh combined, her flesh and the flesh-coloured fabric. The deep crease of her cleavage made him grind his teeth together and he had to clench his fists to avoid pressing her back against the pillows so that he could ravish her.

And now she was gently but firmly pulling down the zipper and tugging the trousers down.

'Becky…' He groaned.

'I like it when you lose control…' she said in a ragged voice. He had stepped out of the trousers and she knew that he was having to restrain himself from pushing her back against the mattress so that he could do what came so naturally for him, so that he could take control of the situation.

No way.

She tugged down the boxers and circled her fingers firmly around his massive erection. She felt it pulse and then she delicately began to lick it from the head, along the thick shaft, trailing wetness up and down and around until he couldn't contain his groans. His hand was tangled in her hair. He wanted to keep her right there, doing what she was doing, even though, at the same time, he also wanted to tug her away so that she could stop taking him to that point of no return.

She took him into her mouth, sucking gently, then firmly, then back to gently, building a rhythm that was exciting her as much as it was exciting him. He was groaning, urging her on, telling her how he liked it. Before she'd met him, she would never have thought that she could be this intimate with a man, intimate enough to taste him like this. She'd never thought that she would be able to hear him say the sort of things Theo said to her in the height of their lovemaking…telling her where to go, what to do, urging her to do the same…describing all the things he wanted to do to her until she was burning up and frantic with desire.

'Stop,' he ordered gruffly, but it was too late, as she pushed him over the edge.

It was the last thing he'd wanted. He'd wanted slow and thorough. But it just went to show the effect she had on him. He hadn't been able to stop himself and he cursed fluently under his breath as he came down from a mind-blowing orgasm.

'Shame on you,' he chided, settling onto the bed with her, depressing the mattress with his weight so that she slid towards him, her body pressed up hard against his nakedness. 'I wanted to take things easy...' He pushed some of her hair behind an ear and then nibbled her lobe, which sent little arrows of beautiful sensation zipping through her.

She squirmed and wriggled against him, then slid one thigh sinuously up along his leg, relieving some of the aching between her legs.

'Naughty girl,' he admonished softly, grinning. 'You know you're going to have to pay dearly for making me lose control like that, don't you?'

He'd missed this—missed it much more than he'd ever imagined possible. Having her here in bed with him made him feel...weirdly comfortable, as though the inevitable was happening, as though he was meant to be here, doing this.

Finishing business, he thought, shrugging off a suddenly uneasy feeling he couldn't quite define.

He smoothed her thigh with his hand. She was warm and he paused to ask her whether she was up to it.

'You took something for your cold, I'm assuming?'

'Since when are you a fussing mother hen?' Becky laughed and leaned up to kiss him. His lips were firm and cool and so, so familiar. It amazed her how readily her body could recall his.

For a second, just a second, Theo stilled, then the moment was lost as he curved his fingers under the lace, finding her breasts, cupping them, moving to tease her nipple between his fingers. He gently pushed her flat against the bed and levered himself into the most advantageous position for exploring her body.

He started with her mouth. She'd taken him over the edge, but he was building fast to another erection, and this time he was going to take her all the way…feeling her wrap herself around him.

He kissed her slowly, tracing her lips with his tongue, then tasting her the way a connoisseur might taste vintage wine. He gently smoothed her hair away from her face, kissed her eyes, the sides of her mouth, then her neck.

She arched back slightly and shivered as those delicate kisses wound their way along her neck and then across her shoulders.

Her staccato breathing sounded as loud as thunder in the quiet of the bedroom. It was all she could hear. It was louder than the gentle background whirring of the ceiling fan, which she had become accustomed to keeping on all night, and punctuated with small whimpers and little, gasping moans.

She was desperate to rip the lace nightwear off but he wouldn't let her. Instead, he traced his tongue over the fabric, inexorably finding her nipple and then suckling hard on it through the lace, rasping it with his tongue until he found a gap in the lace through which it peeped, dusky pink, a hard button standing to attention.

'You're going to wreck this brand-new top,' she rebuked with a breathless giggle as she watched him toy with the intricate lace pattern until he had engineered two slightly bigger gaps, which he proceeded to position expertly over her nipples so that they were now both poking through.

'You shouldn't have bought it,' he countered, glancing at her and meeting her fevered eyes. 'You should have stuck to the baggy cotton tee shirts, then you wouldn't mind if I ripped it to shreds to get to your delectable body.'

'I was only obeying orders and replacing my wardrobe, as per your request...'

'Since when do you ever obey orders?' Theo asked huskily. 'You're the most disobedient mistress I've ever had.'

'I'm not your mistress!'

'You prefer "lover"?'

'I'd prefer you to stop talking.' *Wife*, she thought. She'd prefer *wife*. But *lover* would do, just as these snatched few days and nights would also have to do.

'Happy to oblige.' Theo took his time at her breasts. He sucked her nipples, giving them both the attention they deserved. He liked the way they stuck out at him through the lace, perfect, pouting and slickly wet from his tongue. He was almost reluctant to lift the top higher, to free them from their constraints, but he wanted to hold them in his hands. He had big hands and her breasts filled them, heavy and sexy. He massaged them and she writhed as he did so, tossing and turning, her eyes drowsy and unfocused with lust.

This was how he liked her. It startled him to realise that he had pictured this almost from the very moment he had left the cottage, having been marooned there by the snow. He hadn't just had her on his mind. He'd stored all sorts of images of her and projected them into a place and time where they would be doing just what they were doing now. Making love.

He nuzzled the undersides of her breasts, then trailed languid kisses along her stomach. Her skin was as soft and as smooth as satin. He paused at the indentation of her belly button, explored it with his tongue and heard her tell him that she needed him, that she was burning up for him. Her legs were already parted and he could smell the sweet, musky scent of her femininity.

She was breathing fast, panting, her stomach rising and falling as if she were running a marathon.

He cupped her between her legs and felt her wetness through the lace shorts, then he slipped his hand underneath and ran his finger along the tender, sensitive slit of her womanhood, finding and feeling her pulsing core.

The lace shorts restricted movement of his hand and he moved the barrier to one side. In a minute, he would take off the damned things completely, but right now he was enjoying watching her face as she responded to the gentle probing and teasing of his fingers.

Her eyelids fluttered, her nostrils were flared and her mouth was half-open. Her breathing was raspy and uneven, halfway between moaning and whimpering.

She was the very picture of a woman at the mercy of her body's physical responses and he felt a kick of satisfaction that he was the one who had brought her to that place. She might make a big song and dance about his unsuitability but she couldn't deny how much he turned her on.

Which was probably why his mother had not questioned their relationship. Normally so perceptive, Marita Rushing had not doubted for an instant that they were seriously involved. Yes, she might have wanted to believe it, and so had avoided gazing too closely for discrepancies in the perfect picture on display, but something about their interaction had convinced her that they were truly an item. Theo could only ascribe that to the physical pull between them which had transmitted itself to his mother by some sort of osmosis, making the pretence very, very real.

'You have no idea how much you turn me on,' he breathed in a rough undertone and Becky looked at him with darkened eyes.

'You could try telling me. I need convincing after you've spent so long ignoring me...'

'I like to think of it as a slow burn...' He eased the shorts off and she half-sat up, tugged the top over her head and flung it to the ground, then lay back, propping herself against the pillows.

Theo paused, taking time out to look at her, so supple and soft and so very, very feminine. The height of femininity, with her rounded curves, her long hair and open, honest face.

He straddled her and then knelt, his legs on either side of her, so that he could continue his lazy exploration of her glorious body. He had to keep telling himself not to rush because he wanted to, badly. He had to make himself slow down, although it was nigh on impossible when he moved down her body and began to lick her between her legs, tasting her, savouring her dewy wetness in his mouth. He nudged his erection into some good behaviour because there was no way he was going to allow himself to lose control again. Once had been bad enough.

Becky could barely breathe. It was exquisite having him down there, head between her legs, his hands under her bottom, driving her up to his mouth so that not even the slightest fraction of sensation was lost.

She hooked her legs around his back and flattened

her hands at her sides. She could feel the steady rhythm of an orgasm building and eased away from his mouth, panting, not wanting to come, wanting and needing him inside her.

Theo straightened, lying lightly over her so that he could deliver a few little kisses to her mouth. 'You have no idea how long I've wanted this,' he confessed unsteadily. He pushed himself up and Becky traced the corded muscles of his arms.

'How long?' Becky made her voice light, teasing and mildly amused. She hoped that only she could hear the desperate plea to have something, *anything* to grab on to, that would turn this into more than just sex for him. It would never be love or anything like that, but affection, maybe… Would that be asking too much? She was only human, after all.

'Pretty much as soon as I stepped out of your front door.' He dealt her a slashing, wicked grin that made her toes curl.

'You could have stayed a little longer.'

'Unfortunately…' Theo nuzzled the side of her neck so that some of what he was saying was lost in the caress '…there was a certain little something called *reality* to be dealt with. Playing truant can only last so long…'

'A bit like what we're doing here.' Becky laughed lightly, although her heart was constricted with pain.

'This is a bit more than truancy.' Theo looked down at her seriously. 'It's not just about having some fun and then pushing on. There's someone else in the equation.'

'But essentially it *is* just fun and pushing on. I mean, we're here and we're in bed together, and then we'll leave and that'll be that…'

Theo shrugged. He wasn't going to cross any bridges until he was staring them in the face. 'I plan on bringing my mother back as soon as possible,' he admitted. 'It's all very well and good, her being out here—and I'm sure she's enjoying the weather, my aunt's company and my aunt's kids and grandchildren—but that's a form of truancy in itself, wouldn't you agree?'

'Maybe...'

'And, as for us pushing on... I admit things are slightly more complex on that front than I'd originally imagined.'

'How so?' Becky felt her racing heart begin to stutter. Tense as a bow string, she waited for him to elucidate.

'All this talk is killing the mood.' Theo shifted to turn onto his side and pulled her into position so that they were facing one another, belly to belly. 'I thought my mother would have been delighted to discover that I was capable of more than having flimsy relationships with unsuitable women. I imagined that that would have given her a fillip, so to speak. Bucked up her spirits and stopped her from having worst-case scenarios in her head about me remaining a bachelor for the rest of my days, because somehow I was incapable of forming bonds with any woman that might be permanent. I intended to insinuate that you might not be the one for me, but certainly there was a woman out there who would be...a woman who wasn't a supermodel with nothing much between her ears...'

'Not all models are like that.' Becky thought of her clever, lovely sister.

'I know,' Theo admitted. 'But maybe I've just made it my mission to find the ones who are. At any rate, I was perhaps a bit short-sighted. I also thought that I'd be able to break things off between us gently. A process of gradually growing apart because of the distance or my work commitments or your work commitments. No need for you to put in an appearance—just a slow and gradual demise which could be explained away without any visits from you. I had no idea that my mother would jump on board this charade with such rich enthusiasm or that she would...' he sighed and searched for the right words, and then shot her a crooked, sideways smile '...fall in love with you the way she has. It poses a problem, although it's not something we can't work with.'

'What problem?'

'It'll wait. I can't talk any more, Becky...' He dipped his fingers into her and slid them up and down. 'And neither can you, from the feel of things.'

He didn't give her time to pick up the threads of the conversation or even to dwell further on it, because he lowered himself down the length of her agitated body, hands on her sides, mouth kissing, licking and nibbling.

She gave a husky groan as he buried his head between her legs again, teasing with the same lingering thoroughness as he had earlier teased her tight, sensitive nipples. She curled her fingers into his hair, arched back and bucked in gentle, rotating movements, urging on his inquisitive tongue to taste every bit of her.

Her body was on fire and she feverishly played with her nipples, driving yet more sensation through her body. She was so close to coming...

But, when she could stand it no more, he reared up and rustled about, finding protection, giving her body a little time to breathe and for those almost-there sensations to subside.

She couldn't wait to have him inside her. Like him, she hadn't stopped wanting this. Unlike him, so much more was attached to her wanting, but for the moment she couldn't even begin to go down that road, not when she was burning up.

He inserted himself gently into her. He was big and

every time they had made love he had been careful to build his rhythm slowly, had eased himself slowly into her, before thrusting deeper and firmer.

She loved the feel of him in her, loved it when he began to move with surety and precision, knowing just how to rouse her, just where to touch her and when for maximum effect. It was as though her body had been groomed to respond to him in ways that she knew, in her heart, it would never, ever respond to any other man.

And this time it was no different. He pushed deep and hard and she automatically bent her knees, taking all of him inside her and feeling the rush of her orgasm as it hurtled towards her, sending her to a place where nothing existed but the sound of their breathing and movement, and then a splintering that was so intense that the world seemed to freeze completely.

Distantly, she knew that he was coming as well, felt the tension in his big body as he reared up with a strangled groan of completion and satisfaction.

She wrapped her arms around him, her eyes still closed and her breathing still laboured, shuddering as she came down from the high to which she had been catapulted. He stayed still for a while, his arms encasing her. It was such an illusion of absolute closeness that she wanted to cry.

Instead, she whispered softly, stroking his face until he opened his eyes and looked at her. 'You were telling me that there's a problem, Theo…'

'Isn't it usually the unthinking man who breaks the post-coital mood by talking? Or falling asleep? Or getting up to work?' Theo half-joked, kissing the tip of her nose.

'I wonder which of those three would be your preferred choice of atmosphere-breaking?' Becky darted a kiss on his mouth, which deepened into something more intense.

'With you...' Theo murmured, cupping her breast and absently playing with her nipple, rolling the pad of his thumb over it, thinking that he could easily dip down to suckle on it and just stay there until they were both ready to make love all over again, which, judging from the way his penis was behaving, would be sooner rather than later. 'With you, I could happily go for the repeat performance option...'

'Not yet.'

Theo flopped onto his back and laughed ruefully. 'Okay. Here's the problem.' He sighed and took a few seconds to get his brain back into gear before shifting onto his side to look at her. 'I don't think it's going to be easy for you to simply vanish from my life overnight, whilst I paper over your disappearance with as many limp excuses as I can think of. My mother may have had her spirit sapped by her ill health and worries but she's still vigorous enough to do something like demand a meeting with you to find out why we aren't making wedding plans. I asked you for a fortnight. It might not be long enough.'

'It has to be, Theo. I have a life to be getting on with.' She pushed herself away from him and then kept her hand flat on his chest to stop him from coming any closer.

'I get that.' Did he? Honestly? He didn't think that a few more days of this was going to be nearly enough to get her out of his system.

'I'm not going to be at your beck and call just because you think you might need me to put in an occasional appearance.'

'What about being at my beck and call because I can't seem to keep my hands off you and I don't want you to disappear from my life?'

If he hadn't said that…

If he'd just let her keep thinking that all he wanted was a continuation of the business arrangement they had embarked upon…

He didn't want her to disappear from his life. She knew that it was silly to read anything behind that but her romantic heart couldn't help but be swept away by the notion of fate having brought them together, delivered them to this place, this here and now, where possibilities were endless, if only he could see it.

'I know you don't mean that,' she muttered, confused and hearing the uncertainty in her voice with some alarm.

'I've never meant anything more in my life before, Becky,' Theo told her with driven urgency. He could sense her capitulation but he didn't feel the expected triumph. Instead, he felt a rush of heartfelt honesty that took him by surprise. This wasn't just about his mother. Oh, no…this was about *him*. She was a fever inside him and he knew that just a little bit longer with her would douse it. Overpowering *need* had never cut so deep.

'It's not practical, Theo, and besides…'

'Besides what…?' She didn't answer and he looked at her with deadly seriousness. 'Tell me you don't feel this too, Becky. This has nothing to do with my mother. I would be asking this of you were my mother not a factor in the equation. I don't want to let you go…'

Just yet, Becky reminded herself, clutching at sanity the way a drowning man clutched at a life raft. *You don't want to let me go just yet*…

She couldn't afford to let herself be lured any further along the road than she already had been. She was in love with him. Each day spent with him was a day deeper in love for her. She had cracked this time, had argued herself into a position of being able to justify her surrender.

So was she going to do that again? Until she was finally dispatched at some point in the not-too-distant future?

Theo knew that this was not only a tall order but an extremely rash one. It would be difficult to write her out of his life abruptly, but it could be done. There were always ways and means when it came to solving thorny problems. But he still really wanted her, and wanted her so badly that the need took precedence over clear judgement.

He was involved with her because of the cottage. Break up with her when they returned to England, and he could still buy the place after the dust had settled. They would have had a few sex-filled days in the Cotswolds and a dalliance in the sun generated from the extraordinary circumstance that had brought them together.

Continue, for whatever reason, when they returned to London, and like it or not they would be indulging in a full-blown relationship. What else could he possibly call it? Whatever she said about him not being her type, how long before that would change? Would she inevitably be seduced by a lifestyle she had never envisaged for herself? Once upon a time, he had doubted that she would fit in to his world, not that he'd really given a damn. He'd been wrong. Looking at the ease with which she'd pulled off the expensive couture clothes she had bought, he realised she fitted in just fine.

Haute couture was something a woman could get accustomed to very easily. How long, then, before she became just another woman trying to talk about marriage and planning things that would never materialise?

But none of that seemed to matter because the sex was just so good.

And anyway, he argued with himself, he would have *some* contact with her afterwards because of the practice he had promised to buy for her. He would have to have her input in sourcing somewhere suitable. It wasn't as though they could just walk away from one another without a backward glance.

There and then, he made his decision. The purchase of the cottage would have to be jettisoned. That had been an error of judgement, given everything that had come afterwards, and she would never find out about any of it. At any rate, Becky would soon be busy changing jobs and facing the challenges of living somewhere else. They would see one another but not regularly. His mother might see her again a few times but that would be it. Harmless dinners out where he would be able to manage the conversation.

It would be a shame about the cottage, but you won a few, you lost a few.

He slipped his hand between her legs and kissed her, a long, lingering, persuasive kiss. This was what he knew, the power of sex, and he was going to force her to admit to it too. He wasn't going to let her walk away in a haze of high-principled apologies and rambling, earnest lectures about what made sense and what didn't. If she walked away, then she was going to face what she was walking away from. Explosive, mind-blowing sex.

It was hitting below the belt, but Theo was nothing if not a man who knew how to take advantage of the situations life threw at him.

Becky moaned, her whole body quivering as he began devastating inroads into her self-control. He moved his fingers and touched her until she wanted to scream and beg him to take her. Her mind slipped its leash and she imagined all sorts of things she wanted him to do to her. She imagined what it would be like to pin down those powerful arms of his, restrain them with a nice leather strap and then torment his body by making love to him oh, so slowly…

She imagined them naked in a field making love under a black, starry sky, and touching one another in the back row of a cinema like a couple of teenagers…

And then the slideshow ended because none of that would happen if she walked away now.

She didn't want any of that to happen. She knew the consequences of prolonging this disastrous union.

But she still reached down anyway, held his erection in her slight hand and began massaging it before climbing on top of him and letting herself surrender…

CHAPTER TEN

HOW COULD YOU...? How could you do this...?

Ten days ago, that was exactly what Becky had wanted to scream and shout at the man who once again had become her lover, against her better judgement.

She had thought at the time that being bedridden for a day with a cold virus would give her breathing space. In fact, as it had turned out, being bedridden had placed her in just the right place for him to stage his very successful assault on what precious little had been left of her common sense.

She'd folded faster than the speed of light and they had spent the remainder of their stay in Italy unable to keep their hands off one another. Much to his mother's obvious delight.

And, after they had returned to England, she had kept telling herself that it was just a matter of time before it all fizzled out. That work commitments and all the details that had to be sorted out with her job and the new practice would reduce their time together until they simply drifted apart though lack of proximity. He wasn't the sort of man who could ever do a long-distance relationship or indeed any relationship where the woman he wanted was inaccessible.

Certainly, she had had to return to the Cotswolds, had

had to begin the process of dismantling her life there and beginning the search for somewhere new where a practice could be profitable. Yet, somehow, she seemed to have seen him over the ensuing fortnight with more regularity than she might have imagined, and then his mother had returned from Italy, earlier than he had anticipated.

Becky stared numbly around her, back where she had started at the cottage, which had now been renovated to a standard that was eminently saleable.

In fact, she barely recognised the place.

She blinked rapidly, squashing foolish tears at her own naivety. There was no such thing as a free lunch and especially not in the rarefied world that Theo occupied.

At the time, she had thought, unwisely, that the cottage and the practice were part of the deal that he had hired her to undertake. Play the game and she would be rewarded—and she had played the game, not for the rewards, but for the pleasure of playing because she had missed him. He had phoned and she had got herself in a lather and called upon her pride but, in the end, she had thrilled at the thought of just seeing him again and being with him again.

But, of course, the picture was a lot more complex than the one that had been painted for her benefit.

She paused to gaze at herself in the mirror in the newly painted hall. She'd dumped all the finery, the expensive dresses, the designer shoes and underwear.

This is who you are, she told her reflection. *A pleasant enough looking vet who's lived her entire life in the country. Not some glamorous sex kitten powerful enough to turn the head of a man like Theo Rushing.*

What on earth had got into her?

She knew, of course. Love had got into her. It had roared into her life and she had been knocked off her feet without even realising it because it had come in a format she hadn't recognised.

She'd expected someone like Freddy. She'd expected cuddles, kisses and, face it, polite, enjoyable sex.

She hadn't expected sex of the bodice-ripping variety, so she had written it off as lust until, of course, it had all been far too late for her adequately to protect herself.

Love had turned her into a puppet that had walked back into his arms, even though she had known that it was never going to be reciprocated. Love had effectively switched off all the burglar alarms that should have been up and running, protecting her.

And, disastrously, love had made her begin to hope.

She'd begun to think that he might just feel more for her than he had anticipated. People said one thing, but life had a way of getting in the way of all their well-grounded intentions.

Look at her!

Had it been the same for him? It surely wasn't just about the sex…? There'd been many times when they hadn't been rolling around on a bed, when they'd talked, when he'd given her advice on setting up a practice— brilliant, sensible advice from a guy who had done his own thing and come out on top.

It hadn't been the same for him. He'd had an agenda from the word *go* and, oh, how she had wanted to scream and shout when she had found out. Instead, she had absented herself and taken off to France for a week to be with her family, who had been overjoyed to see her.

For a while, she had almost been distracted enough to see a way forward. She had revelled in her sister's pregnancy and obvious happiness. She had allowed herself to be congratulated on her ambitions to move on and set up a practice while she had skirted around the precise explanation as to how, exactly, she was managing to do that. She had waffled a lot about excellent references, possible bank loans and the possibility of someone willing to invest for a share of the partnership...

Now she was back, though...

She peered through the window in the hall by the front door.

For the first time in ten days, ever since she had found out from his mother details of his past which he had conveniently kept from her, she would be seeing him.

She had no idea what was going through his head but she hadn't wanted him to know what had been going through hers. At least not then, not when she had been so boiling mad, so humiliated and mortified, that her emotions would have done the shouting and that would have made her incoherent and vulnerable.

And, when she confronted him, she wanted to be cool and detached.

She also wasn't even certain that she would mention anything at all. Perhaps she would just tell him that she felt that what they had had run its course. Maybe he had got the hint, because she hadn't been returning his calls, and on the couple of occasions when he had managed to get through to her she had been vague and distant, practically ending the conversation before it had begun.

She ducked away from the window the second she heard the throaty purr of his car and the crunch of gravel as it swerved into the little courtyard in front of the house.

Nerves gripped her. The doorbell sounded and she wiped her perspiring palms on her jeans and took a deep breath.

Experience told her that, when she pulled open the door, his impact on her would be as strong as it always was. Absence and time apart were two things that never seemed to diminish it. Unless he had gained two stone in the space of ten days and lost all his hair and teeth, his devastating good looks would still make the breath hitch in her throat and the flood of emotion she felt for him would still make her feel weak and powerless.

Not wanting to appear over-keen, she allowed him to stand pressing the doorbell for a few seconds before she opened the door.

And there he was.

The weather had changed from those heady few days when he had last been in the Cotswolds. Spring had long since arrived, and with it pale blue skies and wispy clouds were scurrying across the washed blue backdrop as though hurrying on urgent errands. The trees were in full bloom and the flowers were poking out wherever they could, eager to feel the first rays of sun on them, blues and violets and reds and pinks clambering out of the bushes and hedgerows and tumbling across fences and yellow stone walls.

It was Saturday. No work, hence his arrival at four in the afternoon, just a few hours after she herself had arrived back from France. He was long and lean in faded black jeans and a black polo shirt, casual jacket hooked over one shoulder. He'd propped his shades up and he looked every inch a drop-dead-sexy movie star.

And she felt all those predictable responses she always did whenever she clapped eyes on him.

'Theo,' she managed, stepping aside and then slightly back as he brushed past her.

His clean, woody scent filled her nostrils and made her feel faint.

'So...' Theo turned to look at her. His face was impassive. His body language was cool and controlled. Neither bore any resemblance to what was going on inside him because she'd spent the past ten days playing an avoidance game that had got on his nerves. She'd vanished off to France on a whim. She'd contrived to view possible practices up for grabs without him, even though he was going to be funding whatever purchase transpired.

'What's going on, Becky?'

They hadn't made it out of the narrow hall and already it was clear there were going to be no pleasantries to paper over the awkwardness of what she was going to say. Ending something was always tough but she was going to be ending this with an edge of bitterness that would live with her for ever, and that made it all the tougher.

'I thought I would show you the practice I'm thinking would be suitable. The head vet who runs it is retiring and he's looking for someone to take over. It'll be a similar sort of size to the one here and, if anything, the work will be less demanding and probably a lot more profitable because it's in a town.' She began edging towards the sitting room.

Two weeks ago, she would have flown into his arms and they wouldn't have made it to the bedroom.

If he hadn't got the message already that things were over between them, then he'd have to be blind not to be receiving the message loud and clear now. And he wasn't blind. Far from it.

'I know buying the practice was all…er…part of the deal that we had…'

Theo stayed her with one hand and spun her round to face him. 'This is how you greet me after nearly two weeks of absence, Becky?' He stepped closer towards her, a forbidding, towering presence that filled her with apprehension, nerves and that tingling excitement that was now taboo. 'With polite conversation about business deals?'

She whipped her arm away and stepped back, anger rising like a tide of bile at the back of her throat.

'Okay,' she snapped, reaching boiling point at the speed of light. 'How else would you like me to greet you? You must have guessed that…that…' She faltered, and he stepped into the sudden leaden silence like a predator sensing weakness.

'That…? Why don't you spell it out for me, Becky?'

'It's over. I…I'm moving on now and it's time for this to end.' She looked away because she just couldn't look at him. She could feel his grey eyes boring into her, trying to pull thoughts out of her head.

He knew. How could he not? One minute she had been full on and the next minute she had left the building. He'd tried to get in touch with her, and, sure, she'd picked up a few times, but conversation between them had been brief and stilted. He would have called a lot more because her silence had driven him crazy but pride, again, had intervened.

He felt sick. What was it they said about pride being a person's downfall? Except it had always been so much part and parcel of his personality. He wanted nothing more now than to shrug his shoulders and walk away. Let his lawyers deal with whatever had to be done in connection with the practice, sort out whatever paperwork needed sorting out.

He couldn't and he was afflicted by something alien to him. A wave of desperation.

He needed to move so he headed for the kitchen, barely glancing at the renovations his money had paid for. She was saying something from behind him, something about paying back whatever money he lent her. He spun around and cut her short with a slice of his hand,

'Why?' he grated savagely. 'And you can drop the

"time to move on" act. The last time we saw one another you were wriggling like an eel under me and begging me to take you.'

Becky went bright red. Trust him to bring sex into it—trust him to use it as a lever in his line of reasoning—yet why should she be surprised when it was the only thing that motivated him? That and the cool detachment that could allow him to see manipulation as something acceptable.

She moved to stand by the sink, pressed up against it with her hands behind her back because she was too restless to sit at the kitchen table.

'Maybe,' she burst out on a wave of uncontrolled anger that was heavily laced with fury at herself for ever, ever having thought that he might actually have proper feelings for her, 'it's because I've finally decided that having a bastard in my life is something I can do without!'

Theo went completely still. For once, his clever mind that could be relied upon to deal with any situation had stalled and was no longer functioning.

Their eyes met and she was the first to look away. Even in the grip of anger, he still exerted the sort of power over her that made her fearful because she knew how out of character it could make her behave.

'Explain.' He felt cold inside because he knew what she was going to say and, in retrospect, marvelled that he had ever thought that she wouldn't find out, marvelled that he had ever felt he could carry on having this relationship and then walk away from it with her none the wiser.

'You didn't just *happen to come here* while you were out taking your car for a little spin in the middle of nowhere, did you, Theo?' She had regained some of her self-control and her voice was low, but steady.

'You weren't just the *poor marooned billionaire* unfortunate enough to wash up on the doorstep of a country bumpkin with a house falling down around her ears, were you? You came here because you wanted to buy the place. Your mother told me. She told me how much she'd been hankering to return to the house where she and your father had lived as a young couple. She told me how she'd left in a hurry after he'd been killed in a road accident. She said that she'd never wanted to return but that lately she'd been wanting to make peace with her past and especially now that you seemed to be so happy and settled.' She laughed scornfully but her cheeks were bright red and her hands were shaking. 'When did you decide that it made more sense to check out the place and see for yourself how much it was worth? When did you decide that you would sleep with me so that it would be easier to talk me into selling it for the lowest possible price? The power of pillow talk and all that? Did you decide to put your little plan on hold temporarily because using me as a fake girlfriend was more important than yanking the house out from under my feet?

'After all, you'd already slept with me—why not keep it up for a few more weeks until your mother was over her little turn? Then a clean break-up and a speedy purchase! You'd already done the groundwork to get the place up to your standards. Were you ever going to tell me that you were behind the purchase? Or were you going to string me along for a while longer, until you got me to the point where you could convince me to sell it for a song before regrettably letting me go, like all those women you dated before me?'

Theo raked his fingers through his hair.

Consequences he had put on hold were ramming into him with the force of a runaway steam engine and fact was so intricately weaved with conjecture that he was well and truly on the back foot.

But that didn't bother him. What bothered him was that he had blown it.

He'd blown the only good thing to have happened in his life with his arrogance, his misplaced pride and his driving need to exert control over everything.

'Let me explain,' he said roughly, which provoked another bitter laugh, and he couldn't blame her. He couldn't have sounded more guilty of the accusations hurled at him if he'd tried.

'I don't want you to explain!'

'Why did you let me drive here if you didn't want to hear what I had to say?' he countered in a driven voice. He badly wanted to get closer to her, to close the distance between them, but it would be a big mistake. For once, words were going to have to be his allies. For once, he was going to have to say how he felt, and that scared him. He'd never done it before and now...

She hated him. It was written all over her face. But she hadn't, not before. No, she might have protested that he wasn't her type, but they'd clicked in a way he'd never clicked with a woman before.

He should have told her the truth when he'd had the chance in Portofino. He'd started but had allowed himself to be side-tracked. Now, he was paying a price he didn't want to pay.

'You're right. I did come here with the sole intention of buying this place. My mother had been making noises about wanting to return here. I had the money and I saw no reason not to take back what, I felt, had been taken from her at a knockdown price.' He held up his hand because he could see her bursting to jump in and, if nothing else, he would have his say. He had to. He had no choice.

'You used me.'

'I exploited a situation and at the time it felt like the right thing to do.' He looked at her with searing honesty and she squashed all pangs of empathy. 'I don't like having this conversation with you standing there. Won't you come here?'

'I don't like thinking that you used me. So that makes both of us not liking things that aren't about to change.'

Come nearer? Did anyone ever take up an invitation to jump into a snake pit?

And still her body keened for him in a way that was positively terrifying.

'Sleeping with me was all just part of your plan, wasn't it?'

'I would never have slept with you if I didn't fancy you, Becky. And fancy you more than I've ever fancied any woman in my life before. Okay, so you might think that what I did was unethical, but—'

'But?' She tilted her head to one side in a polite enquiry. At least he'd fancied her. He wasn't lying. That, in itself, was a comfort. *Small comfort*, she quickly reminded herself.

'But it was the only way I knew how to be,' he said in such a low, husky voice that she had to strain to hear him.

Unsettled, she felt herself relax a little, although she remained where she was, pressed against the counter, careful not to get too close. And she wasn't going to ask him what he meant either!

But her keen eyes noted the way he angled his big body so that he was leaning towards her, head lowered, arms resting on his thighs and his hands clasped loosely together. That looked like defeat in his posture, although she was probably wildly off the mark with that one. She seemed to have turned being wildly off the mark into a habit as far as this man was concerned.

Theo dealt her a hesitant glance.

He had such beautiful eyes, she thought, shaken by that hesitancy, such wildly extravagant eyelashes, and when he looked like that, as though he was searching in fog to find a way forward, was it any wonder that something inside her wasn't quite as steely as it should be?

'I've always been tough,' he admitted in the same low, barely audible voice and she took a couple of tentative steps towards him, then sat at the table, but at the opposite end. Theo glanced across and wondered if he dared let his hopes rise, considering she was no longer pressed against the counter like a cornered rat preparing to attack. 'I've had to be. Life wasn't easy when I was growing up, but I think I told you that.'

'Whilst omitting to tell me other things,' Becky pointed out with asperity, although her voice wasn't as belligerent as it had previously been.

'Granted.' He hung his head for a few seconds, then held her eyes once again. 'My mother was always unhappy. Not that she wasn't a good mother—she was a great mother—but she'd never recovered from my father's death. Love cut short in its prime will always occupy top position on the pedestal.' He shot her a crooked smile. 'She got very little for the cottage in the end. She sold low and, by the time the mortgage was paid off, she barely had enough to buy something else. She had to work her fingers to the bone to make sure we had food in the larder and heating during winter. That was what I saw and that was what, I guess, made me realise that love and emotion were weaknesses to be avoided at all costs. What mattered was security and only money could give you that. I locked my heart away and threw away the key. I was invincible. It never occurred to me that I wouldn't have to find the key to open it because someone else would do that for me.'

Becky felt prickles of something speckle her skin. She took a deep breath and held it.

'It made financial sense to buy the cottage cheap. My plan was to go there, fling money on the table and take what should have been my mother's as far as I was concerned. But then you opened the door and things changed—and then we slept together and after that everything kept changing. I kept telling myself that nothing had, that I was still going to buy the cottage, but I was in freefall without even realising it. Becky, I wanted to tell you why I'd shown up on your doorstep, but I'd boxed myself in and I couldn't get a grip to manoeuvre myself out.'

He shook his head ruefully. She was so still and for once he couldn't read what she was thinking. It didn't matter. He had to plough on anyway.

'In the end, I wasn't going to buy it,' he confessed heavily. 'I'd made that decision before we returned to this country. The only problem was that I never followed through with the reasoning because, if I had, I would have realised that the reason I dumped the plan to buy your house for my mother was because I'd fallen in love with you, and to do anything as underhand as try and buy you out, even if you agreed to sell, would have felt... somehow wrong.'

'You what? Say that again? I think...I think I must have missed something...'

'I've been an idiot.' Theo looked at her steadily. 'And I don't know how long I would have carried on being an idiot. I just know that the past ten days have been hell and, when you told me that you wanted me out of your life just now, my world felt like it was collapsing.

Becky...' He searched to find the words for a role he had never played before. 'I realise you don't consider me the ideal catch...'

'Stop.' Her head was buzzing from hearing stuff she'd never in a million years thought she'd ever hear. She was on cloud nine and now the distance between them seemed too great when all she wanted was to be able to reach out and touch him. She saw the shadow of defeat cross his face and her heart constricted.

'I *did* think that you weren't the sort of guy for me. I'd always made assumptions about the sort of guy who *would* be for me and you didn't fit the bill. There was so much about you that I'd never come across in my life before.' She smiled, eyes distant as she recalled those first impressions when he'd appeared on her doorstep in all his drop-dead, show-stopping glory. 'But you were irresistible,' she confessed. 'And it wasn't just about the way you looked, although it was easier for me to tell myself that. Everything about you was irresistible. I was hooked before I even went to bed with you, and then you disappeared without a backward glance.'

'Not so,' Theo murmured. 'If only you knew.' He patted his lap and she obediently and happily went to sit there. She sighed with pleasure because this was where she belonged. Close to him. If this turned out to be a dream, she was hoping not to wake any time soon.

'When you got in touch, I was so excited, then I realised that you'd only got in touch because you wanted something from me. That I was the only woman who could deliver that something, because I was plain and average and the sort of girl boys don't mind taking home to their mothers.'

'You're the sexiest woman I've ever known,' he assured her with a seriousness that made her smile again.

'The bonus is that you're also the type of woman I was proud to introduce to my mother.'

'I put down that "no sex" clause,' Becky said thoughtfully, 'but I was still excited to be seeing you again. Through it all, even when I was so angry—because some of the things you said, like me having to buy a whole new wardrobe to be a convincing girlfriend, were really offensive—I was still excited. It was like I could suddenly only come alive in your company.' She sighed. 'Which brings us right back to where we started. With the cottage and your reasons for showing up.'

'I think there's something my mother wants a lot more than a cottage.' He dropped a kiss on the side of her mouth and then, as she curved into him, looping her arms around his neck, the kiss deepened and deepened until he was in danger of forgetting what he wanted to say. Eventually he drew back and looked at her. 'She wants a daughter-in-law and I've realised that there's nothing more I want, my darling, than a wife. So…will you marry me?'

'You called me your darling…'

'And will you let me call you my *wife*?'

'My darling husband-to-be… Yes, I will.

* * * * *

LET'S TALK
Romance

For exclusive extracts, competitions
and special offers, find us online:

 MillsandBoon

@MillsandBoon

@MillsandBoonUK

@MillsandBoonUK

Get in touch on 01413 063 232

MILLS & BOON

THE HEART OF ROMANCE

A ROMANCE FOR EVERY READER

MODERN

Prepare to be swept off your feet by sophisticated, sexy and seductive heroes, in some of the world's most glamourous and romantic locations, where power and passion collide.

HISTORICAL

Escape with historical heroes from time gone by. Whether your passion is for wicked Regency Rakes, muscled Vikings or rugged Highlanders, awaken the romance of the past.

MEDICAL

Set your pulse racing with dedicated, delectable doctors in the high-pressure world of medicine, where emotions run high and passion, comfort and love are the best medicine.

True Love

Celebrate true love with tender stories of heartfelt romance, from the rush of falling in love to the joy a new baby can bring, and a focus on the emotional heart of a relationship.

Desire

Indulge in secrets and scandal, intense drama and sizzling hot action with heroes who have it all: wealth, status, good looks…everything but the right woman.

HEROES

The excitement of a gripping thriller, with intense romance at its heart. Resourceful, true-to-life women and strong, fearless men face danger and desire - a killer combination!

To see which titles are coming soon, please visit

millsandboon.co.uk/nextmonth

GET YOUR ROMANCE FIX

Get the latest romance news,
exclusive author interviews, story
extracts and much more!

MILLS & BOON

Desire

Indulge in secrets and scandal, intense drama and plenty of sizzling hot action with powerful and passionate heroes who have it all: wealth, status, good looks…everything but the right woman.

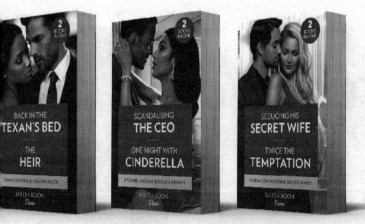